KARLUK BONES

A Kodiak, Alaska Wilderness Mystery Novel

ROBIN BAREFIELD
Alaska Wilderness Mystery Author

Author Masterminds Charter Member

PUBLICATION
CONSULTANTS
We Believe In The Power Of Authors

PO Box 221974 Anchorage, Alaska 99522-1974
books@publicationconsultants.com—www.publicationconsultants.com

ISBN: 9781594339905
eISBN: 978-1-59433-891-5
Library of Congress Catalog Card Number: 2019955315

DEDICATION

For Mike

PRESENT DAY
SATURDAY, MAY 24TH
2:34 A.M.

"Fire! Wake up! Fire!"

The cry yanked me from a pleasant dream in which my camping companions and I sat around the campfire roasting marshmallows. Now I realized the smoky inspiration for my dream emanated not from a campfire but a forest fire.

I struggled to sit in my sleeping bag while my fingers fumbled with the zipper. *Did we leave our campfire burning? No, I remember Geoff throwing water on it, and then we all watched until the last curls of smoke evaporated.*

I'd worn my clothes to bed, so as soon as I struggled out of my bag, I crawled through the fly of the small tent. Smoke filled the air, and my friend and colleague, Geoff Baker, my friend, Dana Baynes, and her new beau, Jack Parker, all stood, staring to the north. I followed their gazes and saw the flames.

"What do you think?" I asked.

"It looks like a campfire got out of hand," Geoff said.

"It's so dry," Dana said. "It's bound to spread before they can put it out."

"And the wind is blowing this way," Geoff added.

"We'd better help," Jack said.

"You're right," I said, "but I fear only Mother Nature will be able to extinguish a blaze in the middle of this dead, dry vegetation."

"I'll dump out our food buckets," Geoff said. "We can use those to scoop up lake water to throw on the fire."

"Sure," Dana said, "we'll do a bucket brigade."

I doubted anything we did would help, but if we stayed where we were, we'd burn alive. "I suggest sticking anything you can't live without in your pocket," I said.

"Good point, Doc. I'll grab my phone," Geoff said.

"I'm taking my raincoat just in case," Dana added.

I nodded. "I hope we need our raincoats. Rain is the one thing that will extinguish this fire."

Geoff, Jack, and I carried our bear-proof food buckets, now empty of their contents, and Dana shouldered a pack full of first-aid gear. She also carried a small camp shovel.

We hiked along the shore of Karluk Lake. It was a dark, chilly night. Correction, it was a dark, chilly morning. Darkness rarely visits Kodiak in late May, but I'll testify it is dark at 3:00 a.m. We wore headlamps to light the beach along the lakeshore, and I glued my eyes to the ground so I wouldn't stumble over a large rock or a tree branch. The smell of smoke grew stronger with each step.

As we neared the blaze, I watched the flames grow in intensity and slowly but steadily spread toward the south and our camp.

"We should have packed our stuff and moved it out of the line of fire," I said.

"I don't think we could move our gear far enough to get it out of the fire line unless we brought it with us and stashed it upwind from the flames," Geoff said.

We clung to the lakeshore and skirted around the edge of the fire. As we neared the tent camp where the blaze had started, we saw four young men frantically packing their tents and gear and moving everything down the beach. Miraculously, it looked as if the flames had not touched their camp.

Dana ran toward the men. "Is everyone okay?" She called.

One of the young men stopped in his tracks and looked toward her, obviously surprised by her presence. "Our campfire got out of control," he said. "I thought we put it out but guess we didn't."

The man slurred his speech and seemed confused. At first I thought he had a natural physical or mental impairment, but then I realized he was intoxicated, or more likely, he hadn't completely sobered up from being drunk. I took in the entire scene and watched his camping companions stumble to move their gear, their actions clumsy and awkward. They were all in the no-man's-land between drunk and sober, the period of the night when you wake up and curse yourself for drinking too much alcohol. I admit I'd been there a time or two, and now I tried to muster some forgiveness for them stupidly getting drunk and letting their campfire burn out of control.

Forgiveness was not on Dana's mind, and she immediately understood the situation. She dropped her pack on the ground and stood, hands on hips, glaring at the young man who had spoken to her. "Are you drunk?"

"Maybe," he said. "I'm not quite sober."

"You are camping on an island with 3,500 bears." Dana walked toward him, her voice was as loud as I'd ever heard it. "Many of those bears live near this lake."

The young man looked at the ground and said nothing.

"If you want to camp on this refuge, you need to be responsible." Dana gestured to the spreading fire. "You started a fire by not putting out your campfire."

"We tried to put it out," the young man said.

"You tried?" Dana was now only about four feet from the poor guy, all five feet nothing of her intimidating the young man as she screamed up at him.

Although the situation was dire, I nearly laughed as I watched the much larger man cower while petite Dana approached him. He flinched at each of her words as if she were slapping him in the face, and I thought she might punch him when she got a few steps closer.

"I saw a video the other day," Dana said. "An observant camper watched and videotaped a bunch of yahoos like you and your friends. They ate breakfast around their campfire, threw a little water on the fire, packed their gear, jumped in their raft, and headed down river. A few minutes after they'd left, a curious bear began sniffing their campfire. He put his paw on the hot embers, burned his paw and limped away, holding his burned paw in the air." She took another step toward the young man, who was now backing away from her. "I thought their lack of regard for the environment was disgusting until I see what you idiots managed to do here."

I stood, caught up in the drama of Dana and the young camper, until Geoff thumped me on the shoulder.

"Here, Doc," he said, handing me a full bucket of lake water. "Let's get this bucket brigade going." He looked at Dana and the cowering campers. "Yo!" he yelled. "We need some help here; we have a fire to put out."

The campers seemed happy for any excuse to escape Dana's withering gaze and sharp reprimand. They found two more food buckets in their gear, emptied the contents, and hurried to stand in line between the lake and the burning fire.

I knew I couldn't be the only one in this group who saw the futility of fighting a spreading wildfire with buckets of water, but buckets were all we had, and we needed to do something. There was no firefighting agency to call in the middle of the night to help put out a fire on the Kodiak National Wildlife Refuge. If the fire was still burning by morning, we could notify the National Wildlife Refuge office in Kodiak, and perhaps they could ask for assistance from the Department of Natural Resources. Dana was a biologist for the Kodiak National Wildlife Refuge so she would know what to do. At present, Dana stood in the bucket brigade between the four campers, still lecturing them. If they weren't sober by now, they would be soon, and between excessive alcohol, smoke, and Dana's piercing voice, I didn't envy any one of them the headache he would have for the next several hours.

We continued the steady progression of bucket passing as the sky slowly lightened. At 5:00 a.m., my arms felt numb, my shoulders screamed with pain, and I had one of the worst headaches of my life. My comrades and I silently passed buckets, refusing to admit defeat. A little after 6:00 a.m., Mother Nature decided to lend us a helping hand. It started as a drizzle, but soon the rain pelted us in sheets.

I stepped out of the bucket line and said, "I think we can stop now."

Slowly, we all dropped to the ground and sat in the pouring rain. For the first few minutes, the rain felt good, but then I began to shiver. I found my raincoat on the ground where I'd discarded it hours earlier and pulled it on over my sodden clothes. The raincoat didn't add much warmth, but at least I wasn't getting any wetter.

We sat and watched the fire smolder for the next several hours. We couldn't tell from where we sat whether the flames had reached our campsite, but I knew at the very least, our gear would smell like smoke.

Geoff, Dana, Jack, and I had planned to get an early start for our raft trip down the Karluk River, but now, none of us seemed to have the energy to make the trek back to our camp to pack our gear and head out on the river. Even Dana's outrage at the campers had cooled as we sat and made small talk with them. They were four college kids from Indiana who had consumed too much alcohol and did something stupid. Luckily for all of us and for the Kodiak National Wildlife Refuge, the often-cursed Kodiak rain solved the problem.

At 8:30 a.m., my camping buddies and I finally decided to hike back to our camp and see if we still had any belongings. We walked silently along the lakeshore in the pouring rain. I didn't think I would ever feel warm and dry again. I fantasized about going home, taking a hot shower and crawling under every blanket I could find. The idea of a raft trip did not appeal at all to me now, and I hoped my comrades felt the same way.

I watched the ground, picking my way carefully over the slippery rocks. Wet smoke filled my nostrils, adding to my pounding headache, and I knew my eyes must be a shade of red only seen on monsters in horror movies. I heard Geoff say something, but my raincoat hood muffled his voice.

I pulled down my hood and looked at him. "What?"

"I think we can cut through the woods here," he said. "The undergrowth has burned away, but I don't see any lingering fire. The rain must have put it out."

"I don't know," Dana said. "Everything is still smoldering."

"We can always cut back to the lakeshore if it looks hot," Jack said.

I followed the group as we headed inland away from the lake and in a direct line to our campsite. Only the bottoms of the trees had been burned here, but the undergrowth had melted into a mat of black goo. I wondered what this meant for our camp; the fire had traveled further than I'd realized.

We stomped over the sodden, charred remains of ferns, cow parsnip, wild celery, and wildflowers, all burned to shriveled, unrecognizable bits. I focused on my feet and concentrated on each step. We came to a still-smoldering dead tree, and Geoff pointed it out to us as we walked around it. Ten minutes later, Geoff came to an abrupt stop and kneeled on the ground. I was the last person in line and wasn't paying attention to the people in front of me. When Geoff halted, everyone else but me stopped walking, and I smashed into Jack's back.

I pulled the hood off my head. "Sorry," I said to Jack. "What's up?"

Dana crouched beside Geoff to see what he was looking at. I heard her say, "We have part of a skull and a scapula; anything else?"

"I don't know," Geoff said. "Let's look around."

"Human?" I asked.

"Yes," Dana said, "but it's probably hundreds, if not thousands, of years old. People have lived on Kodiak Island, and especially around Karluk Lake, for a very long time."

I knew she was right, and a native burial site probably had been uncovered by erosion and or animal activity. The fire had burned away the vegetation and leaves, completely exposing the bones.

"Still," she said. "They don't look ancient. They haven't decayed much, but they don't appear recent, either."

Jack and I both joined Dana and Geoff. The skull had yellowed but was not yet pitted from spending centuries in a shallow grave.

"I don't know," Jack said. "They could easily be a hundred years old."

I knew nothing about aging bones, so I remained quiet. We all stood and began searching near the bones to see if we could find anything else. Slowly, our search radius increased in diameter.

"I have something," Jack said.

We examined Jack's find and decided he'd found the long arm bone. A few minutes later, Dana found two leg bones. "A femur and a tibia," Dana said.

We speculated whether the bones all belonged to the same skeleton. If a burial site had been unearthed, bones from several skeletons easily could have been scattered by foxes or even bears.

Several minutes later, I found something that brought me up short and made me begin thinking about our bones in a new light. I picked up the item and stared at it for several minutes, lost in thought about what it could mean.

"What do you have, Doc?" Geoff asked.

"A belt buckle," I said. "The belt must have deteriorated, but the buckle is made of brass. It has some sort of insignia on it, but I can't quite make it out."

My three companions approached me. Jack took the buckle from me and switched on the headlamp he still wore. "Air Force," he said.

I trusted Jack's assessment. He had been an officer in the Air Force before retiring. He was now a meteorologist with NOAA. He had informed us to pack good rain gear for this trip, and now I knew why.

"I doubt ancient Alutiiqs wore brass belt buckles," Geoff said.

"We don't know if the belt buckle is related to the bones," Dana reminded us. "We don't even know if all the bones belong to the same skeleton."

"Yes," I said, "but I'm now wondering if we should report this," I waved my hand toward the bones we'd laid out on the ground and then pointed at the buckle, "to the troopers."

"No," Dana said. "We don't have enough to warrant bringing the troopers all the way out here."

"We could take photos of what we have and send it to them. Then they can make their own decision about whether the bones are worth investigating," I said.

"I'll do it," Geoff said, and began snapping photos with his phone.

"Wait a minute," Jack said. "Why don't we look a little longer and see if we can find anything else."

"What about our raft trip?" Dana asked.

"Dana, darling," Geoff said. "I don't know about you, but I think I'm over the idea of a raft trip."

"I guess so," Dana mumbled. "This was supposed to be a fun weekend, and here we are, covered in smoke and soot, searching for bones."

I didn't think I should point out that my heart started racing the moment I found the belt buckle. I could not stop speculating about what happened to the person who had worn the belt. *Are these his bones, and if so, how did he die? Did he die from natural causes? Was he mauled by a bear? Did someone murder him? What caused his skull to break, and did the skull fracture cause his death, or was his skull broken after he died? Why were his bones never recovered? Who was he or she? I guess it could have been a woman, but the long leg bones plus the large belt buckle made me think the skeleton belonged to a man. When did he die? The bones aren't recent, and the belt buckle has been exposed to the elements for a long time, but how long?*

I continued to search the area where I'd found the buckle. A few minutes later, I found an old wristwatch.

At the same moment I picked up the wristwatch, I heard Geoff yell, "Got something!" He held up a pocket knife.

"I have this." I held up the wristwatch.

"What kind is it?" Dana asked. "If we know the model, maybe we can Google it and narrow down a time frame."

"Unless the guy was wearing his father's or grandfather's watch," Jack said.

Dana gave Jack a withering look. "You're a lot of help," she said.

"It's a Timex, an early digital model. My Dad had one that sort of looked like this, but I never saw him wear it. He said it was a piece of junk." I shrugged at Dana and handed her the watch.

Dana studied the watch for several minutes. "You're right," she said. "I think it's first-generation digital. It must be a few decades old."

"What about the knife?" Jack called to Geoff.

"I don't think it will help us much with a date. It's a Swiss Army knife, and it's rusted shut," Geoff said.

We searched for another hour, but by then, we were exhausted. We'd been up most of the night fighting a fire, and now, after this long search for bones and personal effects, we had nothing left in the tank. We found a few more small bones and bone scraps which could have been part of the skull or nothing at all. We weren't even sure they were human.

"Let's leave everything here for now," I said, "and I'll call Sergeant Patterson with the Alaska State Troopers and ask him if he wants us to bring the bones and other things to town or leave them here."

"Tell him I photographed and took GPS waypoints on each item," Geoff said.

"I don't think the troopers will care about these bones," Dana said. "They might not be ancient, but they are old."

We were thrilled to see our camp intact. Everything smelled smoky, but nothing had burned. Jack handed me his satellite phone, and Dana recited the troopers' phone number from memory. Since in her job as a Fish and Wildlife biologist she often worked with the troopers, she probably should have been the one to place the call, but she seemed to think we were making much ado about nothing, so I didn't feel she would be the best one of us to relay the information to the troopers.

I took the satellite phone and walked toward the lakeshore until I picked up a signal. When the trooper dispatcher answered, I asked to speak to Sergeant Dan Patterson. I doubted the senior trooper would be in his office on a Saturday, and I expected her either to ask me more questions or connect me with a junior officer, but a moment later, a gruff voice said, "Patterson."

"Sergeant Patterson," I said. "My name is Jane Marcus. You don't know me, but we have a mutual acquaintance."

Patterson didn't even pause. "Dr. Marcus," he said, "how is our esteemed friend?"

"Fighting crime," I said.

"On the back of a white steed," he said and laughed. "I actually had a nice, long conversation with him the other day."

The comment stung me. I hadn't spoken to FBI Special Agent Nick Morgan in more than three weeks. I thought he was immersed in a hot and heavy investigation in Indiana and was too busy for small talk, but apparently he had time to call his buddy Sergeant Patterson and have a nice long chat.

Agent Nick Morgan had provided FBI assistance on two cases on Kodiak Island, and I'd met him on his first trip to the island when we'd become friends. On his next trip to Kodiak, I thought we'd moved to the next level of our relationship, but five months had passed, and despite several long phone conversations, I felt him drifting away from me.

"Anyway," Patterson said, "I'm sure you didn't call me to talk about Nick."

His words snapped me out of my reverie. "Yes," I said. "My friends and I are camping near Karluk Lake, and we found some human bones. The bones are several years old, but I don't think they are ancient."

"Okay," he dragged out the word.

"We also found a belt buckle, a pocketknife, and a watch," I said. "It's a digital watch." I didn't point out it was an ancient digital watch. If Patterson believed we'd found recent bones, he'd be more eager to investigate.

Patterson paused for several moments and then finally said, "Hmmm."

"I know this might not be anything you want to investigate, but my friend took photos and marked the spot on his GPS. We can bring the bones and other items to you," I said.

"Let me think for a minute," Patterson said.

I paced and waited, wondering if he thought I was crazy for bothering him with bones obviously years, if not decades, old.

"I think I want to look at this scene myself," he said.

"We already moved some of the bones," I said.

"That's okay. I don't think their exact placement is important, but I'd like to get a feel for where you found the bones. I can't get out there today, and it will probably be after the weekend before I make the trip. Would you be willing to fly back out there with me and show me what you found?"

I hated flying in small planes, but what could I say. "Sure, just give me some notice, and I'll get off work."

I gave Patterson my cell number, and Patterson recited a number to me where Geoff could send the photos of the bones. I reported the conversation to my group, and Dana seemed surprised Patterson wanted to invest the time and resources to examine the old bones.

"Maybe he can match them up with an old missing persons case," Geoff said.

"I doubt it," Dana said.

"Should we call Kodiak Flight Services and see if they can pick us up this afternoon?" Jack asked. "I know I'm not in the mood for a raft trip with this weather and after all we've been through."

The rest of us agreed, and he placed the call. The dispatcher told Jack their planes were busy until 4:00 p.m., so he reserved the time slot and we returned to our tents for a long nap.

1976

Jay Bently and Terry Schwimmer hauled their duffel bags, rifle cases, and four cardboard boxes out the door of the Wien Airlines terminal at the Kodiak Airport. They grabbed one of the two taxis idling in front of the airport and asked the driver to take them to the Baranof Hotel.

They unlocked the door to their hotel room, dropped their gear on the floor, removed their coats and headed for the bar. After four beers and a hamburger each, they laughed and chatted. Their spirits soared in anticipation of their upcoming hunt.

Bently and Schwimmer had been buddies and housemates in Eagle River, Alaska, for the past eighteen months. Both men had been airplane mechanics in the United States Air Force at Elmendorf Air Force Base near Anchorage, and they also both had been discharged from the Air Force two months earlier. When their names were drawn for bear-hunting permits on Kodiak Island, the ultimate bear-hunting location in the world, they decided this would be their final Alaska adventure before returning to "real life." Bently planned to return to Iowa and work with his aunt and uncle on their farm, while Schwimmer hoped to land a job as a jet mechanic in Seattle.

The men decided to turn in early so they would be ready in the morning for their flight into the Kodiak wilderness to Karluk Lake. They planned to spend two weeks bear hunting. They decided to hunt together and drew straws to see who would go after the first nice bear they saw. Schwimmer drew the long straw so he would have the first choice. If Schwimmer decided a bear wasn't big enough for him, then Bently would have the option of shooting it. If both men rejected the bear, then Schwimmer would have the first choice at the next bear. They'd read *Outdoor Life Magazine* and had heard all the stories. They expected to be surrounded by huge bears, so it just would be a matter of picking the right one.

They worried a little about camping in the middle of so many bears. Their goal was to be the hunters, not the hunted. To keep from attracting bears to their camp, they packed only freeze-dried food and granola bars and just enough food for twenty days. They only planned to camp fourteen days, but they knew the weather in November on Kodiak Island could be nasty for days at a time. If it was too snowy or windy, floatplanes would not be able to fly, and they would be forced to spend a few extra days in their camp. They wanted to have plenty of food on hand in case of bad weather. Schwimmer had put on a few pounds over the last year, and he told Bently this hunting trip would be a good time to jump-start a diet.

PRESENT DAY
WEDNESDAY, MAY 28TH
10:20 A.M.

Would I be going on this wild goose chase if this woman wasn't Special Agent Nick Morgan's lady friend? Patterson wondered. He thought he knew the answer to the question, and it bothered him to think he could be swayed so easily. Still, he had said he would fly out to Karluk Lake and examine bones that were sure to be ancient, so he might as well get this task done and put it to rest. Dr. Marcus told him when he'd called her yesterday she would meet him at his plane in Trident Basin, and true to her word, she, or some woman, was standing at the end of the floatplane dock when he arrived. He carried a backpack that held evidence bags, a thin duffel, a camp shovel, and a good camera. He couldn't think of any other forensic gear he would need for this trip. The photos of the bones Marcus's friend sent him indicated a few intact bones and a heap of small pieces of bones probably not even human. Some of the bones, including the femur, wouldn't fit into evidence bags, so he'd brought the duffel for those.

Patterson walked down the dock and shook hands with the trim, dark-haired woman. "You must be Dr. Marcus. I'm Dan Patterson."

"Please call me Jane, Sergeant."

"Only if you call me Dan," he said. "Thank you for taking time to fly out to Karluk Lake today," Patterson said, but what he was thinking was, *You are wasting both of our mornings with this nonsense.*

Jane was a good-looking woman, and he could see what physically attracted Morgan to her. Her dark hair was pulled into a ponytail, and although fine lines radiated from the outside corners of her big brown eyes, these lines were the only indication of wear and tear, and Patterson wondered how old she was. Her slender frame appeared muscular under her hiking clothes.

Jane was a fish biologist at the marine center, and Patterson knew Morgan admired her quick mind and valued her opinion. She already had been at the center of one Kodiak crime and on the fringes of another. Patterson didn't think she was the type of person who went looking for trouble, but she didn't shy away from it when she found it. This time, though, he thought she had only found a bunch of old bones and was making more out of them than necessary.

Patterson and Jane climbed into the de Havilland Beaver. They each put on headsets, and Patterson started the plane. While it was warming up, Jane told Patterson she had brought her friend, Geoff's, GPS. She explained Geoff had marked the original location of each bone and item they'd found with a waypoint. "We put the bones in a pile but left the watch, belt buckle, and knife, in the same general area where we found them." She paused. "We did handle the items, though, so our fingerprints are on them."

Patterson fought back a snort of laughter at the thought of finding usable prints on a belt buckle or watch sure to be decades old. He simply nodded and taxied the plane into the channel. He talked briefly to the tower located at the Kodiak Airport, increased the throttle, and soon they soared into the air. The day was cloudless and calm, the sort of day Patterson preferred for flying. Over the years, he'd been forced plenty of times to fly in dicey conditions, and he knew he was a good pilot and could fly in marginal weather when necessary. Sometimes, a violent situation in a village, a crime at a remote wilderness cabin, or a deadly fire at a secluded site required the troopers to respond quickly regardless of weather conditions. If Patterson felt he could get himself and the other troopers to the scene safely, he always agreed to make the flight, but if he decided conditions were too unstable for a safe trip, he never hesitated to tell his superior officers he would not fly until the weather improved. So far, no one had questioned his judgment on when to fly and when to stay put.

Today's mission was not the sort he would undertake in marginal weather. The bones weren't going anywhere, and it made little difference whether he examined them today or three weeks from now. As it turned out, though, he had an unusually light caseload right now, and when he saw the beautiful forecast for today, he decided to call Jane Marcus and finish this task. He had to admit this beat sitting in his office doing paperwork. Here he was with a good-looking woman sitting next to him flying over the rugged landscape of the most beautiful place he'd ever worked. A smile broke out on his face when he thought about his wife, Jeanne. She'd kick him in the shin right now if she could read his mind.

Patterson and Jane made small talk during the flight. Patterson, no doubt from a twinge of guilt, told Jane about his wife, who was a radiology technician and had recently taken a job at the Kodiak hospital. Jane explained her work with plankton at the marine center. They both avoided the topic of Nick Morgan. Patterson thought Nick and Jane were involved in a relationship, but he wasn't sure and decided it best not to bring up the subject.

When they reached Karluk Lake, Jane pointed to the spot where she and her friends had camped. Patterson circled the area charred from the fire.

"It's a good thing it rained," he said, "or the fire might still be burning."

"It was very lucky," Jane agreed. "We threw buckets of water on the fire all night, and it kept spreading, but two hours of Kodiak rain did the trick."

"I guess rain comes in handy at times," Patterson said.

Patterson landed the plane on the lake and taxied to the area where Jane said she and her friends had camped. After securing the plane to the shore, he told Jane to lead him to the bones. Jane held the GPS in front of her and followed its marked trail to the waypoint where they had stacked the bones. Twenty minutes later, they reached the bones.

"They're still here," Jane said. Patterson heard the note of relief in her voice and realized Jane feared looking foolish in his eyes. *She is an intelligent woman, a scientist with a Ph.D., and she probably does not want me to feel she's leading me on a wild goose chase. She really believes these bones should be analyzed, and maybe if she is concerned enough about the provenance of these bones to involve the troopers, then I should extend her the courtesy of taking this mission more seriously.*

He bent and examined the bones. He saw a partial skull, a humerus, a femur, a tibia, part of a pelvis, four small bones, probably belonging to the hands and feet, and several bone scraps. He turned the bones over in his hands and studied each one carefully, and then he sat on the ground. Jane stood quietly watching him.

Patterson blew out a breath through closed lips and looked up at Jane. "I don't know, Jane," he said. "I am certainly no expert, but these look old to me. They could only be a few decades old, but they could also be over a century old." He reached down and picked up the femur. "This one does stir my curiosity, though. As I said, I'm no expert, but this is a long femur, and I would guess it belonged to a tall man," he shrugged, "perhaps making it unlikely it belonged to an Alutiiq man who died two hundred years ago."

"Is it worth sending them to a forensic anthropologist?" Jane asked.

Patterson mulled over the question for a minute. "Yes," he finally said. "It wouldn't be a rush job, but I'd like to hear what a forensic anthropologist has to say about the bones. Some of these scraps might belong to the skull, and if an expert can piece them together, it could help us identify the individual. Why don't you show me what else you found."

Jane led Patterson first to the belt buckle, then the wristwatch and the knife. Patterson examined each item before dropping it into an evidence bag.

"You realize these items might have nothing to do with the bones or with each other," he said.

"Of course," Jane said. "This must seem crazy to you."

"I'll wait to hear what the forensic analysts have to say before I make a judgment. This could be something," he shrugged, "or nothing."

"One thing," Jane said. "If they determine these bones are old and probably from a nearby burial site, I'd feel terrible for disturbing them and would like to return them to where we found them. Would I be able to?"

"Of course," Patterson said. "I'll make certain the bones are returned to you if we determine they are older than a few decades. If they are more recent, though, we will have to look back through missing persons' records to determine who you found."

Patterson and Jane searched the area near the bones for an hour but found nothing else. Patterson bagged the smaller bones in evidence bags and carefully placed the long bones and skull in the duffel bag. He packed the evidence bags in his backpack and carried the duffel bag back to the plane.

Patterson and Jane remained quiet on the return flight to Kodiak. Patterson knew Jane must have been disappointed by his lack of enthusiasm over the bones and other objects. She had misread his reaction, though. While he wasn't ready to open an investigation into these bones, something about the bones, and especially the watch, belt buckle, and knife made a spot in the pit of his stomach rumble just a bit. He felt this was a historical find, but a recent historical find, not an ancient one.

20

PRESENT DAY
TUESDAY, JUNE 17ᵀᴴ
11:00 A.M.

I reclined in my desk chair and checked my cell phone for messages. I had recently given the students in one of my classes a test and now faced the daunting task of having to grade the pile of papers. I hoped my cell phone would provide me with a momentary distraction, and I was not disappointed. I'd missed three calls and had one voice message. One of the calls was from my boss, Peter Wayman, but I didn't recognize the other two numbers. I headed straight for voice mail.

"Jane, this is Dan Patterson with the Alaska State Troopers. I have news on your bones. Give me a call at your leisure."

I was surprised he had information already from the crime lab. I didn't expect anything for months. The bones did not relate to a current crime, and there was no evidence a crime had even occurred.

As much as I wanted to hear the news about the bones, I thought I would be wise and return my boss' call first. If Peter had bothered to check the class schedule on his computer, he would have seen I was teaching a class at the time he tried to call me, but Peter never paid attention to the mundane activities of the marine center. His forte was raising money, a skill for which the rest of his minions and I remained grateful because it kept us employed.

"Jane," Peter said, "How are you?"

I'd seen Peter in the hall two hours earlier, but I politely said, "Fine, Peter, and you?"

"I am well, Jane, thank you for asking. The reason I called you was to ask if you are free for dinner tomorrow night."

The question took me back. Peter had never invited me to dinner. "Sure," I said, because there was no other acceptable answer.

"You've heard of Tamron International?"

"The oil company?"

"Yes," Peter said. "They are considering giving the center a substantial grant, but they'd like to meet a few of our scientists first, so I thought I'd introduce them to you and Dr. Norman. You're both working on projects they can easily understand and embrace."

My head began to ache at the thought of this ordeal. My colleague Sam Norman was studying arrowtooth flounder, trying to find a way to stabilize the enzyme, which when heated, causes the meat of the fish to melt into goo. My research involved plankton, both phytoplankton and zooplankton. As our oceans warm, we must understand changes in plankton populations in the ocean. My most exciting research, and what I knew Peter would want me to discuss over dinner with the Tamron folks, involved the deadly blooms of plankton responsible for killing more than fifty whales near Kodiak. I knew there had been at least one toxic bloom over the past summer, and I felt certain several deadly blooms had occurred over the last three years. I also believed the whales had consumed the poisonous algae and had died as a result, but I couldn't prove the algae had killed them. Despite necropsies on five whales over the past year, the marine biologist was unable to determine the cause of death in any of the whales. Since the whales were bloated and partially decayed before they washed up on a beach where they could be necropsied, they yielded little scientific information. Everyone loves whales, and I knew Peter believed the Tamron people would be thrilled to open their wallets to help save them. Think of the great publicity they'd receive from saving whales in the North Pacific. I could easily imagine the television commercial of a humpback leaping into the air with the Tamron logo in the upper-right-hand corner of the screen.

"I'd be happy to go to dinner and talk about my research," I said and wondered if I sounded more sincere than I felt.

Next, I called Dan Patterson. He must have given me his personal cell phone number because I didn't have to go through a dispatcher. He answered the phone himself.

"Patterson."

"Hi, Dan. This is Jane Marcus returning your call."

"Jane, yes, I thought you'd like an update on your bones."

"I'm surprised you have any news yet; I thought it would take months."

"I was surprised, too. This is just a preliminary report, but we got lucky. An anthropology professor at UAA has a graduate student studying bone chemistry from old bones to learn about the diet and nutritional status of Inuit populations hundreds of years ago. She would have to explain it to you, but apparently, different foods have unique chemical signals, and by studying bone chemistry, a scientist can learn a great deal about the diet of an individual."

"Yes," I said. "I saw a documentary about dietary bone chemistry not long ago where anthropologists used bones dug from old graves to determine the health and diet of early colonists in the U.S."

"The graduate student mostly has been looking at Inupiat populations and at bones hundreds of years old, so when she heard the medical examiner had our bones, she asked to examine them," Patterson said. "The medical examiner was all too happy to hand off old bones to someone who would give him a free anthropological assessment, and the student hasn't disappointed; she has already covered the basics."

"What did she find?" I was getting impatient.

"The bones belonged to a young adult male," Patterson said and paused.

"Okay," I said.

"He was probably close to six feet tall, and he was Caucasian."

"Interesting," I said. "Could they tell how long ago he died?"

"They gave me a ballpark figure of between thirty and fifty years."

It took me a moment to process this information. *What could have happened to him? Why was he at Karluk Lake? Did many people camp at Karluk Lake fifty years ago? Did he still have living relatives who had been wondering all these years what had happened to him?*

"They found something else, too," Patterson said, "and for now, I'd like to keep this information quiet. Can I count on you not to tell anyone?"

"Sure," I said, "what is it?"

"The ME and forensic anthropologists think a bullet shattered the skull. From the fragments you found, the anthropologist reconstructed a portion of the top of the skull, and while they can't be certain a bullet parted the skull, their best guess is a gunshot wound."

"Wow!" I said.

"Interesting, I agree," Patterson said, "but this is a very old, cold crime or suicide, and it's not at the top of my to-do list."

"I understand," I said, "so what's next?"

"Things are quiet here right now. I know from experience the calm won't last, but while we have it, I assigned a trooper the task of pulling old files from 1960 through 1990 to see if we have any missing persons' reports that fit the description of what we know about this individual. I gave the task to a smart young man, and if the kid doesn't die inhaling dust from all those old files, he might find something."

"Will you call me if he does?" I asked.

"Of course, Jane. After all, you started this investigation."

I called Dana and Geoff to tell them the news about the bones, leaving out the part about the bullet hole in the skull. I was surprised Patterson had told me about the bullet hole, and I planned to honor his wish not to tell anyone else the information.

"You're not going to let this go, are you?" Dana said. "Poor Sergeant Patterson has just encouraged the wrong woman."

"I'm not touching this case," I told Dana. "I'm just a bystander."

"Uh huh," Dana said.

True to my word, I did not hound Patterson over the next week, but I did think about the case, imagining wild scenarios to explain how the young man died when and where he did. I Googled everything I could think of to learn more about bones and the information they could provide anthropologists. I learned bones are a lasting encyclopedia of the living person to whom they had once belonged. If the bones were well preserved, a scientist could determine the sex, race, and health of the individual when he died. If the scientist could extract DNA from the bones, she could even determine the individual's identity. I also learned the diet of an individual affects not only bone growth but also bone chemistry. This was the field of interest for the Ph.D. student at UAA.

Six days after Patterson had called to tell me the news about the bones, Dana phoned me at my office.

"Your bones made the *Kodiak Mirror*," she said.

"How did a reporter find out about them?" I asked.

"I think it's a reprint from an Anchorage paper," Dana said. "It probably came from the university."

"What does it say?"

"Not much," Dana said. "It's just a blurb about how a UAA graduate student is helping troopers learn more about bones found near Karluk Lake on Kodiak Island after a forest fire exposed them."

"Does it say anything else about the skull?" I asked.

"No, there's nothing about the skull, and I hate to break it to you, but there's nothing about you in the article."

"Darn," I said. "I thought this was my chance to be famous."

"I know, I'm sorry," Dana said and then laughed.

PRESENT DAY
FRIDAY, JUNE 27TH
7:30 A.M.

Jake Shepherd retired at age sixty from flying jets for Delta Airlines and returned to his roots as a floatplane pilot on Kodiak Island. His wife, Inga, was not thrilled to move from Atlanta to Kodiak, away from her four kids and eight grandkids and away from warm weather and sunshine. She knew Jake had always dreamed of returning to Kodiak, though, so she moved north with him and spent at least part of the year in Kodiak, sneaking back to Atlanta as often as she could to spoil her grandchildren.

Jake had grown up on Kodiak and began his flying career as a floatplane pilot on this island. Once he'd accumulated the required number of flight hours, he became a commercial pilot for a charter service named Sea Air Kodiak. In 1977, about a year after he'd moved on to flying freight planes out of Anchorage, one of Sea Air Kodiak's planes crashed, killing five people. Amid lawsuits from the passengers' families, the charter service went out of business.

Jake moved from freight planes to small passenger planes and finally up to co-piloting jets all over the world. By the time he retired, he was a chief pilot for Delta. He was proud of all he'd accomplished, but flying a jet felt nothing like flying a small floatplane, and there was no place he'd rather fly a floatplane than Kodiak Island.

Kodiak, with its rugged terrain, changing weather conditions, and extreme tides, challenged a pilot every day he was on the job. Jake never felt bored as a floatplane pilot. Unlike piloting a jet, flying a floatplane never seemed routine. Flying a floatplane made him feel alive and young again, and right now, feeling alive meant everything to him.

When Jake retired from Delta, he didn't think anyone would want to hire an old pilot who hadn't flown a floatplane in years, but he contacted Steve Duncan, the owner of Kodiak Flight Services. Steve was the son of John Duncan, a pilot Jake had known well back in his floatplane days. Jake had stayed in touch with John until John's death from cancer five years earlier, and he knew John's son was doing well with his charter operation.

To Jake's surprise, Steve hired him immediately. Jake knew he would have to go through a training period, but it had gone well, and he'd been flying on his own for the past year, enjoying every minute of it and not complaining too much about Inga's frequent escapes back to Atlanta.

Today was one of those rare bluebird days on Kodiak. Calm, cloudless days were special treats in June on the island, when the temperature and dew point hovered at the same level, creating dense fog which forced mariners to turn on their radars and pilots to stay on the ground and stare out at a wall of gray.

Jake was flying the de Havilland Beaver today. He checked the board in the Kodiak Flight Services' office to see how many flights had been assigned to him. It looked like a full day of flying, and he considered a full day of flying on a beautiful day a dream come true. He saw his first flight would be to Afognak Island, followed by a drop off at Karluk Lake and a pickup on the other side of the lake. Then, he had a flight to Olga Bay, a quick run to Raspberry, and two more flights to Afognak.

Jake waved to the dispatcher, headed out the door, and down the ramp to start loading gear on the plane for the first flight. As he neared the airplane, he breathed in the salty smell of the ocean commingled with the pungent aroma of airplane fuel. He smiled. Those were the two best odors in the world.

1976

SATURDAY, OCTOBER 23RD
7:00 A.M.

Bently was the first to jump out of bed when the alarm clock chimed, and he had his gear packed and ready to go in twenty minutes. Schwimmer took time for a shower, but both men were packed and waiting an hour before their scheduled pickup by Jarvin Flight Service. They decided to head down to the dining room for breakfast because they knew it would be their last chance for a hearty meal for two weeks.

Seventy-five minutes later, Bently and Schwimmer sat in the Jarvin Flight Service van on their way to Lily Lake to check in for their flight. It was 9:00 a.m., and the sky had brightened to a hazy blue. A light wind ruffled the Sitka spruce trees.

At the flight service office, they paid for their air charter both to Karluk Lake and the return flight back to Kodiak in two weeks. On the small day calendar on the wall, Bently saw their flight as well as six other flights listed for the day. Below those flights, someone had written "pickups" followed by the names of three more parties. Bently smiled. He and Schwimmer were just beginning their adventure instead of ending it like the parties listed at the bottom of the calendar page.

The lady behind the counter motioned for Bently and Schwimmer to load their gear on the scale to be weighed. Next, she asked each man to step on the scale. A few minutes later, a young man put their gear back into the van and told Bently and Schwimmer his name was Mark, and he would drive them to the floatplane ramp.

The morning air sliced through Bently's down jacket, and he wished he'd worn his heavy raincoat as a wind block. As soon as they got to Karluk Lake, he'd pull the raincoat from his pack and wear it. He knew he needed to stay warm and hydrated. His cold-weather survival training was still fresh in his mind.

Bently and Schwimmer helped Mark load their gear into a cart and then followed him down the ramp to the floatplane. Mark stopped at a Cessna 206 and began handing their duffel bags and other gear to a man standing on the float of the plane. This guy had long, dirty-blond hair pulled into a ponytail. He wore a heavy, wool jacket, but his head and hands were bare. As soon as he'd packed the gear into the rear of the plane and secured the cargo net, he turned and smiled at Bently and Schwimmer. He held out his hand. "I will be your pilot on this beautiful day."

Bently shook the pilot's hand. He guessed the man was in his late twenties or early thirties.

"You boys heading out on an adventure?" the pilot asked, his blue eyes gleaming as he took in their camo gear.

"Yes sir," Bently said. "We're going bear hunting."

Bently thought from his appearance the pilot looked as if he would be more at home in a commune in California than piloting a floatplane in Alaska, but he was trying to learn to not judge people by the way they looked and the clothes they wore. His ex-wife had told him repeatedly he was too judgmental.

"Bear hunting, eh?" the pilot said. "I hope you packed warm gear. We're expecting a big storm in a couple of days."

"We'll be okay," Bently assured him.

Bently motioned for Schwimmer to take the front seat.

"It will be yours on the way back," Schwimmer said as he crawled into the plane. Bently took the seat directly behind Schwimmer.

The pilot pushed the throttle forward for takeoff, and the plane skimmed over the water. Schwimmer turned and smiled at Bently, his deep, blue eyes magnified by his wire-rimmed glasses. Bently grinned back and gave Schwimmer a thumbs-up. Bently pulled off his cap and rubbed his short-cropped hair. *This is really happening, I'm in a floatplane on Kodiak Island, heading for the biggest adventure of my life.*

Bently stared down while they circled the town of Kodiak, and then they left civilization behind and flew through a narrow mountain pass, the mountains covered with a blanket of snow from the previous storm a few days earlier. According to the weatherman, Kodiak would be hit with another storm in two days when fifty-knot winds and heavy snow were expected to pummel the island. Bently hoped the forecast was wrong, but at least by then they would have their camp set up and could huddle in their tents and eat MREs and drink coffee laced with whiskey until the storm passed. He might even have his bear down by then. Even though Schwimmer had drawn the long straw, Bently thought he would get a bear before Schwimmer did because Schwimmer wasn't much of a hunter. Bently wasn't sure Schwimmer even wanted to kill a bear. He just came along for the adventure.

They edged over snow-white mountains, frozen lakes, and deep bays. The snow extended all the way to the beach but was only a dusting down low. Where they would camp at Karluk Lake was 370 feet above sea level. It was low enough so they shouldn't have to worry about setting up camp in deep snow.

As they continued to fly southwest, Bently noted fewer spruce trees and more brown vegetation. He knew from his research he was looking at deciduous trees, including cottonwoods, alders, willows, and birch. By the time they reached Karluk, alders and willows would be the predominant large vegetation. He knew it was tough to penetrate or see through a thick stand of either willows or alders, and he probably wouldn't see a bear standing in an alder patch, even if he was only a few feet from it. Adrenaline raced through him. He had been dreaming about a Kodiak bear hunt since he was a kid, and now he would have a chance to face off against the monarch of the woods.

"Does Karluk Lake ever freeze?" Bently heard Schwimmer yell his question to the pilot.

"Sometimes," the pilot yelled, "but not until late winter. The lake won't freeze while you're there, but from the sound of it, you might get two feet of snow on your tent." He smiled at Schwimmer. "I'm glad I'm getting off this rock for a while."

"Where are you going?" Schwimmer asked.

"Hawaii."

Bently could see the huge smile the pilot flashed at Schwimmer.

"Yeah, which island?" Schwimmer asked.

"Maui. Have you been there?"

"No," Schwimmer said, "but I'd like to go."

"Do you like flying here on Kodiak?" Bently asked.

The pilot laughed. "I love it. I complain a lot, but it's great. I love it so much, I'm thinking about buying part of this airline from old man Jarvin." He glanced at Schwimmer. "That's a secret. Don't tell anyone."

Bently stared out the window wishing Schwimmer and the pilot would quit talking so he could concentrate on the scenery below him. The jagged terrain appeared wild, untamed, and uninhabited. Since his divorce from Julie, he'd felt lost, his mind a jumble of emotions, but he knew he would find peace at Karluk Lake. He couldn't care less if it snowed; in fact, he welcomed it. *Bring it on!* He wanted all nature could throw at him, and when he came out the victor with a beautiful bear hide in hand and an adventure story he could someday tell his grandkids, he would look at the sky and laugh. Maybe he should have come on this trip alone. He liked Schwimmer, but Schwimmer was a talker, and Bently wanted peace and quiet for the next two weeks.

Bently tried to ignore the chatter from the front of the plane, but the voices raised above the roar of the engines were loud and hard not to hear.

"I did two tours in 'Nam," the pilot said. "I flew choppers. To be honest, I thrived on the excitement, but now I'm ready to settle down and get married. I plan to pop the big question to Emily when we're on Maui."

Bently never would have pegged this long-haired hippie as a veteran. Bently hated pilots. He'd worked with them in his job as an airplane mechanic for the last eight years, and he knew pilots were egomaniacs who believed they controlled every situation. He especially didn't want to hear about this guy's love life. Bently's split with Julie was too recent and painful for him to hear about someone else's happiness.

Finally, the plane crested a ridge, and Karluk Lake lay in front of them. Bently knew it was Karluk because he had studied the map of the lake so many times, he had it memorized. The pilot circled and landed smoothly on the water. Ice rimmed the edge of the lake, and a quarter-inch of snow covered the ground above the waterline. The pilot nosed the plane into shore at the exact point where Bently had told the dispatcher he wanted to camp. The pilot drove him crazy, but he was good at what he did.

Bently exhaled a deep breath when the plane took off, circled, and headed back toward Kodiak. He and Schwimmer stood alone in the middle of their camping gear. The brisk autumn air smelled pure, and not a sound marred the silence.

"Should we start setting up our tents?" Schwimmer broke the spell and shattered the illusion of peace.

Bently again wished he had come alone on this trip and hoped he could convince Schwimmer to hunt by himself. He regretted agreeing to Schwimmer's request to hunt together.

"Sure," Bently said, and began hauling gear up to a flat spot where they could set up camp. They spent the next hour erecting tents, unfurling sleeping pads and bedrolls, and storing rations.

"I'm gonna find a little hill or something to glass from to see if I can spot any bears," Bently said.

"Don't shoot anything today," Schwimmer said.

"Yeah, I know," Bently said. "Same day airborne—got it," he continued, referring to the law restricting hunters from shooting big game the same day they flew, in either an airplane or a helicopter. The purpose of the law was to keep hunters from unfairly spotting game from the air and then landing and shooting it. Spotting game from the air was considered unsportsmanlike and a violation of the rules of "Fair Chase."

Four hours later when Bently returned to camp, he found Schwimmer sitting in his tent in his sleeping bag, reading a novel.

"Is this how you hunt?" Bently asked.

"I can't shoot anything today, what's the point of going out hunting?" Schwimmer asked.

Bently shook his head. "The point," he said, "is to enjoy nature, get familiar with the terrain, and look for animals."

"Did you see anything?" Schwimmer asked, either unaware or not caring about Bently's annoyance with him.

"No," Bently said, "nothing." He crawled into his tent and tied the fly. He stretched out on his sleeping bag, and the next thing he knew, he heard Schwimmer softly calling his name. He looked up, surprised. It was pitch black.

"What time is it?" he asked.

"It's 6:30," Schwimmer said.

"In the morning?"

"At night," Schwimmer said. "I heated some water on the propane stove. Do you want an MRE?"

"Sure," Bently said. He sat up, confused, and he fought to get his bearings. He had been in the apartment he'd shared with Julie, and they were eating

Mexican food and laughing about something that had happened at work. He wanted to go back to sleep and return to his dream, but he reminded himself Julie had moved back to her Momma's house in Memphis. He would never see Julie again. His marriage had ended, and it was time for him to move on with his life.

Bently untied the tent fly and crawled out of the small tent. The temperature had dropped ten degrees, and he felt cold and stiff from sleeping on top of his bag instead of inside it. He wore layers of warm clothes, but the cold, moist air seeped through to his skin.

Schwimmer handed him a cup of coffee. "You must have been tired," he said. "You slept nearly three hours."

"I guess so," Bently replied. Schwimmer had lit a gas lantern, and it illuminated a bright circle in front of their tents.

"You okay, man? You don't seem like yourself," Schwimmer said.

"I'm fine, but I can't wait to start hunting."

"Which way do you want to go tomorrow?"

"I think we should split up," Bently said. "You pick the way you want to go, and I'll go the opposite direction."

"I thought we decided to hunt together," Schwimmer said. "Wouldn't it be better if we didn't separate, you know, in case one of us has a problem? You can shoot the first good bear we see. I have no issue with that."

"We won't have any problems, and it'll be better if we go separate directions," Bently said firmly.

Schwimmer shrugged. "Okay, man, it's up to you."

PRESENT DAY
FRIDAY, JUNE 27TH
2:30 P.M.

Steve Duncan stared at the stack of papers in front of him. At times like this, he hated his job. All he wanted to do was fly, but owning your own charter airlines meant less flying and more paperwork. All three of his Beavers and the 206 would be busy most of the day, and he knew this should make him happy, but his feet would not leave the ground all day. Here he sat, chained to his desk, filling out government forms, paying bills, and sending out invoices. Instead of hiring another pilot, he needed to hire a good bookkeeper, but it seemed good bookkeepers were harder to find than pilots, and he hated training people.

"Come in," Steve called in response to the rapid knock on his office door. He welcomed the diversion, but when he saw the worried look on Charli's face, a knot began to form in the pit of his stomach. Charli had been his dispatcher for ten years and had worked for another airline before he'd hired her. Besides his head pilot, Stan, Charli was his most valuable employee, and if she looked concerned, it meant he had a problem somewhere in his operation.

Charli closed the door behind her, and Steve watched her.

"Jake is overdue," she said.

Steve felt the knot morph into a ball of fire in his stomach. Less than two years earlier, one of his planes had exploded midair, killing the pilot and his five passengers. Steve did not think he could live through another loss like that. He had felt responsible for each person on the doomed plane, even though he had done nothing to cause the explosion. Only recently had he again been able to sleep through the night without waking to nightmares of exploding planes and grieving relatives. For a time, he had even considered selling Kodiak Flight Services and finding another line of work. He knew he'd never be happy doing anything else, though, and instead of selling his interest in the airlines, he took out a loan and bought out his partner. Now, the headaches were his and his alone.

Charli ran a hand through her long hair, which was now more gray than brown. She took her job as a dispatcher seriously, and daily, she was under a great deal of stress. Steve had watched her age over the last few years.

"How long overdue?" Steve tried to keep his voice calm.

"He left at 9:30 with one passenger for Karluk Lake. He was supposed to drop him off and then pick up two people on the other side of the lake and two people in Uyak Bay and then head back to town. He said to give him two-and-one-half hours, so I expected him back around one."

Steve checked his watch. It was a little after 2:30 p.m. "One of the groups probably wasn't ready to go, and he had to sit there and wait awhile."

"I know," Charli said, "but he always calls when he's delayed. You know how careful he is."

Steve did know. Jake was a good pilot who went by the book. Jake had flown planes all over the world, and you didn't get a job like that by being sloppy. Steve rubbed his forehead and then looked at Charli. "Let's give him another hour before we start to worry. Tell his next group of passengers he's running late and ask them if they'd like one of our van drivers to take them somewhere in town until their plane is ready." Steve knew these were unnecessary instructions for Charli. She excelled at handling people, especially restless customers waiting to board a floatplane. Steve needed to feel in charge of this situation, though, and telling Charli what to do helped him slow the rising panic he felt.

"Okay, I'll keep you posted," Charli said as she turned and left his office.

Steve pushed the chair away from his desk. He'd never be able to concentrate on paperwork now. Jake Shepherd was a first-rate pilot, and Steve had felt silly when he'd checked him out in the Beaver. He knew Shepherd could teach him a thing or two about flying, but the old pilot carefully paid attention to everything Steve said, and he even took notes in the small notebook he kept in his shirt pocket.

Steve believed Jake and the Beaver he was flying were fine, *but why hasn't he called the office to let Charli know he's running late? Maybe his satellite phone died, or perhaps he did something silly and got the plane stuck on the shore at Karluk and is too embarrassed to call and tell Charli what happened.* Jake was the kind of guy who would want to fix the problem he'd created before calling his boss to assure him everything was okay.

Steve felt some of the stress drain from his body. He felt eighty percent certain Jake Shepherd was alive and well. The plane might be damaged, but planes could be fixed. Steve again leaned over the paperwork on his desk and began filling out forms.

His desk phone rang ten minutes later.

"Duncan," he said.

"Steve," Charli's voice shook. "I have Sergeant Patterson with the Alaska State Troopers on the line. He says it's urgent."

"Connect me," Steve said.

"Sergeant Patterson, this is Steve Duncan," he said a moment later.

"Mr. Duncan," Patterson said, "I just received a frantic phone call from a woman on a satellite phone. The call cut out twice, and between the poor reception and the hysterical woman, I'm not sure what we have."

"What did she say?" Steve's heart pounded, and he fought to control his composure.

"She said one of your planes is tied to the shore on Karluk Lake, and the pilot is dead, sitting in the cockpit."

No—did Jake have a heart attack or a stroke? He isn't a young man, but he sailed through his physical with flying colors. He bragged that the doctor told him he had the heart of a man half his age. Still, these things happened, and at least he wasn't in the air with passengers when he died.

"Did the woman say anything else? Is she sure he's dead and not just unconscious?" Steve asked.

"She said he has a bullet hole in his head," Patterson said. "She told me his eyes are wide open, staring at nothing."

Steve couldn't think of anything to say. Of all the terrible scenarios he had envisioned from the moment Charli told him Jake was overdue, he had not, could not, imagine Jake had been murdered, shot while he sat in the cockpit of his plane. *Why would someone want to kill Jake?*

"Are you okay?" Patterson asked.

Steve realized he hadn't said anything in some time, but *what could he say?*

"What do we do now?" Steve asked. He wasn't sure his question made sense.

"If you're up to it, I'd like you to fly me and another trooper out to the crime scene. I could fly our plane, but you might see something we don't. After all, it's your plane and your pilot."

"Can I take another pilot with me?" Steve asked. "I can't leave Jake's plane sitting out there."

"Of course," Patterson said. "We need to take photos at the crime scene, and once we get the plane back to town, the crime scene techs will have to examine the plane, but once they're done, we'll release it to you."

"I'm ready to leave whenever you are," Steve said.

"I want to grab a few things, and then we'll be there," Patterson said.

Steve ignored the curious, worried stares of his office staff as he left his office and crossed to the bathroom. He removed his glasses, splashed water in his face, and stared at his reflection in the mirror. He was only 36 years old, but lines creased his forehead and radiated from his eyes. His short-cropped, brown hair was mostly gray and getting thinner by the day. He needed to get out of this business, or the stress would kill him before he turned fifty. He replaced his glasses, took several deep breaths, and walked out of the bathroom and into the main office to tell his staff the bad news.

PRESENT DAY
FRIDAY, JUNE 27TH
4:10 P.M.

Steve asked Rusty Hoak, one of his pilots, to fly to Karluk Lake with him and the troopers to help bring the plane Jake had been flying back to town. They were already down one plane, and diverting another plane and pilot threw the charter service's full schedule into disarray, but a few late flights and disgruntled passengers were the least of Steve's worries.

"Did you have any flights to Karluk this morning?" Steve asked Rusty as they stood on the dock waiting for the troopers.

"No, the only flight I had to the west side was a trip to Uyak this morning," Rusty said. "I dropped off Jeb White and some bear viewers at Fuller's lodge."

Steve nodded. "Did you talk to Jake on the radio?"

"No," Rusty shook his head, and Steve saw tears snaking from his soft brown eyes.

"I talked to Roy, though. He had a flight to Karluk at about the same time." Rusty said. "I think he was headed to the north end of the lake, but he might have seen something."

Roy Tayler was another pilot for Kodiak Flight Services. Steve made a mental note to talk to Roy and find out if he saw Jake's plane at Karluk. As rattled as Steve felt, though, he wasn't sure he would remember to do anything when he got back to town.

Steve's hands shook as he gripped the yoke of the plane for takeoff. Sergeant Patterson, who sat in the seat next to him, asked him if he was okay, and Steve nodded, fighting back the bile rising in his throat.

Steve told Patterson and Trooper Mark Traner everything he knew about Jake Shepherd on the one-hour flight to Karluk Lake. Jake had an exemplary record with Delta Airlines and had flown every model of big jet all over the world. Steve said he would never know as much about flying and planes as Jake Shepherd had. "He was a walking, talking, aircraft encyclopedia," Steve said. "You could ask him anything, historical or current about airplanes, and he knew the answer. I had some great conversations with him."

"Why did he quit flying for Delta, only to take a job here that must pay much less?" Traner asked.

Steve smiled at Patterson. "Trooper Traner must not be a pilot," Steve said.

"No, he's not," Patterson said, "or he would know the answer to his question."

"Flying a floatplane is a way of life," Steve said. "It's much more than a paycheck; it gets in your blood. Jake told me when he was young, his parents and then his wife pressured him to think bigger. They wanted him to fly bigger planes and bring home a bigger paycheck, so he did, but he said he always dreamed of someday returning to Kodiak and his roots as a floatplane pilot." Steve laughed. "He told me his wife, Inga, said when he retired from Delta, she would leave the grandkids in Atlanta and move to Kodiak with him if he still wanted to fly floatplanes. Jake said she really never believed he would do it, and when he got a job flying for me and told Inga he was ready to move, she was not happy."

Steve stared straight ahead in silence for a few minutes, and then he said, "I suppose Inga can move back to Atlanta, now."

"Where is Inga now?" Patterson asked

Steve understood Patterson's question. If Jake had been murdered, Patterson would look hard at those closest to him. "Not at Karluk Lake," he said. "I've met Inga Shepherd, and there is no way she would spend the night in a tent in the middle of a bunch of brown bears. I think Jake told me she'd gone back to Atlanta for a few weeks. She spent more time in Atlanta than in Kodiak."

"Do you know if Jake had any enemies?" Patterson asked.

"No," Steve said. "He was always cordial to everyone. His passengers loved him, and he took the time to get to know the office staff and the kids who drive the vans and load the planes for us. The other day, he brought Charli, our head dispatcher and office manager, flowers for her birthday. He was just that kind of guy, very thoughtful."

"He didn't mention any problems he had with anyone?" Patterson asked.

"No," Steve said, "nothing I can think of."

Steve remained quiet for several minutes, and then said, "There was one thing about Jake, though. He couldn't stand pilots who flew recklessly, and he let a few of the younger pilots know how he felt. Mostly they just had words, but a couple weeks ago, one kid took a swing at Jake when Jake threatened to report his carelessness to the FAA."

"What happened?" Patterson asked.

"Jake caught the kid's fist and bent his arm behind his back. He told him to grow up, and I guess the kid meekly walked away," Steve said.

"Who was the kid?" Patterson asked.

"His name is Jordan Gregg," Steve said. "He flies for Emerald Island Air."

"He's a commercial pilot?" Patterson's voice rose a notch.

"Yes," Steve said. "I called him a kid, but he's probably pushing thirty. He acts like a kid, but he isn't one."

"What did he do to anger Jake?" Traner asked.

"Jake was flying over Terror Flats when he saw Jordan buzz another Emerald Island Air plane. Jake said he came dangerously close to the other plane," Steve said.

"Why did he do it?" Traner asked.

"I guess his buddy was flying the other plane," Steve said, "and Jordan thought it would be funny to buzz him. To be honest, I've seen similar behavior between some of the Emerald Island Air pilots but nothing as bad as what Jake described to me. I have heard rumors those pilots pull some crazy stunts, though."

"Jake never said an unkind word to anyone who didn't deserve it," Rusty said from the backseat. "He gave a few pilots a dressing down for their own good. He didn't want them to kill themselves. He didn't think they took flying seriously enough."

"I understand, and I appreciate his motives," Patterson said, "but since Jake has apparently been murdered, we need to take a hard look at those pilots. When you two get back to the office this evening, would you please write down all the pilots Jake confronted?"

"Sure," Steve said, "but do you really think a pilot killed him?"

"At this point, everyone is a suspect," Patterson said.

PRESENT DAY
FRIDAY, JUNE 27TH
5:20 P.M.

A light breeze rippled Karluk Lake when Steve circled. This was Patterson's second visit to the lake in a little over a month, but this time, they were headed to the other side of Karluk. Patterson couldn't pick out the white and teal Beaver until Steve circled low over it. He landed smoothly on the surface of the lake and taxied up next to Jake's plane. The four men climbed from the airplane and jumped to the shore. A young, muscular man with a buzz cut and tattoos peeking out from under his long-sleeved, black T-shirt strode down the beach to meet them, a shotgun slung over his right shoulder.

"Tammy," he indicated with a jerk of his chin at the young, sobbing, blonde-haired woman sitting on the beach, "found him like this," he jerked his chin again, this time at Jake's plane. "We had nothing to do with it. I told her we should mind our own business, but she'd already called you."

Patterson thought it intriguing the young man volunteered his confession of innocence before being asked. The person first on the crime scene is always a person of interest, at least in the preliminary stages of an investigation, but this young, tough guy had with one statement made himself even more interesting to Patterson.

"What is your name?" Patterson asked.

"Why do you need to know my name?" Mr. Tough Guy asked.

Patterson leveled his gaze at the man-child and took two steps closer to him. "Because you and your friend discovered the plane and the dead pilot. We need your names for the record."

The young guy turned and looked at the blonde woman. "I told you, Tammy," he said. "Now, you got us all mixed up with the police."

The young woman sat with her head in her hands and did not acknowledge his comment.

"Name!" Patterson said. He'd pulled his notebook from his pocket, his pen poised to write.

"Brian Decker," he spat the words at Patterson. "She," he turned and jabbed a finger at the young woman, "is Tammy Monroe."

Patterson asked him to spell Tammy's name and then asked him to explain how they came to find the plane and the dead pilot.

"Tammy!" Brian yelled. "Get your butt up here and tell your story. This is your fault, not mine."

Tammy pushed herself off the ground and took a few wobbly steps toward Patterson. Patterson closed the distance because he feared she would fall if she tried to walk any further. She was very thin and looked no older than sixteen. Brian appeared to be in his twenties, and Patterson wondered if he was camping with an underage girl and that was why he was so reluctant to talk to police. Her eyes and nose were red from crying, and her limp, blonde hair clung to her wet face.

"Would you like to sit down, Miss?" Patterson asked.

"I'm okay," her voice rose barely above a whisper.

"How old are you?" Patterson couldn't help himself because she looked like a child.

"Seventeen." Her voice shook.

Patterson guessed she was no more than 14 now that he got a closer look at her, but he reminded himself he would get nowhere if he antagonized her and her friend. He had just one more personal question, and then he would move on to the issue at hand.

"Are you okay? Are you here voluntarily with Brian?"

"Hey!" Brian yelled. "What's that supposed to mean?"

"Yes," Tammy said. "He's my boyfriend."

"Tell me how you came to find the plane and the pilot," Patterson said.

Tammy opened her mouth to begin her tale, but instead, a sob escaped. She cried for a minute, took a deep breath and tried again. "We've been camping here for a week, and a plane was supposed to pick us up late morning, around 11:00 a.m. We had our gear packed and stacked at the top of the beach, but the plane didn't show up. I called Kodiak Flight Services on the satellite phone, and the lady said the pilot was probably running behind, and he'd be here soon." She took a ragged breath. "Brian told me to chill and said we were in no hurry because our flight back to Anchorage doesn't leave until 7:00 p.m. He stretched out in the sunshine and took a nap."

When Tammy took a break in her monologue, Patterson quickly asked, "Do you live in Anchorage, or are you traveling through Anchorage to someplace else?"

"We live in Anchorage," Tammy said, "or at least I do. Brian lives in Eagle River."

"So, Brian was napping, and what did you do?" Patterson asked, hoping to nudge her back into her story.

"I decided to walk along the lakeshore. I walked quite a ways before I saw the plane on the shore. With the sun glinting off the water, it was hard to see; it kind of blended into the water and the beach. Once I saw it, I realized it was a Kodiak Flight Services plane, and maybe the pilot landed in the wrong place and was looking for us. I ran toward the plane to tell the pilot where we're camped."

"Did you see anyone near the plane?" Patterson thought Tammy would have mentioned if she'd seen someone on the shore next to the plane, but the question had to be asked. You never knew what crazy, obvious detail people would omit from their account.

"No," Tammy said. "I thought it was weird I didn't see the pilot, but I figured he was either hiking around looking for us or sitting in his plane waiting for us to show up. To be honest, I didn't think much about anything. I ran as fast as I could toward the plane. I never suspected I would find . . ." She put her hands to her face as a fresh torrent of tears burst from her eyes.

Patterson had never seen anyone cry as effectively as Tammy Monroe. Her tear ducts would soon run dry. He waited for the sobs to stop. Tammy hugged herself, pulling her jacket tight.

When Tammy reined control over herself again, Patterson asked, "When did you realize something was wrong?"

"Not until I got to the plane." Her voice dropped to a whisper, and Patterson had to step closer to hear her.

"I saw the pilot sitting in the plane, so I called to him. When he didn't seem to hear me, I thought he had earbuds in his ears and was listening to music or something. Brian always has earbuds in his ears and doesn't hear anything I say." She looked at Brian and then back at Patterson. "I walked up to the window on the pilot's sided of the plane. It was open, so I reached in and touched his arm, and then I looked up at his face." Tammy sank to the ground and buried her face in her hands.

This interview could take the rest of the afternoon, Patterson thought, and he probably would learn nothing useful from Tammy Monroe.

"Stop being so weepy," Brian said to Tammy. He walked to her, helped her up from the beach, and supported her as she wobbled. He whispered something in her ear, and then louder he said, "Get on with the story, honey. The sooner you tell them what happened, the sooner we can get out of here."

Tammy nodded as she fought back the tears. "He had a bullet hole in his forehead, and his eyes were open wide. I knew right away he was dead. I know CPR," she said, "but I knew it was too late for that. There was nothing I could do."

"How soon after you found the body did you call the troopers?" Patterson asked.

"Right away. I still had the sat phone in my pocket."

"How did you know who to call?" Patterson asked this question purely out of curiosity.

Tammy handed the satellite phone to Patterson, and a smile crept onto her lips. "My Dad," she said, "is a worrier. He wasn't happy about Brian and me flying out to the wilds of Kodiak Island. He rented the sat phone for me and then covered it with labels for every law enforcement agency on the island and made sure I knew which number to call depending on my emergency."

"You have a smart dad," Patterson said. "Be sure to thank him for us."

Tammy looked down at the ground. "I will," she said in a soft voice.

"Tammy," Patterson said. "Did you touch anything on the inside or outside of the plane?"

"I don't think so," she said. "I don't know."

"What about you, Brian? Can you give us your account of what happened?"

Brian sighed and shrugged his shoulders. "What's to tell? Tammy came running down the beach, crying and all hysterical-like. I couldn't make sense out of what she was saying, but she kept insisting I come with her, so I followed her here. I saw the dead pilot, and then she told me she'd called you guys. We sat on the beach and waited for you to arrive, end of story."

"Did you touch anything inside or outside of the plane?" Patterson asked.

"I didn't get in the plane if that's what you're asking, but I might have touched the window or the metal on the outside. I don't know."

"Mark," Patterson turned to face the other trooper who stood a few feet behind him. "Get their fingerprints so we can exclude them when the techs run the prints on the plane.

"Sure," Mark said. He opened his backpack and removed his forensic field kit.

"I don't like this," Brian said.

"It will only take a minute," Patterson said. He neglected to say the fingerprinting process was voluntary and Brian and Tammy could refuse to be fingerprinted. These prints would be tossed out of a court of law, but Patterson wanted to know more about this young couple, and fingerprints, even if they weren't admissible in court, were a quick way to learn why Brian wanted nothing to do with the police.

After Brian and Tammy had been printed, Steve told them another plane would pick them up in about an hour. As the couple walked glumly down the beach back to their campsite, Patterson removed a camera from his pack and began shooting photos of the Beaver, the rope tying it to the tree on the bank, and the area around the crime scene.

"I only see two sets of tracks on the beach," Patterson said. "We need to take a close look at Tammy's and Brian's boots." He looked at Traner.

"Yes, sir. Do you want me to catch up with them and do that now?"

"They're not going anywhere for a while," Patterson said. "Let's look at the crime scene first. We might have other questions for them. I'll take several photos of the shoe prints, and you look around carefully to see if you see more in the wet mud."

Traner did not find more footprints near the plane, so Patterson gave the nod, and he, Traner, and Steve approached Jake's plane.

Rusty walked to the other Beaver and sat on the float. He propped his elbows on his knees, cradled his chin in his hands, and stared at the gentle waves caressing the shore beneath the pontoons. Patterson understood why Rusty did not want to see what had happened to his co-worker and friend. Steve, on the other hand, probably felt it was his responsibility to know what had happened to Jake.

The Beaver looked intact with no visible damage. As they neared the plane from the front, the sun's glare on the glass prevented them from seeing the interior. Once they walked around the nose to the pilot's side, Patterson saw the pilot's window slid open. *Had Jake opened the window, and if so, why? Was it hot in the plane? Had he opened it to speak to someone? Did it matter? If someone approached his plane, he probably would have opened the window to talk to the person. On the other hand, why not just open the door to have a conversation? Maybe Jake had opened the door, and the killer closed it. It would be much easier to shoot a pilot through an open door than through the small window.*

Patterson and Traner slipped on nitrile gloves once they reached the pilot's side of the plane. Steve stood behind the two troopers. Now, Patterson could clearly see Jake Shepherd sitting in the pilot's seat, eyes open wide, staring at nothing.

"I think we should print the door handle before we do anything else," Patterson said. "I'll have technicians print the entire plane once we get it to town, but we should print the door handle now. It's likely Jake opened the door to talk to someone, and that's when he was shot. If so, then the killer must have shut the door, and maybe we'll get lucky and find some prints."

"The door handle must be covered with prints," Steve said. "How will you be able to separate them?"

Patterson shrugged. "This is a long shot, but I want to dust it now before we touch it and possibly smudge the killer's prints."

While Patterson and Steve discussed the problem, Traner assembled the tools he needed to dust for prints. Patterson stood back while Traner climbed the steps of the plane and meticulously dusted powder on the door handle.

"Nothing," Traner said after a few minutes.

"No prints? That's not possible," Steve said.

"It's possible if someone wiped clean the door handle with a cloth," Patterson said.

Steve's blue eyes opened wide under his wire-rimmed glasses.

Patterson climbed up to the door and turned the handle. He snapped several photos of Jake's dead body and the interior of the plane. Except for the hole in the middle of Jake's forehead, the dried blood on his face, and his open eyes with their unfocused gaze, everything looked normal inside the de Havilland Beaver. Patterson felt certain the killer had been outside the plane when he'd shot Jake. Jake had likely been shot from a distance of no more than six feet. *Jake must have trusted his killer to let him or her approach so closely. Even if his killer was an adversary and not a friend, Jake must not have been afraid of the person.*

Patterson carefully examined Jake's body, looking for blood from other bullet holes, but he only saw the exit wound from the one bullet in the back of Jake's head toward the top. Patterson noticed the corner of a small, bound notebook protruding from Jake's shirt pocket. He asked Traner for an evidence bag and then carefully held only the corner of the notebook while he slid it from Jake's pocket. A pen was clipped to the cover of the book, and Patterson dropped both items into the bag. He hoped Jake had been considerate enough to jot the name of his killer in the book before he died. *If only it could be so easy.*

Patterson called to Traner, "Get a bag, and let's get Jake packaged."

Patterson turned his attention to Steve. "Do you mind flying this plane back to Kodiak? We'll put Jake's body in the rear. I'd like you to wear nitrile gloves and touch as little as possible. As soon as I get back to town, I'll call my office and have two troopers and the forensic techs come down to the dock. They'll go over the plane as quickly as possible and release it to you."

"What about Jake's body?" Steve asked.

"The troopers will take care of it. We'll send it up to Anchorage to the Medical Examiner's office. I'll call Dr. Libby up there and see if he can do the autopsy. He is very good," Patterson said.

"I'd like Rusty to fly me back to town," Patterson said. "After you leave, Steve, Mark and I will search around and under the area where Jake's plane sat on the beach to see if we missed anything." He looked at Traner. "Mark, after we're done, I'd like you to stay here and walk down to Brian and Tammy's camp and take photos of their footwear. I'll fly back out here with our plane and bring camping gear. You and I will spend a night in the woods and find out who else is camped in this area."

"Yes, sir," Traner said. He looked pleased with the idea of a night out of town.

Patterson pressed a reluctant Rusty Hoak into service to help move Jake out of the airplane, into a body bag, and back into the plane. Steve donned nitrile gloves and climbed into the cockpit. Rusty untied the plane, and he, Patterson, and Traner pushed the plane away from the beach and into deeper water, spinning it so the nose pointed away from the beach. Once Steve had room to maneuver, he started the engine, taxied a few minutes to let the plane warm up, and then smoothly skimmed across the water and into the sky.

As soon as the plane departed, Patterson and Traner began to study the area on the beach where it had been. Patterson shot several more photos, and then both troopers walked the entire area, searching the ground, and hoping to find anything to give them a clue to the identity of Jake's killer.

"I have something," Traner said.

"Patterson approached him, and Traner held out the brass shell casing. Patterson dropped the casing into an evidence bag and then peered at it through the clear bag and studied it for several seconds.

"You don't see many of these anymore," he finally said.

"No, sir," Traner said. "It's a 30-30 shell, right?"

"It is, and we have another question for Brian and Tammy, and it's one I should have asked them while they were here."

"What type of gun or guns they have in their camp," Traner said.

"Exactly," Patterson said. "I saw the shotgun slung over Brian's shoulder, but it might not be the only gun in their possession."

"You don't think those two kids killed Jake, do you?" Rusty asked.

"At this moment, Brian Decker sits at the top of my list of suspects," Patterson said. "But, I haven't started investigating yet."

"Why would that kid shoot Jake?" Rusty said. "Jake was here to take them back to town. You don't kill your pilot."

"Rusty," Patterson said, "when I became a cop, one of the first things I learned was violent crimes usually don't make sense. We know Jake sometimes confronted people, especially young men when he felt they were doing something wrong or stupid. I can imagine a scenario where Mr. Brian said something derogatory or even hit poor Tammy, and Jake lost his temper and yelled at Brian. Then, Brian, who was already angry with Tammy, pulled his gun, and before he had a chance to cool down, he shot Jake in the head. After he came to his senses, Brian forced Tammy to call us, and they arranged the little skit they performed for us here on the beach."

"Tammy really seemed upset," Rusty said.

"I have no doubt her tears were real, but then they would be if she'd just watched her boyfriend shoot a man," Patterson said. "Mind you, I'm not saying Brian killed Jake; I'm just saying we can't rule out Brian or Tammy yet."

1976

SUNDAY, OCTOBER 24TH
6:10 P.M.

Schwimmer was already in camp when Bently returned. The weather had been beautiful all day, sunny and cold. It was after 6:00 p.m. now, though, and beginning to get dark. Schwimmer was brewing a pot of coffee on the small camp stove and sat above it, warming his hands.

"Hey man, how did it go?"

Bently didn't know why, but this simple question irritated him. He forced a steadying breath and tried to maintain his composure. "I saw seven bears today but nothing worth going after. How about you?"

"I saw three," Schwimmer said.

"Were any of them big?"

Schwimmer hesitated a beat before answering. "Man, to be honest, I can't tell. That's why we should hunt together. I need your help judging size. I've never been around bears before."

Bently threw his pack on the ground. "You think I've ever seen a Kodiak bear before now? I told you; look at the shape of the bear. If it's square, it's small. If it's rectangular, it's bigger. A bigger bear has a longer neck, and its head appears small in relation to the rest of its body. Boars are heavier than sows through the shoulders. A big bear's moves are more deliberate, and they walk at a steady pace. A young, smaller bear has jerky motions. It runs, it stops, it rolls on the ground, things like that. Be sure the bear you go after doesn't have cubs because it's illegal to shoot a sow with cubs. I told you all of this before."

"Okay," Schwimmer said. "You don't have to get mad at me. I just think it would be more fun to hunt together and help each other. If you go after a bear, I can watch it through the spotting scope and give you hand signals to direct you to it, and you can do the same for me."

"I don't need your help." Bently scooped up his pack, tossed it into his tent, and climbed in behind it.

An hour later, Bently emerged. He looked into Schwimmer's tent where he found his friend in his sleeping bag reading a book with a flashlight.

"Sorry," Bently said. "I didn't mean to yell at you earlier, but I need some time alone on this trip."

"That's cool, man."

Bently held up the bottle of whiskey. "You want a drink to help you sleep?"

PRESENT DAY
FRIDAY, JUNE 27TH
8:00 P.M.

Rusty did not have much to say on the flight back to town, and his silence suited Patterson fine. Patterson's mind raced, organizing the steps he would follow in the investigation into the murder of Jake Shepherd. At first glance, this seemed like an impossible crime, but Patterson had investigated enough crimes to know by the end of the day, he would likely have one or possibly several suspects in mind for the murder of Jake Shepherd. Most murders weren't well-planned, and criminals usually made stupid mistakes. Someone saw something, and Patterson believed he would have the perpetrator of this crime in prison in a matter of days, if not hours. *Still, whoever murdered Jake took the time to wipe his prints from the door handle of the plane. It would take a cool, calculating individual to wipe his prints from the plane while anyone flying over Karluk, out in a boat on the lake, or hiking down the beach could see him—or her.*

Patterson acknowledged Brian could have killed Jake in a fit of rage, and then he and Tammy had at least an hour to manipulate the crime scene and wipe away prints before the troopers arrived. He wanted to find out as much as he could about the young couple. If Tammy was as distraught as she seemed, Patterson felt he could easily break her, and if she knew who killed Jake, he'd get it out of her. If she had just been acting for the troopers, then she should be on Broadway because she gave a believable performance. He'd soon learn more about Brian and Tammy.

Meanwhile, tonight, he and Traner would interview everyone camped near the spot where Tammy found Jake. He had only noticed one campsite when they were landing, but there could be more. The dense vegetation near the lake could hide an entire town. He also wanted to talk to Jake's last passenger. He was camped on the other side of the lake, so Patterson doubted he saw anything related to the murder, but perhaps Jake said something during the flight that would help unravel this mystery.

When the plane pulled up to the dock in Kodiak, Patterson saw Steve standing on the pontoon of Jake's plane, guarding the body until the troopers arrived to remove it from the plane. Patterson called Irene, the trooper dispatcher, just before they landed, as soon as he could pick up a cell signal. He asked her to send three troopers and the crime scene techs to Trident Basin. While he waited, he joined Steve and stood silently next to Jake's plane.

While the troopers maneuvered Jake's body out of the plane, Steve ordered one of his freight handlers to place a pallet on the forklift and drive it down the steep ramp to the floatplane dock. The troopers carefully loaded Jake's body onto the forklift, and the forklift driver slowly ascended the ramp to the parking lot. Steve followed behind the forklift, and a quiet group gathered to pay their respects. Patterson noted the gathered group included not only Kodiak Flight Services employees but also employees from the other three air charter services based out of Trident Basin. Many in the assembled crowd cried, and some bowed their heads. Patterson saw Rusty standing at the back of the crowd, a handkerchief held to his face as he looked at the ground.

Once the troopers placed Jake's body in the back of a trooper SUV, Patterson called Irene. "What do you have for me?" he asked.

"I got ahold of Dr. Libby, and he said he'll do the autopsy as soon as possible. He said he'd do it tomorrow if we can get the body there in time."

"Have you contacted the airlines?"

"Yes, sir. They have room on the 10:00 p.m. flight. Will that work?"

"We'll have to hurry, but we should make it. Thanks, Irene, and thanks for staying late."

"Is there anything else?"

Patterson paused for a moment. He needed to be in three places at once. He wanted this investigation to proceed swiftly and meticulously, but he couldn't waste too much time if he planned to fly back to Karluk Lake tonight. These were the longest days of the year, but it was already 8:30 p.m., and he not only needed to get back to Karluk before dark, but he wanted to arrive there in time to interview some of the parties camped near where Jake's plane had been found. Some of those campers probably planned to raft down the Karluk River soon, and then they would fly back to wherever they came from, and that could be anyplace in the world. If a camper killed Jake, only a narrow window of opportunity existed for Patterson to catch the murderer. He knew he had a good team of troopers, and he needed to delegate parts of the investigation to them.

"Yes, Irene," he said. "If you don't mind staying a little later, I'd like you to call the dispatchers for all the floatplane charter services in town and find out how many parties they have in the field at Karluk Lake right now and how many they picked up there today. We need all the information they have on the passengers to and from Karluk, and if they flew folks back to town from Karluk, ask if they know where those people were planning to stay tonight. I'd like to intercept and question them before they leave the island. If they've already left Kodiak, then we'll need to track them down and interview them by phone."

"Got it," Irene said. "I'm not sure the airlines will be open this late, but I'll give it a shot."

"If their offices are closed tonight, then call them first thing in the morning."

"Yes, sir."

"I'm flying back to Karluk tonight, and I'll have Randy and Peter take the body to the airport.

Report whatever you find about the campers to Sara, and she will be in charge of setting up interviews as soon as possible. Also, if you could mark the camping spot of each party on a map, it would be a big help."

"I'm on it," Irene said.

"Thanks, Irene. You're the best."

While Patterson was speaking to Irene, the crime scene techs arrived, and Patterson hurried down the ramp to Jake's plane to talk to them. They would, of course, inspect the entire plane, but he wanted to let them know the pilot's door handle had been wiped clean of prints.

Next, Patterson called Sara. Sara had only worked as a trooper on Kodiak for the past four months, but the young woman impressed Patterson. She had a quick mind, a good work ethic, and excellent people skills. If she remained a trooper, he believed she would move quickly up the ranks.

Sara was off duty, but she didn't hesitate when Patterson asked her to go to trooper headquarters and help Irene map camper locations and then bring the information to him at Kodiak Flight Services. Meanwhile, Patterson caught up with Steve and asked if he knew when Brian Decker and Tammy Monroe were due to arrive back in town.

"Let's ask Charli," Steve said. "She's the one who runs this place."

Charli was already back at her desk answering phone calls when Patterson and Steve entered the office. She put the caller on hold and looked expectantly at Steve as they approached her.

"Has someone picked up the Decker party yet?" Steve asked.

"Stan has them." She looked up at the clock. "They should be here in fifteen or twenty minutes."

"Sergeant Patterson wants to talk to them before we take them to the airport, so make sure they don't sneak out of here."

"I'll hold them as long as I can." She looked at Patterson.

"I'll be outside," Patterson said. "I'm sure I'll see them, but if I don't, yell at me."

Patterson wanted to run back to headquarters, pack camping gear, and then come back here and warm up his plane, but he couldn't afford to miss Brian and Tammy. He reminded himself to delegate. He noticed Ted, one of the young troopers who had helped move Jake's body, standing at the top of the ramp watching the activity around Jake's plane. He called to him and sent him back to headquarters to pack the camping gear.

Twenty-five minutes later, Patterson watched a Kodiak Flight Services Beaver glide in for a landing and pull up to the floatplane dock. The pilot emerged from the plane, and a few moments later, he saw the thin frame of Tammy followed by bulky Brian step onto the float and then onto the dock. Patterson met the pair at the top of the ramp.

"Hi, Tammy," he said. "How are you doing?"

"Okay, I guess." The girl started shaking as soon as she spotted Patterson.

"We told the other trooper dude everything we know," Brian said.

"I just have a couple more questions," Patterson said. He kept his tone light. He wanted Tammy and Brian's cooperation, and he already knew Brian was a powder keg waiting to blow. He hoped Tammy figured this out about her boyfriend before it was too late, but Patterson wasn't a relationship counselor.

"We have a flight to catch." Brian puffed himself up like a rooster.

"This won't take long, and I'll make certain you get to the airport on time."

"What do you want, then?" Brian asked.

"Do you have any guns with you other than the shotgun I saw you with earlier?" Patterson asked.

"The other trooper already asked us about guns," Brian said.

"The faster you answer my questions, the faster you'll get to the airport," Patterson said.

Brian let out a long sigh. "Yes, we'd be idiots to go camping on Kodiak without bear protection. I have a .308 Winchester, and Tammy's dad loaned her his Colt .45. We also have bear spray."

"Did Trooper Traner look at your guns?" Patterson asked.

Tammy nodded.

Brian said, "Yes, he looked at our guns." He stretched out the words to let Patterson know he was bored by this line of questioning.

Patterson knew Traner well enough to know he would have done a thorough job of examining the firearms, and since neither was the same caliber as the shell casing they found on the beach, he didn't think either weapon had been used to kill Jake. While the shell casing could have been left on the beach by someone other than Jake's murderer, the casing looked new, not like a brass casing weathered by years of exposure to the harsh Kodiak climate. Patterson had no doubt the casing they found on the beach had been fired out of the barrel of the murder weapon.

Patterson switched to a new line of questions. "Did you see or hear any planes low overhead or landing on the lake this morning?"

"We saw planes everywhere the entire time we were there," Brian said. "I thought we were going to the wilderness, but it was like camping in the middle of the freakin' freeway."

"What about this morning?" Patterson gently brought the subject back to his question. "Tell me about the planes you saw today."

To Patterson's surprise, Tammy answered his question.

"One plane circled above us, and it was about time for us to be picked up, so I thought it was our plane. Then it circled again maybe fifteen minutes later, but it never landed." She paused for a moment and then amended her statement. "At least I didn't hear it land."

Patterson thought about what Tammy had said. "Could it have been two different planes you saw circling above you?"

Tammy looked at Brian, and when he shrugged, she said, "I guess. I didn't really look at them. We were busy tearing down camp and hauling gear to the lakeshore." She blushed. "We overslept."

"What about other campers?" Patterson asked. "Was anyone camped near you?"

"We saw some obnoxious guys fishing one day," Tammy said. "They were out in a boat, and one guy kept standing up and screaming obscenities, and the other guy in the boat yelled at him to shut the—you know—up."

Tammy blushed again, and Patterson wanted to smash Brian's nose for taking advantage of this sweet, young girl. He felt sorry for her poor parents. He was certain they didn't want her camping with Brian, but Tammy was at a tough age. *If they restricted her too much, she might rebel and do something stupid like run off and marry Brian. If they gave her some leeway while quietly discouraging her relationship with Brian, though, they might help her see the light, so she'd eventually dump the guy and move on with her life.* At times like this, Patterson was glad his son was grown and he didn't have teenagers. As soon as this thought entered his mind, his stomach dropped. How could he even think such a thing?

"There was the kid, too," Tammy said, and looked at Brian. "Didn't you say you saw a kid?"

Brian nodded. "The second evening we were there I saw a kid skipping stones across the lake. I never saw him again, though."

"What did he look like, and how old was he?" Patterson asked.

"How should I know? I don't know nothin' about kids." Brian looked at the ground and finally said, "He had blond hair cut short, and I guess he was ten or so. He was several hundred yards down the beach, so I can't tell you if he had blue or brown eyes or a mole on his left cheek. He was a kid skipping rocks."

"I understand," Patterson said, fighting to remain calm. "I appreciate any information you can give me." He looked from Brian to Tammy. "Did you see anyone else while you were at Karluk?"

Tammy slowly shook her head, and Brian said, "No, man, we didn't go to Karluk Lake to see people. We wanted to be alone and enjoy the wilderness."

Patterson abruptly walked away from the pair before he did or said something he would regret. Brian Decker had to be at least twenty-five years old, and although Tammy appeared to be younger than 17, he had believed her when she'd told him she was 17. He'd also believed her when she'd said her father knew she was camping with Brian. He'd wanted to ask the pair for driver's licenses, but he didn't want to antagonize them. He needed their help to solve Jake's murder.

Since Brian and Tammy lived in Anchorage, Patterson knew he could find out everything he needed to know about the pair. He'd pull up their driver's licenses and look at Brian's police record, and he had no doubt the young man had a record. He figured he'd find a few misdemeanors and maybe even a felony or two in Brian's past. If he discovered Tammy's age was younger than she'd said, he'd alert the police in Anchorage.

Patterson returned to the Kodiak Flight Services office. He asked Charli if they had a van available to run Tammy and Brian to the airport, and she said she'd take care of it. Meanwhile, Ted returned and told Patterson he packed the camping gear in his SUV and was parked near the second ramp, above the float where the trooper plane was docked.

Patterson turned and began to walk with Ted toward the second ramp when he heard a female call his name. He turned and saw Trooper Sara Byram hurrying toward him. When she approached, her brown eyes blazed with focus, and her rosy cheeks betrayed her excitement at being called in to assist with a big investigation.

"Sir," she said, "Irene and I talked to every charter company except Kodiak Vistas Charter Service."

"Good job, Sara," Patterson said. "That was fast work. What do you have? Let's sit on that bench." Patterson pointed to a small, wooden bench twenty feet in front of them. Sara handed him a map, and he spread it on his lap. Several numbered marks covered the topographic map of Karluk Lake. Patterson studied the marks while Sara explained them to him.

"We identified twelve parties who might have been in the vicinity when Jake was murdered. Three parties were supposedly heading down the river on rafts, but they had boats, so they were mobile, and I don't think we can rule them out. Kodiak Flight Services dropped off two of the groups, and Emerald Island Air dropped off the third."

"I agree the rafters are longshots, but we need to talk to them when they get back to town. Will you make sure you or one of the guys meet their planes?"

"Yes, sir," Sara said. She looked at him with wide eyes and nodded so seriously, Patterson nearly laughed. Most young troopers ached to show they could handle responsibility and wanted to perform well, so they could move up the ranks. Unfortunately, though, female troopers often had to perform at twice the level of their male counterparts before their superiors noticed and respected them. If Patterson did nothing else while he was stationed on Kodiak, he promised himself he would shower Sara Byram with accolades and make certain his superiors took notice of this stellar trooper in the ranks.

"Who else do we have?" Patterson asked.

"Three more parties are camped at Karluk getting ready to raft the river," Sara said. "All three plan to start down tomorrow." Sara stabbed a point on the map at the head of the Karluk River. "Two parties are camped in the cabins near the river, but the third party is camped here." She pointed the tip of her pen at a dot with the number three beside it.

"How far is their camp from where we found Jake's body?" Patterson asked.

"About two miles," Sara said.

"So, they're camped a mile north of Tammy and Brian's camp," Patterson said.

"Approximately, yes." Sara nodded.

"Tammy told me about an obnoxious group of guys she saw out in a boat," Patterson said. "I think we've found them. Who dropped them off?"

Sara looked at her notes. "Eagle Charters, sir."

"Traner and I will interview those campers," Patterson said. "What else do you have?"

"Emerald Island Air dropped off a group of four bear viewers at Jason Meckel's lodge at the south end of the lake near O'Malley Lake."

Patterson knew Jason Meckel was a bear-viewing guide who owned a small lodge on Karluk Lake and catered to tourists who wanted to see the majestic Kodiak bear. Meckel had a reputation as a hothead and had filed at least twenty complaints the previous summer about low-flying aircraft. Patterson tried explaining to Meckel there was little he could do about the airplanes because most of his complaints involved Fish and Wildlife planes landing at the refuge research facility on Camp Island, a small island near the south end of Karluk Lake. He told Meckel the planes sometimes had no other option but to fly low over O'Malley and his lodge. He'd even tried joking that planes must fly low to land, but Meckel hadn't been appeased, and he kept filing complaints.

Patterson hadn't considered Meckel's lodge or the Camp Island research facility. All the employees of the lodge plus the researchers would have to be questioned. He suddenly felt weary. This investigation hadn't even started, and it already seemed out of his control. Both Camp Island and Meckel's lodge were several miles from where they'd found Jake. He doubted the murderer was one of the researchers or an employee or guest at Meckel's lodge, but he couldn't rule out anyone this early in the investigation.

"Tell Peter I want him to charter out to Karluk tomorrow and interview everyone at Camp Island and at Meckel's lodge," Patterson said. "He can take someone with him to divide the work." He looked Sara in the eye. "I need you to stay in town and organize things until I get back."

"Yes, sir," Sara said with a slight quaver in her voice. "How long will you be gone?"

"I plan to be back tomorrow, but you never know. The forecast is calling for fog tomorrow morning, and if it persists, I could be stuck a day or two. This investigation can't wait for me to return to town. We need to immediately question possible suspects and anyone who could have seen something. The longer we wait, the harder it will be to track down leads."

"I understand, sir. I'll get things moving on this end," Sara said.

"You've told me about seven groups, so we have five left."

"Yes, sir, and the other five groups are just camped at the lake. I'm not sure if they are hikers or bear viewers, or simply like to camp in the woods."

"Are any of them camped near where we found Jake?" Patterson asked.

"First of all," Sara said, "I should mention none of these groups has a boat, and since three of the groups are on the other side of the lake, I'd say they are long shots. The closest group to where you found Jake is a party of four. Jake dropped them off a few days ago, and they are supposed to be there another three days. They are camped approximately two miles south of where you found Jake." Sara looked down at the map. "Two parties of two people each are camped near the river on the north end, but neither group has plans to raft the river. One of those parties is on the east shore of the lake and the other is on the west shore. Then, there's a group on the west side of the lake near the south end."

"What about the guy Jake dropped off before he was killed?" Patterson asked.

"He is also on the other side of the lake." Sara pointed at a dot near the southwest side of the lake with the number twelve beside it.

"This is great work, Sara. I'll take the map with me." Patterson said. "I'll give you a call tomorrow morning around 10:00 to check in. Go home and get some rest. There's not much more you can do tonight, and tomorrow will be a busy day."

Sara started to walk toward the parking lot, but Patterson called to her.

"Sir?" she asked.

"I nearly forgot." He pulled two bags out of his jacket pocket. "Get this evidence to the crime-scene people." He handed Sara the two bags, one held Jake's notebook and the other contained the shell casing. "Tell them to process the notebook as soon as possible. It probably won't help us find Jake's killer, but you never know."

PRESENT DAY
FRIDAY, JUNE 27TH
10:45 P.M.

Patterson still had plenty of daylight for the return flight to Karluk Lake. He wondered, though, if he and Traner would have enough light to find and interview any of the parties camped near where they'd found Jake's plane. Since the family group planned to camp three more days before their scheduled pickup, he and Traner could wait to talk to them until the following morning.

Patterson's priority was to interview the party of six guys camped two miles from where they found Jake. The men were planning to raft the river in the morning and would likely be on the river two days or longer. He knew the men had at least one and probably two or even three boats. They might have been out on the lake when Jake was murdered, and they possibly saw something of interest to aid the investigation.

When Patterson landed and pulled up to the beach, Traner stood waiting for him. Patterson motioned for Traner to get into the plane.

"What's up, sir?" Traner asked as he tightened his seat belt.

"Before it gets dark, I want to interview a party of six men camped toward the north end of the lake. I thought we could get there quicker by plane than on foot." Patterson said.

"Yes, sir. I did some hiking this evening and located their campsite. I also found the camp of a family about one-and-one-half miles south of here."

"We'll catch them in the morning," Patterson said. "I want to talk to this group of men tonight because according to the dispatcher at Eagle Charters, the men plan to start down the river sometime tomorrow morning." Patterson glanced at Traner. "Did you talk to them?"

"No, sir," Traner said. "I thought I should wait for you. The only people I talked to were Tammy and Brian. I photographed their shoes and checked their guns. They didn't have anything that would take a .30-30 cartridge. At least, they didn't show me a firearm capable of shooting a .30-30 cartridge. I asked if I could search their bags, but Brian said, 'No.'"

"Brian isn't the sort to cooperate with law enforcement," Patterson said as he brought the plane in for a landing. He and Traner quickly tied the Beaver to a tree and hiked up the path toward the camp.

As soon as they stepped onto the trail, they heard voices and laughter. They followed the sounds up the path to a small clearing in the brush.

"Hello," Patterson said loudly, hoping not to surprise the men.

He heard frantic movements, and when he entered the clearing, two men held rifles trained on him.

"Whoa." Patterson held up his hands. "I'm Alaska State Trooper Sergeant Dan Patterson. Trooper Mark Traner is behind me. Lower your weapons."

Both men pointed their rifles at the ground, but Patterson noticed they still held the guns firmly. He wondered if he should have considered this a potentially volatile situation. Maybe he should have entered the campsite with his gun drawn, and he hoped Traner, who was still behind him in the brush and not visible to the men around the campfire, had his weapon in his hand and ready to use.

"Whataya want?" a rotund, balding man who looked to be in his sixties seated on the far side of the fire asked, his words slurred as if he had a mouthful of peanut butter. He held a bottle of whiskey in his right hand and seemed to have trouble focusing on Patterson.

"We'd just like to ask you gentlemen some questions," Patterson said.

"How do we know you're really a trooper?" one of the armed men asked. This man appeared to be in his forties and was short with sandy hair.

Patterson handed the man his ID and showed him his badge. The man nodded and laid his rifle on the ground. The other rifle bearer followed suit, and Patterson advanced toward the fire. He heard Traner re-holster his gun.

"We ain't done nothin' wrong," the drunk said.

Patterson took in the scene. He counted three bottles of whiskey and one of rum. He'd bet none of these men was sober, and the idea of firearms and alcohol made him uneasy. He needed to tread lightly here. Traner walked up beside him and stood, legs spread, his hands resting on his gun belt. He looked prepared to draw his weapon if the situation deteriorated.

"Do you know a pilot was murdered today two miles south of here?" Patterson asked.

"No," several of the men said, and they all shook their heads.

Drunks didn't lie well, and Patterson knew they weren't telling the truth. *Do they simply not want to be involved in a criminal investigation, or are they hiding something?*

"You didn't see the pilot or the plane on the beach?"

Head shakes all around.

"I noticed three rafts pulled up on the beach—were you out in those today?"

"Yes," the man sitting to the left of the drunk near the fire said. "We were out fishing. We were all over the lake, but we stayed near each other."

"And you plan to float the river tomorrow?" Patterson addressed the question to the same man.

"That's right," the man said. "We're gonna fish our way down the river."

Patterson looked down at the notes Sara had given him. She'd obtained the names of the individuals in this party from the dispatcher at Eagle Charters. "Which of you are Bobby and Donald Brinker?"

The men remained motionless for several moments, and finally, the tall, thin man who looked to be in his early sixties standing the farthest away from Patterson spoke. He had been one of the men pointing a rifle at Patterson when he'd walked into their camp. "I'm Don Brinker." He pointed at the overweight drunk still sitting by the fire. "That's my brother Bobby."

"None of your damn business who we are," Bobby Brinker said. His black eyes reflected the light from the fire. Two brothers couldn't look any less alike than Bobby and Don Brinker did. Don was tall, thin, sported a full head of wavy, brown hair, and had a full beard, while his brother was short, fat, nearly bald, and clean-shaven. They both had dark eyes, but while Don's were big and hard to read, Bobby's beady eyes looked mean.

"Where are you and Bobby from?" Patterson addressed the question to Don.

"None of your damn business," Bobby bellowed, and struggled to stand before the guys sitting on either side of him pulled him back to the ground.

Don looked at his brother. "Shut up, Bobby."

The sharp command induced Bobby to open his bottle of whiskey and take a slug.

Don's gaze slowly returned to Patterson's face. "I'm from Wasilla, and Bobby lives in Kodiak. These guys," he waved his hand at the rest of the group, "are my friends, and all live in the Palmer-Wasilla area. Bobby invited us down to Kodiak to spend a few days fishing with him, and that's all we've been doing. We're just six guys fishing, drinking, and getting away from our wives. We've been together the entire time, and we don't know anything about a dead pilot."

Patterson felt Don had just offered an alibi for the entire group when none had been requested. His interest in this group of men grew.

"I understand," Patterson said. "Listen, I have your names from the Eagle Charters dispatcher. Let me just get everyone straight so I can put a name with a face. After that, I'll leave you alone." The men said nothing, so he looked down at his list and said, "Which one of you is Ronald George?"

The man sitting to the right of Bobby raised his hand. George was a thin, bespectacled man of about fifty.

"David Landry?"

"That's me," said the sandy-haired man who'd asked to see Patterson's badge.

"How about Jeremy Lawson?" Patterson asked

"That's me," the man sitting to the far left by the fire said. Lawson looked young and fit with short, dark hair.

"Okay, so," Patterson pointed to the man sitting to the left of Bobby. "You must be Greg Sparks."

"That's right." Sparks was lean and muscular with a shaved head and a long, black beard.

"One more question," Patterson said. "Did you see any low-flying airplanes late this morning or early this afternoon?"

"At least three," Ronald George said.

"Right," Sparks agreed. "We were talking about all the noise. It was like fishing in the middle of an airport."

"Did you notice what kind of planes they were?" Patterson asked.

"One was a 206, and the other two were Beavers," Landry said.

"David is a pilot." Sparks volunteered.

"Are you a commercial pilot?" Patterson asked.

"No, no," Landry said. "I'm just a private pilot. I fly for fun when I have time."

"How long will you guys be on the river?" Patterson asked.

"You said one more question ten questions ago," Bobby yelled.

"Shut the—keep your mouth shut, Bobby," Don said. He turned to Patterson. "We plan to spend three nights on the river."

Patterson looked around the group of men. He wanted them to understand he believed they knew more than they were saying. "We'll want to interview you again when you get back to Kodiak."

"Like hell, you will." This time, Bobby managed to struggle to his feet. Sparks and George hopped up and held Bobby's arms while he thrashed.

"I hope you guys know it's illegal and stupid to consume alcohol while you are operating a boat," Patterson said as he turned to leave. None of the men responded to his comment.

1976

Bently stared through his scope at the bear walking across the alpine meadow. He wasn't small, but he wasn't big. On day twelve, this bear would be good enough, but this was only day three, and Bently wanted something bigger.

At 2:00 p.m., the snow started, and by 2:30, it began to blow. Bently knew it was time to head back to camp. Not only would he be unable to glass in a blizzard, but it would be dangerous to get caught away from camp in such weather. He began the two-mile hike back to his tent. As the snow grew heavier, he relied on his compass to point him in the right direction, but even then, he had trouble finding camp, and he almost walked past the tents, not recognizing the lumpy, white forms. He immediately began brushing the snow off the tents. They needed to remain vigilant, or the weight of the snow would collapse the tent poles, leaving them without shelter.

The snow fell so fast, visibility diminished to a few feet, and Bently realized he would need to clean the pop tents every hour, or even less, to keep them from collapsing. He wouldn't get much sleep tonight.

He looked around him and for the first time since returning to camp, he thought about Schwimmer. *Where is he? He probably has a compass with him, but does he know how to use it?* Bently considered himself a competent outdoorsman, but even he had nearly walked past the tents in the driving wind and snow, and conditions had steadily worsened since he'd arrived in camp. The wind whistled, blowing the heavy snow at a forty-five-degree angle. These were the worst blizzard conditions Bently had ever seen.

Bently thought about what he should do. How could he search for Schwimmer in these conditions? He had no idea even where Schwimmer had gone hunting today, and he'd never be able to find him in this weather.

He looked at his watch. It was 4:00 p.m. It would be getting dark soon. Could he find enough dry wood to start a campfire? Schwimmer might be able to see the glow of a fire through the heavy snow. Bently felt a mixture of fear and rage. He worried Schwimmer was wandering aimlessly through the blizzard and would die from hypothermia, and he was angry the idiot didn't know enough to come back to camp before the storm got bad. They both knew a severe snowstorm was predicted for today, and because of the dire forecast, Bently had chosen not to wander far from home. *Is Schwimmer so stupid he doesn't know how dangerous a blizzard can be, especially when camping in the wilderness?*

PRESENT DAY
SATURDAY, JUNE 28TH
1:35 A.M.

It was nearly dark by the time Patterson and Traner landed at their campsite. Patterson wished they had set up their camp while it was still light, but with the aid of the moon and headlamps, they erected their tents in a small clearing in the brush above the lakeshore. Both men were too tired for food and decided to save their freeze-dried meals for breakfast. Patterson badly wanted to review his notes and organize his thoughts about this case, but first, his brain needed a few hours of downtime.

"Let's get some sleep," Patterson said. "We'll go over the case and plan the rest of our interviews in the morning."

"Yes, sir," Traner said. "Do you want to get an early start?"

"Let's have a bite to eat around 7:00 a.m."

Just then, Patterson heard a noise behind him in the brush, and he casually turned to see what had caused it. His headlamp illuminated a young buck with spike antlers. The deer raised his head above the foliage and locked eyes with Patterson. The animal froze for several seconds and then resumed munching on the vegetation, seemingly unconcerned by the humans.

Mark laughed, and Patterson began breathing again, hoping Traner hadn't noticed how edgy he was. Trooper Sergeant Dan Patterson didn't want to let his subordinate know he felt uncomfortable camping in the middle of the Kodiak National Wildlife Refuge. Of course, he'd be a fool not to be wary and vigilant when spending the night protected by nothing more than a flimsy tent while sleeping in the heart of the largest concentration of huge brown bears in the world. Wary and vigilant were a long way from scared, though, and he didn't want to lose his cool in front of Traner.

Patterson could tell Traner also was nervous about spending the night in the woods surrounded by bears. Traner tried not to act uncomfortable, and he would never utter his concerns, but Patterson noticed he talked louder than necessary and kept glancing behind him. Maybe this night in the woods would be a bonding experience for the two men. Patterson considered Traner a brilliant investigator, and he had good people skills. For some reason, though, Traner had built a wall not only between himself and Patterson but also between himself and his fellow troopers. Patterson thought Traner feared to get close to any of his colleagues after the brutal murder of his friend and fellow officer a few months earlier. Guys, and especially law enforcement officers, didn't talk about their feelings, though, and Patterson knew it would take time before Traner let down his guard again. Still, *if they fended off a brown bear together tonight, perhaps the event would speed the healing process.* Patterson let out a long sigh. *What a terrible idea.*

Patterson was stretched on his back in his sleeping bag when his alarm sounded. He'd been awake for an hour thinking about the case and all he needed to do that day. His back was killing him. Ted either didn't know sleeping pads should be included with camping gear, or he chose to punish Patterson and Traner by excluding them from the gear. Patterson hoped it was the former because he didn't need his own people sabotaging him.

Patterson crawled from the tent and tried to stretch the pain from his back, but the exercise only made it worse. Traner stumbled from his tent still half asleep.

"What a miserable night," Patterson said. "How did you sleep?"

"It took me a while to get to sleep with the wilderness noises, but then I slept great."

"Your back doesn't hurt?"

"No, sir."

Patterson shook his head. "Let's get some coffee and food and head to the family's campsite. You know where it is, right?"

"Yes sir, I walked up to it yesterday. It's a bit of a climb."

"Great," Patterson mumbled, "just what my back needs."

As they hiked up the hill toward the family's campsite, Patterson's thoughts drifted from the case to his wife, Jeanne. Thoughts of her also had been part of the reason he hadn't slept well. Jeanne was forty-two years old and had been trying to get pregnant since they married fourteen years earlier. Patterson had been married briefly in his early twenties, and he had a twenty-two- year old son in the Marines. He had a good relationship with his son, and he didn't feel the need to have another child. He knew how important a baby was to Jeanne, though, and he supported her wish. A year earlier, they'd decided to use a chunk of their savings to pay for fertility treatments, and to their great surprise, three months ago, she'd gotten pregnant. Jeanne had been over the moon with excitement and immediately started buying and making baby clothes. Under her direction, Patterson had turned their spare room into a nursery, complete with a mural of Humpty Dumpty.

Jeanne had miscarried a week earlier. Physically, she was doing fine, but her deep depression worried Patterson. Both he and the doctor told her they could try again, but she said she'd had enough. It had been a roller coaster ride, and she wanted to get off and move on with the next chapter of her life. Nothing Patterson said helped. He didn't think she would take her own life, but he'd never seen her so down, and it worried him. He didn't like leaving her alone overnight, but maybe she needed time alone.

He definitely didn't want to leave Jeanne alone two nights in a row, but he might not have a choice in the matter. When he'd called headquarters a few minutes earlier on the satellite phone, Irene informed him it was foggy in town. Patterson immediately called one of Jeanne's good friends and asked her to check on Jeanne.

Patterson watched his feet as he walked over the uneven terrain. Traner led him up a rough trail, probably made by bears or deer. So far, he'd stepped in two holes, tripped over a rock and climbed over countless fallen trees. His lower back screamed with pain at each event. At forty-five, he was no kid, and today, he felt like an old man. He'd already outlived his father by nine months. His father, an Anchorage police officer, had dropped dead from a heart attack at age forty-four.

Traner came to an abrupt stop, and Patterson, whose eyes were still fixed on the trail, smacked into his back. Patterson looked up to see what had caused Traner to stop so suddenly. Twenty feet in front of Traner, a man stood in the center of the trail. The man was medium height. A stocking cap covered his hair and mirrored sunglasses shaded his eyes. His pale skin hinted at a life spent mostly indoors. He wasn't holding a gun, but his threatening demeanor alerted Patterson.

Patterson quietly reached down and unsnapped his holster. "Hi there," he said, trying to make his voice sound as friendly as possible.

"Can I help you?" The man stood, arms crossed, and legs spread wide, blocking the trail.

Patterson pushed past Traner and walked a few steps toward the man. "I'm Sergeant Patterson with the Alaska State Troopers, and this is my colleague, Trooper Traner. A pilot was murdered yesterday, and we found him in his plane on the lakeshore near here. We'd like to ask you and your family a few questions about the incident." Patterson did not know if this man was part of the family group camped nearby, but he wanted to alert the man that he and Traner knew there was a family camped on this hill.

"We had nothing to do with any murder," the man said.

"I'm not suggesting you did, sir, but you might have seen something which could prove useful in our investigation," Patterson said.

"We can't even see the lake from our campsite, so I'm sure we can't help you."

"Please, sir," Patterson said, "this will only take a few minutes. We would like to speak with your entire family."

The man stood motionless for several moments, and Patterson wished he could see his eyes. His mirrored sunglasses revealed nothing, and his defensive stature did not change. Finally, the man shrugged, turned, and headed up the trail.

Patterson and Traner followed the man to a cluster of three tents hidden behind the alders and willows.

"Marla," the man called, "we have company."

An attractive blonde with shoulder-length hair crawled from one of the tents, stood, and wiped crumbs from her jeans.

"Kids, come out here," the man said.

A child crawled from each of the other two tents. The oldest was a girl, who Patterson placed at thirteen or fourteen years old. The younger child was a boy of about twelve. The woman and the two kids approached the man and stood close to him—too close. Patterson felt there was something off about this family.

"I can't remember your names," the man said to Patterson.

Patterson introduced himself and Traner to the group and then said, "What are your names?"

No one said anything for several seconds. The woman and the kids looked at the man, and the man faced forward, his eyes unreadable behind his sunglasses. Finally, he said, "I'm Hiram Madison, this is my wife, Marla, our daughter Ann, and our son, John."

Patterson nodded. "It's nice to meet you folks. As I was telling Hiram, a pilot was shot and killed yesterday. He was found dead in his plane less than two miles north of here."

The woman's eyes widened, but no one said anything.

Patterson looked from one family member to the next while he asked, "Did you see anything out of the ordinary yesterday?"

The family replied as one with a chorus of headshakes.

"What about planes?" Patterson continued. "Did you notice any planes flying low overhead yesterday?"

Again, headshakes were all he received as an answer to his question.

While Patterson thought about what to ask next, Hiram said, "We took a long hike through the brush yesterday. We saw four deer and two bears, but no humans and no planes."

"We saw a rabbit," John blurted, and then slapped his hand over his mouth and glanced at his dad.

Hiram didn't look at his son, but Patterson detected concealed anger when he said, "Yes, John, we saw a rabbit."

"How long are you folks planning to camp here?" Patterson asked.

"Three more days," Hiram said.

"And where are you from?"

"Southern California," Hiram said.

"Have you seen any other campers since you've been here?"

Hiram seemed to consider the question for several moments and then said, "Two days ago, we walked along the shore of the lake for a short distance, and we heard men in boats yelling at each other. I couldn't make out what they were saying, but they sounded drunk."

"They were yelling at each other? Did they sound angry?"

"Maybe," Hiram said. "I couldn't tell."

"Do you have any firearms with you?" Patterson asked.

Hiram shook his head. "We only have bear spray," he said.

Patterson doubted the veracity of this statement, but he had no reason to search the campsite.

"Okay," Patterson said. "I'll give you one of my cards, and I'd like to get your contact information."

"I'd rather not give it to you," Hiram said.

"Sir," Patterson said. "This is a murder investigation. I don't want to involve you and your family, but I need to be able to get ahold of you if we have more questions."

Hiram sighed, and then looked at his wife. "Give them what they want, Marla."

A few minutes later, Patterson felt Hiram Madison's eyes boring through his back as he and Traner left the small encampment and started down the trail.

"Sir," Traner said, after they'd walked about 100 yards.

Patterson, who was now in the lead, stopped and turned around. "Yes?"

"Look up." Traner pointed to the top of a cottonwood tree near the trail.

"That's how he knew we were coming." Patterson stared at the small trail camera and then nodded to let Madison know they were onto him. Patterson wondered if trail cams surrounded the Madisons' campsite. If so, Hiram Madison was beyond paranoid. *There was definitely something wrong with this family.*

Patterson and Traner returned to their camp and packed their gear. As they stuffed it in the plane, Traner asked Patterson what he thought of the Madison family.

"I don't know what to make of them," Patterson said. "There's something strange going on, and I plan to find out what it is."

"You don't think they kidnapped the two kids, do you?" Traner asked.

Patterson slowly shook his head. "The kids seemed happy enough," he said, "but they obviously have been told not to say anything unless their father gives them permission. We'll see what we can learn about them when we get back to town. Right now, let's interview Jake's last passenger on the other side of the lake, and then we'll head back to the office if the fog has cleared. I'll call Irene now and get a weather check."

Traner crawled into the Beaver while Patterson placed the call on the sat phone.

"Has the fog lifted?" Traner asked a few minutes later when Patterson climbed into the plane.

"Still down on the ground," Patterson said. "I guess we'll run down Jason Meckel and talk to him and the rest the staff at his lodge." Patterson had hoped to pass along these interviews to his troopers, but if they couldn't fly back to town, he and Traner might as well spend the day conducting interviews with as many possible witnesses to Jake's murder as they could find.

"But first," Patterson said, "let's talk to Jake's last passenger."

Lance Crane greeted the Beaver as they landed, and he helped secure the plane by tying it to an alder on the shore. Patterson guessed Lance was in his mid-to-late sixties, but he stood lean and straight at nearly six feet tall. He held out his hand to Patterson. His deep blue eyes sparkled with intelligence and the hint of a question.

"Lance Crane," he said. "How are you gentlemen today?"

"I'm Sergeant Patterson with the Alaska State Troopers, and this is Trooper Mark Traner."

"I see," Crane said. He took a step back and folded his arms. "Is there a problem?"

"Yes sir, I'm afraid so. The pilot who flew you out here yesterday was murdered."

Crane recoiled as if he'd been slapped in the face. "Jake?"

"Jake Shepherd, yes." Patterson nodded.

"When did it happen? This morning?" Crane asked.

"No sir, he was shot yesterday after he dropped you off here," Patterson said.

"When he got back to town?" Crane asked.

"No," Patterson said. "He was murdered across the lake and north of here a few miles. He was shot while he sat in his plane, and we think he was killed less than an hour after he left you."

"Who killed him? Did you catch his murderer?"

Patterson shook his head. "No, we didn't, and we didn't find much at the murder scene other than a shell casing."

Crane sat on the ground, his eyes glazed and unfocused. "He told me he was picking up two people on the other side of the lake. Could they have killed him? But why? Why would someone kill his own pilot? It doesn't make any sense."

"No sir, it doesn't," Patterson said. "Jake's plane was found over a mile south of the pickup spot for his next party. We have no idea why he would have landed there. We're hoping he said something to you."

Crane shook his head. "Jake was in a great mood. We had a nice conversation. We both were floatplane pilots back in the day. I flew out of

Haines all over Southeast Alaska for thirty years. Jake moved from floatplanes into the big time with Delta, but he said he never got the thrill of flying small planes in Alaska out of his blood. We talked a lot about how times had changed." Crane pulled a handkerchief from his pocket and wiped his eyes. "Shot to death? What a ridiculous way for an old pilot to die."

"Did you see which direction Jake flew after he left here?" Patterson asked.

Crane shrugged. "I stood on the shore and watched him take off and circle." A small smile creased his lips. "I love watching a floatplane take off. Once he was airborne, he circled, and I think he headed straight across the lake, but I began hauling my gear up into the woods to my camping spot, so I didn't watch the plane for more than a few minutes. I assumed he headed across the lake to pick up his next party." He pointed toward the woods. "My camp is a good hundred yards from the lake. I like peace and quiet."

"Do you still fly planes in Haines?" Traner asked.

Crane slowly shook his head. "I retired six years ago. I'd live in Alaska if I had my way, but my wife wanted to move to Portland to be closer to the kids and grandkids. I come to Alaska every summer, though, and camp someplace remote like this. I'll never get Alaska out of my blood, but my wife said good riddance to the state." He shrugged. "She hasn't been back since we moved."

Crane's statement about his wife reminded Patterson of Jake's wife, Inga's, supposed hatred of Kodiak. *Did Inga hate Kodiak enough to kill her husband? If Jake had a large life insurance policy, Inga might have had more than one reason to wish her husband dead.* Patterson made a mental note to check on Jake's life insurance. Jake had been a pilot for Delta Airlines, and they probably insured their pilots well.

"Do you remember if the small window on Jake's side of the plane was open?" Patterson asked.

"I couldn't say," Crane said, but then he turned his head to the side. "Wait a minute, now, yes, it was open. I remember Jake sticking his hand through the window and waving as he began to taxi for takeoff. Why?" he asked. "Was he shot through the window?"

"We don't know yet, sir," Patterson said. Patterson did not believe Jake was shot through the window, but he didn't want to offer up every detail from the crime scene so early in the investigation. Patterson believed Jake opened the door for his murderer, giving the killer an easy, straight shot, but the open window suggested Jake might have been talking to his murderer before he opened the door. On the other hand, if the window was already open before Jake's murderer approached the plane, then the open window might mean nothing at all to the investigation.

Crane pushed himself up from the ground. "Who could have shot him? There can't be many campers here."

"What about other planes?" Patterson asked. "Did you notice any other planes circling the lake yesterday soon after you were dropped off?"

Crane laughed. "This place is nearly as bad as Lake Hood in Anchorage. I heard planes all day and into the late evening. I'm beginning to rethink my decision to camp here. I was hoping for a quiet camping spot; I could have stayed in Portland if I wanted noise. I spent most of the day hiking through the woods on game trails, so while I heard several planes, I didn't see many of them." He paused a few moments, lost in thought. "I did see a plane not long after Jake left, but I doubt this will help you."

"Why is that, sir? Can you describe the plane? What color was it?"

"Yes, Crane said. It was another Kodiak Flight Services Beaver."

"You're sure it wasn't Jake flying over you again?" Traner asked.

"No, the plane had a different tail number," Jake smiled. "When you're a pilot, you notice tail numbers."

Patterson felt his pulse quicken. "Do you remember the tail number of the second Beaver?"

Crane looked up at the sky and then shook his head. "There was a time when I would have remembered it, but I must be getting old. Maybe it will come back to me."

"Yes, sir," Patterson said. "If you think of it, please let me know. Have you seen or heard any other campers since you've been here?"

Crane shook his head. "I've been trying hard not to see other people, and so far, I've been successful."

"I understand, sir," Patterson said. He handed Crane a card with his name and phone number on it. "Will you call me if you think of anything else?"

"Yes, sir," Crane said. "I'll do anything I can to help you catch Jake's murderer. Do you think other campers here at the lake are in danger?"

Patterson started to shake his head but then shrugged. "I'd like to say Jake's murder was an isolated incident, but I don't know enough yet to make such a claim. I suggest being watchful. How long are you planning to stay here?"

"Until Monday," Crane said. "I'm not worried. I'll remain vigilant."

"Do you have a firearm with you?" Patterson asked.

"Absolutely," Crane said. "I have my trusty 12 gauge." He paused a moment. "Could you tell what type of gun was used to kill Jake?"

Patterson paused, debating over how much information to release but then decided it wouldn't matter if he told Crane about the rifle shell. "We don't have the autopsy report yet, of course, but we found a .30-30 shell at the scene," he said.

"A .30-30 carbine?" Jake snorted a laugh. "Really, that's what you found?"

Patterson nodded. "Why?"

"I knew several pilots who carried Marlins back in the day because they're short and easy to carry in the plane, but I don't know any pilot who still carries one," Crane said.

"What did you carry in your plane, sir?" Patterson asked. He was intrigued to think the .30-30 shell might have come from a pilot's gun.

"I always carried my shotgun when I flew. I'd leave it in my duffel in the rear of the plane."

"Thanks for the information," Patterson said. "You've given us plenty to think about."

Crane waved Patterson's card in the air. "I'll call if I think of anything else."

Patterson and Traner returned to the plane, and Patterson piloted the Beaver toward the south end of the lake. As they were circling to land, he saw a mother bear with two newborn cubs. The trio was walking calmly along the lakeshore until they heard the roar of the Beaver, and then the mother ran into the brush with two small bundles of fur on her heels. A man in hip boots, a green cap, and a brown coat marched from where he had been concealed in the brush out onto the beach and raised his fist in the air at the circling plane.

"That wasn't a cool move," Patterson said. "Not only did I scare a sow and her two cubs, but I also antagonized the very man I plan to interview next."

Patterson considered his options and landed near Meckel's lodge. The lodge was much smaller than he'd expected, consisting of only two cabins. He assumed the guests stayed in the smaller cabin, and the larger cabin must be where the staff stayed and where everyone ate.

After securing the Beaver to a tree, Patterson and Traner walked up to the larger building. Patterson knew the staff must have heard the plane circle and land, but they hadn't bothered to meet the troopers on the beach. He took in the cabin with its dark green paint and brown trim. He knocked on the dark brown door, and a moment later, a young, petite woman with her black hair pulled back in a ponytail opened the door.

Patterson introduced himself and Traner, and the young woman opened the door wider.

Patterson and Traner followed her into a small sitting room. The smell of chicken and baked rolls washed over him, and he felt his stomach rumble. An older woman walked into the room, wiping her hands on a dish towel. She had a sturdy build and curly, red hair. Tattoos peeked out from her short-sleeved T-shirt. She frowned, and Patterson went through the introductions again for her.

The first woman introduced herself as Amy, and the second woman said she was Becca. They didn't offer last names, but he'd have Traner get their contact information before they left.

"Someone murdered a pilot at the other end of the lake yesterday," Patterson said.

Amy opened her eyes wide, but Becca's expression didn't change. "We're interviewing everyone who was on the lake or in the area yesterday," Patterson said.

Amy looked at Becca, and Becca easily supplied the answer. "Amy and I were here, but we didn't see anything. We were busy because four bear viewers arrived yesterday for a seven-day stay."

"I think we saw them on the beach. You work for Jason Meckel?" Patterson asked.

Both women nodded.

"Are any other employees here?"

Amy shook her head, and Becca answered. "There's one other guide, but he's in town right now. He's supposed to fly out today if the weather improves."

"And he wasn't here yesterday?" Patterson asked.

"He's been in town four days," Becca said.

"What about Jason? Did he mention seeing anything strange yesterday?"

"No," Becca said.

"What was he doing yesterday?" Patterson asked.

Becca paused, and Patterson sensed she didn't want to answer for her boss. Amy remained quiet and looked at the wood floor.

"Yesterday morning he went out in the boat. He was working on the outboard. Then the guests arrived a little before noon, and he met them. They ate lunch, and he took them for a boat ride," Becca said.

"So, he could have been anywhere on the lake in the morning?" Patterson asked.

Becca shrugged.

Interesting, Patterson thought. He needed to interview Mr. Meckel, but he'd wait. He knew if he approached him now, Meckel would not appreciate the troopers talking to him while he had tourists, and the man rightfully would give Patterson an earful about spooking the bears he and his guests had been watching. Meckel had a temper, and Patterson was in no mood to be yelled at this morning.

"Do either of you ladies know Jake Shepherd?" Patterson asked.

"The pilot?" Becca asked.

"Yes," Patterson said. "He flew for Kodiak Flight Services."

"Sure," Becca said.

Amy nodded.

"Someone murdered him yesterday," Patterson said.

Amy's mouth opened wide. She put her hands to her face and took a step back.

Becca responded to the news by crossing her arms over her stomach. "Why?" she asked.

"That's one of the things we're trying to find out," Patterson said.

"Did Jake ever fly you or your guests?"

"Yes," Becca said. "Kodiak Flight Services used to do all our flying."

"Used to?" Patterson asked.

Becca and Amy exchanged a look. "Well," Becca said. "Jason had a falling out with them, so now we usually use Emerald Island Air."

"What happened between Jason and Kodiak Flight Services?" Patterson asked.

Both women stared at each other for a long while. Finally, Becca said, "You really should ask Jason. He'll already be mad at me for saying too much. He might even fire me."

"Becca, I promise you I won't tell Jason you told me anything of interest," Patterson said. "I don't plan to interview him now because he's in the field with guests. I'll catch him this evening or early tomorrow morning, and I'll let him think I learned about his issue with Kodiak Flight Services from Steve, the owner of the airlines."

Becca remained quiet for several moments, and then sighed and said, "You'd find this out anyway, so I might as well tell you. Jason got into a yelling match with Jake Shepherd a couple weeks ago. We needed propane, and Jason wanted to fly the empty tank back to town with Jake, but Jake said, 'No.' He said it wasn't legal to fly hazardous materials with guests, and the FAA considers even an empty propane tank hazardous. It was only a small tank, but Jake wouldn't put it in the float. They had a screaming match on the beach, and Jason punched Jake."

"Did he hurt Jake?" Traner asked.

"He knocked him down," Becca said, "and Jake kept rubbing his jaw."

"What happened next?" Patterson asked.

"Jake got in the plane and left. Jason called Kodiak Flight Services, gave them a piece of his mind, and then contacted Emerald Island Air and moved all our charters to them," Becca said. "They don't mind flying empty propane tanks with guests."

Jake wondered if he should let the FAA know Emerald Island Air flies propane tanks while hauling passengers. He personally felt the "hazmat" issue had reached ridiculous proportions, but the law was the law. Still, he had enough on his plate right now, and he didn't want the FAA in the middle of his investigation.

Patterson asked the women a few more questions, and then Traner wrote down their contact information, and the two troopers thanked them for their assistance.

Once Patterson got back to the plane, he again called his office.

"What's it look like in there, Irene?" he asked.

"Better," she said. "I think it's starting to lift."

"Great," Patterson said. "I hope to see you soon."

Next, he called the tower to see if conditions had risen above minimums.

He was told they were up to five miles and eight hundred feet. Planes were beginning to fly.

He passed along the good news to Traner, and they climbed in the plane for the hour flight back to town.

"I'll fly back out either this evening or early tomorrow morning and talk to Jason Meckel," Patterson said. "Since he had conflicts with Jake, he's a person of interest, but he had tourists with him yesterday afternoon, so I think it's unlikely he could have gotten away from them long enough to motor to the other end of the lake, kill Jake, and motor back to continue his sightseeing tour." Patterson shook his head. "I could be missing something, though, and that's why we ask the questions, right?"

"Yes, sir," Traner said. "He could have killed Jake before his guests arrived."

"It would have been tight, but it's possible," Patterson said. "We need to find out exactly when he returned to the lodge."

PRESENT DAY
SATURDAY, JUNE 28TH
1:50 P.M.

The ceiling dropped steadily as they approached Kodiak, and they were fifty feet above the ocean for the last seven miles of the flight. Patterson knew he didn't have to tell Traner to keep an eye out for boats. Traner was on full alert, his face pasted to the window watching for fishing boats, tugs, or even the passenger ferry from the mainland. A collision with a boat's superstructure would likely prove deadly.

Patterson powered down for landing and noticed Traner's muscles relax as he finally looked away from the window.

"It's a little soupy in here today," Patterson said.

"Yes, sir," Traner replied.

"Why don't you take the rest of the afternoon off," Patterson said. "I'll need you rested and at the top of your game tomorrow."

Traner nodded. "If you're sure, sir."

Patterson climbed from the floatplane onto the dock and stretched. He rubbed his back and wondered if he had bruised it; he must have slept on a boulder. He and Traner secured the plane and unloaded their camping gear from the rear.

They'd walked a few steps toward the ramp leading up to the parking lot when an excited Sara Byram flew down the ramp toward them.

Sara's auburn hair, normally pinned in a neat bun, was pulled into a loose ponytail, and it swung back and forth as she raced toward them. Patterson and Traner stopped and waited for her. She came to an abrupt halt directly in front of Patterson.

"Good morning, Trooper Byram," Patterson said.

"Sir," she nodded at Patterson and then at Traner, "and sir."

When she didn't say anything else, Patterson prodded her. "Did you have something to tell us?"

"Yes, sir," Sara said. "I learned an interesting bit of information. Tammy Monroe, the girl who found Jake," she paused and looked expectantly at Patterson.

Patterson nodded, "Yes, go ahead."

"Tammy's father is a pilot with Delta. I talked to the personnel office in Salt Lake, and Jake and Daniel Monroe both were based in Atlanta at the same time." The words tumbled from Sara's mouth; her brown eyes opened wide, and her pupils dilated.

Patterson smiled. The more he got to know this young trooper, the better he liked her. "Good work, Sara," he said. "Now, find out if they ever flew together and if so, did they like each other?"

"I'm on it," Sara said. She reached for some of Patterson's camping gear and helped carry the gear up to Patterson's SUV.

Patterson found the connection between Tammy's dad and Jake interesting, and it was something they needed to investigate, but he couldn't imagine any reason Tammy's father would send his daughter to Kodiak to murder Jake.

As they were stuffing gear into the SUV, Patterson said to Sara, "Talk to Charli, the Kodiak Flight Services dispatcher, and find out if Tammy and Brian requested Jake as their pilot or if Jake was randomly assigned to them."

"Sir?" Sara asked.

"If they asked to have Jake as their pilot, I want to know why, but if Jake just happened to be the pilot scheduled to pick them up, I think it's unlikely they came to Kodiak planning to kill Jake." Patterson paused. "I can imagine Brian losing his temper at something Jake did or said and shooting him in the heat of the moment, but I'd need a lot more evidence before I could believe Brian or Tammy premeditated this murder."

Sara nodded. "I understand."

"Check it out thoroughly, though," Patterson said. "I don't want to leave any stone unturned. Do you have anything else for me?"

"Not much yet, sir," Sara said. "With the weather down in town, we haven't been able to get out to Karluk to talk to the rafters, and none of the campers have flown to town from Karluk. Do you want me to interview the staff at Kodiak Flight Services or any other pilots?"

"You're in charge of corralling the rafters returning from Karluk, and I'd like you to send two troopers out to talk to the biologists and others at Camp Island. I'll handle the Kodiak Flight Services staff and the various pilots who had altercations with Jake," Patterson said. "Mark and I questioned the family, the six fishermen, and Jake's last passenger. We also talked to everyone at Meckel's lodge except Jason Meckel. I'll fly back to Karluk tomorrow morning and catch him before he starts his day."

"Do you think Meckel could have killed Jake?" Sara asked.

Patterson shrugged. "I think he's an unlikely suspect, but he recently punched Jake in the nose, so he warrants closer scrutiny. Also," Patterson said, "I want to meet with the primary troopers involved in this investigation. Let's do it tomorrow at 4:00 p.m. Maybe we'll have made progress by then."

"Yes, sir," Sara said and hurried back to her vehicle.

Patterson rubbed his lower back. Sara's energy made him feel very old.

Patterson needed to talk to Steve, Charli, and the other employees of Kodiak Flight Services, but first, he'd check in at headquarters. He wanted to call his wife, but he knew this was her first day back at work at Providence Hospital since her miscarriage. It would be a tough day, and he didn't care what catastrophes occurred on Kodiak Island today, he planned to be at home to meet his wife when she got off her shift at 6:00 p.m.

The moment Patterson walked through the door at the trooper's station, Irene looked up from her desk and announced, "Dr. Libby finished the autopsy on Jake this morning and wants you to call him."

"And good afternoon to you too, Irene," Patterson said. "What else do I need to know?"

Irene ignored Patterson's sarcasm, "Wise was called out on a bad car wreck on the Chiniak Highway. He called in and said it will tie him up all day."

"Who's here?" Patterson asked.

"Sara, Simpton, Boyle, and I took the liberty of calling in Deetry."

"Good thinking, Irene," Patterson said. "Put Deetry on call to respond to anything on the road system. If he needs backup, I'll see he gets it. In the meantime, I want everyone else on Jake's homicide. Make sure they know Sara is in charge, and she will be handing out assignments."

"Boyle won't like that," Irene said.

"I'm not worried about what he likes," Patterson said. "I sent Traner home for the day, so if you need more help, call in Harrington."

"Yes, sir," Irene said.

Patterson proceeded to his office and shut the door. He stretched and rubbed at his sore back. Then he rummaged through the top drawer of his desk, found the bottle of Advil, and popped two in his mouth. He'd just sat down in his desk chair when he heard knuckles rap his door.

"Yes, Irene?"

Irene cracked open the door and stuck her head into Patterson's office. "I forgot to tell you that Jane Marcus called this morning. She wants you to call her back."

Patterson blew out a long breath between clenched teeth. He had a lot to do today and didn't want to deal with Jane Marcus and her ancient bones. "Thanks, Irene," he said. He leaned back in his desk chair, but the motion only made his back pain worse.

He decided to get Jane out of the way first so he could concentrate on his murder case. He would have to contact his superiors in Anchorage. For now, he thought he and his team could handle this investigation, but they needed to solve the case in days, not weeks, because many of the possible suspects would soon scatter to distant places. If they didn't make headway in the next few days, he would be forced to ask for help from a special investigator. He hated to ask for help from Anchorage; it was an admission of defeat.

"Hello," Jane answered on the third ring, sounding breathless.

"Jane, this is Dan Patterson. Did I call at a bad time?"

"No," Jane said, her breaths still coming at a rapid rate. "I just ran up the steps from my lab." She laughed. "I think I need to start jogging more. I'm out of shape."

"Irene said you called this morning," Patterson said. "What can I help you with?"

"Sorry to bother you, but I was wondering if you've heard anything about the bones."

Patterson sat forward and propped his elbows on his desk, but this position only made his back pain worse. "No, Jane," he said. "I have other, more pressing matters to deal with right now. I don't have time to fool with a bunch of old bones." He was in too much pain to hide his impatience.

"Okay," Jane said. "Again, I'm sorry I bothered you."

"No problem." Patterson disconnected and immediately regretted the conversation. He thought for a few minutes and then slowly punched Jane's number into his phone.

This time, Jane answered on the first ring. "Yes?" The word was clipped, and Patterson detected annoyance in her tone.

"Jane, sorry I sounded short with you," he said. "It's been a rough two days. You've probably heard about the pilot who was murdered."

"No. Who?" Jane asked.

Patterson knew on an island with only 13,500 people, there was a good chance Jane knew or at least had heard of Jake.

"Jake Shepherd. He flew for Kodiak Flight Services."

Jane said nothing for a moment but then said, "I didn't know him, but poor Steve. This is the second terrible thing he's had to endure recently."

"I know," Patterson said, "and he's taking it hard." He paused. "Anyway, I have my hands full with the investigation, so I don't have time for much else right now."

"I understand," Jane said.

Patterson massaged his temples. He knew he was overly tired and probably not thinking clearly. He should keep his mouth shut, but instead, he said, "Would you like to see what you learn about the bones on your own?"

After a short pause, Jane said, "Yes, I would if you'd allow it."

"Let me be clear, Jane," Patterson said. "I know your reputation. You're very intelligent and have an excellent, deductive mind, but you sometimes take chances you shouldn't. You're not a cop. I want you to discuss anything you find with me. Don't question anyone until we've discussed things first, okay?"

"Got it," Jane said. "In other words, don't go rogue."

"Exactly," Patterson said.

"I've already Googled the watch we found at the scene, but I'd like to take another look at it and the other items we found."

"No problem," Patterson said. "Come over to trooper headquarters anytime, and I'll make sure Irene knows it's okay for you to look at those items."

"What about the bones? Jane asked.

"They're up in Anchorage at UAA. I'll call the anthropology student and her professor and tell them they can share any information they have about the bones with you. You can call them or even fly up there and talk to them in person," Patterson said. "My suggestion would be to try to narrow down the time frame of death, and then we can search for missing persons in that time frame."

"Got it," Jane said. "I'll do my best. Thank you."

"I have my hands full with this current investigation, and I won't be able to provide you much help, at least for a while," Patterson said, "but you can always call me with any thoughts, findings, or ideas."

1976

Bently couldn't find enough dry wood to start a fire in the driving snow. Instead, he spent the next two hours yelling Schwimmer's name every few seconds. By 6:30, he was nearly hoarse, and his anger had mounted into a seething rage. If this fool froze to death, Bently knew he would feel as guilty as if he'd murdered him, and he'd have to spend the rest of the hunt looking for Schwimmer's dead, frozen body. They had no way to call for help. They hadn't brought radios with them, and Bently hadn't seen a plane fly overhead since they'd arrived. He wouldn't be able to report Schwimmer's death until the plane came to get them on their scheduled departure day.

Bently continued to yell and fume. Could Schwimmer be so far away he couldn't hear him yelling?

Finally, at 7:05 p.m., just after Bently had yelled Schwimmer's name five times in a row and had decided to take a coffee break, he heard a faint cry. He stood and took two steps in the direction of the sound. Had he imagined it?

Bently remained still and concentrated. Now, all he heard was the howling wind. He pulled down his hood and listened.

"Help."

This time, he had no doubt. Schwimmer was nearby, and he sounded weak.

"I'm coming!" Bently yelled and ran toward the direction where he'd heard Schwimmer call.

Ten minutes later, Bently saw the weak beam of Schwimmer's flashlight through the driving snow. Schwimmer was stumbling in the opposite direction from their camp. Bently grabbed his arm and turned him around. Schwimmer's body shook.

This is good. If he's shivering, he's not too far gone; I should be able to warm him up. Bently supported Schwimmer under his arms and guided him back to camp. Schwimmer kept dragging his feet and tripping, his body shaking violently.

"Keep going, buddy. You're almost there." What Bently really wanted to do was punch him in the nose as hard as he could, but he knew, for now, he needed to fight back his feelings and play the role of caregiver.

Once they reached camp, Bently helped Schwimmer peel off his wet outer clothes. His long johns felt dry, so Bently didn't remove those. Bently then rummaged through Schwimmer's pack for a warm shirt and wool pants. It was like dressing a little kid. Schwimmer offered no assistance in pushing his arms and legs into the clothes. As soon as he had buttoned Schwimmer's shirt and zipped his pants, Bently pulled Schwimmer's sleeping bag around him.

"Stay put," Bently said. "I'll make you some food and bring you a cup of hot water. We need to get some heat and sugar in you."

Bently didn't know if Schwimmer was alert enough to swallow food and hot water, but with Bently's assistance and coaxing, he managed. After a few bites of food and the two cups of hot water Bently forced him to drink, Schwimmer dropped into a deep sleep.

While Schwimmer slept, Bently dealt with the task of sweeping snow off the tents every half-hour. His anger toward Schwimmer grew during his sleepless hours. Maybe he should have let Schwimmer freeze to death when he'd had the chance. Perhaps Schwimmer would die during the night, and Bently could truthfully say he'd done everything he could to save him.

PRESENT DAY
SATURDAY, JUNE 28TH
3:20 P.M.

I knew I should have declined Sergeant Patterson's offer to investigate the mysterious bones on my own. My curiosity outside the laboratory often brought trouble. My nosiness had recently resulted in someone planting a bomb at the Braxton Marine Fisheries Center. One of my colleagues had been killed in the explosion, and I'd come close to losing my job. I'd worked hard to claw my way back into the good graces of my boss, Peter. If I did anything to negatively impact the center again, I had no doubt I'd be packing my bags and dusting off my résumé. Now, Peter had chosen to showcase me and my research in front of possible, wealthy donors to the center. As much as I hate begging for money, I needed to keep my head down and perform as commanded.

I promised myself I would only research the old bones, and I would not stray outside the strict guidelines Patterson had just given me. I had to admit, though, the thought of solving another mystery excited me, and *how much trouble could I find researching decades-old bones?*

I'd already Googled the wristwatch with the aid of the photos Geoff had snapped, and a very helpful *Timex* website informed me *Timex* manufactured this watch model, or a model similar to this watch in the 1970s. I wanted to confirm the model number at the watch, and if this was the correct model, I'd know for certain it was manufactured sometime in the 1970s. If—and this was a big "if"—the watch belonged to the bones, the bones could not be older than 1970. If the belt buckle, watch, and bones were all related, then the individual must have been in the Air Force at some time. Of course, it was possible he just knew someone in the Air Force or bought the belt at a garage sale, but to begin with, I would assume my guy was in the Air Force in the 1970s.

I'd wait a couple days before calling the anthropology student in Anchorage and heading over to trooper headquarters to take a closer look at the knife, watch, and belt buckle. Tonight, I again needed to put on a dress and a smile and dazzle Peter's possible moneybags.

PRESENT DAY
SATURDAY, JUNE 28TH
3:30 P.M.

Dr. Libby sounded tired, and Patterson wondered if the medical examiner had planned to be in the lab on a Saturday, or if he'd come in specifically to handle this autopsy because Patterson had requested him. Patterson respected the expertise and thoroughness of this medical examiner. Libby had helped him link a string of recent murders on the island and had provided valuable insight for catching the murderer.

"Dr. Libby," Patterson said. "Thank you for taking this case."

"No problem," Libby said. "I'm always happy to help you with cases down there on your little island. It looks as if you have another murderer in your midst."

"I'm afraid so," Patterson said. "I imagine the autopsy was straightforward. There's no mystery about how Mr. Shepherd died."

"No," Libby said. "A gunshot to the head is often lethal. The exit wound is higher than the entrance wound, so the shooter was below the victim. You should find a bullet either in the plane or at the crime scene."

"The techs haven't given me their report on the plane yet," Patterson said. "Hopefully, they will find the bullet. Do you have any thoughts on the caliber of gun used?"

"Not from the autopsy," Libby said, "but I do have one interesting finding."

Patterson squirmed in his desk chair, trying to find a comfortable position. "Yes?"

"Jake Shepherd had terminal colon cancer. Stage IV. He had to be in a great deal of pain. If he had gunpowder residue on his hands, I would suspect suicide, but I think he was shot from a distance of approximately six feet, so suicide is out of the question."

"No gun at the scene, either," Patterson said. He thought for a moment. "You say he was in pain?"

"I'm sure he was in excruciating pain. I'd estimate he only had a few months to live."

"How was he flying airplanes?" Patterson asked.

"Good question. I sent Jake's blood work off for a toxicology analysis. When we get it back, we'll know if he was taking painkillers. He never would have passed his physical if he had opiates in his system," Libby said.

"But you think he could pass it with cancer?"

"Possibly," Libby paused. "If he took his physical several months ago, received it from someone other than his normal doctor, and told the doctor nothing about his symptoms, the doctor would have no way of knowing he had cancer. He wouldn't need a colonoscopy to pass his pilot's physical."

"If he was in pain and not taking any medicine to control the pain, he would have been cranky," Patterson said, thinking out loud.

"I don't know about Jake Shepherd, but I certainly would be cranky," Libby said.

"Thank you, Doctor. You've put Jake's personality into perspective for me."

"Always happy to help. I'll give you a call when the tox screen comes back."

No wonder Jake confronted so many people in the last few months of his life. The poor guy must have been in terrible pain. Patterson felt certain the tox screen would come back negative for opiates. Jake desperately wanted to fly floatplanes as long as he could. Another disturbing thought occurred to Patterson: *Could Jake have paid or convinced someone else to shoot him and take him out of his misery? Maybe he chose to die in a floatplane on Karluk Lake.* A case that yesterday seemed to be solvable within a matter of hours continued to get more and more complicated.

PRESENT DAY
SUNDAY, JUNE 29ᵀᴴ
7:10 A.M.

Patterson looked down at the quiet streets of Kodiak as he headed for Sharatin Pass. No clouds marred the baby-blue sky this morning, and he would be able to fly over the spine of the island on his way to Karluk Lake to interview Jason Meckel and his guests. He wanted to arrive early before they headed out for their morning bear-viewing trip.

Patterson decided to do this interview himself because he'd met Jason Meckel, and the man had a temper and would not be easy to interview. Patterson felt he could rule out Meckel if the guide was with his guests at the approximate time someone murdered Jake. Still, he knew Meckel could be violent, and his employees said he was out working on the outboard on his boat Friday morning. He could have murdered Jake before his guests arrived.

The previous day, Patterson checked Meckel's record and learned Meckel had been charged with assault four times and convicted twice. Once, he'd beat a man so badly, the guy spent a month in the hospital recovering from his wounds. *If he and Jake got into a fight, who knows what Meckel could have done to him.*

Patterson stared down at the Coast Guard base and the small golf course. He had wanted to interview Steve and Charli the previous afternoon, but since Steve was out of the office flying, taking up the slack with the loss of Jake, Patterson decided to wait until today to interview both Steve and Charli. Charli assured him Steve would be in the office late morning or early afternoon, so Patterson planned to corral the pair once he returned to Kodiak.

He flew into Sharatin and was greeted by smooth air instead of the usual turbulence in this small mountain pass. The beautiful, calm day should have lifted his spirits, but he couldn't stop thinking about Jeanne. He arrived home early the previous evening and grilled steaks for dinner. Jeanne got home at 6:30, and he could see she was both mentally and physically exhausted. She only ate two bites of steak and none of her baked potato or salad. She apologized to him for her lack of hunger and then went to bed. He knew it would take time for her to recover from the blow of losing her baby, but how much time? *Should he encourage her to seek medication or therapy for her depression?* He didn't think she was suicidal, but he didn't know.

Suicide brought his thoughts back to the case. *Did Jake hire someone to shoot him, and put him out of his pain?* A shot to the head certainly would beat a slow, painful death from cancer, and he could imagine an old pilot wanting to die in his plane. If he hired or convinced someone to kill him, it had to be a pilot, someone who could arrive and leave quickly, and who would be crazy enough to take the chance of being caught shooting a man in the head in broad daylight. Patterson believed the "suicide-by-proxy angle" was a viable theory at this point in the investigation, but if this theory were true, then they were searching for either Jake's very good friend or a pilot who needed money badly enough to agree to kill Jake for it.

Karluk Lake was a flat, black mirror when Patterson landed near Meckel's lodge. Jason Meckel trotted down to meet the plane when Patterson pulled up to the beach. Meckel frowned as he approached the Beaver, and Patterson stepped out on the float to greet him. The pain in Patterson's back had eased since the previous day, but after an hour of sitting in a plane, pain jolted him again as soon as he stood.

"Are you the ass who buzzed me and scared away the bears yesterday?" Meckel asked.

Here we go. "I apologize," Patterson said. "I didn't see you or the bears until I was too close."

"You people have rules about flying too low over your precious refuge. Do the rules not apply to you?"

Meckel looked like a bodybuilder. He stood about 5 feet 10 inches, Patterson guessed, and he was all muscle. His biceps bulged from under his T-shirt, and his T-shirt adhered to his abs. His tight jeans revealed well-formed leg muscles, and Patterson noted he'd hurried out of his cabin wearing his slippers. Hair was nearly absent from the top of his head, but a dark fringe around the bottom half of his head morphed into black sideburns, a mustache, and a neatly-trimmed beard. He probably wore a cap to cover his bald head when he went out in public. His eyes shined an odd color between yellow and green, and he reminded Patterson of a silver fox with eerie, glowing yellow eyes. His crooked nose suggested he liked to fight.

"Again, I apologize," Patterson said, "and I don't want to take up too much of your time this morning because I understand you're busy."

Meckel stood silent, arms crossed over his chest.

"Did you hear about the shooting two days ago?" Patterson asked.

"Yeah, I know. Someone blasted away Jake Shepherd, probably because they got tired of him telling them how to live their lives," Meckel said.

"You didn't like Jake Shepherd?"

"No, I did not," Meckel said evenly, "but I didn't kill him if that's what you're asking."

"Mr. Meckel," Patterson said, "I'm interviewing everyone who was on the lake Friday, and I'd like to know where you were Friday late morning and early afternoon."

"Right here. Well, not here, but I was over at O'Malley Creek with my clients. We were bear viewing." Meckel said.

"The clients you have in camp now?"

"That's right."

"I understand your clients arrived in the early afternoon. What were you doing before they got here?" Patterson asked.

"I was working on my outboard," Meckel said. "I never left this end of the lake. Besides, the clients arrived before noon, and I was back at camp well before the plane arrived."

"I heard you punched Jake and knocked him down," Patterson said.

"Yeah, so what? Punching is a long way from shooting. The guy was obnoxious, but if I went around shooting every obnoxious guy I know, there wouldn't be anyone left."

"Did you see anything unusual Friday morning?" Patterson asked.

Meckel shrugged. "Seemed like there was more air traffic than normal," Meckel said.

"Did you recognize the planes?" Patterson asked.

Meckel stared into the distance for several moments and then said, "I saw at least three Kodiak Flight Services planes, two Emerald Island Air planes, including the one carrying my clients, a refuge plane, and one or two other planes."

"Did you note the tail numbers of any of the planes?" Patterson asked.

"If you're asking me who was flying the planes," Meckel said, "Jordan Gregg brought my clients, and I think Buddy Stark was flying the other Emerald Island Air Beaver." He paused for a moment. "Of course, it could have been Henry Sheld. He sometimes flies the Beaver."

"What about the Kodiak Flight Services planes?" Patterson asked.

"I saw Jake go over," Meckel said, "and I also saw the Beaver Roy Tayler flies, and then their 206. I don't know who was flying it, and I have no idea who was flying the other planes."

"Do you mind if I talk to your clients?" Patterson asked. He expected Meckel to object because what businessman wants his clients to think he's in trouble with the law?

To Patterson's surprise, Meckel shrugged. "Talk to them if you want, but they're from Poland and don't speak much English."

Meckel was right, the four Polish gentlemen spoke almost no English, and Patterson did not know a word of Polish. After twenty minutes of gesturing and thumbing through the Polish/English dictionary the men carried with them, he felt reasonably certain Jason Meckel had been nowhere near Jake's plane at the time Jake was murdered. Meckel said he had seen nothing unusual Friday morning or afternoon, so Patterson thanked him and climbed back into the cockpit of the Beaver. The interview had gone well. Meckel provided some potentially helpful information about which pilots had been near Karluk Lake when Jake was murdered. Patterson also now believed he could mark Jason Meckel off the suspect list, and he was happy to subtract rather than add another name.

Patterson flew down the middle of Karluk Lake and then circled the perimeter. He noted the six men had disappeared from their campsite and presumably now were floating down the Karluk River. They planned to spend a leisurely four days and three nights fishing their way to the mouth of the river, so they should be back in Kodiak by Tuesday afternoon. At least Patterson would know where they were for the next few days.

Patterson saw no sign of the strange family, but he guessed they were still camped in the thick brush on the hill above the lake. He did catch a glimpse of Jake's last passenger Lance Crane's camp, and he imagined the man shaking a fist at him for flying over his tent and disturbing his peace and quiet.

Despite a flurry of activity near the river, the lake seemed quiet this morning, and Patterson again thought about the strange crime scene. *How could someone commit a violent murder in this peaceful, wilderness setting without leaving any clues?* He reminded himself they did have a bullet cartridge, and perhaps the crime scene techs would uncover more evidence in the interior of Jake's plane. Patterson hoped they would finish examining Jake's notebook soon. He was anxious to look at it.

PRESENT DAY
SUNDAY, JUNE 29TH
11:30 A.M.

Patterson touched down in Trident Basin at 11:30 a.m., and the sun beat on his shoulders as he tied his plane to the dock. According to the forecast, the temperature would soar to nearly eighty degrees today, a heat wave for Kodiak, and Patterson knew he'd hear nothing but complaints all day about the extreme heat.

When Patterson walked into the Kodiak Flight Services office, Charli looked up from her desk and pointed to Steve's office. "Steve said to send you straight in when you got here."

Patterson knocked softly on Steve's door and then opened it. Steve sat in his desk chair, staring into the distance. His eyes looked red and tired. When he saw Patterson, he scooted his chair up to the desk.

"Sergeant Patterson, please come in and have a seat."

Patterson crossed the room, shook Steve's hand, and then sat in the chair facing his desk. "Thanks for making time for me today," he said.

"I want you to find Jake's killer as soon as possible, and I'll do anything I can to help."

"I found out something interesting from the medical examiner yesterday," Patterson said. "Did you know Jake had cancer?"

"No," Steve said. "No way. He passed his physical."

"It was colon cancer," Patterson said, "and if he wasn't taking opioids to control the pain, there would be no reason he wouldn't pass his physical."

"But if he started taking painkillers after the physical, it would mean I had an impaired pilot working for me."

"I haven't received the tox screen back yet, but I'll let you know what we find," Patterson said.

Steve shook his head. "I wish he'd told me, but if he had, I would have been forced to ground him, and I know how much he wanted to fly floatplanes. I guess he thought he'd keep flying until he got too sick." Steve seemed lost in thought for a moment and then said, "Now I understand why he's had such a short fuse lately."

"That's one of the things I want to talk to you about," Patterson said. "You mentioned he got into an argument with the Emerald Island Air pilots, and we know Jason Meckel punched him. Who else did Jake confront?"

"The Meckel thing," Steve said, "was not Jake's fault. Jason Meckel is a jerk, and I told him I won't fly him or his guests again. We were following the law, and if he can't accept that, then we don't need his business. Poor Jake just happened to be the messenger."

"How about other pilots besides Jordan Gregg? Did he have any problems with other Kodiak Flight Services pilots?"

"Maybe some, but I don't know. I guess I don't want to hear about conflicts between my pilots. I have enough other things to worry about."

Patterson sighed. "I'm not trying to make Jake look bad, Steve. It's possible another pilot landed, pulled up next to Jake, shot him and took off again. That scenario makes more sense than a camper walking down the beach to shoot him. We didn't find footprints near Jake's plane, and a pilot could have killed Jake without ever stepping onto the beach. If he asked Jake to land so they could talk and then pulled up beside him on the beach, he could have stepped from his floats to Jake's without leaving a trace he had been there."

"You'd be able to see an imprint of the floats in the mud," Steve said.

"Then perhaps he pulled up behind Jake's plane and tied to it." Patterson shrugged. "There'd be no marks in the mud if he left his plane floating."

"I guess," Steve said. "The beach has a lot of rocks, couldn't someone step on rocks without leaving footprints in the mud?"

"It's possible," Patterson said, "and I'm not saying it was a pilot who killed Jake, but we have to consider all the possibilities. Unfortunately, solving a crime means untangling the victim's life and revealing his secrets."

Steve remained quiet for several moments and then nodded. "As I said, I'm the boss, and my employees don't tell me everything. Why don't you talk to Stan, my head pilot, or to Rusty? I'm sure they both know more than I do about the interpersonal relationships of my pilots." He shrugged. "On the other hand, Charli knows more about what happens around here than anyone."

"What can you tell me about Jake's wife?" Patterson asked.

"Inga?" Steve tilted his head and seemed to be lost in thought for a moment. "To be quite honest," he said, "I think she's snooty and believes she's too good to live in a small town in Alaska. I also think she resented Jake for moving back here. She spent far more time in Atlanta near her kids and grandkids than she did here."

"How did Jake feel about her prolonged absences?" Patterson asked.

"It didn't seem to bother him," Steve said. "He joked about his 'absentee wife.' I could be wrong, but I never felt they were close. I didn't detect any warmth between them." He flashed a sad smile. "Who knows what goes on in a marriage?"

Patterson thought about his own marriage and nodded his head.

"One more thing," Patterson said. "Do you carry life insurance on your pilots?"

"No," Steve said. "I'm required to provide medical insurance, but this is another reason I hired Jake. He didn't want to be added to our insurance plan because he already had health insurance through Delta. I'm thrilled when a pilot saves me money."

Patterson made a mental note to have Sara check on Jake's insurance when she contacted Delta. He thanked Steve and told him to call if he remembered anything else, no matter how small.

Charli escorted Patterson to the small conference room and closed the door. Patterson sat at the head of the table, and Charli sat next to him and turned her chair to face him.

Patterson noticed Charli's puffy face and the dark circles around her big, light blue eyes. She'd pulled her beautiful, long hair into a severe ponytail. She looked at him, her lips formed a tight slash across her face as if holding back a sob. She was taking Jake's death hard.

Patterson spoke in a low voice, holding Charli's gaze as he said, "I'm so sorry for your loss."

Those words were all it took; the normally tough-as-nails dispatcher began to sob. A torrent of tears ran from her eyes, and she held a wad of Kleenex to her face. She sat hunched over for several minutes until she calmed her emotions and regained her composure. "Sorry," she said.

"No problem, Charli. Of course, you're upset. Do you feel like answering a few questions for me?" Patterson asked.

Charli nodded as she sat straight in the chair. "I want to," she said. "I want you to catch the bastard who killed Jake."

"I've been told Jake sometimes had a temper," Patterson said. "Did you ever see him get mad at anyone, or did you hear about him losing his temper?"

"Oh, yes," she said. "Jake didn't suffer fools quietly. I always got along with him, but he let me know if he thought I didn't give him enough flying time or if I sent him to the logging camp too many times in a week. The logging camp run is just a short flight to Afognak, and it gets boring after a while. Jake wanted adventure. He liked being sent to tough locations, places that were difficult to get into or out of. He also liked flights to the mainland or to the small, distant islands in the archipelago." She smiled. "I try to divide the flights evenly between the pilots, but I'll admit I had a soft spot for Jake. I mean, the guy brought me flowers on my birthday. How sweet is that?" She dabbed at her eyes again but fought back the tears.

"How about Karluk Lake? Did he like flying there?" Patterson asked.

"He liked the Karluk run. We fly down there a lot in the summer, so there's at least two or three Karluk flights on the board every day."

"What about on Friday? Were any of your other pilots in the vicinity where Jake was killed either late Friday morning or early afternoon?"

Charli frowned. "None of our guys would hurt Jake."

Patterson shook his head. "Charli, I need to cross my 'Ts' and dot my 'Is,' so help me out here."

"Okay," she said after a moment's hesitation, "but I'll have to check my logbook in the office."

Patterson nodded. "We'll take a look at it before I leave."

Patterson took a deep breath, leaned toward Charli, and looked into her eyes. "Charli, I'm not asking you to rat out the pilots, and I won't tell anyone a word you tell me, but if you want to help me find Jake's killer, we need to know what went on during the last weeks of Jake's life. Why would someone want to kill him? I don't believe a stranger randomly shot a pilot who was sitting in a plane on the beach at Karluk Lake. Someone hated Jake enough to kill him, and it's my job to find out who that was. Do you understand? I need you to tell me everything you know about Jake's skirmishes with pilots or anyone else."

Charli blinked and then slowly nodded. "Okay," she said. "He did have a temper, but from what I saw, he was usually in the right when he got mad at someone. He just said what he thought and moved on with his life. Not everyone was okay with his behavior."

"Like who?" Patterson urged.

"The other day he yelled at Billy, the kid who helps load freight. Billy was so upset he nearly quit, and I had to talk him down."

"Why did Jake yell at him?" Patterson asked.

"Billy said Jake was furious because he thought Billy had loaded his plane wrong."

"How did he load it wrong?"

"Oh, pilots are particular about how the plane is loaded. Part of it, of course, is proper weight distribution, but some of it is because every pilot likes freight loaded a certain way, and they get pissy if the freight guys forget. I guess Jake had shown Billy twice how he wanted things piled in his plane, and when Billy still did it wrong the third time, he yelled at him."

"Is Billy still here?"

"He is. He's a good kid."

"Was he working here the day Jake was killed?"

"No," Charli said. "He took a few days off so he and his friends could . . ." Her eyes got big, and she stared at Patterson. "So he and his friends could float down the Karluk River." She paused a minute, and red blotches sprouted on her pale cheeks. "He'd never hurt Jake, though."

"I imagine it's a coincidence," Patterson said, "but I will need to talk to him. Is he back here yet?"

"Tomorrow," she said.

"Who else?" Patterson asked.

"Jake got into it with two pilots from Emerald Island Air."

"What were their names?" Patterson asked

"Jordan Gregg and Buddy something-or-other. I don't remember his last name," Charli said. "Their dispatcher—Daisy—called and gave me a piece of her mind, as if it was my fault the pilots got into it. I told her Jake yelled at her pilots because they did something stupid, and she should worry about her own airlines instead of mine."

"Did he have words with any of the other Kodiak Flight Services pilots?" Patterson asked.

Charli shrugged. "Probably, but I don't think there were any serious issues. Everyone here is upset about his death."

"Charli, did you know Jake was sick?" Patterson asked.

"No, what do you mean?"

"He had stage IV colon cancer. It was terminal," Patterson said.

Charli's hands flew to her mouth. "No!" she said, and Patterson thought she was about to begin crying again.

"He had to be in a great deal of pain if he wasn't taking painkillers, and narcotics would show up on a random tox screen," Patterson said.

"A few days ago," Charli said, "Jake returned from a flight, and his next group was ready to go, but he told me he needed a few minutes because he had a bad headache. He went into the pilots' lounge and stayed there for fifteen minutes. When he came out, I was so busy, I never asked him if he got rid of the headache." Tears trickled down her cheeks. "I should have said something."

"Charli," Patterson said, "you couldn't have known. Jake kept the news to himself. He apparently didn't want anyone to know he was sick."

She nodded and brushed at the tears. "I feel bad for him."

"Do you know Jake's wife?" Patterson asked.

Charli wrinkled her nose. "I met her," she said. "She was nice enough to me, but I got the feeling she thought she was better than me. I know she thinks Kodiak is a Podunk town, and Jake told me she believed working here was beneath him. I think she wanted to live out her years as the retired Delta pilot's wife."

Patterson consulted his notebook. "I think that's all I have for now." He handed Charli one of his cards. "Give me a call if you think of anything else."

"I will," she said.

"Before I leave, will you check to see which of your other pilots were in the vicinity of Karluk Lake when Jake died?"

"I'll check." Charli's back stiffened, and she stood.

Patterson knew Charli was doing this task under protest. He followed her to the main office where one of the office staff stood explaining to a group of four men their flight would leave an hour later than planned. Charli walked behind the tall desk, punched at the computer keyboard, and studied the screen.

"Let's see," she said. "Roy had a flight to Uyak Bay. Uyak is just over the mountain from Karluk. He left twelve minutes before Jake. Rusty flew to Karluk to drop off rafters and left twenty-two minutes after Jake, and John flew that direction a little over an hour after Jake."

"Could you write down those names and times for me, and also, add the tail numbers of the planes they were flying?" If Lance Crane remembered the tail number of the plane he'd seen circling Karluk Lake a short time after Jake departed, Patterson wanted to know who was flying the plane.

Charli scribbled down the information and handed the note to Patterson. He glanced at it.

Jake Shepherd to Karluk - departed at 9:02 N4412
Roy Tayler to Uyak - departed at 8:50 - left 12 min. before Jake N4416
Rusty Hoak to Karluk - departed 9:24 - left 22 min. after Jake N4414
John Saner to Fraser Lake - departed at 10:06 - left 64 min. after Jake N7635X

"Are any of these pilots here now?" Patterson asked.

Charli shook her head. "It's John's day off, and Rusty and Roy are both flying. They have tight schedules all day. We're down a pilot, so the other guys have heavier loads."

"What time will Roy and Rusty be done for the day?" Patterson asked.

Charli consulted the computer. "Maybe by 8:00 p.m."

"I'll try to be here at 8:00 p.m. then. Please tell them to hang around so I can talk to them." Patterson said. "I know they'll be tired, and I'll only take a few minutes of their time."

"Okay," Charli said. "But I'm sure neither one of them would hurt Jake."

Patterson's gaze softened. "I know, but they could have seen something important."

Patterson had his hand on the door handle, preparing to leave the Kodiak Flight Services building, when Charli called to him.

"Sergeant," she said. "I thought of something. I don't know why it didn't come to me until now, but it might be important."

Patterson turned and walked back to the front counter.

Charli lowered her voice. "A few days ago, Jake flew a family, mom, dad, and two kids, to Karluk Lake. When he got back here, he told me he recognized the guy."

"Who was he?" Patterson asked.

"I don't remember all the details," Charli said, "but I think he was a builder in Miami, and he testified at the trial of some big contractor, providing evidence against the guy for violating codes and using subpar materials in his buildings. These weren't homes, they were big office buildings. Anyway, after he testified, the contractor told him in open court for all to hear that he would track him down and kill his wife and kids and then he'd kill him."

"Jake was sure this is the same guy?"

Charli nodded. "I guess it was big news in Miami. Jake said he flew out of Miami for eight months a few years ago, and this trial was in the news when he lived there."

"Do you remember how many years ago this happened?" Patterson asked.

Charli blew out a long, slow breath and closed her eyes. Finally, she said. "I think he said it was six or seven years ago, but I can't be sure."

"Did this guy know Jake recognized him?"

"Jake told him," Charli said. "He said the color drained from the man's face, and the wife and kids looked scared. The man told Jake he had no idea what he was talking about, and Jake said it hit him all of a sudden that the family must be in hiding. I don't know, maybe they're in the witness protection program?"

"Did the man or Jake mention the trial again?"

"No," Charli said. "Jake said the man barely uttered another word to him, and the wife and kids wouldn't even look at him."

"Interesting," Patterson said. "Do you remember if Jake told you the man's name?"

"He did, but I don't remember it. All I know is it wasn't the name he gave us."

Patterson thought he already knew the answer to his next question, but he needed to confirm his suspicions. "What name did he give you?" he asked.

Charli punched a few keys on her computer keyboard. "Hiram, Marla, Ann, and John Madison."

This was the mysterious family of four he and Mark had climbed the hill to question. The same family who had mounted a trail cam high in a tree so they could see anyone climbing the one trail to their campsite.

1976

After three days of blizzard conditions, the snow and wind finally stopped sometime during the night. This morning dawned clear and cold with at least four feet of snow on the ground. Bently didn't know how far he could hike slogging through the snow, but he had to get out of camp for a few hours. He was sick and tired of sitting in his tent, and he couldn't stand to be around Schwimmer any longer. He never realized what a whiner the guy was.

Schwimmer had been very lucky, and it seemed to Bently the guy should be happy. He hadn't suffered any frostbite, and while he'd been mildly hypothermic, he seemed fine now. He'd eaten too much of their food because he said he needed to recover his strength, and now, he should want to get out and do something on this gorgeous day. Instead, Schwimmer said he had no intention of hunting until some of the snow melted, so Bently left him alone in camp as he began stomping a trail down to the lake. He didn't bring snowshoes with him on this adventure because he'd read this side of Kodiak didn't get much snow at the lower elevations, especially in the fall. He just needed to get to the lakeshore, though, and then he could hike along the beach where waves had melted and dislodged the snow.

He reached the lake in fifteen minutes and picked up his pace along the edge of the water. He felt his head clear with each step taking him further from the confines of their small campsite. He didn't care if he ever saw Schwimmer again. The guy was a wimp, and anymore, Bently barely could stand to talk to him.

Bently hiked around the shoreline until he stood below the small hill he had glassed from a few days earlier. He knew he'd have to fight through heavy snow up the hill if he wanted to get to the top. Before he'd left camp, he'd duct-taped his rain pants to his boots, so he didn't think he'd get too wet slogging through the snow. He thought about it for a few minutes and then finally went for it.

One hour and twenty minutes later, he made it to the top of the hill. He felt exhausted and wet when he summited the peak of the mound. He didn't know if he was wet from sweat, if the snow had soaked through his rain pants, or if it had worked its way down through the waistband. One thing for sure, the snow hadn't entered from the boot line because the duct tape had held firm. He knew he'd have to head back to camp before long. The temperature hovered in the teens, and it wouldn't be wise for him to spend too many hours in wet clothes in this weather.

He stomped down the snow and sat on it. He'd come this far; he at least wanted to glass for an hour or two. It would be easy to spot tracks in the fresh snow, but unfortunately, he would never be able to fight his way through the deep snow to reach a bear even if he saw one. Still, he glassed.

He saw nothing for an hour. His only hope was to see a bear near the lake where he could get to it. He thought it made sense bears would get out of the deep snow and head to the lakeshore where they could walk more easily, but he saw no tracks and no bears.

He was getting ready to call it a day when he saw something move on the far shore of the lake. He set up his spotting scope to get a better look at the animal. He adjusted the focus on the scope and realized he wasn't looking at a wild animal. It was a man wearing beaver or otter furs, walking the shore of the lake and dragging a small sled behind him. The man loped at a slow gait, and Bently got the impression he was old. *What is he doing out here by himself?*

Bently watched the man for several minutes, but when he started to shiver, he decided to head back to camp.

PRESENT DAY
SUNDAY, JUNE 29TH
1:20 P.M.

Patterson was getting nowhere with the U.S. Marshals Service. When he'd returned to his office after interviewing Charli, he'd researched the Madison family. On the surface, their records looked clean. They had Social Security numbers, passports, and the parents had driver's licenses, but when he tried to dig deeper, their trail disappeared.

Marla had posted her résumé on a job-search site. According to her employment history, she had most recently worked at a florist's shop in Albuquerque, New Mexico. Patterson dialed the number next to the name of the shop, but a recording said the number was out of service. Next, he Googled the shop and found no web page or address listing. He suspected the shop did not exist and probably never had.

Next, he searched for news stories about the trial of an accused contractor in Miami. After twenty minutes, he found what he was looking for. Four years earlier, Sylvester Roberti had been on trial for major code violations on two large condominium complexes he had constructed in the heart of Miami. The prosecution had provided several witnesses to testify against Roberti, but the most damning testimony came from Marcus Cole, a young builder who had worked with Roberti. Cole had agreed to testify against Roberti in exchange for the prosecution dropping all charges against him. After Cole testified and walked past the defendant on his way to the rear of the courtroom, Roberti said loud enough for those around him to hear, "You and your family are dead."

Patterson found a photo of Marcus Cole and studied it. Hiram Madison had been wearing dark sunglasses and a ball cap when Patterson and Traner questioned the family, but the man in the photo resembled the man who had introduced himself as Hiram Madison.

Patterson took the next logical step and called the U.S. Marshals Service but was told by a very officious receptionist to call back on Monday, and one of the marshals would talk to him. He thought for a few minutes and then decided to tap into his federal connection. He dialed FBI Special Agent Nick Morgan.

Morgan answered on the second ring. "Dan, how are you?"

"Is this a bad time to ask for a favor?"

"I'm in Columbus, Missouri, consulting on a case right now. I've been flying back and forth nonstop between here and Houston, where we're looking for a serial killer. It's nice to catch my breath and listen to a friendly voice for a change. What can I do for you?"

"I heard you caught the guy in Indianapolis," Patterson said.

"Yes, but not until after he'd murdered five women."

Morgan was a profiler for the FBI, and his job took him to grisly crime scenes all over the country. Patterson wondered how he did it. Patterson met Morgan the previous winter when Morgan had consulted on a string of murders on Kodiak, and the two men quickly became friends. Patterson felt comfortable asking for his help with the U.S. Marshals Service.

"We have a situation here on Kodiak," Patterson said.

"Not another serial killer, I hope."

"No, thank God, but this is a puzzling case, and I've run into a snag." Patterson explained about Jake's murder and the strange family camped within walking distance of the murder scene.

Morgan barked a short laugh. "Dan, you'll need more than that on the Madison family before you convince a U.S. Marshal to give up his secrets. Those WitSec people take their jobs seriously."

Patterson sighed. "I was afraid you'd say that. Of the suspects we've found so far, Hiram Madison had the best motive to murder Jake. If he feared Jake would expose him and put him and his family in danger, he might have decided to eliminate the threat."

"I'll be happy to talk to the Marshals Service for you," Morgan said, "but I think you need more evidence against Madison before I make the call."

ROBIN BAREFIELD

Patterson thanked Morgan and disconnected. He hoped Hiram Madison wasn't their guy because he'd be tied up in red tape for years if he had to deal with the U.S. Marshals Service.

A light knock sounded on Patterson's door. "Come in," he called.

The door opened slowly, and Jan Carter, one of the crime scene techs, entered his office.

"What do you have for me, Jan?" Patterson asked.

"Sir, we've processed the notebook. We found Jake's fingerprints on it but no other prints. Sara said you wanted it back as soon as possible."

Jake held out his hand for the evidence bag containing the notebook. "Thanks, Jan. Did you find anything else of interest in the plane?"

"Yes, sir," Jan said. We dug a bullet out of the ceiling of the plane. "Jake's killer must have been below Jake's level because the trajectory of the shot was an upward angle."

"Makes sense," Patterson said. "Jake was in the plane, and his killer must have been on the beach a few feet below Jake. What is the caliber of the bullet?"

"A .30-30, sir."

Patterson nodded. The shell they'd found was from the killer's gun. "I don't suppose the murderer left us a nice, readable fingerprint on the shell casing," he said.

Jan shook her head. "Unfortunately, we found no prints on the casing," she said.

"Anything else?"

"Two more things, sir," Jan said. "We found a duffel bag in the rear of the plane with a sleeping bag, water, granola bars, extra socks, and a 12-gauge shotgun."

"Jake's survival bag in case he found himself stranded someplace."

"Yes, sir, and no prints besides Jake's on the gear."

"What else?" Patterson asked.

"The photos of the boot impressions on the beach match those of the photos Mark took of the boots worn by the two campers who found Jake."

"No surprise there," Patterson said. He thanked Jan for the information and slid Jake's journal into his top desk drawer. He then called Emerald Island Air, introduced himself, and asked if either Jordan Gregg or a pilot named Buddy were working today.

"Buddy Stark is here," the dispatcher said. "Jordan won't be in until tomorrow."

"Is Buddy flying, or is he there right now?"

"He's here, but he has a flight leaving in about twenty minutes."

"Tell him I'm on my way, and I need to talk to him before he leaves."

The Emerald Island Air office occupied a small, log building next to Kodiak Flight Services. Patterson parked and walked in the front door. A small woman about forty looked up from her computer screen and smiled.

"Are you Daisy?" Patterson asked.

The woman shook her head. "I'm Mia. Daisy has the day off."

"Nice to meet you, Mia." Patterson shook her hand. "Where will I find Buddy?"

"He's down on the dock loading the plane. He said to send you down there."

Buddy Stark was a tall, thin man with a receding hairline and a bad complexion. Patterson guessed he was in his late twenties or early thirties. When he saw Patterson approaching, he walked toward him, and they shook hands.

"I don't have much time," Buddy said. "I'm supposed to leave in a few minutes."

"This won't take long," Patterson assured him. "I want to talk to you about Jake Shepherd."

"I wasn't at Karluk Lake when he was killed," Buddy said. "I don't know how I can help you."

"I heard you and Jordan Gregg had an argument with Jake."

"Oh, man." Buddy shook his head. "This is ridiculous." He continued to shake his head as he took a step back from Patterson, head down, eyes glued on the dock. "Listen," he said. "I felt bad about that argument the moment it was over, and I feel terrible about it now. The truth is," he looked Patterson in the eyes, "Jake had every right to scold us like little kids because that's how we acted, and I told Jordan the same thing. I will never again buzz anyone with my plane, and it's all because Jake Shepherd made me feel like the idiot I was. I owe him a debt of gratitude, and I'd planned to thank him."

"What about your friend, Jordan? Did he feel the same way about the situation?"

Buddy shook his head. "You'll have to ask him how he felt. I don't want to speak for Jordan," he said. "I will say I know Jordan well enough to know he would never kill anyone, especially over an argument."

Patterson believed everyone was capable of murder, and he also knew the only person you could ever know completely was yourself, and even then, you could surprise yourself.

PRESENT DAY
SUNDAY, JUNE 29TH
4:00 P.M.

Troopers Sara Byram, Brad Simpton, Peter Boyle, Mark Traner, and Patterson gathered around the table in the small conference room at trooper headquarters. A carafe of coffee and a plate of Irene's homemade chocolate-chip cookies sat in the middle of the table. Patterson wondered when Irene had found the time to bake cookies. She'd put in two long days at the station since Jake's murder.

"We need to see what we have and organize our investigation," Patterson said. "We have only a short window of opportunity to interview possible witnesses rafting down the river or camping near the lake, so they should be our priority over the next few days. I would also, if possible, like to try to nail down our most high-profile suspects at this point. Sara, why don't you start? What have you learned about the campers?"

"Brad and Peter flew out yesterday afternoon to talk to the biologists at Camp Island, and I've interviewed three rafting groups who returned to town today. They were on the river when Jake was murdered, though, and they didn't know anything," Sara said.

"I did find out something interesting about Tammy's dad, though," Sara continued. "Gerald Monroe and Jake Shepherd both flew for Delta out of Atlanta from 2012 through 2014. I talked to a personnel director about both pilots." Sara's large brown eyes flashed with excitement as she relayed what she had learned. "Jake and Gerald flew together eleven times. Jake was the lead pilot, and Captain Monroe was co-pilot." Sara paused a moment. "At first, that's all the personnel director would tell me, but she finally admitted Gerald Monroe and Jake Shepherd had gotten into a physical altercation in the crew lounge before one of their flights. She had no idea what they'd fought about, but Monroe asked to be transferred as far away from Jake as possible. The personnel director found it ironic that both men had ended up in Alaska."

"Did the personnel director know Jake or Gerald Monroe personally?" Patterson asked.

"No," Sara said. "She made it clear she didn't know the men well, and she didn't know who'd started the argument. She said she heard no other complaints about either pilot."

Patterson sighed. "I hate coincidences as much as any of you do, but I can't believe Gerald Monroe would send his daughter and her boyfriend to Kodiak to shoot a pilot because he didn't like the guy." He looked at Sara. "This is good work, Sara, but I don't want you to spend too much time on it. Did you call Charli at Kodiak Flight Services and ask if Tammy or her boyfriend requested a particular pilot for their flight?"

Sara nodded. "Charli said no, they did not request Jake as their pilot on either the drop-off or the pickup, and Stan Edwards was the pilot who dropped them off."

"Let's wait on this angle for now," Patterson said. "If necessary, we'll dig deeper and learn more about the argument between Jake and Monroe, but let's save it."

Sara nodded and wrote something in her notebook.

"What about you, Mark?" Patterson asked. "Have you learned anything about our party of six guys?"

Traner cleared his throat and consulted his notes. "Robert and Donald Brinker grew up in Kodiak. Robert, or Bobby as he is called, still lives in Kodiak. He's a diesel mechanic and has his own business. His brother Don lives in Wasilla and works in construction. He works with Jeremy Lawson and Ronald George, and the other two guys, David Landry, and Greg Sparks, are friends. Landry is a firefighter, and Sparks owns a pizza place in Wasilla." Traner placed his notes on the table and made eye contact with Patterson. "Get this, though. Bobby and Don Brinker went to high school with Jake. Bobby was in the same grade as Jake, and Don was two grades behind them."

Patterson sat back in his chair. "That is interesting. Good work, Mark. Keep digging."

Traner nodded. "Do you want to wait until they get back to town to interview them again?" he asked. "I could intercept them on the river."

"No," Patterson said, "we know where they are for the next two days."

"Brad, Pete, what did you guys find out from the Camp Island biologists?"

"Absolutely nothing," Brad said. "None of them saw anything. I'm checking their backgrounds now, but I've found no obvious connections between them and Jake."

Patterson told the group about Jake's terminal cancer and what he'd learned from Charli and Steve. "I've interviewed Buddy Stark. He claimed he held no animosity toward Jake, but even though Buddy didn't say so, I got the feeling Jordan Gregg isn't as forgiving as his friend. I'll interview Gregg tomorrow. Tonight, I plan to interview Roy Tayler and Rusty Hoak. Those were two of the three Kodiak Flight Services pilots in the vicinity of Karluk Lake during the time frame when Jake was murdered. John Saner has the day off, so I'll catch him tomorrow. According to Lance Crane, he saw a Kodiak Flight Services Beaver not long after Jake dropped him off. He remembered the plane had a different tail number than Jake's, but he couldn't recall the number. I want to find out who was flying that plane."

Patterson paused a moment and then said, "I have one more interesting piece of information, but unfortunately the U.S. Marshals Service slammed the door in my face."

"I bet this has to do with that strange family," Traner said.

"The Madison family," Patterson nodded. "I am fairly certain they are in the witness protection program. Jake was the pilot who dropped them off, and he recognized Hiram Madison as Marcus Cole, a man who testified in a trial in Miami against a very dangerous guy. Jake, who we now know was not good about keeping his thoughts to himself, told Cole he recognized him. Cole and his family are in hiding, so Cole must have been alarmed to learn his bush plane pilot knew who he was. My question, though, is was Cole worried enough to radio Jake, ask him to land, walk up to the plane, and shoot him in broad daylight?" Patterson shook his head. "I think Cole is a long shot, but Pete, I want you to take a good hard look at the family and see if you think we should beg the Marshals Service to let us interview them again."

"The situation could have been more complicated," Pete said. "Maybe Jake landed there to talk to Cole about something, and Cole shot him."

Patterson shrugged. "Could be. It's best to keep an open mind."

Patterson looked around the table at the assembled troopers. "I think all these leads are possibilities, but time is not on our side. I want to concentrate on the most likely suspects and be certain we corral the rafters and campers for interviews before they leave the island. Sara is in charge of keeping track of the rafters and campers, so work with her when she needs you to intercept and interview someone. Mark and I will interview the six fishermen when they get to town."

"Mark, I would also like you to look into Jake's will if he had one and any life insurance policies he had. Sara, why don't you call your contact at Delta and confirm they offer life insurance policies to their pilots."

Patterson ended the meeting and returned to his office. He slid the evidence bag containing Jake's journal from his top desk drawer. Even though the crime scene techs had already examined the journal, Patterson wanted to handle it as little as possible and get it locked away in the evidence room where it belonged. He carried the journal to the front office and opened it to the first page, placing it on the photocopying machine.

"Sir," Irene said. "If you need something photocopied, I can do it for you."

"Thanks, Irene," Patterson said, "but this is evidence, so the fewer people who touch it, the better."

Patterson made five copies of the journal. He stapled the pages together and then carefully carried everything back to his office. He placed the journal into another evidence bag, initialed the seal, and carried the bag to their small evidence room. He logged in the evidence and then dropped the bag into an empty box he labeled with the case file number. They didn't have much evidence for this crime, and he hoped the journal and the bullet would be enough. The entries he'd glimpsed while copying Jake's journal looked like code, and he wasn't sure he'd be able to decipher Jake's scribbles.

PRESENT DAY
SUNDAY, JUNE 29TH
7:50 P.M.

Rusty Hoak stood waiting in the lobby of Kodiak Flight Services when Patterson arrived. He held his cap in his hands, and his tousled brown hair looked as if he had been running his fingers through it. Patterson shook his hand, and Rusty led him to the conference room.

"I don't think I can tell you anything about Jake, but I'll help if I can." He pinched the bridge of his nose. "Man, I still can't believe he's dead."

Patterson and Rusty took seats at the table, and Patterson said, "I understand you had a flight to Karluk leaving about the same time Jake left for Karluk on his last flight."

"I guess so. Jake was loading his plane when I left."

"You didn't talk to him over the radio when you were in the air?"

"No. At the time, I didn't even know we were both going the same direction. I was in my own little world."

"Did you see his plane when you were at Karluk?"

"I did, but it wasn't where his body was found. It was on the other side of the lake, a long ways from where he died," Rusty said. "I checked the schedule after I heard what happened to him, and his plane was at the point where he dropped off his last passenger. I was on my way back to town, so he'd probably just landed."

"What time was it when you saw his plane?" Patterson asked

"It must have been a little after 11:00 a.m."

"Did you see any other planes in the vicinity of Karluk?"

"The only other plane I saw at Karluk was an Emerald Island Air Beaver."

"Do you know who was flying it?" Patterson asked.

"Yeah, it was Jordan Gregg. I talked to him."

"What did you guys talk about?"

Rusty shrugged. "The weather, where we were headed, the usual stuff. He didn't sound angry, if that's what you want to know."

"I also talked to Roy on my way back to town," Rusty said. "I know he was flying to someplace on the west side of the island."

"Roy Tayler?" Patterson asked.

"That's right. He left about a half hour after I did."

"I plan to talk to Roy next," Patterson said. "What can you tell me about Jake? I understand he had quite a temper and no qualms about confronting someone who did something he considered wrong."

Rusty nodded and laughed. "Yeah, we called him the 'pilot police.' I think he'd worked for a regimented airline too long. He forgot that bush flying is laid back. Sure, we have rules, but sometimes we fudge a little. If a load is ten pounds overweight, we look the other way, and we are often forced to fly below minimums. You do what's necessary to get the flight done, and Jake had trouble relaxing the rules. He went strictly by the book. I'm sure in time, he would have mellowed, but he made a lot of enemies with other pilots."

"Like who?" Patterson asked.

"The Emerald Island Air pilots hated him, and the Sea Quest Air guys weren't too fond of him, either." Rusty's eyes suddenly opened wide. "I'm not saying any of those guys disliked him enough to kill him. They just kept their distance from him."

"Can you tell me anything else about Jake?" Patterson asked.

Rusty paused and looked down at the table.

"What is it?" Patterson finally asked.

"I don't know if I should say this, but I heard Jake talking to his wife on the phone the day before he died, and they were having a nasty argument."

"Did you hear any of it?"

"This is really none of my business," Rusty said.

"Rusty, in order to find out who murdered Jake, I need to know everything I can about Jake and the people around him."

Rusty tapped the table and let out a long sigh. "I heard Jake tell his wife she could divorce him if she wanted, but he would see to it she got nothing."

Interesting. "Did you hear anything else?" Patterson asked.

"No, I left the pilots' lounge when I realized he was talking to his wife."

Patterson gave Rusty a card and urged him to call if he thought of anything else. As soon as Rusty opened the conference room door, Roy Tayler walked into the room. Roy towered over Rusty, and Patterson guessed he was six feet two or six feet three. His shaggy, brown hair nearly reached his shoulders, and his brown eyes were both darker and harder than Rusty's. He was also several years younger than Rusty, and Patterson guessed he was in his mid-twenties.

"Are you ready for me, yet?" Roy asked. "I'm supposed to fly up to Anchorage with my girlfriend this evening, and she'll kill me if I miss the flight again."

"This will only take a few minutes," Patterson said. "Please, shut the door and have a seat."

Roy did as directed, sitting in the chair Rusty had just vacated.

"I guess this is about Jake," Roy said.

"Yes," Patterson said. "What did you think of Jake?"

"I respected him," Roy said. "He was too serious and strict at times, but man, the guy was a legend. I tried to soak up some of his knowledge and skill."

"Did you ever have a run-in with him?"

Roy shook his head, "No, but I take flying seriously. I don't know if I want to fly floatplanes all my life or move into cargo planes and finally passenger jets. I haven't decided, but I know I want a clean record and a good reputation. Jake even told me once he thought I was the best young pilot flying on Kodiak, and he saw great things in my future. His praise meant a lot to me."

"I understand you had a flight around the same time as Jake's final flight left town."

Roy raked through his hair, leaving a strand sticking straight up in the middle of his head. "I think I left Kodiak a few minutes after Jake."

"Rusty said he talked to you when you were in the air. Do you remember a conversation with Rusty?"

"Sure. Rusty and I talked on the radio. I think he was somewhere near Karluk too, but I didn't see him."

"Did you see or talk to Jake?" Patterson asked.

Roy shook his head. "No, I'd remember if I talked to Jake on his last flight."

"What about other pilots? Did you talk to anyone else?"

"I think I talked to Jordan Gregg briefly, but it might have been later in the day when I talked to him," Roy said.

"Did you ever see Jake get into arguments with other Kodiak Flight Services pilots?"

"Sure," Roy said. "He yelled at us all at one time or another, especially lately. If the least little thing bothered him, he felt he had to speak his mind."

"Anything in particular?"

Roy stared at the table for several moments as if lost in thought but finally shook his head. "I don't remember anything serious. He just couldn't let anything go."

Patterson handed Roy his card. "That's all I have for you now, Roy, but call me if you think of anything relevant."

Roy shook Patterson's hand and left the room.

Patterson knew he should go back to his office and organize his thoughts on this case, but Jeanne had headed straight to bed as soon as she'd arrived home that evening, not even attempting to eat dinner. He hated to admit it to himself, but he was beginning to worry she could be suicidal. He had never seen her so depressed, and he didn't want to leave her alone longer than necessary.

PRESENT DAY
MONDAY, JUNE 30TH
7:00 A.M.

Patterson arrived early the next morning at the Emerald Island Air office, hoping to catch Jordan Gregg before he started flying for the day. He waited only twenty minutes before the young pilot walked through the door. Daisy, the dispatcher, was polite but cool when Patterson interviewed her about "her pilots." She admitted to the dispute between Jordan Gregg, Buddy Stark, and Jake, but she claimed Jake started it, and her pilots did nothing wrong.

As soon as Jordan Gregg arrived, Daisy called him over to the desk and whispered in his ear. He turned and walked toward Patterson, his hand extended and an easy smile on his lips. Jordan Gregg had red, curly hair, a mustache, and a closely cropped beard. His hazel eyes met Patterson's, and the two men shook hands. Patterson guessed the pilot was around twenty-five years old. He stood approximately five feet, six inches tall, and although he wasn't overweight, he could be called pudgy.

"I have a few questions for you," Patterson said. "Is there somewhere we can go to talk?"

Gregg motioned to the door. "Let's go outside."

Patterson was surprised when they walked outside. The morning fog had dissipated, and patches of blue suggested a sunny day or at least a sunny few hours. After all, this was Kodiak and the weather was bound to change two or three times during the remainder of the day. Patterson breathed in a pungent mixture of damp earth, ocean, processed fish, and aviation fuel. Gregg led him to a quiet corner of the parking lot.

"Is this about Jake Shepherd?" Gregg asked.

"Why do you ask?"

"Because it was no secret I hated him, and I'm sure it's no secret I was flying near Karluk Lake around the time he was murdered," Gregg said.

The man's direct approach surprised Patterson, and he decided to let Gregg take the lead. "What can you tell me about all of this?" he asked.

"First of all," Gregg said, "I'm not a murderer, and second, I'm not stupid enough to kill someone in the middle of the day."

"Yes, but Jake was killed in the wilderness," Patterson said, "in a secluded area."

Gregg exhaled a bark of laughter. "If you think Karluk Lake is secluded, you haven't been there lately. Between bear viewers, fishermen, and rafters, the place is hopping. I worry more about other air traffic there than I do near Kodiak. Only an idiot would murder someone on the lake in the middle of the day."

"Yet someone did," Patterson said.

"Well, I don't know how I can prove it, but it wasn't me," Gregg said.

"Why don't you tell me what happened between you and Jake," Patterson said.

For the first time, Gregg's eyes left Patterson's and dropped to the ground. He crossed his arms over his chest. "I didn't have any passengers, and neither did Buddy. I guessed I buzzed Buddy when we were over Terror Flats, and a few minutes later, he buzzed me. If I'd known Shepherd was anywhere in the area, believe me, I never would have done it. That old fart thought he was the only pilot who knew how to fly."

"By Buddy, do you mean Buddy Stark?" Patterson asked.

"That's right," Gregg said. "Maybe we shouldn't have done it, but Shepherd threatened to report us to the FAA. Who does that, man?"

"Did you have any other disagreements with Shepherd?"

"Not since then, but he was on everyone. At the dock, he'd let you know if he thought you pulled up too fast, if the fuel hose was in his way, or if he thought we left our freight on the dock too long. He complained about everything. No one liked him, and anyone who tells you anything different is lying." Gregg again locked eyes with Patterson. "If you need a suspect for his murder, I suggest you look closer to home."

"What do you mean?" Patterson asked.

Gregg shook his head and kicked a small rock. "Nothing, except even the pilots and ground crew who worked with Jake didn't like him."

"Did you see Jake at Karluk Lake on Friday morning?" Patterson hoped to unsettle Gregg by the sudden change in topic, but Gregg seemed unphased.

"I saw his plane on the beach, but not at the spot where he was found a few hours later. It was across on the other side of the lake."

"What time was it when you saw the plane?"

"I don't know," Gregg said, "maybe 11:30."

Patterson nodded. He needed to find a pilot who had seen Jake's plane on the beach where he was murdered. If he could find a pilot or camper who saw the plane across the lake, then maybe they could narrow down the time frame for when he was killed.

"Did you talk to anyone on the radio when you were over Karluk Lake?" Patterson asked.

"Hoak," Gregg said. "I talked to Rusty Hoak for a few minutes, but that was it."

"Did you hear Jake talk to anyone on the radio?"

"Not on the frequencies I was monitoring, but he could have been on another channel."

Patterson thanked Gregg for his time and asked him if he had any plans to leave the island.

"Not at the moment," he said.

Patterson walked across the gravel driveway to Kodiak Flight Services. At 7:50 a.m., the office buzzed with activity. Two young women worked the front counter, and Patterson saw Charli behind the radio, mic in her hand as she conversed with pilots. Patterson feared he was already too late to catch John Saner before the pilot started his busy day of flying. He spotted Rusty Hoak as he walked out of the pilots' lounge and he called to him. Rusty stopped walking when he saw Patterson and took a step back, eyes wary.

"Rusty," Patterson said, "can you point me toward John Saner?"

"I think he's down on the dock loading his plane," Rusty said.

Patterson hurried from the office and down the ramp to the dock. Pilots, freight handlers, and passengers crisscrossed the dock, and Patterson regretted not asking Rusty for a description of John Saner. He walked up to a kid no older than sixteen who was dragging a heavy fuel hose down the dock. "Is

John Saner down here?" he asked. The boy pointed toward the 206 at the end of the dock. Patterson thanked him and walked toward the plane.

When he neared the plane, he saw a man around forty years old instructing a teenage boy on the proper way to load a plane.

"Excuse me," Patterson said. "Are you John Saner?"

Saner eyed Patterson's uniform and stepped off the float of the plane and onto the dock. He held out his hand and nodded. "What can I do for you?" he asked.

"I'm investigating the murder of Jake Shepherd," Patterson said. "I understand you flew to Karluk not long after Jake left on his last flight."

Saner shrugged. "I think I left an hour after Jake, so I didn't leave here right after him."

"Did you see or talk to Jake during your flight or at Karluk?"

"No. I mean, I saw his plane at Karluk, but I didn't talk to him."

"Where was his plane when you saw it?" Patterson asked.

"On the east side of the lake where he was found, why?"

Bingo! Someone finally admitted seeing Jake's plane in its final resting spot.

"What time was it when you saw his plane?" Patterson asked.

Saner stared at the dock for several seconds. "I saw it after I dropped off my group and was headed back, so it would have been around noon."

"Did you see anyone near the plane?"

"No. I didn't think about it at the time, but of course, now I wonder. Maybe Jake was sitting in his plane waiting for his group to arrive."

Or, maybe he was already dead.

"What did you think of Jake?" Patterson asked.

Saner shrugged. "He was okay but a bit of a pain in the ass to the younger pilots. He mostly left me alone."

"Do you know anyone who would want to kill him?"

Saner shook his head. "No, I don't."

The answer was too quick; Saner hadn't even thought about it. Patterson believed Saner was holding back something. Did the pilot have someone in mind for Jake's murderer? Was the person a friend or a co-worker he didn't want to betray?

Patterson asked Saner a few more questions but learned nothing else. At least now he knew Jake's plane had been sighted on the east side of Karluk Lake at noon, and since Saner hadn't seen activity around the plane, it was likely the perpetrator had murdered Jake and left the scene by then.

1976
SUNDAY, NOVEMBER 1ST

Bently spent the day on his hill glassing the lakeshore. He hadn't seen a bear or even a set of tracks since the snowstorm. The last two days had been freezing, and the snow hadn't melted, but Bently forged a decent trail to the top of the hill and carried with him a tarp to sit on while he glassed.

He hadn't seen the strange, old man in the last two days. He'd told Schwimmer about the man, and Schwimmer had been frightened by the idea of a man wandering around the lake. Bently assured Schwimmer the man was several miles away and wasn't likely to see them, but Schwimmer seemed upset. Bently wondered why before this trip he had never noticed what a crybaby Schwimmer was. The man still refused to leave camp to go hunting and said he planned to wait until the snow melted before he continued to hunt.

PRESENT DAY
MONDAY, JUNE 30TH
9:00 A.M.

I played hooky from work. I'd accumulated sixteen vacation days and five sick days, so I thought I could afford to use one or two to check into the case of my mysterious bones. I knew these bones were old, and there was no rush to find out how they came to be in the forest near Karluk Lake, but I couldn't stop thinking about them. Maybe the individual had relatives who were still alive and had spent the last decades wondering what had happened to their loved one.

I called the number Patterson gave me for the anthropology professor in Anchorage. She answered after only one ring, and I introduced myself.

"Yes," she said, "I received a message from Sergeant Patterson asking me to share our findings with you. It's my graduate student, Ying Lee, who is analyzing the bones. Hang on a second, and I'll transfer your call to her."

With a name like Ying Lee, I expected to hear someone with a strong Chinese accent answer the phone. When a woman with no foreign accent came on the line, I berated myself for racial profiling a person based on her name.

"Hey," she said. "Nice to meetcha, and thanks for sending the bones my way. They're fascinating."

"Would it be possible to meet and go over your findings?" I asked.

"Absolutely," she said. "You're in Kodiak, right? How soon can you make it to Anchorage?"

"How about Wednesday?"

"I can meet with you anytime Wednesday morning," Ying said.

"I'll take the early jet up there. How does 11:00 a.m. work?"

"Great," Ying said.

I wondered if I could cancel my Thursday classes and spend a few days in Anchorage on a mini getaway to what in Alaska passed for "the big city." I could shop, get my hair cut, take in a movie or two, and recharge my batteries.

Next, I drove to trooper headquarters. A heavyset woman around sixty with short-cropped gray hair greeted me when I walked through the door. When I told her my name, she grabbed a set of keys, stood, and led the way down the hall. I saw or heard no one else as I followed behind her. She opened the door to what she told me was the property room. She asked me to sit in the chair by a small table, and she disappeared through a second door. A few minutes later, she returned with a miniature tote labeled with the number 5283 followed by Karluk – Cold.

"I'm Irene," the woman said. "I'll leave you alone to look at the contents of this box. When you're done, put the lid back on the box, and let me know you're leaving so I can return the box to its proper place." She put her hands on her hips and looked down at me, her face stern. "Do not break the seal on the evidence bags. They're transparent, so you can clearly see each object through the bag. If you break the seal, you will ruin the chain of evidence. Do you understand?"

"Yes, ma'am," I said. I felt like a schoolgirl.

Irene turned abruptly and left the room, and I looked at the three small bags in the container. I picked up the knife first, but I didn't see anything about this generic Swiss Army knife that would prove helpful in identifying the bones or narrow down the time frame of death.

Next, I picked up the brass belt buckle with the U.S. Air Force insignia on it. I turned it over in my hand while I thought. The nearest Air Force base was Elmendorf, in Anchorage. I felt it was a long shot, but if I could narrow down the time frame, I would call the base and ask if anyone had disappeared during that time.

I picked up the third bag containing the watch. This digital watch was an antique, and I had already researched it based on the photos Geoff snapped when we'd first found it in the woods. I'd studied a website dedicated to the history of Timex watches and learned as much as I could about this model. When it had worked, the gold, rectangular watch displayed the time, and only the time, in red numerals. According to the website, Timex manufactured this model in the early 1970s. The watch was a prototype and didn't sell well because it was priced higher than similar styles sold by other watchmakers.

I again wondered why anyone would wear such an expensive, delicate watch into the wilds of the Kodiak National Wildlife Refuge. The watch was sure to shut down in the cold, damp air, leaving the wearer with only a blank display. *Maybe the watch had sentimental value to the wearer, and he never took it off.* I peered through the evidence bag, squinting at the back of the watch and the gold band to see if there was an inscription, but I saw nothing. I also saw no model number, but this had to be the same model watch I had seen on the Timex website. It looked identical.

Perhaps experts could tell me more about the origin of the knife, belt buckle, and watch, but for now, I hoped the items would provide me with a time frame for when they had been left in the woods near Karluk Lake. I also hoped the items had all been left in the woods by the man whose bones we had found, because so far, the watch and belt buckle provided me the only clues to his identity.

I returned the items to the box and thanked Irene for her help. Just as I was climbing into my car, my phone vibrated. I glanced at the display and groaned.

"Good morning, Peter," I said.

"I just checked your office," Peter said, "but you weren't there, and Betty says you're taking a personal day?"

"That's right," I said. *Thanks for ratting me out, Betty.*

"Listen," he said. "Some good news. One of the Tamron people—Corban Pratt—do you remember him?"

I had a bad feeling about where this conversation was headed. "Yes, I remember Corban." *How could I not remember him? The guy was gorgeous and quite a charmer.* He'd set off all the warning signals in my brain because I knew from experience his type offered nothing but trouble.

"He wants to stop by your lab today and look at your work. I hate to ask this of you, Jane, but would you mind coming in for a few hours? I believe he's seriously thinking of giving us a sizable grant, and a chunk of it might go to your research."

I slapped my hand down on my steering wheel and accidentally hit the horn. The loud noise made me jump.

"Are you okay? Are you driving?" Peter asked.

"I'm fine, and sure, I'll come into the lab and get things ready for Mr. Pratt."

My day off suddenly evaporated.

PRESENT DAY
MONDAY, JUNE 30TH
1:15 P.M.

Patterson walked into trooper headquarters, and when Irene held her hand in the air, he stopped and stood by her desk while she finished her telephone call.

When Irene disconnected, she handed him several message slips and said, "You'll be interested in the call I just received."

"Who was it?" Patterson asked.

"He identified himself as David Landry and said he was a member of the party of fishermen you interviewed Friday night at Karluk Lake. He said to tell you he was with Bobby and Don Brinker."

Irene had Patterson's attention. "Of course, I remember him. Where did he call from? I thought they were spending another night on the river."

"He was on his sat phone," Irene said. "He and another member of the party," Irene looked at her notes, "Jeremy Lawson, left the rest of their group and decided to come out a day early. Eagle Charters is picking them up at 2:00 p.m., so they should be back to town by 3:00 p.m." Irene looked up at Patterson. "He says he needs to talk to you."

Patterson rapped his knuckles on Irene's desk. "I'll be there to meet him, then."

Fifteen minutes later, Sara knocked on Patterson's open office door.

Patterson looked up from the case notes he was reading. "Sara, what is it?"

"It's the Madison family, sir. Charli just called and said a dispatcher for an airline in Homer contacted her and said to cancel the Madison family's return flight because they just picked them up."

"And flew them back to Homer?" Patterson felt his blood pressure spike and his face grow hot. He hated working with the federal government.

"Yes, sir," Sara said.

"Let's hope one of them isn't our murderer, or this case will never be solved," Patterson said.

Patterson then told Sara about his planned meeting with David Landry and Jeremy Lawson, and her eyes widened at the news.

"I wonder what they want to tell you," she said.

"Hopefully I'll be done talking to them by our 4:00 p.m. meeting, but if not, will you get things started for me?"

"Yes, sir," Sara said. "Mark and I are making headway on Jake's will and life insurance, so we should have something to report at the meeting. The other guys are talking to campers and rafters as they return to town, but I don't think they've learned much yet."

Patterson parked in the small lot in front of Eagle Charters at 2:30 p.m. Eagle operated out of Lily Lake, a lake in the center of town. Larry Mendoza owned the small charter company, and he was also the lone pilot and chief mechanic for the airline. Larry had a great reputation and was a favorite pilot for many locals. Patterson had flown with him twice and liked, respected, and felt safe with the older pilot. Unlike Jake Shepherd, Larry seemed to get along well with the other pilots in town, and he once told Patterson the only way to stay sane in the charter flying business was to be your own boss and your only employee. Of course, he wasn't his only employee; his wife, Louise, dispatched for him. When the pair decided to take a vacation, they simply shut down their business for a month.

It struck Patterson that Larry might be the perfect person to give him insight into the local pilot world and how the pilots felt about Jake. After he talked to Landry and Lawson, maybe he'd try to run down Larry for a chat.

Larry Mendoza landed his Beaver like a pro, skimming the lake surface at 3:05 p.m. As Patterson watched him taxi the plane up to the floatplane dock, he checked his watch and called Sara, asking her if she could contact the others and move the start of the meeting to 4:30 p.m.

Patterson walked to the dock and waited for the men to climb from the plane and unload their gear. As the two passengers walked toward the office, he intercepted them. Both men shook his hand.

"We're hoping to catch the afternoon jet back to Anchorage," David Landry said.

"Put your gear in my SUV, and we can talk on the way to the airport," Patterson said.

The two men complied, and then Landry crawled in the front passenger seat of the SUV, while Lawson took the rear seat.

"Since our time is limited," Patterson said, "I'll let you get right to the reason you wanted to talk to me." Patterson removed his phone from his pocket. "Do you mind if I record this meeting?" he asked.

"That's fine," Lawson said.

Landry nodded.

"Go ahead then," Patterson said as he exited the parking lot onto Mill Bay Road.

"We lied to you the other night," Landry said.

"Explain," Patterson said.

"We knew a pilot had been killed, and we weren't together the entire day."

"Okay." Patterson's pulse quickened. "How did you know a pilot had been killed?"

Landry stroked his beard. "We didn't know until later in the evening. Bobby told us. He said he called one of his employees in Kodiak, and the employee said he heard a rumor a pilot had been murdered at Karluk Lake."

"Did you see Bobby call someone?" Patterson asked.

"I did," Lawson said. "I saw him walk toward the beach with his sat phone, but I don't know who he called. He was so drunk, I'm surprised he could punch a number into the phone."

"You said you weren't together the entire day," Patterson said.

"We were out on the lake in three boats," Landry said. He jerked a thumb toward the back seat. "Jeremy and I were in one boat, Greg and Ron were in another boat, and Don and his fat slob of a brother, Bobby, were in the third boat. Bobby had two shots of whiskey in his coffee for breakfast and drank at least four beers on the lake that morning, but he was mad at Don for forgetting to bring the bottle of whiskey out in the boat. He finally convinced Don to get into our boat while he took their boat back to camp to get the whiskey."

"Let me get this straight," Patterson said. "Bobby Brinker returned to your camp alone in one of the boats?"

"Right," Landry said. "We headed on down the lake and didn't see where he went, but he was gone for over two hours. When he got back to us, the bottle of whiskey was nearly gone, and he was so drunk he couldn't see straight."

"What time was this?" Patterson asked.

"I wasn't wearing a watch," Landry said, "but I know he left before noon because Don told us he had no idea his brother had become a full-blown alcoholic, and he mentioned how much he'd had to drink, and it wasn't even noon yet. Don left the whiskey in camp on purpose, hoping Bobby would sober up during the day. Of course, we all had beer, so Bobby managed to find alcohol."

Patterson felt the entire bunch of guys should be arrested for consuming alcohol while operating a boat, but he decided to keep this thought to himself for now.

"I know Bobby was gone for over two hours because when he returned, Don looked at his watch and said it was 2:20 p.m. and he asked Bobby what he'd been doing all that time."

"What did Bobby say?" Patterson asked.

"He told Don it was none of his damn business," Landry said.

"Where do you think he was?" Patterson asked.

"I have no idea," Landry said, "and I didn't notice any airplanes on the beach, but I knew Bobby hated that pilot Jake."

"What about you, Jeremy?" Patterson looked in the rearview mirror at Lawson. "Did you see where Bobby went when he left your group?"

"I wasn't paying attention," Lawson said. "We were talking and fishing, and I was happy not to have the loudmouth around for a while."

"What makes you gentlemen think Bobby might hurt Jake Shepherd?" Patterson asked.

"Because he couldn't stop talking about how much he hated the guy," Landry said. "The other day, Jake stopped to drop off a party, and he spotted us. Bobby was drunk as a skunk, standing up in the boat bellowing at the sky, and Jake taxied over to us. He told us that alcohol and boats don't mix. He didn't recognize Bobby, but Bobby knew who he was."

"Bobby started screaming at Jake the minute he saw him," Lawson said.

"What did he say?" Patterson asked.

"Most of his tirade was obscene," Landry said, "but he told him he hadn't changed since high school, and he was still the same know-it-all prick he had been back then."

"Jake looked at Bobby for several seconds, and then he seemed to recognize him, and he laughed," Lawson said. "He told Bobby he could have predicted back in high school Bobby would turn into a fat drunk. Bobby told Jake he didn't know anything about him. To which Jake replied he knew everything he needed to know about Bobby."

"What happened next?" Patterson asked when neither man continued.

"Nothing, really," Lawson said. "Jake got in his plane and left. I don't think he meant anything by what he said, but Bobby flipped out."

"I don't understand." Patterson regarded Lawson in the rearview mirror, but Landry was the one who answered.

"Bobby couldn't stop talking and ranting about Jake. He went on all afternoon and evening while he got drunker and drunker. When he's wasted, he's hard to understand, but both Jeremy and I got the feeling Jake knew something about Bobby from their high school days, and from what Jake said to him, Bobby thought Jake was threatening to expose his secret."

"Do you have any idea what this secret is?" Patterson asked.

Both men shook their heads. "That's just it," Lawson said. "It was probably something stupid like Bobby pulled the fire alarm, and Jake saw him do it. Bobby blows everything out of proportion, and he has a terrible temper."

"If you take a second helping of beans before he gets his first helping, he's likely to punch you in the nose," Landry added.

"But do you think he could kill Jake?" Patterson asked.

"Oh, yes," Landry said. "If he'd had his gun with him in the boat when Jake came over to talk to us, I have no doubt he would have shot Jake. He can't think straight when he's drunk, and he was very drunk that day."

"What type of gun did he carry?" Patterson asked.

"The only gun I saw was a Ruger .308 rifle," Landry said. "But he's the type of guy who would carry several guns when one would do the job."

"Did you have a radio in your camp?" Patterson asked. "Would Bobby have had any way to contact Jake when he was flying over the lake?"

"We had two handheld VHFs and two sat phones," Landry said.

"We were thinking he could have called Jake at home and told him he wanted to talk to him for a few minutes if he had a flight to Karluk," Lawson said.

"What makes you think he called him on the sat phone to set up a meeting?" Patterson asked.

"To be honest," Landry said. "I don't think Bobby was ever sober enough during our camping trip to plan something as complex as a rendezvous with Jake."

"The first night on the river," Lawson said, "David and I started talking, and we realized we needed to tell you the truth. Bobby probably had nothing to do with the murder, but he hated Jake, and he was in the right place at the right time."

"After Trooper Traner and I visited you the other night, what did Bobby say?" Patterson turned onto the road leading to the airport.

"He got so drunk that night he passed out. We put out the campfire and left him sleeping on the ground," Lawson said. "The next morning, he could barely move. His brother had to pack his gear, and we had to pour Bobby into one of the rafts."

"Yeah," Landry said. "Talk about a terrible camping trip. I can't wait to get back to work."

"The first night on the river," Lawson said, "Bobby was hitting the sauce again, but he wasn't as drunk as the night before. I heard him say he was nowhere near Jake's plane. No one had even mentioned the possibility that Bobby could have killed Jake, but once he began denying it, David and I started wondering if he did set up a meeting with Jake and then murdered him."

Patterson thought about the tidy crime scene with no footprints on the beach and no fingerprints on the door handle of the plane. *Could a drunk Bobby Brinker pull off such a meticulously executed murder?*

Patterson pulled into the small airport lot and parked near the door to the Alaska Airlines terminal. "How did you guys get away from the others?"

"We told the truth," Lawson said. "At least most of it. We said we were sick of Bobby and we wanted to go home. No one questioned us."

"I think they all wanted to come with us," Landry said. "The other guys are closer friends with Don, though, so I think they felt duty bound to stick it out with him."

Patterson thanked the two men and helped them carry their gear up the ramp and into the lobby of the Alaska Airlines building.

Patterson again consulted his watch. It was 3:53 p.m. If he hurried, he could sneak in a quick meeting with Larry Mendoza, the owner of Eagle Charters.

Patterson found Larry and his wife, Louise, sitting on padded stools behind the counter in the Eagle Charters office, sipping coffee.

"Sergeant," Larry said, "I saw you talking to my last two passengers. Do you need some information from me?"

"Nothing about your passengers," Patterson said. "I just wanted to get your take on the Kodiak pilot scene."

Mendoza laughed. "You're a pilot. Aren't you part of the scene?"

Now it was Patterson's turn to laugh. "Hardly," he said. "I'm a cop, so no one tells me anything."

"I'll let you boys gossip," Louise said. She stood, clutching a purse in her right hand. "I have a few errands to run, and then I'll be back to get you." She stared her husband in the eyes. "I want to get home before eight tonight."

"Yes, dear," Larry said and smiled at Patterson. "This is the first night in a week I haven't had late flights. I'm looking forward to making it through an entire movie without falling asleep in my chair."

"I know the feeling," Patterson said.

"What can I do for you?" Larry asked. "I assume this is about Jake Shepherd?"

"That's right," Patterson said. "I'm trying to learn as much as I can about Jake, and it didn't take me long to learn Jake made some enemies in town."

Larry let out a sigh while he slowly shook his head. "With his blunt approach, I don't know how he climbed the ranks at Delta. I see young pilots do stupid things, and it probably irks me as much as it did Jake. Flying a plane anywhere should never be taken lightly, but pulling stunts while flying a plane around Kodiak will eventually get you and probably several other people killed."

Mendoza paused for a few seconds. "I don't have to tell you how challenging it is to fly around this mountainous island with its ever-changing weather conditions. It's no place for kids to play, but we were all young once, and I'm sure even Jake pulled some idiot stunts early in his career." Mendoza shrugged. "I try to nurture young pilots, not lecture them. Jake had few people skills. It was as if he needed to teach everyone else how to live."

"How did you get along with Jake?" Patterson asked.

"Me?" Mendoza asked. "Fine. I didn't have problems with Jake. I really didn't talk to him much, to be honest, but he flew out of the basin, and I fly out of the lake, so we didn't see each other often. We occasionally passed along weather conditions when we were both in the air, but that's the extent of my relationship with Jake Shepherd."

"What can you tell me about Jake's interactions with other pilots?"

"Ah, the gossip," Mendoza said. "I know he yelled at two of the Emerald Island Air pilots for buzzing each other. They thought he was going to report them to the FAA, and they were hopping mad." He shrugged. "Nothing ever came of it, though."

"Anything else?" Patterson asked.

Mendoza sat back and regarded Patterson for several moments. "Are you asking me what I think you're asking?"

"I don't understand," Patterson said.

"Do you want to know if any of the local pilots hated Jake enough to somehow lure him into landing at Karluk Lake and then shoot him?"

"Not exactly," Patterson said, "but since you brought it up, let's cut to the chase. Do you know anyone who wanted Jake dead?"

Mendoza sighed and took a long draw of coffee. Finally, his hazel eyes met Patterson's. "I think you need to talk to Steve Duncan about the pilots in his shop."

"What do you mean?" Patterson asked.

Larry Mendoza stood and began tidying the office. "I've already said too much," he said. "All I know are third-hand rumors, and they're probably wrong."

Patterson left the Eagle Charters office feeling confused and cranky. Larry Mendoza was the second pilot today to suggest at least one Kodiak Flight Services pilot had a reason to murder Jake, but who, they wouldn't say. He'd have to re-interview Steve and Charli, and this time, he'd take a hardline approach.

PRESENT DAY
MONDAY, JUNE 30TH
4:37 P.M.

When Patterson entered the conference room at trooper headquarters, he saw Sara Byram, Brad Simpton, Peter Boyle, and Mark Traner sitting quietly around the table. While he and Sara had given some of the other troopers assignments on this case, he wanted to keep the core investigators to a minimum. He needed to keep track of all the moving parts in the case, and the fewer people he managed, the better. He trusted and respected the four troopers he faced as he sat at the table. He believed together, they could solve this case and find Jake's murderer.

Patterson began the meeting by telling the others about his conversation with Landry and Lawson.

"Bobby might have wanted Jake dead," Traner said, "but the crime scene looked perfect, not the work of a drunk."

"I don't know," Peter said. "My uncle is a drunk. He has his first gin and tonic with breakfast and doesn't stop for the rest of the day. By evening, he's a sloppy mess, but he functions fairly well in the morning and early afternoon."

"Bobby Brinker is a bully, and bullies are cowards," Patterson said. "When he returns tomorrow, let's get him in here and sweat him. If he's drunk when he gets back to town, we'll put him in a cell until he's sober."

The troopers nodded.

"I think we've narrowed down our timeline," Patterson continued. "When I interviewed John Saner, one of the pilots for Kodiak Flight Services, he told me he saw Jake's plane on the east side of the lake, around noon.

Rusty Hoak saw Jake's plane on the west side of the lake at 11:00 a.m., and Jordan Gregg spotted Jake's plane in the same spot near 11:30 a.m. These aren't exact times, but I think we can conclude Jake flew to the east side of the lake approximately between 11:30 a.m. and noon and was probably killed soon after."

"What I don't understand," Simpton said, "is what was Jake doing for all that time? If he left town at 9:00 a.m., he should have arrived at Karluk around 10:00 a.m. What did he do for the next hour?"

"His last passenger was an old floatplane pilot," Sara said. "They probably flew here together back in the day and had a lot to talk about."

"Keep in mind," Patterson said, "we have Charli's scheduled departure times, not the actual departure times. As we all know, floatplanes rarely depart on schedule, so it's likely Jake left Kodiak later than 9:00 a.m."

The troopers nodded, and Patterson studied his notes to organize his thoughts.

"What about the 'WitSec' family?" Sara asked.

"Let's not worry about them for now," Patterson said. "If we keep hitting dead ends with our other leads, I'll take on the Marshals Service. What have you and Mark learned about Jake's life insurance policy and will?" Patterson asked, his gaze locked on Sara.

Sara glanced at Traner and then back at Patterson. "Delta carries life insurance on their pilots, at least they did in Jake's day," she said. "The initial policy was for $100,000, but pilots had the option to increase the value of the policy, and if they did increase it, Delta deducted the additional premium from their paychecks."

Sara paused, and Patterson asked, "Did Jake increase the payout on his policy?"

Sara nodded. "He bumped it up to $500,000."

"That's quite a bump," Simpton said.

Sara tugged at her ponytail. "That's not all." She said. "The policy pays double for accidental death, and murder is included as an accidental death."

Patterson sat forward. "Interesting," he said. "Did you find out who the beneficiary is on the policy?"

"Yes, sir," Sara said. "There's only one beneficiary listed, and it's Inga Shepherd."

"So, if the wife bumps him off before he dies from cancer, she gets twice as much money," Brad said.

"Good work, Sara," Patterson said. "I have an appointment to interview Mrs. Shepherd tomorrow morning at 10:00 a.m. Would you like to join me for the interview?"

"Yes, sir," Sara said.

Patterson noticed the frowns on Boyle's and Simpton's faces. Both troopers were older than Sara and had been on the job longer, so they probably felt they should be asked to accompany Patterson on such an important interview. He hoped Sara's gender had nothing to do with their frowns because he didn't need such nonsense on his squad.

"What about the will, Mark?" Patterson asked. "Did you learn anything there?"

"Yes, sir," Traner said. "It took a while, but I finally ran down Lou Scott, a lawyer here in Kodiak. He told me Jake came in about two weeks ago. He had a will, but he wanted Scott to make changes to it."

"What sort of changes?" Patterson asked.

"He made a few minor tweaks, but the main thing he wanted to change was his beneficiaries. On the first will, he left everything to his wife, but on the new will, he replaced her with his three kids."

"He left his wife nothing?" Patterson asked. "Didn't they own everything together?"

"I asked the same thing," Traner said. "Mr. Scott said Jake showed him a prenuptial agreement. Inga asked Jake to sign the prenup before they got married because her family owned a great deal of real estate and stocks, and she wanted to keep her assets separate from Jake's. Scott said Jake laughed and told him she and her parents had squandered their wealth, and she didn't have much left. He didn't want her to spend all his money and leave nothing for his kids to inherit, so he took her off the will."

"That move could have been mean-spirited," Patterson said, "or perhaps he thought she'd have enough from his life insurance."

"Or maybe he hadn't gotten around to changing the beneficiary on his life insurance, and she thought she'd better kill him before he had the chance," Boyle said.

"Good point, Peter," Patterson said. "The widow looks more and more interesting all the time."

"Don't prenups usually come into play in a divorce?" Sara asked. "Would the prenup be binding for a death?"

Patterson weighed the question. "I don't know, but maybe Jake planned to divorce Inga before he died."

"I asked the attorney the same question," Traner said, "and he said he discussed the issue with Jake. The way the prenup was written, the attorney thought it would hold if Jake died while he and Inga were still married, but he told Jake the only way to make certain Inga didn't inherit anything from him would be to divorce her before he died."

"We know Jake had trouble keeping his mouth shut," Simpton said, "so if he told Inga he planned to divorce her before he died to make certain she didn't inherit anything, she'd have a good reason to kill him before he had the chance to start divorce proceedings."

The room remained quiet for several moments while the troopers considered this point. Patterson consulted his notes and then stood and walked to the whiteboard behind the table. "We have several persons of interest in this case, but for the sake of clarity, let's talk about those at the top of the list." He wrote Inga's name at the top of the board, followed by Brian Decker and Bobby Brinker. "Who else?" he asked the group.

"One of the pilots," Sara said.

"Right," Patterson said and wrote it on the board just as Sara had said it. "Brad," he eyed the trooper. "I want to put you on this because I think it's very important. I've been told twice in recent interviews I need to look at pilots who work for Kodiak Flight Services. When I interviewed the Kodiak Flight Services pilots, they all seemed genuinely upset over Jake's death and claimed they liked him. Either I'm getting some bad information, or at least one of the Kodiak Flight Services pilots didn't tell me the truth. I got the distinct impression John Saner knew more than he was saying about conflicts between Jake and other Kodiak Flight Services pilots, so you might talk to him again. I also want you to look at the other commercial pilots in town. If Jake caught one of them doing something so bad it could cause them to lose their pilot's license, they might have had a reason to murder him."

"Yes, sir," Simpton said. "Any suggestions on where to start?"

"Start with Jordan Gregg," Patterson said. "He knows something about the Kodiak Flight Services pilots, so go at him hard. Suggest you might contact the FAA about his stunt flying if he doesn't help you. He could have been bluffing, but I think he knows something."

Simpton puffed up his chest. "I'll get him to talk."

"Peter," Patterson regarded Boyle. "I would like you to fly up to Anchorage and check out Brian Decker. Discreetly talk to his boss and follow Decker from a distance. See if you can get a feel for what kind of guy he is. He's been in trouble with the law before, but he hasn't been arrested in two years. Has he cleaned up his act or just been lucky?" Patterson stood and paced while he thought. "What I want to know is number one, is Brian Decker the kind of guy who could lose his temper and shoot a man, and number two, is he smart enough to clean up a crime scene and then have his girlfriend call us?"

"What about his girlfriend?" Boyle asked. "Should I talk to her or her dad?"

"Not yet," Patterson said. "First, I want to do a quiet background check on Decker."

"How long do you want me to follow him?" Boyle asked.

"Let's start with two days. Report in frequently, and if you learn anything interesting, we'll either extend the surveillance, or we'll alter our plan. I'll call trooper headquarters in Anchorage and let them know what you're doing. Be sure to give them a call when you arrive in Anchorage and tell them you're headed to Eagle River and will be in the area for two days."

"Yes, sir," Boyle said.

"I'll have Irene get you on the evening flight," Patterson said

Patterson glanced at the list on the whiteboard. "Let's concentrate on this list for now and see where it takes us." He returned to his chair but didn't sit. Instead, he shuffled through his folder and pulled out a pile of papers stapled into several bundles. He handed each trooper a bundle.

"I'm sure you heard we recovered a small notebook from Jake's pocket. Apparently, he kept track of everything from his truck mileage to his floatplane trips to events in his life. Unfortunately, he used abbreviations for much of what he wrote, and it's like reading code. I would like each of you to spend an hour or two over the next day reading through your copy of Jake's journal entries. At tomorrow afternoon's meeting, we'll work together to try to decipher what he wrote. If you figure out something important from his notebook before tomorrow, bring it to me immediately."

Patterson looked around the table at the nodding heads. "Okay, you all have your assignments. That's all for now."

After the meeting, Traner approached Patterson. "Sir, did you want me to check into anything else?" he asked.

"Mark, yes, I have a job for you. I want you to look at Bobby Brinker. Try to find someone who knew Bobby, Don, and Jake when they were in high school. Bobby seemed upset about something Jake knew about him back then, and I'd like to know what that is. The more we can learn about Bobby before we interview him tomorrow, the better."

"Yes, sir," Traner said. "I'm on it."

Patterson checked his watch. It was nearly 5:25 p.m. Time for him to get home so he would be there to greet Jeanne when she finished her shift at 6:00 p.m. He walked into his office and began collecting his things but then sat down in his chair and picked up his photocopy of Jake's notebook.

Much of the book was simply a log. Patterson had no idea why Jake felt it necessary to keep track of the gas mileage for his pickup truck or log every single flight he made when he already recorded the same information on his official air-charter log. Patterson had never met Jake Shepherd, but with each person he interviewed, he gained a fuller picture of Jake's personality. Jake knew a great deal about flying and airplanes, and he loved the joy and thrill of flying floatplanes. He got along well with those he considered his equals in the flying world, but he felt a need to help younger pilots and often offered unsolicited advice. He had no patience with incompetence and carelessness, and possibly as a result of the pain from his illness, his temper flared easily, angering those it was aimed at. Jake's notebook told Patterson the man had been obsessive about recording the minutiae of his life.

The notebook began in January, and Patterson assumed Jake started a new notebook at the beginning of each year. Entries for the first three months consisted of little more than his flight log and the date and number of gallons of gas he put in his truck. Patterson noted a few entries for birthdays and travel dates, mostly for his wife, Inga. These notations were easy to decipher, and Patterson would ask Inga to identify the individuals Jake referred to in each note. These notations included: *Inga to ATL, Inga to ADQ, Josh BD*, and *Caroline BD*. ATL was the airport code for Atlanta, and ADQ was the code for Kodiak. Patterson guessed Josh and Caroline were Jake's children or grandchildren.

It was only after March 20th when Jake's random notes grew in number and became more cryptic. Patterson assumed Jake's cancer was diagnosed around this time, but he hoped Inga could give him more insight into what had happened in March, why Jake's journal entries changed, and what the messages meant. For example, what did *I – A – Who?* mean? Did *I* refer to Inga?

A sharp knock on Patterson's door brought him back to the present. He glanced at his watch with a start. It was 5:48 p.m. "Yes," he called as he stuffed the copy of Jake's journal into his bag.

Irene opened the door a crack and looked into Patterson's office. "I didn't want to bother you while you were in your meeting, but Lance Crane called and said you would know who he is. He said to tell you he remembered the N number." Irene read the message from the small notebook she held in her hands. "Does this make sense to you?"

"Yes, Irene," Patterson said. "Did he say if he is in town?" Patterson really didn't want to take the time to interview him now, but the N number for the Beaver that had circled Karluk Lake shortly after Jake left Lance's camp could be important, or it could mean nothing. Still, if Lance Crane was on his way through Kodiak, Patterson or one of his troopers needed to intercept him.

"He's in Anchorage," Irene said. "He said he remembered the N number because it was on the plane that picked him up from Karluk this afternoon."

"And who was the pilot?" Patterson asked.

"Roy Tayler," Irene said. "Mr. Crane said you can call him anytime. He left his cell number. He plans to spend a few days with a friend in Anchorage, and then he'll fly back to his home in Portland."

Patterson was relieved he wouldn't have to interview Crane now because he wanted to get home to Jeanne. He already knew Roy Tayler had been flying to the west side of the island, but wasn't his flight to Uyak? Why was Roy flying low over Karluk Lake?

1976

Darkness was falling when Bently returned to camp, and he was annoyed to see Schwimmer holding his rifle, pacing back and forth in front of the tents.

"Now what's wrong?" he asked Schwimmer as he tossed his pack and gun into his tent.

"I had company today," Schwimmer said.

"A bear?" Bently asked.

"Not a bear." Schwimmer raised his voice and frowned, his gaze unfocused. He stopped pacing and held his arms wide. "That old man you told me about."

"He was here?" Schwimmer must be wrong. The guy had been several miles from their camp when Bently saw him three days earlier, and he wasn't walking fast.

"That's what I'm saying," Schwimmer said. "He threatened me. He threatened us."

"What are you talking about?" Bently asked. Schwimmer was losing it, and Bently wondered if the old man actually had been in their camp or if Schwimmer had imagined the encounter.

Schwimmer finally looked Bently in the eye and exhaled a deep breath. "He got here a little after noon. He just walked into camp and called out, asking if anyone was here. I was in my tent reading, but I came out right away when I heard him. At first, I thought it must be you because who else could it be?" He shrugged and started to get excited again. "I didn't even grab my rifle because I thought it was you."

"Calm down," Bently said. "What did he say?"

"At first, he didn't say anything. He just stood here staring at our tents. Then, he looked me in the eye and said, 'Who are you, and why are you here?'" Schwimmer shook his head and gulped air. "He's an old guy, all bent over and scrawny, but he scared the hell out of me."

"Why?" Bently asked. "Why should some harmless old man scare you?"

"He's not harmless," Schwimmer said. "He's evil."

"Come on, get a grip. Are you losing your mind?" Bently couldn't believe how frightened Schwimmer looked after an encounter with an old man.

"I'm telling you, man. His eyes were cold and dead. He looked right through me."

Bently was beginning to believe Schwimmer had been hallucinating. *Maybe he'd brought drugs with him on the trip.* Bently realized he didn't know Schwimmer well at all. "So what did he say?" he asked Schwimmer again.

"He said we were trespassing on his land, and he wanted us out of here as soon as possible. I told him we couldn't leave until the plane came to pick us up on the seventh."

"What did he say to that?"

Tears trickled down Schwimmer's face. "He said he hoped we lived that long."

"Get a grip, man. This is a federal wildlife refuge; he doesn't own this land. He was just having fun at your expense."

Schwimmer wiped his eyes. "You wouldn't think he was joking if you'd heard the tone of his voice and the look in his eyes. He plans to kill us."

Bently was tired of Schwimmer and his nonsense. "Are you on drugs?"

"What? No, I don't take drugs. You know better than that."

"Then I think you're losing your mind. There was no old man here today. You imagined the entire thing." Maybe the hours Schwimmer had spent wandering in the blizzard did more to him than Bently realized. "You need to get out of camp and back to hunting. It's not good for you to sit around camp all day."

"No way. I don't want to run into the old man in the wilderness."

Bently laughed. This conversation was so ridiculous he couldn't believe it. "You'll be safer in the wilderness than you are here. He knows where to find you here."

"I don't plan to sit in my tent." Schwimmer's eyes bulged behind his glasses. "I'll hide in the woods where I can see camp, so I'll be ready for him."

Bently blinked and took a step back. Now he was concerned. "What do you plan to do if he returns?"

"Kill him before he can kill me."

"Whoa, buddy. You can't shoot someone because he threatened you."

"You don't understand, Jay. This guy is evil. He'll kill us."

"Terry, I think you're losing your mind. Even if you didn't imagine this guy, you can't just shoot him, and if he is a figment of your imagination, if you are hallucinating, you might shoot me because you think I'm him."

"I'm not crazy, and I won't shoot you, but you'd better be careful out there. If you see him, hide."

"Let's have some whiskey and something to eat. You need to calm down." Bently took a step toward his tent but then turned back to Schwimmer. "How long did he stay here, and did he say what he was doing out here by himself?"

"He only stayed a few minutes, and he said he has a trap line. He's trapping beavers, river otters, and foxes."

"Did he have his sled with him?"

Schwimmer shook his head. "I didn't see a sled."

This was all Bently needed to convince him Schwimmer didn't see the same old man he had seen across the lake three days earlier. That guy had a sled. Of course, the man could have left the sled on the lakeshore while he hiked up to their camp, but Bently didn't believe Schwimmer had seen or talked to anyone. Schwimmer was going crazy, and Bently wondered if Schwimmer would shoot him in his sleep. He crouched and grabbed the flask out of his tent. He wouldn't give Schwimmer much whiskey. He was afraid alcohol might fuel his hallucinations.

Schwimmer calmed down after drinking a cup of coffee laced with whiskey.

"You stay here," Bently told him. "I'll start the boiling water and grab us some dinner."

Bently crawled into Schwimmer's tent where the MREs were stored and grabbed two from the box. He started to leave the tent but then returned his attention to the box of food. After they ate these two MREs, there'd only be eight left. There should be fourteen meals still in the box. He climbed out of the tent and approached Schwimmer.

"Did you store the rest of the MREs somewhere else?"

"No," Schwimmer said.

"Where are they, then?"

Schwimmer didn't say anything for several seconds but finally mumbled, "I get hungry hanging around camp all day."

"What!" Bently yelled. "Are you a complete idiot?"

"There's enough left for us."

"Barely, and what happens if the plane can't get out here to pick us up on time? What do we eat then?"

Schwimmer hunched his shoulders and looked at the ground. "We have granola bars and stuff."

Bently stomped away before he said something else. He didn't want to get Schwimmer agitated again, but he couldn't believe the guy could do something so stupid and selfish. He should shoot the whiny, selfish coward and put them both out of their misery.

PRESENT DAY
TUESDAY, JULY 1ST
7:45 A.M.

I stared out the window of the Ravn Air plane at the churning, dark-green waters of the North Pacific. I should arrive in Anchorage with plenty of time to make my appointment with Ying Lee, the anthropology student at the University of Alaska. My plan to spend a few days in Anchorage had been quashed by Corban Pratt, the Tamron executive, when he'd asked me to dinner, and tonight was the only night he was free. If he hadn't been on the verge of writing a big check to the marine center, I would have kindly declined his invitation, but I knew Peter, my boss, would not be happy with me if I didn't agree to have dinner with Mr. Pratt. I hoped Peter realized, though, dinner was the only thing I'd say yes to. I would only agree to so much in the name of fundraising.

I'd worry about Corban Pratt and his money later. For now, I needed to concentrate on Ms. Lee and what she could tell me about my bones. I drove my rental car across Anchorage to the University of Alaska. I found the guest parking lot and then followed my printout of the campus map to guide me to Beatrice G. McDonald Hall, home of the Department of Anthropology.

I located the GIS/Cultural Research Lab and knocked on the partially opened door.

"Come in," a female voice called. A young woman met me inside the door and introduced herself as Ying Lee. Ying had short, black hair, big blue eyes, and creamy white skin. She motioned for me to follow her, and her petite frame bounced with energy as she led me down the hall and into a small laboratory. My bones, now scrubbed clean, held center stage on the worktable in the middle of the room.

Ying wasted no time with small talk. She walked to the table and held up a portion of the long leg bone we had found. The rest of the bone rested on the table. For some reason, Ying, or one of her associates, had sliced the bone into two pieces. Her blue eyes blazed with intelligence and excitement. Her enthusiasm infected me, and I walked to the other side of the table and focused on her.

Ying held the bone with both hands. "We're very lucky to have a femur," she said, "because the femur offers an easy estimation of height. All I needed to do was measure the bone and then apply a simple formula to obtain an estimate of the individual's height."

"And he was tall?" I asked.

"Well, yes, he was a little above average height—about six feet tall," Ying said.

"So, we know he was male from his height?" I asked.

"I would guess the individual was male from his height, but you also found the pelvis, and I can confirm he was a male from the pelvis."

"Next, I set out to determine the age of the individual when he died. Luckily, I had the skull to examine." She pointed to the skull on the table, and I noticed she had glued several of the miscellaneous bone fragments we'd gathered to the skull. It still wasn't complete, but she had pieced much of it together.

"You see here," Ying said, pointing at an area she had reconstructed on the top of the skull, "these lines are called cranial sutures. The bones that enclose the brain grow together during childhood. As a person ages, these sutures gradually fade. This fading, or remodeling, varies among individuals, but some sutures close at a consistent age in most individuals." Ying pointed to the back of the skull and ran her finger along a faint line. "This is called the lambdoid suture. It generally begins to close at age twenty-one. The closing accelerates at age twenty-six, and the suture is completely closed between age thirty and forty. You can see the suture on this skull is nearly, but not completely, closed."

"So, how old do you estimate he was?" I asked.

"I'd say between twenty-five and thirty years old," Ying looked up from the bones and met my gaze. "This is only my estimate, though. I couldn't swear to it in a court of law, but I think this individual was between twenty-five and thirty years old when he died."

"I understand," I said. "Your estimate gives me somewhere to start. I appreciate it."

A quick smile passed over Ling's thin lips, but then she was all business again. "Again, by looking at his skull, I determined this individual descended from European ancestry. There's not much left of the nasal bones, but the narrow face leads me to believe with little doubt this skull did not come from a Native Alaskan individual."

"Okay," I said. I wanted to make sure I'd understood everything Ying had told me. "We have a fairly tall Caucasian man in his late twenties."

Ying wrinkled her nose. "I don't like the term 'Caucasian,' because race tags can be misleading. All I can really tell you is his ancestors were most likely from Europe."

I nodded and forced myself to remain silent. I wanted to blurt out my questions. *How long ago did he die, and what killed him?* But I knew how much I hated to be interrupted while explaining my research to someone, so I let Ying explain these bones to me in her own style and at her own pace.

She stared at me for several moments as if expecting me to question her, but then she continued. "The question is how and when did this individual die?"

I nodded and watched her expectantly.

Ying pointed to the front of the skull. "I think I know how, but the when part is a big guess."

"What do you mean?" I asked.

"My professor and I are fairly certain this man died from a gunshot wound to the top of the head. I pieced as much of the skull together as I could, and you can see this jagged, roughly round hole in the top of the skull."

"You're sure it's a bullet hole?"

She smiled. "I'm not certain of anything, but I've compared this hole to dozens of known bullet holes in skulls, and it is similar."

"Is there any way to determine what gauge bullet caused the hole?" I asked.

Ying laughed. "If the particular type of bullet becomes important, you might be able to run down an expert who'd be willing to give it a shot." She stopped and laughed at her unintended pun. "This is not my area of expertise, but I do think it is a bullet hole."

"It seems like a weird place to shoot yourself," I said.

Ying looked at me sharply. "Do you have reason to believe this person committed suicide?"

"No, I'm just thinking out loud," I said.

"It's just that . . ." Ying shook her head.

"Just what?" I asked.

"My Ph.D. thesis is linked to studying nutrition in ancient populations. In particular, I'm studying nutrition in communities of Inupiat people. Most of the bones I'm looking at are between 150 and 300 years old. You are a biologist, so as I'm sure you know, teeth and bones contain a protein called collagen. Collagen absorbs chemicals such as calcium, carbon, nitrogen, and strontium from the food an individual eats. Different types of food contain these elements in different ratios, and from studying fossilized bones and teeth, I am attempting to understand the diets of various populations of Inupiat people. Were they healthy? Did they face periods of malnutrition? That sort of thing."

I nodded. "Your work sounds interesting." Her research did sound interesting, but I had no idea why she was telling me about it in relation to these bones.

She seemed to read my mind. "When I received permission to study these bones," she gestured to the bones on the table in front of her, "I thought it would be interesting to see how much the diet of this guy differed from my Inupiat bones." She shrugged. "I know it has nothing to do with your case, or at least I didn't think it did until I started analyzing the bones."

"What do you mean?" I asked. I still couldn't guess where she was going with this.

"This guy," she put her hand on the femur, "was starving to death. If he didn't have a bullet hole in his head, I'd say he did starve to death. I wondered if he shot himself to end his suffering, but you're right, it's a strange angle for a self-inflicted gunshot wound." She shook her head. "It would be possible, though, especially if he used a rifle." She held an imaginary rifle in front of her, pointed at her head.

"Wait a minute," I said, "back up. You think this guy was starving to death?"

"That's one of the few things I can say with any certainty about this individual," Ying said. "His bone mineral density is extremely low. He was emaciated when he died. In fact, his bones are the most emaciated bones I've studied."

"Interesting," I said. "I wonder what happened to him."

Ying studied me, her eyes ablaze. "Isn't it fascinating? I love learning about past civilizations and imaging what the people's lives were like. I feel like a detective sifting through the debris and trying to find the important evidence."

I smiled at this brilliant young woman and was thankful my bones ended up in her laboratory. "When did he die?" I asked. "How long have his bones been at Karluk Lake?"

Ying's shoulders dropped, and the fire in her eyes died. "That's the million-dollar question. It's very difficult to estimate the time since death from skeletal remains. I know he's not ancient, but there's little difference between five-year-old and ten-year-old bones."

"But you told Sergeant Patterson you thought these bones were between thirty and fifty years old."

"Yes, well, I didn't make that estimate," Ying said. "When these bones first arrived, we had a professor here who was visiting from UC Davis, and her field of interest is studying bone chemistry to estimate the time since death. She looks at the citrate content in the bones. She took two slices of the femur back to California with her, and she arrived at the time frame of thirty to fifty years, but she stressed to us, and I told Sergeant Patterson, the time frame was only her best guess."

I smiled at Ying and held out my hand. She took it, and we shook. "I appreciate all you've done. I don't know what it means yet, but I hope to figure it out and maybe even learn who this individual was."

"If you come up with a possible identification and can find relatives, we can attempt to extract DNA from the bones and see if there's a match." Ying said. "We might even be able to tap into a public DNA database."

"Thanks, I'll keep that in mind. I hope I can figure out who you have on your table."

"Will you let me know what you learn?" Ying asked.

"Of course," I said. "If I find out who this guy is, it will be due in large part to your analysis."

After I left the anthropology building, I sat in my car and wrote down all Ying had told me. I knew what I wanted to do next. Before leaving home, I Googled and wrote down the number for the personnel department at Joint Base Elmendorf–Richardson on the outskirts of Anchorage. This was the longest of long shots, but it was worth a try.

I waited on hold for nearly twenty minutes after stating my case to the young woman who answered the phone. Finally, a man with a deep voice greeted me. "Dr. Marcus, this is Major Fanucchi. How may I help you?"

I hated using my "doctor" tag, and I rarely referred to myself as "Dr. Marcus" because I thought the tag sounded both pretentious and misleading. I did have a Ph.D., so while it was accurate, the term "doctor" made everyone assume I was a medical doctor, and when they found out I wasn't, they were usually disappointed, diminishing rather than elevating me in their view. In this instance, though, I wanted to cut through red tape, and I thought "Dr. Marcus" might command more attention than plain old Jane Marcus.

"Major," I said. "I am from Kodiak and am assisting the Alaska State Troopers in a cold-case investigation."

"I see," the major said, a question hanging in the air.

"Human bones were found in the woods near Karluk Lake on Kodiak, and we are trying to match the bones to a missing person."

"I don't understand how I can help you with this," the major said.

"In addition to the bones, we found a belt buckle with an Air Force insignia on it." I paused a moment to let the major think about what I'd said. "I just met with the forensic anthropologist who examined the bones, and she thinks the bones are roughly between thirty and fifty years old. Would you be able to look through your records to see if anyone went on leave and didn't return to duty during that time frame? I guess I'm asking if you have a list of enlisted men or officers who went AWOL from 1965 to 1990?"

Major Fanucchi laughed. "Anyone missing that long would be classified a deserter, especially since a good chunk of the time was during the Vietnam War and the end dates overlap the Gulf War."

"Can you check a list of deserters?"

"Who did you say you work for again?"

I paused. "I am working with the Alaska State Troopers," I said.

"And if I call them, will they confirm you're working with them?"

"Sure," I said. "Call the Kodiak headquarters and ask to speak to Sergeant Patterson. My name is Jane Marcus."

Major Fanucchi told me he would call back within the hour. Since it was only noon, and my flight back to Kodiak didn't leave until 3:40 p.m., I drove to Dimond Center and wandered through the mall while I waited for Major

Fanucchi to return my call. When my phone finally buzzed, I headed to a quiet corner of the mall.

Major Fanucchi was all business. "I checked the list of AWOLs and deserters from the time frame you suggested, and I didn't find anyone unaccounted for," he said. "Everyone showed up eventually. Some were court-martialed, some received a dishonorable discharge, but most were just reprimanded in some way and carried on with their duties."

My stomach fell, and I realized how much hope I had pinned on this wild goose chase.

I was just about to thank the major for his time when he said, "I've been here twenty-seven years, and I got to know Major Kidwell, the officer who trained me, very well. We're still good friends, and he lives in Anchorage. With your permission, I'll ask him if he remembers anything irregular from back in the day. I don't know how an airman could go missing from this base or any other Air Force base without being noticed, but he might remember something unusual. It's a long shot, mind you."

I thanked the major and told him he could call me any time. I didn't expect to hear from him again.

PRESENT DAY
TUESDAY, JULY 1ST
8:12 A.M.

Patterson glanced at his watch as he pulled into the parking lot at trooper headquarters. He was nearly fifteen minutes late, but if he weren't in the middle of an important investigation, he would have stayed home and taken care of his wife. Jeanne looked terrible this morning, with black, sunken eyes and sallow skin. She called in sick to work and went back to bed.

Patterson asked Jeanne if she'd been taking pills, but she said she hadn't even taken the pain pills her doctor had prescribed following the minor surgery after the miscarriage. Patterson checked the medicine cabinet, but he found no narcotics, not even the pain pills he'd helped her pick up at Walmart. Were they stashed in her bedside table? Did she have other pills there? He'd removed his two rifles from the house, but he knew there were plenty of ways to commit suicide if an individual was determined to do so. If Jeanne didn't snap out of this depression soon, he would insist she get help. Maybe he would broach the subject tonight when he got home.

He walked stiffly into trooper headquarters. Irene looked up from her desk. "Sara wants you to know the rest of Brinker party should be in town at Eagle Charters sometime late morning or early afternoon."

"Good morning to you too, Irene," Patterson said.

"Also, Dr. Libby called and wants you to call him back."

Patterson nodded and continued to his office. He closed his office door, settled in his chair, and called Dr. Libby, the medical examiner.

"Sergeant Patterson, good morning," Libby said. "I have the tox screen back for Jake Shepherd."

"What did you find, Doctor?" Patterson asked.

"Absolutely nothing," Libby said. "The man had no trace of narcotics in his system, and with his advanced cancer, he must have been in terrible pain. He was a tougher man than I am."

"He was tough," Patterson said, "but I'm learning he took his pain out on those around him. Could you tell if he was getting chemo or radiation treatments for his cancer?"

"I don't think so," Libby said. "I saw no physical or chemical signs of treatment, and at this point in the progression of the disease, treatment would have only bought him a few weeks or possibly a few months."

Libby had no other information, so Patterson thanked him, disconnected, and began reviewing his notes for his upcoming interview with Inga Shepherd. He looked forward to meeting Jake's widow. Normally, he dreaded questioning the bereaved family of a victim, but from what he had learned about Inga, she might not be too sorry to be rid of her husband. *Did she hate him enough to kill him, though, or was she ruthless enough to have him murdered because his insurance would pay her twice as much for a violent death than it would for a natural death from the cancer eating away at his body?*

Patterson knew how important this interview with Inga would be, and he called Sara into his office to review the topics he wanted to discuss with Inga. At 9:46 a.m., they headed to the Shepherd residence.

Jake and Inga Shepherd's house sat on the hillside high above the Baranof Inn. Jake had often thought this area above the boat harbor and the Port of Kodiak would be a beautiful place to live, but he knew these steep streets provided a challenge to navigate during an icy Kodiak winter. The Shepherd's house was not large, but its exterior sported a fresh coat of driftwood-white paint, and Patterson imagined Jake on his days off sitting behind the large picture window, watching the floatplanes come and go from Trident Basin. This was the perfect vantage from which to watch fierce storms boil the ocean into a white froth or observe the hustle and bustle of the boat harbor on a beautiful summer day.

Patterson and Sara climbed out of the SUV, and Patterson grabbed his backpack from the rear seat. The pack held little other than the scanned pages of Jake's notebook and a spiral notebook in which Patterson had written down the questions he intended to ask Inga Shepherd. As he and Sara ascended the steps to the small deck in front of the Shepherds' house, Patterson inhaled the sweet aroma of ripening salmonberries and wild roses. Up here, earth and wildflowers muted the smell of processed fish.

Patterson knocked on the front door, and a few moments later it was opened by a petite woman with the bluest eyes Patterson had ever seen. He couldn't stop looking at her eyes while he introduced himself and Sara. He'd seen alpine lakes the color of her eyes, but nothing else compared. Once he broke the trance of her gaze, he took in the rest of her. Silver, short-cropped hair framed her tanned face, and while a few creases radiated from the corners of her eyes, he couldn't believe this woman was the same age as Jake. She wore a black turtleneck, black slacks, and no jewelry he could see, not even a wedding ring. Her tight slacks and top revealed an athletic frame and well-developed muscles. She took good care of herself.

"I'm Inga Shepherd," she said. "It's nice to meet you. Please come in."

She ushered them into the great room, and Patterson looked around the interior. He did not believe Inga Shepherd had been involved in decorating this room. The dark wood interior looked like Patterson's dream of the perfect man cave. Fish and deer mounts and a mountain goat pelt adorned the walls. The dark hardwood floor held a variety of green and brown rugs, matching the brown leather couch, which faced the large picture window. A beautiful, rough-wood table filled the space between the couch and the window. Beyond the great room, the open floor plan revealed a small dining room and kitchen.

Inga led Patterson and Sara to the couch in front of the window, and she sat in a rocking chair facing the side of the table. Patterson sat next to the rocking chair, so he could more easily watch Inga's face and her reactions to his questions.

Inga sat with her hands in her lap. Patterson noticed she hadn't offered them coffee or water, and he guessed she didn't want to do anything to encourage them to stay a minute longer than necessary. Patterson asked Inga if she minded if Sara recorded the interview. Inga implied consent by tipping her head to the side. Patterson made sure to ask the question again once the tape recorder was turned on, and this time he requested a verbal response.

The next question out of Patterson's mouth wasn't the one he had planned, but curiosity got the better of him. "Are you here alone?"

A slight smile spread across Inga's lips, and she shrugged. "Yes, Sergeant. I don't know many people in Kodiak, and I have no close friends here. Most of the people I know in Kodiak were acquaintances of Jake."

"And your children?" Patterson let the question hang.

"They're in Atlanta," Inga said. "I'm only here to take care of Jake's affairs, have his body cremated once the medical examiner releases it, and fly him back to Atlanta for a memorial service. Our people live in or near Atlanta."

"I am very sorry for your loss," Patterson said, realizing those words should have been the first out of his mouth.

Inga Shepherd nodded but said nothing.

"Did Jake have many friends in Kodiak?" Patterson asked.

Inga made a swatting motion with her hand, dismissing the question. "Jake had acquaintances here, but none of them were really friends. Jake didn't make friends easily."

"I don't understand," Patterson said.

Inga sighed. "Jake was a lone wolf. Flying a small plane suited him because he liked to be high above the earth all alone." She barked a short laugh. "I guess he got his wish. That's where he is now."

Patterson had learned during his years in law enforcement that people express grief in many ways. Inga Shepherd reminded him of an ice princess; from her glacier-blue eyes to her rigid posture and soft, low voice, she betrayed little emotion. Unfortunately, Patterson didn't know if this was her normal demeanor or if it was an important indicator of how she had felt about her late husband.

Patterson unzipped his pack and removed the spiral notebook, reminding himself to follow the script he had planned and not go off on tangents. "How long had you and Jake been married?" he asked.

"It would have been thirty-eight years next month," Inga said.

Patterson again marveled at how well Inga had preserved her beauty. Of course, maybe she'd had medical intervention. He wasn't a good judge of these things.

"Mrs. Shepherd," Patterson said, "I need to ask you several tough questions. Please don't read too much into these, but you are the only person who can answer them, and I'm sure you understand this is a murder investigation, and we need to question everyone close to the victim."

Inga said nothing but made a waving motion with her hand.

"Let's get this one out of the way," Patterson said. "I think I know the answer, but I need to hear it from you. Where were you when Jake was murdered?"

"I was in Atlanta, Sergeant. I spend at least half of the year in our Atlanta home. Moving to Kodiak was Jake's idea. Kodiak was not my preference."

"What type of relationship did you and Jake have?" Patterson asked.

"I don't understand the question," Inga said. "We were married."

Inga's eyes locked onto Patterson, drawing him into their depths and making him feel as if she were trying to hypnotize him. He looked away for a moment to break their hold. Something about this woman made him very uncomfortable, and he knew she had understood his question.

"Did you and Jake fight?" he asked.

"Are you married, Sergeant?" Inga asked.

"Yes, ma'am," he said

"How long?" Inga asked.

"Twelve years," Patterson said.

"Do you and your wife fight?"

"On occasion," Patterson said. Because he was so worried about Jeanne, he felt very protective of her and hated this woman dragging her into a police interview. He shifted on the couch. He wasn't about to let Inga Shepherd wiggle out of his questions so easily.

"Did you and Jake have serious fights?" he asked.

Inga remained quiet for several moments, and Patterson could tell she was carefully framing her reply.

"We fought about where we lived," she said, interlacing her fingers in her lap and squeezing hard. "I'm sorry, but I hate Alaska, and I especially hate Kodiak. I wanted to live in Atlanta, and Jake insisted he would live in Kodiak until he died." Her gaze hardened a fraction. "I guess he got his wish."

Patterson had lost any sympathy he'd felt for this woman, and while this made questioning her easier, he knew he had to be careful not to anger her to the point where she kicked them out of her house.

"One of the other pilots at Kodiak Flight Services told me he overheard Jake speaking to you on the telephone," Patterson said. "He said Jake threatened to divorce you and leave you with nothing." Patterson paused and watched Inga's reaction. Her icy gaze flickered for a moment, dropped to the floor and returned to Patterson's face. "Did you have such a conversation?" he asked.

"Yes, Sergeant, we did, unfortunately. It was one of the last times I spoke to Jake, so I am left with a final memory of his harsh words."

Patterson really wanted to know what had prompted Jake to speak those harsh words, but he had too much ground to cover with Inga Shepherd, and he couldn't afford to anger her this early in the interview. Instead, he asked, "Was your marriage in trouble?"

Inga looked down at her hands. "I don't know," she said. "Lately, all Jake and I did was fight with each other. He'd always had a hair-trigger temper, but the last few months, he seemed mad at me all the time."

"Did you know Jake had cancer?"

For the first time since he'd entered the Shepherd household, Patterson saw Inga lose her cool. Her hands tightened into fists, and she stopped breathing for a few seconds. Was she shocked to learn Jake had been sick or was she surprised Patterson knew he'd been ill?

Inga's hands slowly unclenched, and the look of calm returned to her face. "How bad was it?" she asked.

"Terminal," Patterson said. "The medical examiner thinks he only had months to live. He must have been in pain, but he wasn't taking anything for it. There were no traces of narcotics in his system."

"Was he getting treatment for it?" Inga asked.

Patterson shook his head. "No traces of any drugs in his system."

"Now I understand why he was angry and mean all the time," Inga said, as she again clasped her hands in her lap.

"You didn't know about his cancer?" Patterson asked.

"No, Sergeant, I didn't know. He wouldn't have told me because I would have insisted he seek treatment, and I would have tried to get him back to Atlanta where he could be properly treated." Inga shook her head. "Instead, all he wanted to do was stay here and fly because he was selfish that way. He'd rather spend the last few days of his life in an airplane than playing with his beautiful grandchildren."

"Are you aware of the terms of Jake's life insurance policy?" Patterson asked.

Inga shrugged. "I know he had life insurance. Delta offered him a policy when he first started flying for them."

"Do you know how much it was worth?" Patterson asked.

"No, I don't remember," Inga said.

Patterson knew Inga must be lying. He felt certain she knew the exact value of Jake's life insurance, but her gaze never faltered. Her cool blue eyes held his without a blink. *This woman was good.*

Patterson nodded to Sara. "Trooper Byram has been looking into Jake's policy. I'll let her explain it to you."

Sara's voice wavered as she began to speak, but she quickly reined in her nerves and met Inga's gaze. Patterson understood the hypnotic hold of Inga's eyes from several minutes of interviewing the woman, and he admired the young trooper's ability to look straight at her while she spoke.

"Delta put me in touch with the insurance company that has Jake's policy," Sara said. "The original value of the policy when Delta set it up for Jake was $100,000, but over the next few years, Jake increased its value to $500,000."

Inga nodded but said nothing. Patterson watched her face. Her countenance didn't change, and again, Patterson felt this news was no surprise to her.

"There's one additional thing," Sara said. "The policy pays double if the insured individual dies from an accident."

Inga slowly shook her head. "But he didn't die from an accident."

"The policy lists murder as an accidental cause."

Inga looked at the floor and seemed lost in thought for several moments. Then, she again looked at Sara. "So what you're saying is Jake's life insurance will pay one million dollars?"

"Yes, ma'am," Sara said, "and you are the sole beneficiary."

"I see," Inga said. There was no sign of surprise, relief, or satisfaction in her response.

"We have to ask this question, ma'am," Patterson said. "Did you have your husband killed so the insurance company would pay you double the amount of his policy?"

Patterson expected an angry or at least an indignant response, but Inga Shepherd slowly moved her focus from Sara back to Patterson. "No, Sergeant," she said quietly but firmly. "I did not have my husband murdered to gain a payoff from his life insurance. I didn't know he was sick, and I didn't know his policy paid double for murder."

Unfortunately for Patterson, Inga Shepherd had no friends in Kodiak he could question to find out if she had mentioned her husband's illness, but he couldn't imagine this cold, calculating woman confiding in anyone.

"Do you think it's possible Jake could have paid someone to murder him?" Patterson asked. "He was probably in a great deal of pain, and a gunshot to the head would be a much easier death than rotting away from cancer. If he staged it to look like murder, he'd know you would receive twice the amount of his insurance policy."

Inga's fists tightened again, and she said nothing for several seconds. "No, I don't think so," she finally said. "I think Jake was the kind of man who would have seen suicide as a coward's way out, and I don't believe for a second he would ask someone else to shoot him. The shooter could be sent to jail for the rest of his life if he were caught, and Jake would never ask someone to risk their freedom for him."

Inga's words sounded emphatic, but her tone was less certain. Patterson reminded himself that suicide didn't pay as well as murder.

"What about enemies?" Patterson asked. "Do you know anyone who would have wanted to kill Jake?"

Inga seemed to weigh the question in her mind. "Jake made enemies because he told people what he thought, and his thoughts were judgmental and harsh. He had no filter, and he always thought he knew best about everything."

"A hard man to live with?" Patterson asked.

"Yes, Sergeant, he was a hard man to live with, which was why I didn't spend much time with him anymore." Her eyes narrowed a fraction. "Back to your question, though, I can't think of anyone who disliked my husband enough to kill him."

"He didn't mention any altercations he'd had while flying on Kodiak?" Patterson asked.

"He didn't talk to me much about his job here." She made a sound somewhere between a chuckle and a groan. "We talked more on the phone when I was in Atlanta than we did when we were in the same house, and our telephone conversations usually turned into arguments." She shook her head. "I know very little about his life here in Kodiak. You'll have to get that information from someone else."

Patterson consulted his notebook and then pulled the scanned copy of Jake's notes from his pack. Inga's focused gaze followed his movements, but she showed no signs of curiosity. Beside him, Sara sat still.

"Mrs. Shepherd," Patterson said. "We found a small notebook in Jake's shirt pocket. Do you know anything about him keeping a notebook?"

Inga laughed, and for the first time, Patterson saw something resembling a smile grace her lips. "Ah, yes, the notebook. I razzed him about his silly notebooks countless times over the years. He started a new one every year, and he still has them all. As a matter of fact, I think he brought them with him when he moved here. Why he wanted to keep them is beyond me."

"Why is that, ma'am?"

"Why would he keep a notebook full of notations he made back in 1980? It wasn't as if he were going to check to see how much mileage his car got back then or ever care again what the weather was like in Paris on March 3rd, 1991. He didn't write anything memorable in those notebooks; they contained useless bits of trivia. He never left in his plane, whether it was a jet or a small floatplane, without noting the exact departure time, and every day when he returned home, he had to write down his mileage before he got out of the car." Inga shook her head. "I think even if the house were burning down, he would write down his mileage before he called 911."

"It appears he did write down birthdates," Patterson said.

"Yes, Sergeant, but most people use a calendar to record birthdates, and anymore, we get alerts on our phone reminding us of special dates. We don't write them in a notebook."

Patterson held up the pages in his hand. "This is a copy of the journal we found on Jake's body, and yes, he did note gas mileage, his flights, the weather, and as I mentioned, birthdates. It also looks as if he chronicled his illness, at least up until he was diagnosed. After that, he noted his blood pressure, temperature, and his pain level."

Patterson watched Inga's face as a single tear snaked from her right eye down her cheek. She made no move to wipe it away.

"He used a sort of shorthand for many of his notes, and I haven't been able to decipher everything. I'm hoping you can help me understand his code," Patterson said.

Inga shrugged. "I'll try, but I make no promises."

Patterson moved over next to Inga's chair and crouched down. "I'll start with February 17th, when Jake believed he had the flu and apparently stayed home from work." Patterson pointed at the notation: *2-17: Flu – no fly.*

Inga nodded. "I remember when he had the flu. It was the day before I left for Atlanta, and I was afraid he'd make me sick before I left. Oh . . ." she

163

put her hand to her mouth. "You're saying it wasn't the flu but one of the first symptoms of his cancer?"

"I can't say, ma'am. He could have had the flu, but you see here on March 3rd," Patterson pointed at the entry, "he made a doctor's appointment, and a few days later, he was diagnosed with cancer." Patterson ran his finger down the page to the March 7th entry and pointed at the notation, which simply read: *3-7: C.*

Inga bent over the journal and followed her husband's entries. "It appears he flew up to Anchorage to see a specialist and decided on no treatment." She let out a deep sigh. "I wish he would have told me."

"On March 22nd," Patterson continued, "Jake wrote '*I-ADQ,*' and I assume this means you were flying back to Kodiak from Atlanta?" He looked up at Inga, whose face now hung only a few inches above his head as she read over his shoulder.

"Right," the frost was back in her voice. "On March 24th '*I-F*' means we had a fight, and the next day, '*I-ATL*' means I flew right back to Atlanta. March 25th was the last time I laid eyes on my husband."

"I see," Patterson said. He continued flipping through the pages of Jake's notebook. "We have '*E-BD,*' '*CO-BD,*' '*J-BD,*' and '*CA-BD.*' I assume those are your kids?"

"Emma is our oldest daughter, and her birthday is February 21st. Kitty, our middle child's son Cole's birthday is May 2nd. Our son, Josh's birthday, is May 4th, and Kitty's daughter, Caroline, has a birthday on June 11th."

"Okay," Patterson said, scribbling down names next to initials, "I have the birthday notations straight. Thank you." He pointed at an April 12th entry. "Can you help me with this one?"

Inga remained quiet for several seconds while she puzzled out the reference. "'*4-12: HM BW -Refuge*? It means nothing to me," she said.

"On April 16th, Jake noted his blood pressure was 126 over 63. His temperature was 100 degrees, and the pain was '*M,*' which I guess means manageable," Patterson said.

"Could be," Inga said.

"On April 23rd, Jake wrote '*CW NP.*' Does that mean anything to you?" Patterson asked.

"No, Sergeant," Inga said.

"What about on May 1st? '*I-A Who*? '*CC*? '*RB*?" Patterson asked.

This time, he heard Inga suck in a small breath as she leaned closer to his shoulder to read Jake's journal entry. When she said nothing, he said, "I assume this has something to do with you since it starts with an '*I*.'"

Inga sat straight in her chair. "I'm sure I'm not the only person Jake knew whose name starts with 'I,'" she said.

Patterson couldn't think of a single person he knew except for her who had a name beginning with the letter '*I*.' "You don't think this notation refers to you?" he asked.

"If it does, I don't know what it means."

"Let's move on, then," Patterson said. He pointed at two more entries in May, but Inga claimed she didn't know what they meant.

"On June 10th, Jake noted his vitals. His blood pressure was higher than previously noted, his temperature was 101 degrees, and he noted '*P-W*,' which I assume means the pain was worse." He looked up at Inga, who nodded.

Patterson shifted to a different position. He'd been squatting beside Inga so long, his legs were beginning to hurt. "Over the last month of Jake's life, he wrote several cryptic entries in his journal, so let me read these to you to see if you can decode some of them."

"I'm not sure I'll be much help," Inga said. "Most of these seem to have to do with his flying."

"On June 15th, he wrote '*PA w/JM HM*.'" He looked up at Inga, but she stared straight ahead and shook her head.

"On June 18th, '*BS-JG DC-FAA*.'"

"I'd say he wanted to report BS and JG to the FAA for doing something, but I have no idea who those people are or what they did," Inga said.

Patterson agreed with Inga's assessment, and he felt certain he knew what the notation meant. At this point, he was just interested in hearing what Inga had to say.

"On June 20th," Patterson said, "Jake wrote '*I-D? No Will*.'"

"Yes, Sergeant. He told me if I divorced him, he would cut me out of his will. We had a prenuptial agreement, you see." Inga said.

Patterson was surprised Inga admitted she understood what this journal entry meant, but in light of the phone call they'd already discussed, she would have been foolish to deny she knew its meaning.

Patterson continued without commenting on Inga's statement. "On June 21st, '*R-DWF-S*?' '*FAA*?'"

Inga remained quiet for a moment and then said, "That means nothing to me."

"On June 23rd, '*I-OOW-LP. Remove,*'" Patterson said.

Inga pretended not to know what this meant, but Patterson didn't believe her.

Patterson stood stiffly and moved back to the couch. "Thank you for your help, ma'am. At least we've deciphered a few of the entries."

"What was the last entry in his journal?" she asked.

Patterson looked down at his notes. "On the day he was killed, he wrote, '*ADQ-Kar Lake-Crane P1.*' Crane was his last passenger, and Jake flew him to Karluk Lake."

Inga emitted a snort of laughter. "His ridiculous journal might have finally had some value if he'd noted who killed him."

Inga Shepherd walked Patterson and Sara to the door, but she didn't offer to shake their hands. Patterson again thanked Inga for her help and expressed his condolences. She simply nodded and held the door open for them.

"What did you think of Inga Shepherd?" Patterson asked Sara when they were back in the SUV and on their way to trooper headquarters.

"Wow," Sara said. "She is one cold lady."

Patterson laughed. "Yes, the ice queen."

"I can't believe she pretended not to know what some of the journal entries Jake obviously wrote about her meant."

"After meeting her, do you believe she is the type of woman who would have her husband murdered to collect his life insurance?"

"Oh, yes," Sara said. "I think we should keep her at the top of our list of suspects."

PRESENT DAY
Tuesday, July 1st
2:34 P.M.

Patterson sat in the small interview room at trooper headquarters and looked across the table at Bobby Brinker. Brinker's face glowed red, from his bald head to his pug nose to his beady eyes. The man looked like a heart attack waiting to happen.

He crossed his arms over his chest and glared at Patterson. "You have no right to hold me."

He was correct. Patterson knew he didn't have the authority to detain Brinker, but he didn't think he'd volunteer this information to the man, or Brinker would simply stand and walk out the door. Patterson intended to play hardball in this interview.

"Mr. Brinker," Patterson said. "I'm going to read you your rights. I am not arresting you, but I won't lie to you. I consider you a person of interest in this investigation and depending on the course of this conversation, you could become my primary suspect, so I think you need to be aware of your rights."

"What in the hell do you mean?" Brinker asked. "You can't believe I killed Jake Shepherd."

Patterson could smell the whiskey on Brinker's breath, and he wondered if the man was sober enough for an interview. On the other hand, Brinker looked like a hardened alcoholic and probably started drinking whiskey in his coffee in the morning. The only way to sober up the man would be to put him in a cell for several hours, and then he'd suffer alcohol withdrawal symptoms and be completely useless.

"I've learned you were not a fan of Jake Shepherd," Patterson said.

"I hated him," Bobby said. "He was a self-righteous prick. I'm glad he's dead, but I didn't kill him."

"Bobby," Patterson said. "I know you went back to your camp and were away from your friends for several hours around the time we believe someone put a bullet in Jake's head."

Brinker's already red face deepened a shade. "Who told you that?"

"It doesn't matter," Patterson said.

"Landry and Sparks. I knew they'd rat me out as soon as they got to town."

"What did you do while you were away from your friends?" Patterson asked.

"Nothing." Bobby slammed his fist on the table. "I drank some whiskey and relaxed. I wanted time alone. I was tired of my brother's friends."

"And you didn't see Jake's plane on the beach two miles from your camp?"

"No. I wasn't looking for a plane. How would I know he was there? Even if I saw the plane, I'd have no way to know who the pilot was."

"You didn't talk to Jake that day?"

"No!"

"Why do you hate Jake so much?" Patterson asked.

"None of your business."

"I know you went to school with him here in Kodiak. Did something happen when you were kids?" Patterson asked.

Brinker said nothing but just stared at the table.

"Bobby, I'm going to find out what happened between you two, so you might as well tell me."

Brinker said nothing, and Patterson found it interesting this loud drunk finally had nothing to say.

PRESENT DAY
TUESDAY, JULY 1ST
2:34 P.M.

While Patterson talked to Bobby Brinker, Traner interviewed his brother across the hall in the conference room. Traner informed Don they knew Bobby's whereabouts were unaccounted for when someone murdered Jake Shepherd.

"I figured those guys called you when they got back to town. I should never have invited my brother on this fishing trip." Don shook his head. "I had no idea his drinking had gotten this far out of hand."

"Sir," Traner said. "Do you believe your brother was capable of killing Jake Shepherd?"

Don let out a long, slow breath. "I'm not sure what you mean by capable," he finally said. "If you're asking me if my brother has the temperament to kill Jake Shepherd, then I'd have to say yes, but if Bobby killed Jake, we'd all know it because he would have told us." He looked Traner in the eye. "My brother is a raging alcoholic. Jake landed and idled up to our boats to talk to us a few days before he was murdered, and he and Bobby got into an argument. If Bobby had a gun in his hand then, I could imagine him shooting Jake right there, but I don't think Bobby arranged a meeting with Jake or saw Jake's plane on the beach and pursued Jake, or any other scenario which would force Bobby to plan and think. Even when my brother was sober, he wasn't the sharpest knife in the drawer, and now he's a barely functioning drunk."

Don's candor surprised Traner. Maybe after putting up with his brother for a week, Don decided he'd had enough of Bobby and didn't want to protect him any longer.

"I know you and Bobby and Jake all went to school together. Why did Bobby hate Jake so much? Did something happen when you were kids?"

Don emitted a long sigh. "Jake thought he knew everything, even back then. He played basketball, ran track, got good grades, and never drank alcohol. Bobby, on the other hand, was a screwup." Don sat back in his chair and rubbed his forehead. "One night when they were seniors, the track coach sent Jake to the office to get some forms for something. It was late in the evening, and the school building was deserted. When Jake got to the office, he found Bobby stealing the history exam for the following morning. Apparently, the secretary had xeroxed the exam for the history teacher and left the copies in the teacher's mail cubicle. Somehow, Bobby figured out the procedure and waited until everyone in the office went home so he could take a copy of the test."

"That's it?" Traner asked. "Bobby hated Jake because he was afraid Jake would expose him for stealing a test back in high school?"

Don shook his head. "No," he said. "Jake then told Bobby's girlfriend, and somehow, Bobby had a beautiful girlfriend named Stephanie Brown." Don snorted. "Stephanie had long, black hair, dark eyes, and luscious, long lashes. I have no idea what she was doing with my brother. Anyway, Jake told her about Bobby stealing the test, and within days, Stephanie broke up with my brother and started going steady with Jake."

Traner waited expectantly, but when Don didn't continue, he said, "Still, there must be something more to the story. After all, Jake didn't end up with Stephanie."

"Oh, there's more," Don said. "Fast forward to senior prom. Stephanie and her girlfriends drank wine before the prom, and when Jake realized she'd been drinking, he gave her hell. He didn't drink alcohol, and he did not believe Stephanie should drink alcohol. I think Stephanie was tired of him by then, and during the night, she and her friends took off for a joyride with a bottle of wine." Don paused and studied the table for several moments. "They missed Dead Man's Curve and shot off the cliff. All three girls were killed. Bobby was still in love with Stephanie, and he blamed Jake for her death."

"Did Bobby still hate Jake enough to kill him?" Traner asked.

My answer remains the same," Don said. "In the heat of the moment, my brother easily could have shot him, as long as he wasn't too drunk to shoot straight, but I don't believe he would go out of his way to shoot Jake, and if he did, he wouldn't be able to keep his mouth shut about it. By the time we got to the mouth of the Karluk River, he would have been bragging about murdering Jake."

1976
NOVEMBER 4TH
9:20 A.M.

Bently hiked as far as he could through the deep snow. The snow had a crust on it now, but it wasn't firm enough to support his weight, so he had to posthole through it, one slow step at a time. He hiked until exhaustion overcame him and then climbed up on a small knob and began to glass. He'd hiked the opposite direction from camp today because he wanted to survey new territory. He hadn't seen a bear since the storm, and he felt defeated. This hunting trip that he had dreamed about for so long had turned into a nightmare. He suspected Schwimmer was the only one of the two who was likely to fire his rifle, and Bently would be lucky if Schwimmer didn't shoot him.

Schwimmer seemed crazier than ever the previous evening when Bently returned to camp. Bently started calling his name as soon as he neared their camp. He didn't know where Schwimmer was hiding in the brush to watch the camp, and if the idiot fell asleep and woke up and heard him walking down the trail, he would likely shoot first and ask questions later. When Bently got to camp, he began heating water for their MREs, and twenty minutes later, Schwimmer finally appeared from somewhere. He looked cold, disheveled, and wild-eyed. Bently wondered if the guy would ever recover from this trip.

Bently pulled his hood tight and held the binoculars to his eyes. It was cold, and a fierce wind blew straight at him. According to the thermometer at camp, it was nineteen degrees this morning, but the wind chill made it feel much colder.

Bently scoured the frozen, white terrain. A brown bear should be easy to see, standing out in contrast to the white background. Bently saw several sets of tracks and areas where bears had plowed through the deep snow, but where were the animals that made those tracks? One set of tracks even skirted above the lakeshore and then disappeared into the thick brush. Bently felt certain a bruin would eventually show itself. If he put in the time, it would pay off for him. At this point, he knew he couldn't be picky. He might not end up with the huge trophy he wanted, but he'd get a bear. If a bear showed itself on a mountainside, he didn't know how he would get to it in the deep snow, but he'd try his best to reach it.

He continued to glass, stopping every hour for a few sips of coffee from his thermos. Despite the insulating properties of the thermos, the coffee got cooler as the day progressed. By 2:00 p.m., Bently began to shiver. He tried not to think about the biting wind while he sat and stared through his binoculars.

Around 3:00 p.m., Bently felt a tap on his shoulder. He thought he'd imagined the sensation, but when he turned and saw the old man standing behind him. He jumped to his feet, and his cold, numb legs barely supported him.

"Whoa there, young fella." The man reached out and put a steadying hand on Bently's arm. "I didn't mean to scare you."

The old man smiled and laughed, and Bently saw the man's few remaining teeth were darkly stained, probably by tobacco and poor hygiene. The man smelled like a wild animal. Bently looked down and saw a dead, bloody fox stretched on the sled behind the man.

"You're a trapper," Bently said. *This looked like the man he had seen a few days earlier, but was he also the guy who had visited Schwimmer at their camp?* Bently could understand how this strange old man might scare Schwimmer. When he smiled, the corners of his mouth turned up, but none of his other facial expressions changed. The smile did not reach his cold, black eyes.

"That's right, I'm a trapper, and you must be the buddy of the guy I talked to the other day."

Bently noticed the ice matting the trapper's scraggly, gray beard. His runny nose dripped into the beard, forming more ice within seconds, but the old man made no effort to wipe his nose.

"Yeah, he's my partner." *Schwimmer actually had talked to this guy; maybe he wasn't delusional after all.*

"Did he tell you, you're hunting on my land?"

The man's expression didn't change. He was several inches shorter than Bently, but Bently felt intimidated and took a step back, nearly falling over his pack.

Bently shook off his fear. "This is a federal wildlife refuge. There is no private land here, and I have the permit to hunt this area." Bently felt pleased his voice hadn't wavered. He tried not to sound confrontational, but he wanted to let the old guy know he wasn't easily cowed.

The trapper's eyes narrowed and grew even darker. Bently would not have been surprised to see flames burst from them.

"This is my land, and I say who can and can't hunt here and who can and can't camp here."

Bently said nothing. He felt his arm shaking, either from fear or cold.

"Your friend said you have plans to leave on the seventh. You'd better be gone by then, and don't come back."

The man turned and started to walk away but then looked back at Bently. "You're wasting your time; you know that, don't you? All this snow," he gestured to the ground around him, "sent the bears into hibernation. They are tucked in for the winter by now."

He turned, and Bently watched him lope away in his awkward gait, pulling the sled with the dead fox behind him. Bently's first thought was he shouldn't have been so hard on Schwimmer. Schwimmer overreacted, no question about it, but there was something otherworldly about this old man. Schwimmer was right, the old guy radiated evil with his hard, black eyes, filthy clothes, and dark, rotten teeth. It was more than just his appearance, though. Every word the man spoke implied a threat, and Bently, like Schwimmer, believed the man would carry out his threat. Bently hoped the weather cooperated on the seventh and the plane could get here to pick them up. He didn't want to find out what the trapper would do if they were stuck here a day or two.

Bently shook his head and sat down on his tarp. He had to get it together; he was starting to think like Schwimmer. Should he tell Schwimmer about talking to the trapper today? No, definitely not. Schwimmer was crazy enough already. There would be no point in ratcheting up his fear a notch.

Bently glassed another hour before calling it a day. If the old man was watching him, Bently didn't want the guy to know his words had spooked him. Maybe the trapper would keep his distance if he thought Bently had a backbone and wasn't a crybaby like Schwimmer.

As he hiked back to camp, Bently's temper started as a low rumble in his stomach and then began to burn. No one or nothing was going to ruin his hunt, not Schwimmer, not a crazy, old man, not snow. *The old man doesn't know what he was talking about. This snow might have sent sows with cubs scurrying to hibernate, but the big, old boars are still out here.* He'd laugh about all of this when he got back to town with his bear hide.

PRESENT DAY

TUESDAY, JULY 1ST
3:07 P.M.

When he heard the knock on his office door, Patterson looked up from the copy of Jake's journal he'd been studying.

"Yes?" Patterson called.

The door opened, and Trooper Brad Simpton entered Patterson's office, shutting the door behind him.

"Brad, please take a seat." Patterson gestured to the empty chair in front of his desk.

Simpton folded his lanky frame into the chair and pulled a small notebook from his shirt pocket. "Sir," he said. "I just finished talking to Jordan Gregg. I went at him hard like you told me, and he finally caved."

"Great, Brad," Patterson said. "What did he say?"

"He said he heard a rumor Jake caught one of the Kodiak Flight Services pilots drinking while on duty," Simpton said.

"You mean drinking and flying?" Patterson asked.

"Yes, sir," Simpton said.

"Who was it?"

"Gregg claimed he didn't know who the pilot was, and he wasn't sure the rumor was true. He said he should have kept his mouth shut."

"But he didn't keep his mouth shut," Patterson said, "and now we need to figure out whether Jake really did catch another Kodiak Flight Services pilot drinking on the job—and if so, who was the pilot?" He smiled at Simpton. "Good work, Brad. Did Gregg say anything else?"

"He said according to the rumor, Jake told the guilty pilot to shape up, or he would report him to either Steve Duncan or the FAA."

Patterson thanked Simpton and then placed a call to Larry Mendoza. He expected the pilot to be flying, but Larry surprised him by answering on the second ring.

"Larry, this is Dan Patterson."

"Now what have I done?" Larry joked.

"I want to pry some information out of you," Patterson said.

"This doesn't sound good."

"It'll be painless," Patterson said. "I'll tell you about a rumor I heard, and you tell me whether you've heard something similar."

"I'm listening," Mendoza said.

"I heard Jake Shepherd observed one of the Kodiak Flight Services pilots drinking on the job, and Jake confronted the pilot, threatening either to report the pilot to Steve Duncan or to the FAA."

"Okay," Mendoza said.

"Is that the rumor you heard?"

Mendoza sighed. "Yes," he said. "It's the rumor I heard."

"Who was the pilot?" Patterson asked.

"I don't know who the pilot was," Mendoza said. "I absolutely have no idea. The rumor surprised me, and to be honest, I'm not sure I believe it. I respect all the Kodiak Flight Services pilots, and I can't imagine any of them being careless and stupid enough to drink alcohol and then get in an airplane and fly."

"Do you know where the rumor originated?" Patterson asked.

"No, I'm sorry, Sergeant. I'm sure by the time I heard the rumor it had passed through several people, and I don't know who started it."

"Where did you hear it?"

"I went to the Brewery for a beer one night after work," Mendoza said. "I sat with a group of six or seven pilots, and they were whispering about it. As I remember, none of them believed the rumor was true."

As soon as Patterson disconnected with Larry Mendoza, he dialed the number for Kodiak Flight Services and asked to speak with Steve Duncan.

"Duncan," Steve answered the phone.

"Steve, this is Dan Patterson, and I have a question for you."

"Sure," Steve said.

"I heard a rumor today about Jake and one of your other pilots," Patterson said.

"What kind of rumor?" Steve asked.

"I heard Jake caught one of your pilots drinking alcohol while on duty," Patterson said.

"While he was flying for me?" Steve's voice rose an octave.

"I believe this happened a few days before Jake was murdered," Patterson said.

"Sergeant," Steve said, "I don't know where you heard this rumor, but if Jake caught one of my pilots drinking on the job, he would have told me, the pilot would no longer be in my employ, and I'd do everything in my power to get his license revoked. I'm sure you understand the seriousness of drinking on the job." Steve's voice seemed to grow in volume with every word.

Patterson rubbed the bridge of his nose, and he tried to make his voice sound as soothing as possible. "Of course, I understand what a serious breach of duty it would be to consume alcohol before or while flying a plane," Patterson said. "I'm just telling you what I heard. If it's true, then the pilot Jake caught would have a good reason for wanting Jake dead."

Steve said nothing for so long Patterson wondered if he'd disconnected, but then, his voice now barely above a whisper, he said, "You need to talk to my head pilot, Stan Edwards. Stan knows more than I do about what goes on with the pilots both on and off duty."

"When would be a good time to talk to him?" Patterson asked.

"He had a flight up to Anchorage today and isn't flying back until tomorrow morning. I'm expecting him to be here sometime late morning. I can make sure he's here around 1:00 p.m. How does that sound?"

"Fine," Patterson said. "I'll be there at 1:00 p.m." Patterson thought this would also be a good time to interview the young freight handler who'd argued with Jake.

"I'll let you know if he gets delayed in Anchorage," Steve said.

Patterson had just dropped the phone in its cradle when it buzzed again. "Patterson."

Sir," Irene said, "I have Jane Marcus on the phone."

Patterson let out a sigh and rubbed the bridge of his nose again. He didn't have time to deal with Jane Marcus today, but he'd told her to dig into the bones, so now he'd better take a few minutes to listen to what she had to say. "Put her through," he told Irene.

"Sergeant?" He heard a quiver of excitement in Jane's voice. *Has she actually learned something about the bones?*

"Yes, Jane, how are you?" Patterson asked.

"Fine. I just returned from Anchorage where I met with the anthropology student who is examining the bones," Jane said.

"Did you learn anything interesting?"

"As you know, the skull has a large hole in it, and the anthropologist feels certain the hole was caused by a bullet."

"Yes, I remember."

"Sir, the bullet hole is on the top of the head, and Ying, the anthropology student, said it would be an awkward angle for a suicide."

"Awkward, but not impossible," Patterson said. "If the shot came from a rifle, the man could have braced the gun on the ground and bent his head toward the barrel before pulling the trigger."

"Maybe," Jane sounded doubtful. "Wouldn't a direct rifle blast blow the skull apart?"

"It depends on the angle and where the bullet exited," Patterson said. "Did you learn anything else of interest?"

"Yes," Jane said. "Ying believes the man was in his late twenties and was starving to death when he died."

"Interesting," Patterson said. "If he was starving to death, maybe he did kill himself. Starvation is a painful way to die. Perhaps he put himself out of his misery."

"Sergeant," Jane said. "Would I be able to look through missing person cases? Ying again stated they believe the bones are between thirty and fifty years old, so I'd like to check the files between those time periods."

Patterson laughed. "Yes, but those are still paper files, so it would be quite a task. Nothing that old has been transferred to the computer." He paused a moment. "Before you clog your lungs with our dust, I have one other suggestion. I know an old trooper who lives here in Kodiak, and he might remember something helpful from thirty or forty years ago. It's a long shot, but I think he could help."

"Should I call him?" Jane asked.

"Let me call him first, and if he wants to talk to you, I'll give him your number."

Patterson signed off with Jane and checked his watch. He still had ten minutes before the 4:00 p.m. meeting, so he placed a quick call to Sid Beatty and asked him if he'd be willing to speak to Jane about any unsolved murders approximately forty years ago. Beatty seemed intrigued, and even a little excited about the idea of digging into a cold case, and Patterson was more than happy to pawn off Jane on him.

PRESENT DAY
TUESDAY, JULY 1ST
3:57 P.M.

Patterson entered the conference room three minutes before the start of the meeting. The other troopers were just arriving, pouring themselves coffee, and getting situated at the table. Patterson consulted his copy of Jake's journal while he wrote some of the cryptic notations on the whiteboard. Once the room quieted, he put down the marker and took his seat at the head of the table.

"I feel we made some progress on the investigation today. We've interviewed Inga Shepherd and Bobby and Don Brinker, and Brad had an interesting conversation with Jordan Gregg."

Patterson proceeded to tell the group about what he and Sara had learned from Inga Shepherd. "By the time we completed the interview, I don't think either Sara or I had much more insight into Inga Shephard than we had when we first walked into her house." Patterson looked at Sara.

"No," Sara said. "Inga Shepherd is one cold fish. She'd never get her nails dirty, but I believe she could have hired someone to murder her husband. She didn't like Jake nearly as much as she likes money."

"She did decipher some of Jake's journal for us, and we'll talk about the journal in a bit, but first, Mark and I will tell you about our interviews of the Brinker brothers."

Patterson went first, consulting his notes as he relayed the details of his interview of Bobby Brinker, and then Traner told his fellow troopers what he'd learned from Don Brinker.

"Shepherd didn't take care of his drunk girlfriend and let her speed off in a car with other drunk kids?" Simpton said. "I like Jake Shepherd less with each passing moment. I'm surprised someone didn't kill him long ago."

"I think we can describe Jake as self-righteous and antagonistic," Patterson said, "but unfortunately, we don't get to pick our victims or our crimes. Brad, why don't you tell us what you learned from Jordan Gregg, and then I have something to add to the subject."

Brad Simpton told the others the rumor Gregg heard about Jake berating a Kodiak Flight Services pilot for drinking while operating a plane.

"Do you believe he didn't know who the guilty pilot was?" Sara asked.

"I do," Simpton said. "I convinced him I'd call the FAA and report his careless flying if he didn't tell me everything he knew. He said the way he heard the story, Jake and the other pilot were having the argument behind one of the Kodiak Flight Services vans. Since Jake was doing most of the talking, the person who overheard the conversation could easily identify Jake's voice, but the other man's replies were barely above a whisper."

"Who overheard them?" Sara asked.

Simpton shrugged. "Gregg said he heard the story third- or fourth-hand. He assumed another Kodiak Flight Services pilot heard them, but he couldn't be sure, and he wasn't even certain the listener was a pilot—or a man, for that matter."

Patterson looked at Simpton. "After you told me about your interview with Gregg, I called Larry Mendoza, repeated the story to him, and asked him if it was the same rumor he'd heard but didn't want to tell me," Patterson said. "Larry admitted he'd heard a Kodiak Flight Services pilot had been drinking and flying, and Jake caught him. He also had no idea who overheard the argument between Jake and the pilot. Larry couldn't guess at the identity of the pilot and said he has the utmost respect for everyone at Kodiak Flight Services and couldn't imagine any of them being stupid enough to drink and fly. When I got off the phone with Larry, I called Steve Duncan, and while he didn't believe the rumor, he set up an appointment for me to meet tomorrow with his head pilot, Stan Edwards. If I don't get anything from Stan, we will need to talk to every pilot in town, beginning with those at Kodiak Flight Services."

"If Jake caught a pilot drinking on the job and threatened him, the guy would have a great motive to murder Jake," Traner said. The other troopers nodded in unison.

"What am I forgetting?" Patterson glanced down at his notebook.

"Have we heard from Peter?" Simpton asked.

Patterson nodded. "Thanks, Brad, that's it. Peter called in this afternoon and spoke with Irene. He talked to law enforcement in Anchorage. Brian Decker has had several run-ins with the law but nothing in the last two years. Peter said he also followed Decker to an AA meeting and talked to Decker's boss. Brian works construction, and his boss said he's a good worker and rarely ever misses work. The boss told Peter that Decker has a chip on his shoulder, and he got into a fistfight with a fellow employee a little over a year ago. Brian put the other guy in the hospital, and Brian's boss told Brian to take anger-management classes or find another job. Apparently, Brian took the classes, and his boss said he's had no further problems with him."

"I don't believe one little anger-management course turns an angry man into a peace lover," Simpton said.

"I agree," Patterson said, "and Peter will follow Brian for two more days. Brian Decker is still near the top of my list of possible murderers, but at this point, our mysterious pilot and Inga Shepherd have edged Brian out of the number one spot."

Patterson stood and walked to the whiteboard. "I asked you all to take a look at Jake's journal," Patterson said. "As I mentioned, Inga Shepherd deciphered a few of the entries for us, but unfortunately, she wasn't much help on the most interesting notations. She knew, or said she knew, nothing about Jake's acquaintances and interactions here on Kodiak. She did point out entries he made about family birthdates, so I've excluded those as well as his airplane log and his strange fixation with the gas mileage for his truck."

Traner laughed. "I don't want to know how much I spend on gas," he said.

"And no one gets good gas mileage driving the streets of Kodiak," Sara added.

"I've written a few of Jake's entries on the board, so let's see if we can decipher them."

"Jake's notations are so cryptic, I'm surprised he could remember what they meant," Simpton said.

"Especially toward the end," Sara said. "He must have known he didn't have much time left. I think he was losing his mind."

"I would," Traner said. "The guy was in horrible pain and facing certain death in a matter of weeks. Have we given up on the idea of suicide?"

"No," Patterson said. "Suicide for hire is still a possibility, but I consider it a long shot. If he hired another pilot to shoot him, why do it on a busy lake like Karluk? He'd more likely choose a secluded spot, and those are easy to come by on this island. It makes no sense that he would ask someone to take the chance or that someone would assume the risk of shooting Jake in the middle of the day on a lake buzzing with activity."

"Buzzing with activity," Simpton said, "but we have yet to find anyone who saw anything suspicious."

"Maybe if he caught a pilot drinking while flying, he blackmailed the guy into shooting him," Sara said.

"You mean shoot me, or I'll report you to the FAA?" Simpton asked.

Patterson turned toward the board. "In addition to the omissions I just mentioned, I've also excluded any entries Jake made about his health. So, let's start here." Patterson pointed to the first item he'd written on the board: "*4-12 HM-BW-Refuge?*"

No one spoke for several seconds, three sets of eyes trained on the board. Finally, Traner said, "The first thing that popped into my head last night was '*HM*' is Hal Michaels; he's a pilot with Sea Quest, but I have no ideas for '*BW.*'"

"Buzzing wildlife?" Sara asked. "Maybe he was wondering if he should report the incident to the refuge?"

Patterson began to nod. "I doubt we will ever know for sure, but Hal Michaels buzzing wildlife fits. Good work, you two. Let's move on." He pointed to another string of numbers and letters: "*5-11 I-A-Who? CC? RB?*"

Again, the room went quiet for a few beats, but then Sara said, "I think I know this one, and I also know why it caused Inga to blush when you showed it to her."

"What do you think it means, Sara?" Patterson asked.

"Inga – Affair - Who? Then he lists two possibilities, '*CC*' or '*RB.*' I don't who they are, though."

"Makes sense," Simpton said, "and we wouldn't know CC or RB because they probably live in Atlanta where Inga spent most of her time."

"No wonder Jake wanted to cut Inga out of his will," Traner said.

"And this gives Inga another motive for wanting Jake dead," Sara said.

"Good," Patterson said. "I came to the same conclusion." He pointed to the next entry on the board: "*5-13 LM-BM-Report?*"

After a few moments of silence, Patterson said, "This one I'm afraid I understand. I think it means Larry Mendoza below minimums, meaning Larry was flying on a foggy day."

"It's impossible not to fly below minimums at times here on Kodiak," Simpton said. "I'm sure Jake did it too. You leave town on a trip when the weather is fine, and by the time you return, you're forced to land in pea soup."

"I agree," Patterson said, and there's no pilot on the island I'd rather fly with than Mendoza, but Larry told me he and Jake got along fine."

"Maybe Jake decided not to tell Larry he observed him flying below minimums," Sara said.

"Perhaps," Patterson said, "but Jake had a problem keeping his mouth closed."

"Even if Jake said something, Larry would probably laugh it off," Traner said.

"I doubt he'd kill him over it, anyway," Patterson said, "but I am surprised Larry didn't mention it to me."

Patterson pointed to the next cryptic string: "*6:15 PA w/JM HM.*"

"Physical altercation with Jason Meckel—hazardous materials," Traner and Simpton said in unison.

Patterson nodded. "It fits the facts. Let's move on." He tapped his finger on the board: "*6-18 BS-JG DC-FAA?*"

"I had some trouble with this one, Sara said. "I get the first and last part. This is when he saw Buddy Stark and Jordan Gregg buzzing each other and was considering reporting them to the FAA, but what does 'DC' mean?"

"Driving carelessly?" Traner said.

"Yes, Mark," Patterson said. "I agree. 'DC' means driving carelessly."

Sara nodded. "Makes sense."

"This one is easy." Patterson pointed to *6-20 I-D? No Will.*

"Inga-Divorce? Remove her from his will," Sara said, and Simpton and Traner both nodded.

Patterson refocused on the board and pointed at the next notation: *6-23: I-OOW-LI? Remove.* "This one took me longer than it should have," Patterson said, "but I believe it means Inga is out of his will, and he is questioning whether or not to take her off his life insurance."

"To me," Traner said, "it means he decided to remove Inga from his life insurance because he didn't put a question mark after the word '*Remove.*'"

"Perhaps," Patterson said, "But we will never know. Either he changed his mind about removing Inga from his life insurance, or he never got around to it before he died. This was, after all, four days before his death."

"If this was a suicide by proxy," Sara said, "You'd think he'd tie up loose ends before he had someone kill him."

"Interesting point, Sara," Patterson said.

"What about this?" Patterson asked as he tapped the next string. *6-24 R-DWF-S?-FAA?*

The room remained quiet for nearly a minute while the four troopers studied the board.

"This one made no sense to me last night," Traner said, "but from what we've learned today, I think I know it."

Patterson, Sara, and Simpton all looked at Traner and waited for him to explain.

"Jake caught pilot 'R' drinking while flying, so should he tell Steve or report the pilot to the FAA?"

The room fell silent again while everyone studied the board. "Maybe," Sara said, "but who is 'R'?"

"Rusty Hoak?" Traner asked.

"Or Roy Tayler," Patterson said. "Both Rusty and Roy fly for Kodiak Flight Services."

"They both seem like responsible pilots," Traner said.

"Both Jason Meckel and Lance Crane told me they saw Roy's plane flying over Karluk Lake near the time Jake died, and according to what Charli told me, Roy shouldn't have been at Karluk Lake then. He flew to Uyak, not Karluk, that morning," Patterson said. "In any case, I have an appointment tomorrow to talk to the head pilot at Kodiak Flight Services, and if we have interpreted this journal entry correctly, I think it helps validate the rumor we've been hearing,"

Patterson stared at the board a few more moments, lost in thought about Rusty Hoak and Roy Tayler. He remembered how broken up Rusty had been over Jake's death. *He didn't even want to help move Jake's body at the crime scene.*

A sharp knock on the door interrupted the meeting. Irene opened the door. "Sorry to interrupt, sir, but I have your wife on the line. She says it's an emergency."

Patterson didn't even remember leaving the conference room and returning to his office. He didn't remember breathing again until he heard Jeanne's voice.

"Honey, what is it?" he asked.

"Dan, you need to come home now. I'm about to hurt myself. I need help."

"Don't do anything." Patterson tried to push the rising panic out of his voice. "I'm on my way."

As he ran through the outer office, Irene handed him his pack. She or the troopers in the conference room had stuffed his notebook and other notes into his backpack. He was grateful for the gesture because he didn't know when he would be able to return to headquarters.

PRESENT DAY
TUESDAY, JULY 1ST
5:15 P.M.

I had just decided to call it a day when my cell phone buzzed. I didn't recognize the number.

"Is this Jane Marcus?" a deep voice asked.

"Yes?"

"My name is Sid Beatty," the man said. "Sergeant Patterson suggested I call you. I used to have his job, and he said you found some bones approximately forty years old, and he thought I could help you with old missing persons cases."

"Yes." I sat on the edge of my desk. "Thank you for calling. Do you have a few minutes to spare to talk to me?"

"I live on my boat in Dog Bay," he said. He gave me the slip number. "It's a forty-six-foot sailboat. You can't miss it."

"You want me to come down there now?" I asked.

"Sure, if you have the time. I'm retired," he said, "so if you'd rather talk tomorrow, I can be here then, too. I might take a trip this weekend, though, so don't wait too long."

"Thank you, Sergeant. I'm leaving my office now; I'll be there in fifteen minutes."

"Call me Sid," he said. "I'm retired."

It took me a few minutes to find the right dock finger, but once I did, I walked toward the boat with the largest mast. Since the commercial salmon season was open, most of the commercial fishing boats had left the harbor, and only the charter sportfishing boats and pleasure boats remained. Very few sailboats populated the two Kodiak boat harbors because there were warmer and easier places to sail than Kodiak, Alaska. The few sailboats in Dog Bay stood out due to their tall masts. As I neared Sid Beatty's boat, I noted its white fiberglass and green trim gleamed in the afternoon sun. Sid obviously spent a great deal of time caring for his vessel.

As I drew closer to the boat, a guy climbed out of the hatch and stepped off onto the dock to greet meet. The man who held out his hand to me looked much younger than I expected. He had the wrinkles and grey hair of a man in his late sixties, but his lean, athletic form suggested a man fifteen years younger.

"Jane, I presume?"

"Yes, and you must be Sid."

Sid Beatty's grey hair brushed the collar of his flannel shirt. He had a two-day's growth of beard, and his deep brown eyes studied me. His smile revealed perfect, white teeth, and I wondered why I had never seen him in Kodiak before now. I felt certain if I'd bumped into him in the grocery store, I would have noticed him.

"Nice boat," I said.

"Come aboard. What's your poison?" he asked. "I have coffee, tea, or whiskey," he laughed as I followed him onto the sailboat and down the hatch into the cozy salon.

I wanted to request whiskey, but I wasn't here to socialize, so I instead chose coffee. I reminded myself this guy was probably married and way too old for me.

"Are you married?" I asked for no good reason when Sid set a cup of steaming coffee in front of me on the galley table.

He took a seat across from me. "Divorced," he said. "My wife got tired of following me around the state to different posts. I can't say I blame her." He smiled. "Kodiak isn't for everyone. She's remarried and lives in Florida now, so I'm sure she's much happier."

"Do you have children?" *What is with me? I need a social life, and a male companion other than an FBI agent I saw once a year and hadn't talked to in weeks.*

"I'm sorry," I said. "Your personal life is none of my business."

Beatty smiled while his eyes studied me. "No problem," he said. "I have one daughter who lives in Indiana with her husband and three sons. I spent two weeks with them last month and couldn't wait to return to the peace and quiet of my boat. What about you? Are you married?"

"No," I said too quickly. I took a long, slow sip of coffee. "I am also divorced, and I don't have children."

"Dan told me you're a fisheries biologist." He laughed. "What he said was, you're a fisheries biologist and a pain-in-the-ass amateur detective."

I felt my face grow hot with embarrassment and forced a laugh. *Is this how Patterson regards me?*

"I should mention he also said you have a brilliant mind, and he respects you."

The heat ratcheted up a notch and I hurried to change the topic of conversation to anything other than me. "I'm nosy," I said. "My friends and I found some human bones, and I can't stop thinking about them."

"Tell me about the bones," Sid said.

Now I was on firmer ground, and I felt myself relax. I began with the fire at Karluk Lake, and our discovery of the bones on the charred ground. I then moved on to describe what Ying had learned from studying the bones.

"Let me make sure I understand," Sid said. "The anthropologist thinks the individual was between twenty-five and thirty years old when he died and estimates the bones have been at Karluk Lake between thirty and fifty years."

"Yes," I said. "I know it's a wide time range, but does anything come to mind? Do you remember any unsolved cases from the seventies or eighties?"

Sid sat back and stared at the ceiling. "I worked three unsolved missing persons cases during my tenure. They were all young women, and two of them were friends who disappeared on the same night." He shook his head. "We never found a trace, and to this day, I have no idea what happened to them." He stared off into space for a while. "But I don't remember any unsolved cases involving young men."

I smiled. "Thanks for trying," I said. "Do you think it would do me any good to go through old case files?"

"Wait a minute," Beatty said. "How could I forget Henry? I did have an unsolved missing male."

"And his name was Henry?"

"No, no," Sid said. "This is a wild story. It's possible Henry could be tied to your bones, but you'd never prove it." Sid took a sip of his coffee. "From the late sixties through maybe 1981 or 1982, a crazy old guy lived and trapped near Karluk Lake. He'd spend the entire winter out there by himself. Back in the seventies, the deer population hadn't yet spread to the south end of the island, so I don't know what he ate." Sid chuckled and shook his head. "I do know some of what he ate, but I'll get to that part of the story in a minute. Henry trapped beavers, foxes, and rabbits, so I assume he ate those. Anyway, he was a tough old guy."

I had no idea where Sid was headed with this story, so I said nothing and waited for him to continue.

"The guy's name was Henry Aurman," Sid said.

"The Aurman from Aurman Plumbing and Heating?" The store was a town landmark, and I'd been told it had survived the '64 earthquake.

"That's right," Sid said. "One of Henry's relatives started the store, but Henry had nothing to do with the business. I think the store is still owned by an Aurman, probably Henry's great niece or nephew."

"Sorry," I said. "I didn't mean to interrupt."

"As far as I know, Henry never married, and he was crazy, or at the very least, eccentric. He claimed the entire region around Karluk Lake belonged to him."

"That's a big area," I said.

Sid laughed. "Yes, it is. The troopers spent a great deal of time dealing with Henry because any time a hunter, fisherman, or camper set up a tent near the lake, Henry threatened the visitors and told them they did not have his permission to camp on his land. He'd tell them he'd kill them if they didn't leave. We threw him in jail numerous times for harassment, but he'd return to Karluk and threaten the next person who dared walk near 'his' lake."

My spine tingled. *Did Henry Aurman kill the man whose bones we found?* "Did he ever kill any campers?" I asked.

"Not to my knowledge," Sid said, "but I always expected one of his confrontations to end in violence with either him or a camper dead. I am certain, though, that Henry murdered at least three men, but they weren't campers; they were his trapping partners."

"What do you mean?"

"Around 1977 or 1978—you'd have to check the file for the exact date— Henry was getting older and wanted help with his winter trapping, so he 'hired,' to use the term loosely, a young man to accompany him during the winter. I believe the deal was that the young guy would help him trap, and

Henry would give him a few hides to sell in payment for his services. The young man was a drifter, looking to turn his life around, and he wanted to learn how to trap, so he eagerly followed Henry to Karluk Lake."

"Did Henry have a house at the lake?"

"He had a shack. It's long gone now, but it had heat. I think most nights he camped near his trapline, but he'd return to the shack to resupply and work on his hides."

"What happened?"

"In May, we received a call from the young guy's brother, and if his brother hadn't called us, I never would have known about the guy." Sid paused for another sip of coffee. "I don't remember the caller's name, but he said his brother had phoned him in November to tell him he'd quit drinking and was planning to spend the winter in the Kodiak wilderness learning to trap from an old man named Henry. He hadn't heard from his brother since. I didn't know Aurman had hired a partner for the winter, but he was the only Henry I knew who trapped, so I flew out to Karluk and found Henry at his cabin."

I sat back in my chair. "Was the young man there?"

Sid shook his head. "Henry admitted he'd hired the guy but said he'd left in mid-December, telling Henry he couldn't stand the cold and isolation any longer. Henry called him a wimp and said he thought the guy missed his alcohol. Henry said he was happy to see him leave."

"Wait a minute," I said. They were camped on a frozen lake in the middle of the winter. "How did the guy leave?"

"Henry claimed the young man planned to hike to the village of Karluk and catch their mail plane back to Kodiak, but he never made it to Karluk— or at least, he never flew from Karluk to Kodiak on the mail plane. They keep lists of their passengers, and he wasn't on any of the lists."

"What did Henry say when you told him his helper never arrived in Karluk?" I asked.

"He said he didn't know what had happened to his trapping buddy, and we didn't have enough evidence to charge Henry with a crime. I suspected, though, either that Henry killed the guy, or the guy got lost in the woods and froze to death."

"Wouldn't he just need to follow the river from the lake to the village?"

"Yes, so I didn't believe he got lost."

"You thought Henry murdered him." A chill ran through me. "Maybe these are his bones I found," I said.

"It's possible, but this guy wasn't the only partner Henry lost."

"Meaning?"

"Rumors floated hinting Henry lost another partner the following year, but no one ever reported the man missing, so the troopers were not involved," Sid said. "Guys who sign on to spend the winter in the wilderness with a crazy trapper aren't social beings, and they don't usually have many resources. They're loners."

"So you never talked to Henry about this guy?"

"No, but two years later, around 1980 or 1981, Henry picked the wrong trapping buddy. When this man didn't return from his winter's expedition, the phone at trooper headquarters rang for two months. We heard from his mother, his two sisters, friends, an aunt or two, and even an employer who expected him to return to his job in Salt Lake City after the end of his winter adventure."

"What did Henry say when you questioned him?"

"This is where the story gets interesting," Sid said. "I flew to Karluk Lake with two other troopers, and we went to Henry's little shack. He wasn't there, so after we knocked on the door, we entered the building."

Sid sat back and regarded me. He looked as if he'd just smelled something bad, or maybe he was trying to decide if he should continue his story.

"What did you find?" I finally asked.

Sid sighed. "We found bones and scraps of meat as if an animal recently had been butchered. We saw jars of canned meat lining the shelves of a makeshift cupboard in the corner of the shack. At first, I thought the bones were bear bones, but then I realized they were human."

Sid waited while I processed his words. "He killed and ate his trapping partners?" I stood as if trying to distance myself from Sid and his horrible tale. I reined in my urge to flee and returned to my seat.

Sid nodded. "I'm sorry; I know this is a terrible story. Imagine how we felt standing in that little shack, realizing what we had found and then knowing Henry could return at any minute and shoot us all. I immediately sent one of the troopers outside to stand guard so we wouldn't be ambushed."

This time, Sid drank a big gulp of his cooling coffee. "Yes, the bones were human, and the nicely stacked jars contained cooked and canned human meat."

"Wow," was the only thing I could think to say. Visions of stacked canning jars bearing human flesh flooded my head. I wondered if Henry had labeled the jars with his dead partners' names, but I wisely pushed the question from my mind before I asked it.

"We dug holes outside his shed in areas where it looked as if the vegetation had been disturbed, and we found more human bones. After the proper experts analyzed the bones, they determined we'd found a good portion of the skeletons of two individuals. From their known or estimated heights and the dental records of the last trapper, we concluded the bones belonged to Henry's last two trapping buddies. Remember, though, we didn't use DNA analysis back then, and we couldn't get dental records for Henry's next-to-last trapping buddy, so we weren't positive about his ID. We do know the first guy who went missing was short, and the second guy, the one who was only rumored to have disappeared, was very tall. The bones we found belonged to a tall man, so we assumed they belonged to trapping buddy number two."

"The bones I found also belonged to a tall guy, so I doubt they are trapper number one's bones either."

"The trapper's cabin was several miles from where you said you found your bones, but Henry could have killed a camper or a hunter. Henry was a mean guy."

"Did you arrest Henry?" I asked

Sid shook his head. "We never found Henry. Two years later, someone found part of the sled he pulled behind him when he was trapping. It had washed up on the shore of the lake, so we concluded Henry tried to walk across the ice while it was still weak, and he fell through and drowned."

"But you never found his body?"

"No, and 'Henry sightings' continued for the next ten years, but none proved credible. I think he died a few months or weeks before we found the human remains in his cabin."

"This is a big help," I said. "I appreciate it."

"You should get the file on Henry Aurman and look through it. It's in a dusty, back room, but it's there at trooper headquarters. Irene will know where it is."

"I'll give her a call tomorrow," I said.

My eyes dropped to my watch, and I was shocked to see how late it was. I was scheduled to meet Corban Pratt for dinner in less than an hour. Peter would never forgive me if I stood up the Tamron executive.

I stood and thanked Sid Beatty for his time, and he promised to call if he remembered anything else. As I hurried up the boat ramp and drove to my house, I pushed the picture of jarred human meat as far as I could to the back of my brain. Once I stopped thinking about cannibalism, I couldn't clear my mind of the image of Sid Beatty's intense gaze and white teeth. *The man had nearly thirty years on me. Why do I find him attractive? I needed to get out more and socialize.*

1976

NOVEMBER 6TH
9:30 A.M.

Bently threw his pack on the ground, grabbed the tarp from its front pocket, spread the tarp on the snow, and sat. Today was the last day of his hunt, and it wasn't looking good. He'd seen one bear yesterday, but it was too high on the mountain to reach. It was the only bear he'd seen in the last week. *Maybe the old man was right; maybe all the bears have already gone into hibernation. Maybe the old bat waved his sorcerer's wand and made the bears disappear.* Bently huffed out a disgusted laugh and pulled his binoculars from his pack. Perhaps this would be his lucky day. The old trapper and Schwimmer and the snow be damned.

Around mid-afternoon, he saw it. He pulled the binoculars away from his face and rubbed his eyes. Had he imagined the animal? Was it wishful thinking? He looked again, and there it was: a chocolate-brown bear frosted with a coating of snow he'd picked up from walking through the alders and willows. The bear stood at the edge of the brush patch now, and Bently wondered how long he'd been right there in the brush. Despite the fact the vegetation had dropped its leaves and the snow provided added visibility, the brush remained so thick, it was impossible to see into it. Dozens of bears probably waited in the protection of the heavy brush for the snow to melt.

Bently pulled his scope from his pack and took a closer look at the beast. His heart thudded, and his hands shook. He ripped his gloves from his hands and threw them on the snow. He wiped his palms on his coat and inhaled a steadying breath. He bent to the eyepiece of his scope and tried to hone his thoughts. It was a big bear and maybe even a huge bear. Bently studied it for only a few minutes. It was his bear if he could get to it before dark. He looked at his watch, but the digital display appeared black. The ridiculous watch only worked intermittently in this wet, cold environment, and he cursed himself for not leaving it at home and wearing a more practical watch on his hunt. He believed darkness would fall in a little over two hours, but the sky was clear. He picked up his gear, struggled into his pack, and pulled on his gloves. It might be stupid and risky, but he was going for it.

A litany of reasons why he shouldn't stalk this bear so late in the day raced through his mind. Even if he managed to get within range and shoot the animal, he'd still have to skin it, and that chore would take him several hours. Then, he'd have to carry the heavy hide down the mountain in the dark over slippery, uneven ground through large patches of thick brush. He was apt to fall and break an ankle, and then what would happen? No one would know where he was, and he'd freeze to death. If he didn't get back to camp before dark, Schwimmer would lose what little sanity he had left. He'd probably think the old trapper had killed him, and Schwimmer would be on guard, ready to shoot the first person who walked down the trail to their camp.

Of course, he didn't have to skin the bear and pack the hide out of the woods tonight. This was the last day of his hunting permit, which meant he couldn't shoot a bear after today, but he didn't have to get the animal out of the woods today. He gave this some thought but quickly rejected the idea. The plane scheduled to pick them up was supposed to leave Kodiak at first light the next morning. They'd need to wake up early, pack their gear, and be ready and waiting on the lakeshore. Ice had formed around the edge of the lake, so Bently wasn't sure where the pilot would want to meet them. They might have to haul their gear to an ice-free spot. If he waited until morning to hike back up the mountain to skin and pack out the bear hide, it would take him most of the day, and the pilot wouldn't wait on him. They had no radio to contact the airlines and change their pickup time, and besides, Schwimmer would pop a gasket if they moved the flight later. He wanted out of here. Bently knew if he shot a bear this evening, he'd have to get the hide back to camp tonight.

Then, there was the crazy old man who thought he owned the land around Karluk Lake. *What would he do if they didn't break camp and fly back to Kodiak in the morning?* Once they got back to Kodiak, Bently planned to talk to the Federal Wildlife Refuge people and report the old trapper. Maybe he was harmless, but he shouldn't be allowed to threaten legitimate refuge users.

Darkness fell while Bently climbed the mountain, fighting his way through snow that continued to get deeper as he gained altitude. The brush patches were the worst. He struggled through each dark thicket, and in the deep snow, he couldn't tell which way to go. He couldn't differentiate uphill from downhill. As he grew more exhausted, he fought for each step. He looked down at his legs, willing them to keep moving as he plowed through the snow, and when he glanced up again, the branch of an alder snapped and hit him in the eye. He stumbled back, fell over a log, and slid nearly one hundred feet down the mountain, only stopping when his head impacted a large rock.

PRESENT DAY
WEDNESDAY, JULY 2ND
9:12 A.M.

I dropped my purse in the bottom desk drawer and was getting ready to shut the drawer when my purse buzzed. Hoping for a miraculous callback from the Air Force major in Anchorage, I recovered my phone and answered.

"Jane," the deep voice said. "Sid Beatty. I know you're probably at work, but I thought of something."

I felt my heartbeat pick up its pace. Why was my body responding to a man I'd only met yesterday? "Sure," I said. "Go ahead, I'm not busy." In reality, I needed to write a test to give my summer session students the following day. I hadn't yet started on the exam. On the other hand, I did give up the previous evening to listen to the wonderful Corban Pratt tell me how amazing he is.

"I thought of something else last night. It was a rumor back in the seventies, but it might be useful information, and it's not anything you will find in a case file because we had no reason to open an investigation."

"I'd love to hear it," I said.

"I know you're at work, and I'm busy all day, but how about drinks this evening at Henry's? I can be there by 7:00 p.m. Does that work for you?"

"Sure," I said, trying to keep the excitement out of my voice.

I stared at my computer for ten minutes, attempting to come up with question number one for the exam, but my thoughts kept drifting to the bones and the strange, old trapper Sid had told me about the previous evening. I picked up the phone and dialed trooper headquarters, announced

198

my name, and asked to speak to Sergeant Patterson. The voice on the phone informed me he wasn't in the office.

"Is this Irene?" I asked.

"Yes, ma'am."

"Would it be okay if I come over to look at an old file?" I asked.

"Yes," Irene said. "Sergeant Patterson told me to make our archived files available to you."

"I'm on my way."

I grabbed my purse and was partway down the long hall to the lobby when I heard the voice of my boss call my name. I stopped and turned to face him. "Good morning, Peter."

"Jane," he said. "How was your dinner with Corban Pratt last night?"

I'm sure Peter wished he could have slipped a bug into my purse before my night out with the Tamron executive.

"It was great, Peter; we had a nice evening," I said.

Peter nodded. "Good, and thank you for agreeing to have dinner with him, Jane. I'm sure you realize how much a grant from Tamron would help the center." In other words, Peter was saying, don't screw this up!

"Of course," I said. "When do you think you'll hear from them regarding the grant?"

Peter shook his head. "I have no idea, but please keep a low profile until we get the word."

I wondered what Peter meant by his comment. *Has he heard I'm snooping into some old bones I found in the woods?* Not much got by Peter, and I'm sure he worried about me pulling some crazy stunt to blow up this grant. *I'm just looking at old files*, I told myself as I hurried out the front door to my car. A soft drizzle began to fall as I made my way through the streets of Kodiak.

Trooper headquarters seemed deserted when I walked in the front door. Irene sat at her desk, but I neither saw nor heard anyone else in the building. Irene stared at the huge monitor on her desk and was keypunching furiously when I walked into the building. As soon as she heard me enter, she stopped what she was doing and turned her attention to me.

"Dr. Marcus," she said. "You made good time."

I laughed. "I'm playing hooky from work, but I can't stop thinking about those crazy bones."

She smiled. "You're a natural detective," she said. "What can I get you, or do you just want me to point the way to the old case files?"

"At some point, I probably will want to sift through old files, but this morning, I am after a particular old file."

"What file do you want?" Irene asked.

"I'd like to see the file on Henry Aurman."

Irene made no comment about the name "Aurman," but she turned back to her computer monitor and began keypunching again. A few moments later, she grabbed a set of keys from her top desk drawer and motioned for me to follow her down the hall. We entered the same room I'd been in before, but this time, I followed her into the storage room.

Row after row of tall shelves filled the room, and labeled boxes covered the surfaces of the shelves. I trailed Irene nearly to the other end of the room before she turned down a row marked with the letter "D." She seemed to know exactly where she was going, and I guessed when she entered Henry Aurman's name into the computer, the program listed the coordinates of Henry Aurman's file.

Irene slowed as she read the numbers on the sides of the boxes. Finally, she pointed to a top row and said, "It's up there." She looked at me. "There's a stepladder back by the door. Will you grab it? You're younger than me, so you can climb up and get the box."

I followed Irene's instructions, and when I climbed up the ladder, I examined the label on the box she had indicated. It read "*1985 A-D.*" I grabbed the heavy file box and carefully backed down the ladder.

I took the cardboard lid off the box, and Irene shuffled through it until she found the appropriate file and handed it to me. The file was over an inch thick.

"Leave the box and ladder here," Irene said. "I'll trust you to put it back where it belongs when you're through with it."

Was I gaining Irene's trust, or had she just decided I was going to be a pain in the butt, and she might as well make it easy on herself?

I took the thick file folder to the outer room and sat at the small table. Much of the folder consisted of photographs taken at Aurman's shack after the discovery of the bones. I found it interesting to read Sid's typed reports about Aurman. He stuck to the facts, but his intelligence seeped through the well-written paragraphs. Sid hadn't left out many facts in what he had told me the previous evening. The only new information I gained from the reports were the dates of the incidents. The first trapper went missing during the winter of 1977/1978. Trapper number two was rumored to have disappeared during the winter of 1978/1979, and the last trapper vanished in the winter of 1980/1981. Sid and two other troopers flew down to Henry's shack and discovered the human remains in May 1981.

I noted the gap of a year between the disappearance of the last two trappers. *Had Henry trapped alone during the intervening year, or had he killed another young man during the winter of 1979/1980?* I was beginning to believe the bones we'd found belonged to one of Henry's victims. *If not one of Henry's trapping partners, the victim could have been a hunter or camper whom Henry felt was trespassing on his land.*

I looked up from the file. *Wouldn't someone have reported this person missing, though?* I could understand a drifter not being missed, and it sounded as if most of Henry's trapping partners were drifters living on the fringe of society. *But someone simply coming to Karluk Lake on a hunting or camping trip would likely have family and friends who would call the authorities and report their loved one or buddy missing when he didn't return from his trip.*

I turned to the photos at the back of the file. Pictures of bones and jars of meat looked innocent enough until you knew the bones and meat were human. I felt bile rise in my throat, and stood and paced, fighting back nausea.

The bones we found couldn't have belonged to any of the missing trappers. The bones for two of the trappers were discovered in or near Henry's shack. Trapper one's bones were never recovered, but according to Sid, trapper one was short, and the bones we'd found belonged to a tall man. *How many people did Henry Aurman kill?*

A sudden thought struck me, and I slid my phone from my purse and called Ying Lee. She answered on the second ring.

Once I identified myself, I told her I had a question about the bones.

"Shoot," she said. "I'll answer if I can."

"This will sound strange," I said, "but did you notice tool marks or cut marks on any of the bones?"

"I don't understand," Ying said.

I explained about Henry Aurman and his cannibalistic ways.

"Yuck," Ying said. She remained quiet for a moment and then continued, "No, I didn't see any tool marks on the bones, but I'll take a closer look. I think it's a long shot I'll find anything, though. We probably would need to use a scanning electron microscope to pick up anything, and those are very expensive to use. These bones are already covered with marks from being exposed to the elements and animals, so it would be difficult to differentiate tool marks."

"Of course," I said. "I knew it was a long shot."

"Jane," Ying said. "I just thought of something. Remember how I told you this guy was emaciated when he died?"

"Yes?"

"Well," Ying laughed. "He wouldn't have made much of a meal for your cannibal."

"I hadn't thought of that," I said and echoed her laugh. "Thanks for pointing out the obvious to me."

1976

NOVEMBER 6TH
6:20 P.M.

Bently had no idea how long he'd been unconscious, and when he opened his eyes, he didn't even know where he was. He stared up at the starlit sky. He was freezing and in the middle of nowhere. He sat, slipped out of his pack, and rubbed his pounding head. Slowly, his memory returned, and he couldn't believe how stupid he'd been. He might have killed himself, and he probably did have a concussion. He stood and checked his arms and legs to make sure he wasn't badly injured. His muscles felt stiff from the cold, but everything seemed to work.

Schwimmer must be crazy with worry and fear by now. He didn't care about Schwimmer's feelings. He was sick and tired of the little weasel, but he was worried Schwimmer would be so nutty, he'd try to shoot him when he returned to camp. He'd have to make plenty of noise and be certain Schwimmer knew it was him and not the old man.

Bently hoisted his pack and then stood, staring down the mountain. He couldn't remember the way back to camp. His head pounded, and the pain clouded his memory. He began to sidestep down the mountain. Maybe he'd remember how to get to camp once he reached the base.

He shined his flashlight on the ground in front of him and took careful steps as he hiked. He followed the trail he'd forged up the mountain; no thinking necessary for the moment. Movement helped clear his head, and the pain subsided a fraction. He wondered if he'd die from the head injury but then decided there was no point in worrying about it because he couldn't do anything for brain trauma. His spine seemed okay, and at the moment, he'd rather have his spine than his brain. In a few hours, he might feel differently, but right now, he needed the ability to move so he could return to the life-saving warmth of his tent and sleeping bag.

He found his way to the glassing hill and then saw the trail back to camp. He forgot about Schwimmer until he was within twenty yards of their tents, and then he began calling his name. Yelling made him feel as if someone were crushing his skull with an ax. After calling Schwimmer's name three times, Bently heard the return bellow.

"Jay! Is that you?"

"It's me," Bently said.

Schwimmer continued to yell his name, but Bently's head hurt too much to respond. All he wanted to do was crawl into his sleeping bag and die.

PRESENT DAY
WEDNESDAY, JULY 2ND
12:50 P.M.

Patterson drove from his home to Trident Basin and the Kodiak Flight Services office. He hated to leave Jeanne alone even for a few minutes, but her friend, Lois, promised she would come over and sit with her as soon as she could get away from her job at the borough courthouse. She thought she'd make it by 3:00 p.m., so Jeanne would be alone a little over two hours.

When Patterson arrived home the previous evening, he found Jeanne sitting in the bathtub, a razor blade on the side of the tub. She'd made a small cut on her wrist before she called Patterson. Luckily, the cut was superficial and required only basic first-aid supplies. Patterson had crawled fully clothed into the tub, put his arms around his wife, and sat there holding her while they both sobbed.

He tried to convince Jeanne to go to the hospital, but she refused. She knew the nurses and doctors at the hospital because she worked there, and she did not want them to see her broken and defeated. She did agree to seek help from a therapist, but unfortunately, when Patterson called the office of the only decent psychologist in town, a recording informed him the doctor was out of town for the Fourth of July holiday and wouldn't be back until the following week.

When she woke up this morning, Jeanne told Patterson she felt better, but Patterson didn't believe her. She ate little for breakfast and immediately returned to bed. Patterson knew Jake's murder case deserved his full attention, but from worry and lack of sleep, he could barely remember what it was he'd wanted to ask Steve Duncan's head pilot.

Patterson parked in front of the Kodiak Flight Services' office and sat in his SUV for several minutes, gathering his thoughts. He pulled the notebook from his pack and reviewed his notes from the previous day. Unfortunately, he had been in such a hurry to get home, he hadn't written down anything from the afternoon meeting, so now, he struggled to remember what they had discussed. He realized he should have asked Mark or Sara to accompany him to this meeting. Either one of them would be sharper than he was now.

At 1:00 p.m., Patterson walked through the doors at Kodiak Flight Services. A large man who looked to be in his mid-thirties crossed the lobby and shook Patterson's hand.

"I'm Stan Edwards," the man said. "It's nice to meet you, Sergeant."

Stan Edwards stood nearly six feet tall and had a muscular frame and short-cropped black hair. He sported a tan, clean-shaven face, his chocolate eyes perched above a Grecian nose. Patterson bet this guy had his share of pilot groupies. He then noticed Stan's large, silver wedding ring and hoped the groupies were in his past.

"Thanks for taking the time to meet with me, Stan," Patterson said. "How was your flight down from Anchorage?"

"Perfect," Stan smiled. "I didn't run into any weather until I was twenty miles from Kodiak."

"It is starting to close in here now," Patterson said.

Stan nodded. "I'm glad I don't have to fly in this stuff. I'm off the rest of the day."

"Can we talk in the conference room?" Patterson asked.

"Sure," Stan said and led the way to the room. Once inside, Stan closed the door, and both men sat at the long table.

"Steve said you have some questions for me about Jake," Stan said.

"Someone killed Jake, either in a fit of anger because he or she hated Jake, or because he or she feared Jake," Patterson said. "My job is to find Jake's murderer, and right now, I am chasing every lead I have."

Stan nodded. "Good," he said. "I want you to find Jake's killer."

"What did you think of Jake?" Patterson asked.

"Sergeant, I will be as honest as I can with you because I have nothing to hide, and I want you to find the person who murdered Jake." Stan paused a moment as if considering his words. "I respected Jake. He had more flying experience in more aircraft than the rest of us combined, and he knew everything about airplanes and aviation history. I admired him."

"But?" Patterson asked when Stan didn't continue.

Stan sighed. "But, I didn't like the guy, and I avoided him when I could. I feel terrible saying bad things about him now that he's dead, but he was overbearing and thought he had all the answers. He hadn't flown float planes in thirty-five years when Steve hired him. Sure, he remembered how to fly the planes, but he didn't remember the culture, or perhaps the culture has changed since he flew floats."

"What do you mean?" Patterson asked.

"He wasn't flexible enough. You don't follow the same rules flying small planes in Alaska as you do flying 757s to Paris. Floatplanes and jets are separate beasts in very different environments. Sure, we have to follow FAA regulations, but sometimes a pilot is forced to fly in low-visibility conditions. You're a pilot, you know what I'm talking about."

"I understand," Patterson said, "and you're not the first pilot I've questioned who has told me Jake was inflexible when it came to rules and pilot conduct. I also understand he liked to lecture other pilots."

Stan laughed. "Oh, yes. I don't know how many times I talked to Jake about keeping his opinions to himself. He was especially bad lately, but Steve told me yesterday you informed him Jake had cancer and was probably in pain, so I guess maybe the pain explains his temper."

"Stan," Patterson said. "I heard a rumor from two different sources about Jake and another Kodiak Flight Services pilot."

"What kind of rumor?"

"I heard Jake caught one of the pilots here drinking alcohol on the job," Patterson said.

Patterson expected Stan to vehemently deny the rumor, but instead, he dropped his head into his hands. Then, he looked at Patterson, stood, and walked to the door. Patterson watched him as he opened the door and called to Charli.

"Have John come in here," Stan said.

"He's loading his plane and getting ready to take off," Charli said.

"We need to talk to him before he goes anywhere," Stan said.

"Okay," Charli said, "but the weather is deteriorating. If he doesn't leave soon, he won't get out of here."

"I understand," Stan said, "but we need to talk to him before he leaves."

Stan shut the door and returned to his seat at the table. "I heard the rumor, but not until after Jake was dead. I still don't believe it, but I've been watching the pilots carefully."

"You haven't told Steve?" Patterson asked.

"No," Stan said. "It's my job to take care of pilot problems. If I determine one of our pilots has been drinking on the job, then I'll go straight to Steve and insist he fire the offending pilot."

A knock sounded on the conference room door, and John Saner walked into the room. Without a cap covering his head and shading his face, Patterson noted Saner's short red hair, ruddy complexion, and light green eyes. Stan began to introduce the two men until Saner told him they had already met. Patterson extended his hand, and Saner shook it before taking a seat at the table.

Stan wasted no time getting to the point. He looked at Saner. "I need you to tell Sergeant Patterson what you told me you overheard Jake saying."

John's eyes widened. "About?" He stared at Stan.

"Yes," Stan said, "about drinking and flying."

"Okay," John said, but he still looked uncertain. Finally, he faced Patterson and began talking.

"This happened three days before Jake was killed," John said. "It was around 6:00 p.m., and I was done for the day, but we still had several flights scheduled. I fly the 206, and we didn't have any more 206 flights, but we had several Beaver flights on the evening schedule. It's light until midnight, so we usually fly until 8:00 or 9:00 p.m. if we have bookings. Anyway, I was walking to my car, and I walked past the big van, the one that looks like a bus, and I heard Jake's voice. At first, I thought he was calling me, but then I realized he was talking to someone else. He sounded really mad."

"What was he saying?" Patterson asked.

"Mind you, I walked in on the middle of his tirade, but I heard him clearly tell the other guy if he ever again saw him take a swig from his flask and then climb into his airplane, he'd tell Steve first and call the FAA second."

"You couldn't tell who he was talking to?" Patterson asked.

"No. The other guy just mumbled his replies. I stood there for a few seconds, but I didn't want to get caught eavesdropping. Jake sounded furious, though."

"Did you repeat what you heard to anyone?" Patterson assumed John was the source of the rumor he had heard from Jordan Gregg and Larry Mendoza, but he wanted to make sure it hadn't come from someone else who had also overheard the conversation between Jake and the other pilot.

John's gaze dropped from Patterson to the tabletop. "I told one other pilot, a friend of mine. He promised he wouldn't say anything." He looked up a fraction and checked Stan's reaction from the corners of his eyes. "I should have kept my mouth shut," he said.

"You immediately should have told me what you heard, and then you should have kept your mouth shut," Stan said, his voice low, his eyes blazing holes through Saner's bowed head.

"John, I appreciate you telling me this," Patterson said. He didn't want Saner to think Stan was telling him to keep his mouth shut now. *Is Stan telling him not to say anything more?*

"I know you didn't see the other pilot, and you couldn't make out his voice, but do you have any idea who he might be? Who was working that night and what planes were at the dock?"

John looked at Patterson. "I don't know. Most of the planes were there when I landed, and I think the only one that wasn't there was the plane Marty was flying."

"Marty?" Patterson asked.

"Marty Johnston," Stan said.

"Were both Rusty and Roy working that night?"

John shrugged and looked at Stan. "I guess so?"

"I'd have to check our records to be certain, but I imagine everyone was working at some point that afternoon and evening," Stan said. "Why are you interested in them?"

"I'll explain in a minute, but before John leaves, I'd like to hear his impression, if he has one, of who Jake was threatening behind the bus."

John shrugged. "I really don't know," he said. "I tried to figure it out, but I can't imagine any of the Kodiak Flight Services pilots drinking and flying. I wouldn't put it past some of those losers at Emerald Island Air, but not our guys." He looked at Stan for confirmation, but Stan's expression didn't change.

"Okay, John," Patterson said. "That's all I have for now." He handed John a business card. "Please call me if you think of anything else."

John took the card and stuffed it in his jacket pocket. He glanced at Stan, and when Stan gave a brief nod, John stood and rushed from the room.

Patterson looked at Stan. "Would you check for me to see who was on duty on June 24th?"

"Sure," Stan said, "but why did you ask about Roy and Rusty? They are both top-notch pilots, and I can't see either of them drinking on the job."

Patterson explained the cryptic entries in Jake's journal.

Stan nodded. "Yes, he was always writing in his journal. Even if he was in a hurry because we were behind schedule, he never left the dock until he wrote down the time and where he was headed."

Patterson pulled his copy of Jake's journal from his notebook and pointed to the entry Jake had written on June 24th: *R-DWF-S?-FAA?*

Stan studied the string of letters for several moments and then shrugged. "I don't get it."

"We think it means R was drinking or drunk while flying, and Jake was trying to decide if he should report R to Steve and/or to the FAA."

"How did you come up with drinking while flying?" Stan asked.

"From the rumor we heard about Jake berating a pilot for drinking on the job and from other notations Jake made in his journal. He has one about a guy who was drinking or drunk while boating, and he used the notation: *DWB.*"

Stan slowly nodded. "June 24th," he said. "The date fits."

"Do you have any pilots besides Rusty and Roy whose name starts with an R, either first or last name?"

"No," Stan said. "Just those two, but neither of them would drink on the job." Stan's words seemed more like a question than a statement.

Patterson thanked Stan for his time and asked if Billy, the ramp kid, was working.

Stan nodded. "He just returned from a little vacation. Check with Charli to see where he is."

Charli told Patterson he would find Billy in the warehouse, so Patterson exited the office and walked to the attached building. The space was mainly a large holding area with gear sorted into piles for upcoming charters. Patterson found a young man loading one pile of gear into a bin on a small forklift.

"Are you Billy Erickson?" Patterson asked.

The kid, who Patterson guessed was between sixteen and eighteen years old, wiped a strand of shoulder-length brown hair out of his eyes, stopped what he was doing, and looked at Patterson.

"Yes," he said as he took in Patterson's trooper uniform.

"I'm Sergeant Patterson with the Alaska State Troopers. Mind if I ask you a few questions?"

"Okay," Billy said as he slowly stood straight. The kid was nearly Patterson's height, but he was rail-thin. "Is this about Jake?"

"It is," Patterson said.

"I need to get this stuff down to the dock." Billy gestured to the gear he had been loading.

"This will only take a minute," Patterson said. "I heard Jake yelled at you a few days before he died."

"He yelled at me all the time," Billy said. "I could never do anything right for the guy."

"You were at Karluk Lake when Jake was killed?" Patterson asked.

"Hey," Billy took a step back. "I didn't kill him. My friends and me were on the river by then. We spent all our time rafting and camping on the river. I didn't like Jake, but I wouldn't kill him. I wouldn't kill anyone."

"Calm down," Patterson said. "I'm not saying you killed him. I have to ask everyone Jake interacted with where they were when he died."

Billy nodded, but he still looked as if he would bolt at any minute.

"Do you have any thoughts about who might hate Jake enough to kill him?"

"No, man. No one here would kill him. It must have been a random camper," Billy said.

"Billy," Patterson said. "You are the eyes and ears of the dock. You help the pilots load the planes before they leave on a trip, and you meet them and help tie up the planes when they return."

Billy nodded.

"Tell me how Jake got along with the other Kodiak Flight Services pilots on the dock."

Billy sighed. "Lately, Jake was always in a bad mood, so we all tried to avoid him. I couldn't help but work with him because I had to load his plane. I admit I was so sick of having him yell at me, I considered quitting. He yelled at everyone else too, but he usually reined in his temper when passengers were on the dock."

"Did you help him load the plane for his final flight?" Patterson asked.

Billy shook his head. "I was already at Karluk on my raft trip by then."

"Did you work the previous day?"

"Yeah, and Jake was in a terrible mood. He and Roy really got into it on the dock."

"What about?" Patterson asked.

Billy shrugged. "I tried to stay out of it. I was loading Roy's plane, and as soon as I finished, I headed back up the ramp before Jake could yell at me."

"Did you hear any of it?" Patterson asked.

"I think they were arguing about the fuel hose. Jake claimed Roy left it out, and it was in Jake's way. All Jake had to do was move the hose, but he liked to yell, so he yelled at Roy until Roy moved it."

"Was Roy upset?" Patterson asked.

"Oh yes," Billy said. "I've never heard so many four-letter words come out of Roy's mouth."

"Did anyone else hear their argument?"

Billy shook his head. "I was the only other person on the dock at the time."

"Do you remember any other big arguments in Jake's last days?" Patterson asked.

"No, man," Billy said. "Most people ignored Jake when he talked. If you didn't take his bait, sometimes he'd leave you alone."

Patterson thanked Billy and returned to the Kodiak Flight Services front office. Charli stood at the front desk, radio mic in hand, talking to a pilot who said he would be landing in seven minutes. As soon as she signed off, she looked at Patterson and smiled.

"Stan asked me to tell you both Rusty and Roy were working on the evening of June 24th."

Patterson thought about the argument Billy had overheard between Jake and Roy. "When is Roy scheduled to fly back to Kodiak from Anchorage?" Patterson asked.

"He's supposed to be back in Kodiak around 11:00 a.m. tomorrow," Charli said.

"Do you have any reason to think he might change his mind and delay his return?" Patterson asked.

"He'd better not," Charli said. "I have him booked for three flights tomorrow afternoon."

"Have you heard from him since he left the island?" Patterson asked.

"He called this morning." Charli turned her head to the side and regarded Patterson. "Why are you so concerned about Roy?" she asked. "He wouldn't have hurt Jake, if that's what you're thinking."

Patterson thought Roy possibly killed Jake, but to Charli, he said, "I just need to talk to him."

PRESENT DAY
WEDNESDAY, JULY 2ND
1:24 P.M.

"Marcus." My voice sounded harsher than I'd intended, but I'd written two-thirds of my exam and wanted to finish it before someone interrupted me again.

"Dr. Marcus, this is Air Force Major Kidwell. I'm retired now, but I worked in personnel at Elmendorf."

I forgot the test and pushed my desk chair away from the computer. "Yes, Major, thank you for calling me." *Did this man know something about a young airman who disappeared back in the seventies?*

"Major Fanucchi called me last evening and told me you'd found some bones and had reason to believe they belong to an airman?"

"Yes, Major. Along with the bones, we found an Air Force belt buckle. Anthropologists determined the bones belonged to a man in his late twenties. I know it's a long shot, but I was wondering if anyone went missing from Elmendorf back in the seventies or early eighties. The anthropologists think the bones are between thirty and fifty years old."

"I see," Kidwell said, "and please call me Anthony. I'm retired and happy to be so." He paused a moment and then continued. "I'm sure Major Fanucchi explained that anyone who took leave and failed to return would be labeled a deserter, and while we had a few of those during my tenure, they all showed up eventually."

"Yes," I said. "He explained that, and he checked the records and said everyone who went AWOL or deserted from Elmendorf during the seventies or early eighties was eventually found."

214

"I remembered something else, though, and this disturbed me at the time, but since it was none of my business, I didn't delve into it."

"Yes?" I stood and began to pace.

"This happened in the mid-seventies, but I don't remember the exact year. I don't even recall the guys' names, but they were two enlisted men who lived off base in Eagle River. They both recently had been discharged from the Air Force, and apparently, before they returned home, they wanted one last Alaskan adventure, so they applied for and were drawn for bear tags on Kodiak."

"For hunting?" I asked.

"Yes, for hunting. I learned this only after the fact, mind you, and I wasn't acquainted with the guys. The only reason I know any of this is because their landlord called Elmendorf when they didn't return to clear out their belongings from their apartment."

"They didn't return from their hunting trip?" I asked.

"No, ma'am. The landlord said they were giddy with excitement about hunting bears on Kodiak Island and told him as soon as they returned, they planned to move out and leave the state. I think they still had a few weeks left on their lease, but after the time expired, their belongings were still in the apartment."

"Do you remember the landlord's name?" I asked.

"No," Kidwell said. "If the complaint had involved active-duty personnel, I would have started a file, but these guys weren't even in the Air Force anymore, so I had no reason to write down the particulars of the call. It did bother me, though, and I gave the landlord the next-of-kin listed in their files."

"Did you ever hear anything else about the guys?"

"I called the landlord a few weeks later to see if they showed up to get their things, and he said they hadn't. He'd found the one guy's sister, and she said she and her brother didn't talk, and she claimed she was his only relative. The other guy had listed his aunt as his nearest relative, and while she and her nephew were still on speaking terms, she had no idea where he was and what his plans were, but she said he'd show up soon."

"That's it?" I asked. "They didn't have any other relatives?"

"Young people often turn to the military when they don't have much of a family life," Kidwell said.

"Do you remember what time of year this was?"

"Yes," Kidwell said. "I do remember the time of year because it was around the holidays."

"Winter," I said. "They must have gone on a fall hunt." I paused a moment while I thought. "Do you think if you looked at the list of men who were discharged in the fall from 1973 through 1977, you might recognize one or both of the men's names?"

"I tried," Kidwell said, "just before I called you. I'm sorry, Dr. Marcus, it's been too long, and my memory isn't great anymore."

"Please call me Jane," I said, "and I think you have a wonderful memory. You've been a big help."

"I'll call you if I think of anything else," Kidwell said.

"Thank you, Anthony."

"Oh, and Jane," Kidwell said as I was about to disconnect. "Will you let me know what you find?"

"I will," I promised.

I called trooper headquarters, and Irene told me Patterson had just walked in the door. A few minutes later, he came on the line.

"Jane," he said, "how are you?" He sounded exhausted, and I knew he must be putting in long hours investigating the murder of the pilot.

I told Patterson what I had learned about the two missing airmen who had come to Kodiak on a hunting trip and never were seen again.

"I guess one of those guys could be your bones," Patterson said, "but it's a long shot."

"Do you think I could find out who drew bear hunting permits back in the mid-seventies?"

Patterson forced a tired chuckle. "I doubt Fish and Game has those records, but it's worth a call to the Game Division here in town."

"I talked to Sid Beatty, and he told me about an old trapper who roamed Karluk Lake back in the seventies," I said.

"Henry Aurman," Patterson said. "I've heard about him. I'm not sure how much is legend and how much is true, but he did cause some trouble back in the day."

"If by trouble, you mean cannibalizing his trapping partners, then yes, he did cause trouble," I said.

"Did Sid confirm that rumor?" Patterson asked.

"They found human bones and jars of human meat in his shed," I said.

"Whoa," Patterson said. "I guess I'll have to pull his file and read it when I have a few spare minutes."

"I know you have your hands full right now with your current case, Sergeant, but I wanted to bring you up to speed on what I'm doing," I said.

"I appreciate you calling, Jane, and great work. I think you should consider a career in law enforcement," Patterson said. "You'd make a good detective."

I laughed. "When I get the boot from the marine center, I might follow your advice."

1976

NOVEMBER 7TH
8:00 A.M.

Bently heard Schwimmer call his name. Schwimmer's voice sounded muffled and a long way off, but he could feel him shaking his arm, so Schwimmer must be in his tent beside him. Bently opened his eyes and looked into the beam of Schwimmer's flashlight.

Bently buried his head in his sleeping bag. "Turn it off, turn it off, turn it off," he said.

"Sorry, man. We need to start packing up camp. Are you up to it?"

"Give me a few minutes," Bently said.

"You want some coffee? I'll bring it to you."

"Sure, whatever."

Schwimmer returned a minute later with a steaming mug of coffee. He handed it to Bently, who was now sitting in his sleeping bag.

"You never really told me what happened yesterday," Schwimmer said.

"Not now." Bently barked the words. They came out harsher than he meant, but why couldn't Schwimmer leave him alone?

Bently felt better after a cup of coffee. His head still pounded, but the cymbals were gone. Every muscle in his body hurt. He blamed the pain on his fall, but it probably was due to slogging through the snow for hours. How many hours had he hiked yesterday? He had no idea. He'd started hiking around 3:30 p.m. and Schwimmer said he got back to camp a little before 9:00 p.m. How long had he been unconscious? He didn't know. He also couldn't remember how far he'd fallen, but it had been far enough to give him a massive headache when he'd slammed into the rock. He refused to think about the monster bear, his bear. Maybe he'd be able to come back in a year or two and look for it again. By then, he hoped the old trapper would be dead.

He had to admit, Schwimmer wasn't as rattled as he'd expected him to be when he was late getting back to camp. Schwimmer was concerned and slightly agitated, but he was ready with a fire and a warm beverage, and then he'd helped Bently into his tent. Maybe Schwimmer was wishing the old man had killed him. Schwimmer was probably as sick of him as he was of Schwimmer. Bently couldn't wait to climb onto the airplane and get back to Anchorage. Soon, he would never again have to talk to Schwimmer.

PRESENT DAY
WEDNESDAY, JULY 2ND
3:00 P.M.

Patterson stood at the head of the conference room table and waited for his troopers to take their seats. He moved the time of the daily meeting from 4:00 p.m. to 3:00 p.m. so he could get home early. He went home once during the day to check on Jeanne and was relieved to find Jeanne's friend, Lois, sitting by her bedside. He could tell both women had been crying, but when he looked in on them, they were locked in quiet conversation. Lois told Patterson she'd taken off early from work and had nothing important to do the rest of the day and would be happy to spend the afternoon and evening with Jeanne. Patterson appreciated Lois' offer, but it was his job to sit beside Jeanne and watch over her until she passed through this depression. *She would pass through it, wouldn't she?*

Patterson looked around the table. Everyone except Peter Boyle was present. Boyle was still following Brian Decker around Anchorage, but Patterson had just spoken to him and told him to return to Kodiak. Decker had done nothing unusual, and the longer Boyle watched the young man, the less Decker seemed like a killer.

Patterson told the group what he had learned at Kodiak Flight Services.

"Do you think it's safe to wait for Roy to return to Kodiak?" Traner asked.

"I think so," Patterson said. "I asked Charli if she talked to Roy again not to tell him I'd been asking questions about him. She didn't like withholding information from Roy, but I believed her when she said she would."

"What about Stan or Steve?" Traner asked.

"I didn't talk to Steve, but I called Stan when I got back to the office and asked him not to tell any of his pilots what we'd discussed. He seemed more than happy to stay out of the fray."

"If one of his pilots has been drinking on the job, he probably hopes we will help him find out who it is," Simpton said. "If Kodiak Flight Services has an accident with a drunk pilot, they'll all be out of jobs."

"Do you want us to ask around about Roy?" Sara asked. "We could talk to bartenders and other pilots."

"No," Patterson said. "I don't want someone spooking Roy before he gets back to Kodiak. Let's lay low until we can bring him in for questioning tomorrow. He is supposed to arrive in Kodiak at 11:03 on Ravn. Mark and Brad, do you want to help me greet him at the airport? We'll bring him back here for questioning."

Both men nodded, and Patterson glanced down at his notes and then around the table at the assembled troopers. "Do we have anything else today?"

"Yes," Sara said. "Jake's remains were cremated in Anchorage, and Inga left late this morning to collect them and take them to Atlanta. She hired someone here in Kodiak to pack up their house. She earmarked a few things she wants to have shipped to Atlanta, but she wants everything else either given to Goodwill or destroyed. She has already put the house on the market."

"She's put Kodiak in her rearview mirror," Simpton said.

"Should we get a warrant to go through the house before everything is gone?" Traner asked.

Patterson thought about Traner's question for a minute and then said, "I don't think so. I can't imagine what would be in the house that would help us."

"Maybe his old notebooks?" Sara asked.

Patterson nodded slowly. "Get a warrant for those. I hope we don't have to decipher thirty years' worth of Jake's notebooks, but we should have them here in case we need them."

"If there's nothing else," Patterson said, "I want you all to go home as soon as your shifts are over. We'll start fresh again tomorrow and find out what Roy Tayler has to say for himself. Maybe we'll get lucky and tie up this case before the Fourth of July."

1976

Schwimmer paced up and down the beach, occasionally stopping to skip rocks across the water. His pacing grew faster and faster as the hours passed. Bently reclined against his duffel bag, trying to sleep but unable to do so because of the noise Schwimmer was making.

"Where are they?" Schwimmer asked for at least the tenth time. "The weather is fine. They should have been here hours ago."

Although clouds filled the sky, the ceiling and visibility were good, and only a gentle breeze caressed the lake.

"The weather could be bad in Kodiak. Maybe it's snowing or something. If they can't see, they can't fly," Bently said. "If they don't come soon, we'd better set up our tents again and prepare to spend another night. Thanks to you, we won't have anything to eat."

"Don't start, man."

"Don't tell me not to start," Bently said. "If we get stuck here several days, you'll hear a lot more from me on the subject."

"We've got more to worry about than food," Schwimmer said.

"And what in your opinion is more worrisome than starving to death?"

"The old man." Schwimmer stopped and sat beside Bently. "He said he'd kill us if we didn't leave today."

Bently had nearly forgotten about the old trapper. His head still hurt, and the pain was pushing everything else out of his brain.

"What's he gonna do?" Bently asked. "We can't leave if the plane doesn't come to pick us up."

"I don't care. He said we had to be gone."

"You're making my head hurt worse. Settle down and stop acting like such a schoolgirl."

PRESENT DAY
WEDNESDAY, JULY 2ND
6:47 P.M.

I arrived early at Henry's and found Sid waiting for me at one of the tables in the bar. He stood as I approached his table.

"I ordered a beer," he pointed to his mug. "What would you like?"

As if on cue, the waitress arrived and took my order for a glass of merlot.

"Are you hungry?" Sid asked.

"No," I lied. I'd worked late at my office and had driven straight from there to Henry's. By now, I figured Sid had eaten, though, and I didn't want him to sit and watch me eat.

"I had a bite to eat on the boat," Sid said. "I gave some friends a ride to their cabin in Kupreanof this afternoon, and I ate on the ride back to Kodiak."

We chatted about Sid's six-hour boat trip to drop off his friends and return to town, and he told me about the whales and sea otters he saw. His descriptions made me want to get out of town again. Except for my whirlwind trip to Anchorage, I hadn't set foot outside the Kodiak city limits since my flight to Karluk Lake with Patterson to check out the bones. I hadn't even driven out to Bell's Flats to visit my friend Dana in several weeks. I'd been stuck in the grind of work and obsessed with a pile of bones. *I wouldn't mind taking a trip on Sid's boat with him.* I pulled myself back to the present with a jolt.

"You said you remembered something else from the 1970s that might pertain to my bones?" I asked. The waitress deposited a glass of wine in front of me, and I took a grateful swallow.

Jake wore a black Henley and black jeans. He was clean-shaven today, his gray hair neatly combed back from his face. I could see he'd put effort into his appearance. Had he done this for me, or did he always try to look his best when meeting someone for a drink?

He smiled at me and took a long draw of beer. "This is the type of information a trooper considers suspect when he hears it, and I probably shouldn't be wasting your time with it now. To be honest, I'm not sure why I even remember it. I'm getting to the age where I can't remember if I ate breakfast, but I recall in great detail something my mother told me fifty years ago." He laughed. "Luckily for you, you won't have to deal with memory issues for a long time."

I felt my face grow hot and wondered if this was a subtle reminder about our age difference.

"Jane," Sid said, "What I'm about to tell you was a vague rumor back in the mid-1970s, and I honestly only remember hearing it once. By the time I heard the rumor, it had passed through several people, and I no longer remember all the details of what I was told."

"I understand the disclaimer," I said. "I'll try not to put too much stock in it, but you must think it bears some truth to repeat it to me now."

Sid shrugged. "The rumor is from the right period and involves Karluk Lake, and those are my only reasons for telling you."

I wasn't sure I believed Sid. I didn't think he would remember a rumor for forty years unless he felt it held some truth, and the harder he worked to disqualify the rumor, the more I wanted to hear it.

"I don't know if I mentioned this to you yesterday," Sid said, "but like Sergeant Patterson, I am a pilot, and back in the day, I was the trooper pilot on the island." He shrugged. "This detail is only important because I heard this rumor through the pilot grapevine, not through my job as an Alaska state trooper."

"Okay," I said. The suspense was killing me. The harder Sid worked to diminish the veracity of this rumor, the more important it began to sound to me.

"I don't recall the year," Sid said, "but I overheard two pilots chuckling and talking about Jarvin Flight Service, a charter airline in Kodiak. I couldn't hear what they were saying, so I asked them." Sid took a sip of beer. "I think they forgot for a minute I was a trooper because I doubt they would so easily have included me in their conversation if they'd remembered I was a cop." He looked at his beer mug and chuckled. "One of the guys told me he heard a rumor about a Jarvin Flight Service pilot dropping off two hunters at Karluk Lake for a fall bear hunt and forgetting to pick them up."

"How could that happen?" I asked.

Sid shrugged. "It shouldn't have happened, and it probably didn't. It makes a good story, and Jarvin Flight Service was having its share of problems at the time. Old man Jarvin, I can't remember his first name, had serious health problems and was getting ready to sell the business. His heart was no longer in running a flying business, and once he stopped running the day-to-day operations, the company began to fall apart."

"But they must have kept a log of which parties they dropped off where, and when they were supposed to pick them up again."

Sid shook his head. "This is what I heard. The dispatchers and office staff at Jarvin Flight Service kept track of their parties by writing the date each party was dropped off and the date they were supposed to be picked up on a calendar."

While Sid drank his beer, I thought about what he'd said. "Using a calendar makes sense," I said. "Isn't that the way most charter companies still do it?"

"Anymore, most use a whiteboard to list the flights of the day, and then they keep a log on the computer plus a handwritten record, but back in the mid-seventies, no one used computers."

I nodded. "So, at Jarvin Flight Service, they just wrote their flights on a calendar."

"Yes," Sid said, "but not just any calendar. "They used a day-of-the-week calendar, you know, one of those calendars where at the end of the day, you tear off the page and throw it away, and the next day's date is at the top for all to see. They wrote the pickup date for a party on the appropriate date, so on that date, they would see it was time to pick up the party."

I still didn't see where Sid was headed with this story, so I just nodded. Sid ran his fingers through his hair, a move so distracting, I had trouble concentrating on his story. What was it about this guy? Was he exuding pheromones? I felt like a schoolgirl with a crush on the teacher.

"According to the rumor," Sid lowered his voice, rested his arms on the table and leaned toward me as if he were about to impart the juicy details of a current scandal and not a forty-year-old rumor. "When the day came to pick up the party of two hunters, it snowed all day with no visibility, so all flights were canceled for the day. At the end of the day, the helpful new girl in the office tore the page off the calendar and threw it away, but she didn't bother rewriting the flights on the page for the next day. That night, the cleaning staff emptied the trash, and the calendar page was gone."

"Surely they must have had a more permanent record of their flights."

Sid shrugged. "I would think so, but anyway, the rumor was these guys weren't picked up because the page listing their pickup had been ripped off the calendar."

"Weren't there other flights listed on the page? What about those?"

Again, Sid shrugged. "I'm sure they had other flights, but they must have remembered the rest and just forgot about the guys at Karluk—or so the rumor goes. I think such an action would be so grossly negligent, I can't imagine it would happen in the first place, and if it did, I think I would have heard more about it than just a hushed rumor."

"What happened?" I asked.

"I don't really know," Sid said. I called Jarvin Flight Service and talked to Jarvin himself. I asked if there was any truth to the rumor, but he denied it. By the time I heard the rumor, it was March, I believe. I flew over Karluk Lake and made several passes. I don't know what I was looking for, but I didn't see any remnants of a tent camp or two guys sitting on the lakeshore."

"What do you think happened to the guys?" I asked.

"If there is any truth to the rumor, I'm sure someone at Jarvin Flight Service eventually remembered they had two hunters at Karluk Lake, and they flew out and picked them up. Our office never received any complaints or calls from friends or relatives searching for two lost hunters. I contacted the Refuge office and Fish and Game, and no one I talked to had heard anything about missing hunters."

The waitress arrived at our table, and Sid requested another round. I was only halfway through my glass of wine and hadn't planned on having another, so I took a gulp of merlot and waited for Sid to continue.

"I never heard another thing about the incident, and I had no reason to use our limited resources to further investigate the situation, so I let it drop, but as you can see, I never forgot it." Sid's mouth curved into a sad smile. "If it really happened, those poor guys must have been terrified and starving."

I remembered what Ling had told me about the bones. She believed from studying the bone chemistry that the individual had been emaciated. *Could he have been one of the missing hunters, and if so, were the bones from the other hunter nearby, waiting all these years to be found?*

"Sid," I said. "The anthropologist who studied the bones my friends and I found told me the individual was starving to death when he died."

Sid sat straight on his stool. "Interesting," he said.

"Is there anyone left from Jarvin Flight Service I could talk to about the rumor?"

Sid nodded slowly. "The dispatcher from Jarvin Flight Service still lives here. She worked at the hardware store for years, but she's retired now. Her name is Abby Long."

"Do you know where she lives?" I asked.

"No, but she's a lifelong resident of Kodiak, so ask around, she'll be easy to find." Sid lowered his voice. "Be careful, though, Jane. Abby is nice, but she's tough. Tread lightly."

Sid and I made small talk while we finished our drinks. I could have easily enjoyed Sid's company for another hour or two, but when he offered to buy another round, I declined. We walked out the door of Henry's together, and I thanked him for his help.

"Let me know if you learn anything useful," he said.

"I'll call and tell you what, if anything, Abby Long says about the rumor."

Sid smiled. "Call anytime," he said.

Was he flirting with me? I sat in my car and slowed my racing heart and reminded myself of the man's age. Why was I so attracted to him?

1976

Bently sat in his tent eating a granola bar and seething. That idiot had eaten all their MREs. They should still have several left for emergency rations in case they got stuck, but Schwimmer ate them all while the weenie stayed in camp scared for his life. Now, a handful of granola bars were all they had. Bently hoped they didn't get stuck here long because the hungrier he got, the madder he got, and he made no promises about what he'd do to Schwimmer. Right now, he wanted to grab his rifle, blast the guy out of his tent, and blame the crime on the old trapper. He took several deep breaths and climbed into his sleeping bag. His head pounded; he needed sleep.

PRESENT DAY
THURSDAY, JULY 3RD
9:00 A.M.

I was stapling and stacking exams in the main office when Peter walked through the door.

"Jane," Peter said. "How are you this morning?"

"I'm great," I said. "I'm about to torture my students with an exam, so what could be better?"

Peter chuckled, but I knew he wondered if I was serious or joking. I'd worked at the marine center for two and one-half years, but Peter still didn't know how to take me, and I knew he considered me a loose cannon, a characterization I wore like a badge of honor.

"Just got off the phone with Corban Pratt," Peter said. "He said he enjoyed a lovely dinner with you the other night."

"Good," I said. "What about the grant?" I'd breathe a big sigh of relief when Peter had the Tamron check in his hand. I worried any false move I made might deter the Tamron people from donating the grant money, and I wanted to be free of the responsibility. Corban Pratt seemed like a nice guy, but he was not my type, and I feared if I rebuffed his advances, the grant money would disappear, and I'd be searching for a new job.

"They're thinking about it," Peter said. He paused for a moment and then walked closer to me. In a lowered voice he said, "Jane, let me know if you hear anything from Corban, okay?"

"Sure, Peter," I said. I grabbed the exams, hurried back to my office, and shut my door. *How did I end up in the middle of an oil company's grant?*

I finished stapling the exams and sat in front of my computer. I'd planned to call my friend, Dana, to find out where Abby Long lived. Dana knew everything about Kodiak and its residents, and I felt certain she would either know where Abby lived or how to find out where she lived. Before bothering Dana, though, I'd see if I could find the information online, and five minutes later, I had the street address for Abby Long. I looked at my watch: it was only a little after 9:30 a.m. I had plenty to do in my lab until my 1:00 p.m. class, but no one would miss me if I slipped out for a few minutes. The polite thing to do would be to call Abby Long and set up a meeting, but I didn't want to give her time to think about what she would say. I needed to catch her off-guard.

Ms. Long's house in the middle of Kodiak was not hard to find. It was a small house, and it probably had been charming at one time. Now, though, it stood in a state of disrepair, with peeling paint, a broken handrail leading up the front steps, and a dangling rain gutter.

I parked in the street and walked to the front door. I rang the doorbell, but when I didn't hear a chime, I opened the storm door and knocked on the wooden inner door. I waited several minutes and then knocked again. I had just decided no one was home and was about to leave when the door whooshed open with a jolt.

"Yes?" The woman who opened the door stood with her bathrobe cinched around her bulky frame, her short, grey hair wet and poking out like spikes from her head. Her bare feet cemented the impression I had just interrupted her shower.

"Sorry to bother you, ma'am," I said, wishing now I had called ahead to set up a meeting. "Are you Abby Long?"

"Yes," she said. Her deep voice portrayed an air of calm, but her frown betrayed her impatience.

"You used to work for Jarvin Flight Service?" I asked.

Her eyebrows lifted, and her eyes widened. "Yes," she said again.

I hadn't prepared for this conversation, and now I feared I might never get through Abby Long's front door.

I introduced myself and then said, "This is a long story, but I'd like to ask you a few questions if it's okay."

I expected Abby Long to shut the door in my face, but she pushed it open and motioned me inside.

"Have a seat," she called over her shoulder. "I was in the shower. I need to dry my hair."

I looked around Ms. Long's front room. A large brown, woven rug covered most of the hardwood floor, and a couch and easy chair dominated the center of the room. Both pieces of furniture faced a large, flat-screen TV, and framed photographs covered the shelves on either side of the TV. Some of the photos appeared yellow with age, while others seemed more recent. I guessed the smiling subjects in the photos represented Abby Long's family. Now, though, it appeared she lived alone.

I settled on the couch and noted a basket of knitting nestled against the easy chair. A half-read romance novel lay on the table next to the chair. Through an open door, I saw a corner of the stove in the kitchen.

Ms. Long returned and sat in the easy chair. She hadn't done much to alter her appearance. She still wore her robe, and it looked as if she'd used a towel to dry her hair and then hadn't bothered to comb it. It now stuck out from her head like a fuzzy, gray halo. Large red glasses perched on her nose and pink slippers encased her feet. I couldn't tell if she wore clothes under her robe.

"What did you say your name is?" Abby Long asked.

"I'm Jane Marcus." I sat forward on the couch and faced her chair. "I'm sorry to bother you, Ms. Long, but I'm helping the troopers with a case, and I have a few questions you might be able to answer."

"Are you a coroner?" she asked.

I laughed. "No, I'm a fish biologist. I work at the marine center. I was camping with friends at Karluk Lake a little over a month ago, and we stumbled across human remains. At first, we thought they might be ancient, but we sent them to a forensic anthropologist and learned they are between thirty and fifty years old."

Abby Long nodded slowly, her black eyes magnified by her thick glasses. "I don't know how I can help you with old bones," she said. Her voice wavered.

Suddenly, Ms. Long jumped from her chair with more speed than I thought possible for her large frame. "I forgot my manners," she said. "I need a glass of water; can I get you anything? No coffee. I can't drink it due to a bad stomach, so I don't keep it in the house."

"Thank you, Ms. Long, water sounds fine."

"Call me Abby," she called over her shoulder as she walked into the kitchen.

Did my question rattle her? If so, maybe this isn't such a crazy rumor.

Abby returned with two large glasses of ice water and handed me one. I took a sip and then set the glass on the coaster on the coffee table.

"Since I was the one who asked Sergeant Patterson with the Alaska State Troopers to take a closer look at the bones, and because I was the one who kept calling to ask him what he'd learned, he finally gave me permission to do all I could to discover whose bones we had found."

Abby drained her glass of water and set the empty glass on the table next to her open novel. "What did you find out?" she asked.

"The anthropologist told me the bones belonged to a young man, probably in his late twenties, and in addition to the bones, we found a watch, a knife, and a belt buckle. The belt buckle had the Air Force insignia on it, and the watch was probably manufactured in the early to mid-seventies."

Abby took off her glasses and used a tissue to wipe sweat from around her eyes.

"I talked to a retired major who was the head of personnel at Elmendorf back in the seventies, and he remembered two retired Air Force guys flying down to Kodiak for a fall bear hunt sometime in the mid-seventies. When they never returned to clean out their apartment, their landlord called the base to find out if anyone knew where they were, but they seemed to have vanished."

"They vanished?" Abby's voice was low, and her rosy red face had paled to a sallow gray.

I nodded. "Yesterday, I talked to a retired trooper here on Kodiak, and he remembered a rumor he heard years ago about Jarvin Flight Services dropping off two fall hunters and forgetting to pick them up." I paused for several minutes and let Abby assimilate all I had told her. "You were the dispatcher for Jarvin Flight Services, weren't you?"

"Yes," she said. She gripped the arm of her chair with a shaky hand.

"Is there any truth to the rumor?"

"No," she said, but then she began to cry.

I sat and watched helplessly while she mopped her face with a tissue and fought to get her emotions under control.

"After all these years," she finally said and sank back in her chair. She stared straight ahead at the black screen of her TV.

I don't know how much time elapsed while Abby sat comatose. *Is she remembering the past or thinking about what to say next?*

"It was 1976," she said after several minutes. She didn't look at me but continued to stare straight ahead. "I know because Dennis Jarvin, the owner of the airlines, shut down the business in May of 1977, and I had to find another job."

"What happened?" I prompted after several more minutes of silence.

"It was a stupid mistake," Abby said. "No, it was sloppy bookkeeping." She sat forward, pushed her glasses up on her nose, and looked me in the eyes. "I always blamed myself because I ran the office, and it happened on my watch."

"What happened?" I asked again.

"Besides myself, two younger women worked in the front office at Jarvin. We wrote the scheduled flights on a daily calendar," she said. "You know, the type where you tear the days off page by page?"

I nodded and felt my pulse race. *The rumor was true.*

"We dropped off two young guys at Karluk Lake to go on a fall bear hunt, and on the day we were scheduled to pick them up, the weather was too bad to fly. As I remember, it snowed all day." She shook her head. "Somehow, the calendar page got thrown into the trash before we rewrote their pickup on the page for the next day."

"Didn't you have a log of scheduled flights somewhere else?" I asked.

Abby sighed. "We should have had a permanent log, and we did keep a log of flights once they happened. The FAA requires a flight log. The problem at Jarvin was nobody was in charge anymore. When I first started there, Dennis Jarvin ran the airlines with an iron fist, and he personally followed the schedule and decided which pilot would fly each flight." She shook her head again. "I don't know if he was sick or just sick of the airlines business. I always suspected he had a drinking problem. For whatever reason, he gradually let things go to pot. It was up to the pilots and mechanics to keep the planes maintained, and it was up to me to run the office and the freight handling. Frankly," her voice rose a notch, "it was too much for me. I now know I should have kept a schedule of flights somewhere other than on a temporary calendar, but at the time, it didn't occur to me."

"When someone scheduled a flight," I said, "You must have written the drop-off and pickup date somewhere."

"Sure, when someone called to make reservations, I'd write it down, but then I'd immediately transfer it to the calendar, and the calendar was what I consulted on a day-to-day basis. You have to understand how many people make reservations and then either change them or cancel them altogether. When a person changed their reservation, I'd change it on the calendar. The reservations book was a hodgepodge of active and canceled reservations."

Abby's bookkeeping seemed more than sloppy in my mind. I believed it rose to the level of negligence, and I wondered if by telling me her story, she'd end up in a jail cell.

"I think what happened was one of the girls—and it wasn't me because I was busy doing other things—" Her fierce gaze betrayed her uncertainty of this fact. "I think when the weather was too bad to fly, one of the girls," she continued, "wrote the names on the calendar on the page for the next day but somehow missed transferring the Karluk group. Maybe she got interrupted partway through the job." Tears spilled from Abby's eyes, and she wiped at them. "I don't know what happened, but they weren't listed the next day. The weather was bad for a few more days, and by the time we finally flew, we were so backlogged with flights, we all forgot about the Karluk hunters."

"Didn't the pilot who dropped them off remember he had a party at Karluk?" I asked.

"He was in Hawaii for a month on vacation," Abby said. "By the time he returned to work, he figured someone else had picked them up."

I lost my train of thought for a moment while I digested Abby's words. *A pilot dropped off two hunters in the middle of the wilderness for a fall hunt in either late October or November and then left on vacation. Meanwhile, the charter office staff forgot about them, and the poor guys were stranded?*

"Didn't the hunters have any way to contact you?" I asked.

"How? People didn't walk around with smartphones in their pockets back in the seventies, and even now," she said, "cell phones don't work in the wilderness here. They might have had a CB or VHF radio with them, but I doubt it, and they certainly didn't lug a big sideband radio on a hunting trip. There were no such things back then as SPOTs or DeLormes or any of the other safety gadgets available today." She looked at me. "Back then, nobody worried about losing contact with the outside world for a few days, and even if they'd had a small radio, such as a handheld VHF, they only would have been able to contact an airplane passing overhead, and there's not much air traffic on the south end of the island in the fall and winter."

"Did anyone call looking for the hunters?" I asked.

Abby began to cry. "Yes," she said through her tears. "A woman called our office in late December. I talked to her, and she told me she couldn't locate her nephew. The last time she heard from him was in late September, and he had a bear hunt planned on Kodiak Island in October. She hadn't heard from him since, and she was wondering if we were the charter service that flew him on his hunting trip. I told her I'd check, so I looked at our flight log for November, and when I didn't see her nephew's name in the book, I told her he didn't fly with us." She blew her nose. "His name sounded familiar to me, though, so after I hung up the phone, I looked back at our flights for October, and there he was. We'd flown him and his buddy to Karluk Lake on October 23rd. At first, I thought our mistake was sloppy bookkeeping. I thought the pilot forgot to log the flight that picked up the party, or maybe I somehow lost the information when I transcribed the daily flights into our logbook. I couldn't remember anyone picking up the party, though, and while our office was hectic during the hunting season, you'd think I could recall the two guys stopping through the office to tell me about their hunting adventure."

"What did you do?"

"I didn't say anything to anyone the day the aunt called our office, but after a sleepless night, I told Mr. Jarvin I had no record and no memory of picking up a party we'd dropped at Karluk Lake on October 23rd."

"What did he say?"

"I remember so vividly," Abby said. "My entire body trembled as I stood in front of him and told him the news. I was afraid of Mr. Jarvin. He never yelled, but he had a smoldering type of anger. I expected he could be violent, the kind of man who holds it all in until he erupts. He told me to get the logbook and let him look at it. He then told me to keep my mouth shut and not say anything about this to anyone. By then, I'd already told my husband my worst fear, but I didn't tell anyone else."

"Did Jarvin fly out to look for the guys?"

"Oh, no," Abby said. "He hadn't flown a plane for several months. He didn't even come into the office every day. I know he talked to the pilot who originally dropped them off because the little twerp yelled at me and asked me why I left his party stranded. He made me cry, and I ran out of the office in the middle of the day and went home. Mr. Jarvin called me two hours later and told me to come back to work. He said they needed me. We didn't have many flights in December, and there was another girl working in the office, so I didn't know why they needed me. When I got back there, Jarvin made it clear it was my responsibility to help clean up the mess of the stranded hunters."

Abby struggled out of her chair and headed to the kitchen with her empty glass. I sipped from my own glass of water while I waited and wondered what the pilot found when he arrived at Karluk Lake.

Abby resituated herself in her chair and continued her story. "Jarvin told the office girl and the extra pilot on duty to go home for the day. Meanwhile, the pilot who had originally dropped off the party flew to Karluk Lake, and we waited for him to return. I was so nervous, and I can still remember Jarvin pacing back and forth from his office, through the main office and back again. He never said a word to me while we waited."

"How long was the pilot gone?" I asked.

"Four hours, maybe longer. It seemed like years," Abby said. "By the time he landed in Kodiak, it was dark, but luckily, he had a full moon, so he could see where he was going. I was worried about him, though."

"What did he find?" I asked. I was certain he had not found the two hunters because if he had, Abby would have told me this news at the beginning of her story.

"Nothing," she said, "just an empty camp. He brought back the tents and sleeping bags and other camping gear, but he couldn't find the hunters, and he said he circled low over the area until it was nearly dark."

"What did you do?" I asked because they must have done something to find the missing hunters. Still, I remembered Sid saying the troopers were never called to help resolve the rumored incident.

"Mr. Jarvin told us to destroy the camping gear, and he ordered us never to speak of the incident again."

"Why didn't he call the troopers to help search for the men?" I asked.

Abby wiped her eyes and blew her nose. "He said to keep our mouths shut, and I did. Except for my husband, I never told another soul until now."

"Do you think the hunters died?" I asked.

Abby shrugged. "I told myself they must have walked to town and flew home."

"From Karluk Lake?"

"I know it's a long way," Abby said, "but people have done it."

"Wouldn't the mountains be covered with snow by then?"

The tears continued to flow from Abby's eyes. "Especially that year," she said. "We had several bad snowstorms in November, so the snow was deep on the mountains."

"The pilot didn't see any bodies or emaciated men at their campsite, though?"

"He said he didn't see anything except their gear."

I pulled a map of Karluk Lake from my purse. I'd printed the map before my camping trip with my friends, and I stuffed it in my purse in case I needed it for my interview with Abby. "Can you show me on this map where the hunters camped?"

Without a moment's hesitation, Abby pointed a shaky finger at a spot near where I'd camped with my friends. She looked up at me. Blotches of red covered her face, and tears dripped off her nose. "Where did you find the bones?" she asked, her voice low and hoarse.

I pointed at a spot near where she had placed her own fingertip, and she let out a low moan, followed by several minutes of sobs.

I stood, walked to the other side of her chair, and picked up her water glass. I patted her back. "Here, Abby," I said. "Drink some water."

She took the glass from my hands and drained most of it. When she handed it back to me, I carried it to her small kitchen and refilled it with tap water.

She was blowing her nose and trying to get herself under control when I returned.

"I should have called the police," she said. "And I would call the authorities if something like that happened to me today. I was just young and stupid." She stared at the floor. "The truth is, I was afraid Jarvin would fire me if I told anyone, and that's a laugh because five months later, he shut down his business, and I was out of a job anyway. By then, of course, it was too late to tell anyone about the hunters."

"Do you remember exactly how long the hunters were in the field from the time you dropped them off until Jarvin sent the plane to rescue them?" I asked.

"We figured they'd been out there eight weeks," Abby said. "They probably had food for two weeks. There weren't any deer on that part of the island back then, but they could have eaten beavers and maybe a river otter. They could have survived for a while."

"If they knew what they were doing," I said.

She nodded. "I talked to them briefly when they came through our office, and I got the idea they hadn't spent much time in the Alaska wilderness."

"I'm guessing Mr. Jarvin is dead," I said.

Abby nodded. "Died two or three years after he closed the air charter service."

"What about the pilot?" Where is he now?" I asked.

"I have no idea," Abby said. "He was just a kid. He moved away from Kodiak before Jarvin shut things down, and I think he took a flying job somewhere on the mainland."

"What was his name?" I asked.

Abby glanced at me quickly and looked away again. "I can't remember his name," she said. "It was a long time ago."

"Did the aunt or any other friends or relatives of the missing men ever call you again?" I asked.

"No," Abby said. "I kept expecting the state troopers to march into our office and demand our books, but nothing ever happened, and so I told myself the men must have made it home safely, or someone would miss them and call the troopers. For a while, I held my breath every time the phone rang. Jarvin was nervous, too. Every day for the next two months, he asked me if I'd had any difficult phone calls, and I knew what he meant." She looked at me again and shrugged. "Nothing happened, though. Life just went on."

I thanked Abby Long for talking to me and told her to stay in her chair. She looked shaky, and I assured her I could find my way to her front door. I reached my hand out to her and received a wet, limp shake. I asked her if she would be alright, and she said she would.

My pulse raced as I walked back to my car. I knew I'd narrowed down the identity of my bones to one of two people. The hunters Jarvin Flight Service dropped off at Karluk Lake in 1976 must have died before the air charter service sent a pilot to rescue them. The man whose bones we'd found was emaciated at the time of his death which made sense because those two hunters would have been starving to death if they'd been out of food for two months.

1976

Bently untied the tent flap and shined his flashlight into the dark. He groaned. He saw nothing but the huge, white flakes directly in front of the beam of the light. He struggled into his boots and parka and crawled out of the tent. It hadn't been snowing long, but it was coming down fast. Before long, they would need to start brushing off the tents.

If this snow continued, they wouldn't get picked up today. Pilots had to be able to see where they were going when they flew over the mountainous terrain of Kodiak, and thick snow would render that task impossible. *Schwimmer will flip out when he sees this snow.* Bently slid back into his tent. *Maybe Schwimmer will sleep another hour or two, and the snow will stop.*

Bently was wrong on both accounts. Ten minutes later, he heard Schwimmer leave his tent. At first, he groaned, and then he cussed several times, with each consecutive expletive increasing in volume. Then, he ran over and began shaking Bently's tent.

"What's your problem?" Bently yelled.

"It's snowing!" Schwimmer said.

"Yeah, so?"

"They can't pick us up if it's snowing, can they?"

"Not when it's snowing this hard."

"We have to get out of here." His voice was a shrill scream.

"Calm down," Bently said. "We'll get out of here soon."

"Hey," Bently said a few moments later. "You still there?"

240

"Yes." Schwimmer now sounded glum and resigned. "Let me know when it stops snowing."

PRESENT DAY

THURSDAY, JULY 3RD
11:22 A.M.

Patterson, Traner, and Simpton stood inside the Ravn Air terminal watching the passengers stream through the doorway. Roy Tayler, his brown hair tucked behind his ears, entered toward the rear of the pack. He was holding hands with a pretty, young woman with long, dark brown hair. Patterson approached Tayler, and Traner and Simpton followed behind him.

Roy's eyes widened when he saw the three troopers headed toward him.

"Mr. Tayler," Patterson said. Nearly every eye in the terminal swiveled in their direction as the troopers singled out Roy as their person of interest.

"Yes?" Roy said. He stepped out of the line of passengers and seemed to be looking for a private corner for this conversation with Patterson. Privacy, though, was not a possibility in the small, crowded terminal.

"We have some questions for you," Patterson said. "Would you accompany us to our headquarters?"

"What's going on, Roy?" the young woman said, clinging to Roy's arm.

"It's nothing, Katy," Roy said. "Put the bags in the car and go home. I'll be home in a while."

Katy regarded Patterson. "What's wrong?" she asked.

"We just need to talk to Roy for a few minutes," Patterson said. "We won't take too much of his time, I promise." He knew he'd just lied to Katy. Likely, Roy would end up in a jail cell before the end of the day.

His words seemed to lessen Katy's anxiety. "Okay," she said. She dropped Roy's arm, picked up their two bags, and headed for the door.

Patterson, Roy, Traner, and Simpton followed her out the door and climbed into a trooper SUV. No one spoke on the way to headquarters. Patterson wanted to give Tayler time to worry and to wonder what they had learned about Jake's murder, and if they suspected he was involved in killing Jake. Once inside trooper headquarters, Patterson led Roy to the conference room, and Traner and Simpton followed. Simpton closed the door, and the men sat around the conference table.

Roy looked expectantly at Patterson.

"I won't lie to you, Roy. You have become a person of interest in the murder of Jake Shepherd."

"What?" Roy said. He leaned forward, arms on the table. "You have to be kidding me."

"You're not under arrest at this time," Patterson continued, "but I think I should read you your rights."

"Are you serious?" Roy asked

"Yes, sir, I am," Patterson said. "And this interview is being recorded." Patterson proceeded to recite Roy's constitutional rights to him. When he was done, he asked Roy, "Do you understand these rights?"

Roy sat, mouth partially open, eyes wide. Sweat beaded on his forehead.

When Roy said nothing, Patterson again asked him if he'd understood his rights.

"Yeah, sure," Roy said, his voice just a whisper.

"Would you like to call an attorney before you're questioned?"

Again, Roy said nothing but looked dazed.

"Sir?" Patterson asked.

"What? No, I don't need a lawyer. I haven't done anything wrong." His voice rose in volume as he seemed to regain his equilibrium.

"We have a witness who saw you flying low over the lake near the time when Jake was murdered," Patterson said.

Roy shrugged. "I flew to Karluk that morning, and I probably was over the lake near the time when Jake was killed."

"Our witness said you were so low, he believed you had either just taken off or were coming in for a landing," Patterson said.

"What? I wasn't that low." Roy said. "I was at least five hundred feet in the air."

"You didn't land when you saw Jake's plane, perhaps to have a chat with him?" Patterson asked.

"No way. I didn't have anything to talk to Jake about," Roy said, "and if I wanted to talk to him, I'd just call him on the radio."

"You didn't pre-arrange a meeting at the lake with Jake so you could work out an issue between the two of you?" Patterson asked.

Traner and Simpton sat quietly while they watched Patterson carefully maneuver Roy into a corner and hopefully wrangle a confession out of him.

"I didn't have an issue with Jake," Roy said.

"Billy, the kid who loads and unloads the planes, told me you and Jake had quite an argument on the dock the day before Jake was killed," Patterson said.

Roy ran his fingers up his forehead and through his long hair. "Oh, that," he said. "It was nothing. I just lost my temper with Jake for carrying on about his usual nonsense. I mean, the man couldn't overlook anything. If the least little thing irritated him, he had to say something. He couldn't let anything go."

"What irritated him this time?" Patterson asked.

"Apparently, I left the fuel hose in his way on the dock, so he gave me a lecture about putting it away properly. Normally, I would have ignored him, but I was in a bad mood, so I yelled at him. The next day, I felt terrible when I heard he'd been killed. I hated to think some of my last words with Jake were words of anger." Roy sighed. "It's like I told you before. Jake could be incredibly irritating, but the guy was my inspiration. He knew more about flying and airplanes than I'll ever know, and he thought I was a good pilot." Roy brushed a tear from his cheek. "I liked to believe he was hard on me because he saw real potential in me."

"Tell me about the morning Jake was killed," Patterson said.

Roy sat back and rubbed his temples. "It was a tough day," he said. "My girlfriend and her four-year-old son live with me. He's a good kid, but he's hyperactive. Katy and I had a fight, and I guess Jackson, her son, heard us. I thought he was asleep, but we got kind of loud. Anyway, the fight apparently upset him. He went back to sleep after our fight ended, but he woke up again in the middle of the night, got out of bed, got disoriented, and fell down the stairs, all twelve of them. Luckily, he just broke his arm, but Katy was a mess. I felt bad, of course, because we had been fighting. We drove Jackson to the hospital, and it took them forever to finally put a cast on his arm and release him. I ended up getting to work late and then Jake was murdered." Roy shrugged. "It was a terrible day."

"You knew Jake kept a journal?" Patterson asked.

"Sure," Roy said. "He wrote down every single flight. He wouldn't leave the dock until he'd recorded where he was headed and how many passengers he had. He was anal about that journal. I think writing everything down made Jake feel he was in control of his life." Roy laughed a sad laugh. "In the end, though, I guess he couldn't control everything."

"We've," Patterson nodded to Traner and Simpton, "been trying to decipher Jake's journal. He wrote his entries in a sort of shorthand, and it's a bit like breaking a code." Patterson chuckled. "He not only kept track of his flights, but he recorded the gas mileage on his truck, birthdays, and other day-to-day activities. It's the other notations I'm interested in, though. In the last few months of his life, Jake ruffled a lot of feathers. He fought with his wife, got punched by a lodge owner, scolded pilots, yelled at fishermen, and the list goes on. Some of his notations are easy to relate to incidents we know happened."

"Like him yelling at the Emerald Island Air pilots."

"Exactly," Patterson said. He reached into his pack and pulled out his copy of Jake's notebook. "There's one entry I thought maybe you could help us with."

Patterson pointed to *R-DWF-S?-FAA?* Roy bent his head over the page Patterson had pushed in front of him. He studied it for nearly a minute.

"I have no idea what this means," Roy said.

"Roy," Patterson said. "We've been asking lots of questions around town. We've talked to Kodiak Flight Services pilots and pilots from other charter services. In the process of questioning folks, we heard a rumor."

Patterson looked Roy squarely in the eyes, and Roy's gaze never faltered. His eyes were locked onto Patterson's, and they showed no sign of deception.

Patterson continued. "Two unrelated individuals told us they heard Jake caught a Kodiak Flight Services pilot drinking while he was on the job."

Roy's face reddened, and his eyes widened. "I don't believe it," he said. "None of our pilots would consume alcohol while they were flying."

"Someone who works for Kodiak Flight Services told us he heard Jake yelling at a pilot for drinking on the job," Patterson said.

"Who?" Roy asked.

"They were behind a bus," Patterson said. "He couldn't see Jake or the pilot. He could make out Jake's voice, but the pilot spoke in a mumble, and he couldn't identify the individual."

Roy's eyes dropped to the table, and he seemed to be lost in thought. Then, he looked at Patterson and shook his head. "I can't help you. I have no idea who would drink on the job. If you were talking about another outfit, like Emerald Island Air, I could believe this, but I can't imagine any Kodiak Flight Services pilot who would be careless enough to drink and fly. If Steve found out, he'd fire the pilot on the spot."

"Roy," Patterson said. He tapped his fingers on the copy of Jake's journal. "We think this entry means pilot 'R' was drinking while flying, and then Jake questions whether he should report the pilot to Steve or even possibly the FAA."

Roy again studied the entry on the page. It took him a few moments to process what Patterson had just said, but then, his head whipped up, his mouth open. "You think 'R' is me?"

Patterson shrugged. "You were seen flying very low at the time and near the spot where Jake was killed. If you feared Jake was about to report you for drinking on the job, then you had a good motive to kill him. A citation for flying passengers while impaired would ruin a future in aviation for you."

Roy stabbed his finger at the copy of Jake's journal. "This isn't me," he said. "I don't even drink alcohol. I don't take drugs. I don't put anything in my body that could mess with my mind. Katy, Jackson, and a career in aviation are my life, and I love it. I plan to be—no, I will be a pilot for the rest of my life."

It was time for Patterson to play his trump card. "Roy, why were you at Karluk Lake on the morning Jake was killed?"

"What?" Roy asked. "I had a flight to Karluk to drop off people."

"According to the schedule Charli showed me," Patterson said, "your charter that morning was to Uyak Bay, not Karluk Lake."

Roy looked confused for a moment, and then his eyes focused. "Wait a minute," he said, "I wasn't flying my plane that morning."

"What do you mean?" Patterson asked.

"Jackson broke his arm, and it took forever at the hospital. I thought I could still make it in time for my 8:45 a.m. flight, but I knew I should help get Jackson home and settled, so I called Rusty and asked him if he'd mind changing flights."

"Rusty flew your plane?" Patterson asked. Wheels churned in his mind. "Why didn't he fly his plane?"

"My plane was already loaded with the freight for Uyak, so it was easier for him to take it instead of unloading my plane and loading the gear in his," Roy said.

"And you flew his plane?" Patterson asked

"Right," Roy said. His flight wasn't scheduled to leave until 9:20 a.m., so I had time to help with getting Jackson settled and drive to work."

Patterson thumbed through his notebook. "You flew N4414, and Rusty flew N4416?"

"Yes," Roy said.

"Is it usual to swap planes like that?" Patterson wondered why Charli hadn't mentioned this flight change to him.

"It's not unusual," Roy said. "We're always making changes at the dock. It drives Charli crazy."

"Would Charli have known you changed flights?"

"Maybe," he said. "We call base as soon as we're airborne, but we don't always talk to Charli; sometimes we talk to one of the other office staff. Charli can tell who we are by our voices, but Rusty and I sound a lot alike, so I'm not sure the rest of the staff could tell the difference between us."

It seemed to dawn on Roy he was shifting suspicion from himself to Rusty. "I'm not saying Rusty did anything wrong." Roy gripped the table. "But you need to talk to Rusty about flying low over the lake because I wasn't flying 16 that morning. I was in 14."

"You didn't land on Karluk Lake to talk to Jake?" Patterson asked again.

"I told you I didn't, and I didn't skim the lake. I flew over the lake at several hundred feet, but I already told you that, and I told you what I saw."

Patterson rubbed the bridge of his nose. This interview wasn't going the way he had planned. He thought if they hit Roy with this evidence, he would cave and confess, but the young man hadn't budged an inch, and now Patterson wondered why Rusty was over Karluk Lake when he should have been in Uyak Bay.

"If Rusty took your flight to Uyak, what was he doing over Karluk Lake?" Patterson asked.

Roy thought for a moment. "I have no idea. Maybe he had a pickup there. I really don't remember. All I know is I talked to Rusty when I was at

Karluk, and he said he was over the lake, or at least I think that's what he said. You'll have to ask him."

Patterson thanked Roy for his time. He escorted him to the front desk and asked Irene to find someone to drive Roy home. Patterson returned to the conference room where Traner and Simpton still sat, deep in conversation.

"What do you guys think?" Patterson asked.

Traner looked up at Patterson. "I think Rusty Hoak is our guy," he said.

"I haven't done a good job on this case," Patterson said. "I've been distracted by a personal matter. I need to check my notes and review the recordings of my original interviews with Rusty and Roy. I believe Rusty told me he left before Jake, but I thought he said he flew to Karluk. Why did he fly to Karluk if his flight was to Uyak? If he flew to Karluk after dropping off passengers in Uyak, it would tack another twenty minutes to his flight."

"Maybe he had a pickup at Karluk," Traner said.

Patterson shuffled through his case file until he came across the note Charli had given him. "This note from Charli says Roy left twelve minutes before Jake and flew to Uyak, and Rusty departed twenty-two minutes after Jake and flew to Karluk."

"That was their original schedule. Maybe Charli didn't know they switched flights," Simpton said.

"Or she was busy at the time and forgot to change their names on the computer log," Traner added.

"Let's take a trip over to Kodiak Flight Services and see if we can find Rusty. While we're there, I'll corner Charli and sort out where these two planes were when Jake was murdered."

1976

NOVEMBER 9TH
12:03 P.M.

The snow continued to fall and was stacked shoulder-high in places. Bently busied himself trying to keep the area around their tents packed down and a trail to the lakeshore open. He also brushed the snow off their tents every hour. He twice told Schwimmer he needed to take care of his own tent, and if he didn't, Bently said he would quit cleaning it, and the tent would collapse on top of him. Schwimmer didn't reply but remained sullenly in his sleeping bag.

Bently wasn't sure when Schwimmer's attitude had switched from paranoid watchfulness and high alert to giving up and accepting his imagined fate. Instead of pacing around their camp with a rifle, he now just stayed in his sleeping bag and waited for the old trapper to arrive and shoot him. When Schwimmer first saw the snowstorm the previous morning, Bently believed he transitioned from cracked to broken. Bently wasn't even sure Schwimmer had eaten today, which was just as well because they only had four granola bars left, and Bently wanted those. He thought he deserved the last four granola bars because Schwimmer had eaten several extra days' worth of food while Bently was hunting.

Bently knew he should sneak into Schwimmer's tent while the man slept and remove all his firearms and knives because if Schwimmer heard someone enter his tent, he'd probably reach for the nearest gun or knife and attack the intruder.

Bently hoped the snow would stop soon and the plane would arrive to rescue him from what was becoming an ever more dangerous situation. He wasn't afraid of the crazy old trapper. At least he wasn't too afraid of the old guy. His biggest fear was Schwimmer shooting him, and his next biggest concern was discomfort from hunger. At least they wouldn't die of thirst in this environment, but how long could they go without food, and how much crazier would a lack of nutrients make Schwimmer?

PRESENT DAY
THURSDAY, JULY 3RD
12:34 P.M.

Irene answered on the third ring. I asked for Patterson, and she told me to hold on a minute. I could hear her tell Patterson I wanted to talk to him, and I heard his loud sigh. Several seconds elapsed, and I expected Irene to tell me Patterson wasn't available, but he came on the line.

"Dr. Marcus, what can I do for you today?" He sounded exhausted, and I knew he had his hands full with the murdered pilot. Rumors about the case had ricocheted around town for the last several days, and the last I'd heard, the troopers hadn't made much progress on solving the murder.

"I know you're busy," I said, "but I learned something related to the bones." I told him about my conversation with Abby Long concerning the two missing hunters from 1976. "I think the bones are from one of them," I said.

"You've done a great job on this case, Jane; you're a good detective," Patterson said. "Keep in mind, though, those guys might have caught a ride with someone else. For all we know, they flagged down a passing pilot, possibly a private pilot from the mainland, and maybe they got a ride all the way back to Anchorage."

"Wouldn't they have called Jarvin Flight Service and told them they were okay, and what about their gear? Abby said all their camp gear, including their tents and sleeping bags, was still there," I said.

"Maybe the pilot who gave them a ride was in a hurry and didn't want to wait around while they packed their gear, or perhaps they were so excited to be rescued, they didn't want to take the time to pack their gear. They just wanted to get out of there," Patterson said. "I'm sure they were mad at Jarvin Flight Service, so why bother to call and tell them they'd gotten a ride with someone else?"

"I guess," I said, but I didn't believe his scenario. I felt certain the bones we had discovered belonged to one of the two hunters Jarvin Flight Service forgot to pick up.

"When I wrap up the case I'm working on, and things settle down a bit around here," Patterson said, "I promise to look at the information you've collected. I don't think we'll be able to make a positive ID on those bones without more information, though."

"I understand," I said, but I was disappointed by his lack of enthusiasm. I expected him to march into Abby Long's house and demand she tell him everything, including the name of the pilot who went searching for the lost hunters.

Abby Long's words consumed my thoughts the rest of the morning, and when I sat in the classroom and watched my nine students hunch over their exams, I wondered if the test even made sense. Had I collated and stapled the exams together correctly, or was each student looking at a muddle of pages? I'd received a few frowns, so the exam was probably too hard.

I watched the group of bowed heads and thought about the bones. I believed I could dig up the names of the two missing hunters. With the assistance of the current and former personnel majors at Elmendorf Air Force Base, I should be able to locate their names by looking through old records. Once I had their names, I could try to locate them. If I found them or at least learned they were still alive in 1977, then I'd I know I was on the wrong track. If, on the other hand, I found no one had ever seen them again after they flew to Kodiak Island on a hunting trip, then I could move forward. If the men had living relatives, perhaps investigators could use DNA to identify them.

Why isn't Patterson more enthusiastic about what I told him? I reminded myself he was embroiled in an active murder case, and he had sounded tired. Maybe once he wrapped up the case of the murdered pilot, he would become more interested in my leads and turn his attention to the bones.

Where was the other hunter? We'd only found one man's bones. *What had happened to the other guy? Maybe the one guy shot the other one in the head and then began hiking to Kodiak, but why, and did he make it to town and then leave*

ROBIN BAREFIELD

the island? Had the crazy trapper shot two men, carved up what little meat they had on their bones, and canned it?

My last thought made me shiver, and I must have made a noise because several of my students lifted their eyes from their exams and looked at me.

Patterson said I needed to find more evidence. *What type of evidence?* I pondered the thought for several minutes while I pretended to read the journal on the desk in front of me. Maybe I should go back to Karluk and take another look. My friends and I had combed the area near the bones, and Patterson and I also had searched the area, but perhaps we should have widened our search radius.

One of my students approached my desk to ask me to clarify one of the exam questions. When she returned to her seat, an idea popped into my mind. At first, I dismissed the crazy thought, but the longer I sat there, the more the idea began to take root and grow in my brain. *Tomorrow is the Fourth of July, and I don't need to be back to work until Monday. I could fly out to Karluk for the weekend and camp near the spot where we found the bones. I'd have several days to search for more bones or other items relating to the remains we'd already found. I might find something to aid in the identification of those bones.*

Who could I ask to go with me on the trip? A vision of Sid Beatty swam into my brain, and I batted it away. Sid was shocked and troubled when I called him to tell him about my conversation with Abby Long. Despite remembering the long-ago rumor, Sid didn't believe it was true. Now, he worried he should have done more at the time to investigate the whispers he'd heard between pilots about the stranded hunters.

I didn't know Sid well enough to invite him on a camping trip. *Maybe Dana would be up for a trip. No, Dana had poo-pooed the bones from the beginning. She'd ridicule the idea of searching for more bones and artifacts. Geoff would probably go with me if he doesn't have plans, but this is the Fourth of July weekend, and Geoff has lots of friends.* No, I decided. I'd go by myself. I had not yet warmed up to the idea of camping in the Kodiak wilderness, especially camping someplace like Karluk Lake where bears would certainly be roaming the lakeshore searching for salmon. I could test myself with a solo camping trip, and a few days by myself in a tent sounded fun. A rare high-pressure area was expected to settle over the island for the entire weekend, and I could imagine sitting on the lakeshore in the sunshine.

After the last exam was handed to me, I stacked them together and carried my things back to my office. I stuffed the exams as well as two biology journals I had been planning to read into my pack. *What better place than the wilderness to grade exams? Maybe fresh air would make me a kinder, gentler teacher.*

I wrote down a quick list of camping gear I'd need. This would be a no-frills trip. I'd fly to Karluk this afternoon and fly home Sunday morning. Would I be able to book a flight this late? This was a big holiday weekend so the air charter companies might not have any available planes for a flight.

I dialed Kodiak Flight Services, my air charter service of choice. They had a Beaver available for a 6:00 p.m. charter, but the 206 was busy all day today. I thought about it but then declined to book the Beaver. A 206 charter would run me $800 one way, and the Beaver cost $1,200 each direction. I didn't need the larger plane and didn't want to spend the money on it.

I had other choices of air charter companies in town with smaller airplanes, but Emerald Island Air was the largest of the bunch, and they had a 206 and a 185. I knew Dana didn't like to fly with Emerald Island Air and considered their pilots careless, but after hesitating a few minutes, I dialed the number for the air charter service. The dispatcher told me their 206 was available at 4:30 p.m. I checked my watch and saw it was already 2:30 p.m. and told the dispatcher I wanted to book the 206 for a flight to Karluk.

I grabbed my list of camping gear, zipped my pack, turned off the office light, and locked the door. I walked down the hall and knocked on Geoff's partly opened door.

"Yo," came the booming voice from inside the office.

I entered the room to find Geoff sitting at his desk with a pile of papers in front of him.

"Are you taking the weekend off?" I asked.

"You bet," he said. "I have friends from Idaho flying in for the holiday weekend."

"What do you plan to do with them?" I asked.

"Nothing special," Geoff said. "We'll cruise the road system, hang out in the bars, and maybe hit Dana's party on the Fourth."

I'd forgotten Dana and Jack were throwing a Fourth of July party, but I didn't regret I'd miss it.

"Sounds like a laid-back weekend," I said.

"You bet," Geoff said. "I'm looking forward to too much beer and endless laughter. What about you, Doc? You'll be at Dana's, won't you? I'll introduce you to my friends. One guy is a wildlife biologist in Idaho. You'll like him." He leaned back in his chair, tugged on his ponytail, and smiled at me. "He's not dating anyone."

I laughed. "Thanks, Don Juan, but I'll miss the party."

"Where will you be?" Geoff asked. "I hope you're not working."

"Don't laugh," I said, "but I'm flying out to Karluk Lake and plan to camp for the weekend. I hope to find more bones or anything else to help me identify the bones we found in May."

"Are you still working on those bones?" Geoff asked.

"I have a charter at 4:30," I said, "so I don't have time to tell you everything now. I'll catch you up on what I've found when I get back."

Geoff frowned. "You're not going to Karluk by yourself, are you?"

"I am," I said, "and I'll be fine."

"Doc, that doesn't sound like a good idea. Salmon have flooded the area by now, and it must be swarming with bears."

My stomach performed an Olympics-worthy flip, and I struggled to maintain my resolve. "I'll be fine. I'm taking a rifle and bear spray. The bears have their salmon; they won't be interested in me."

"Keep the pepper spray on your belt, and wear it all the time," Geoff said. "Rifles are a much better defense than pepper spray, but you won't have the rifle with you all the time."

"Pepper spray is also less lethal," I said. "I hope I don't shoot myself in the face with it, though."

"You're taking a satellite phone, right?" Geoff asked.

"Yes, and the phone is my purpose for interrupting you this afternoon," I said. "I hate to ask you this because I know you will be busy with your friends, but would you mind if we set a schedule for me to check in every day?"

"Absolutely," Geoff said. "Let's make it a morning and an evening schedule. "How about 9:00 a.m. and 8:00 p.m., starting tonight."

"Thanks, Geoff. I owe you one. Have a great weekend and have fun with your friends."

I walked to the main office of the marine center and approached Betty's desk. I saw her spine stiffen when I asked to check out a satellite phone.

"Is this for marine center use?" Betty asked.

"No," I said, "but if there's a phone available, I'd like to use it. I'm flying down to Karluk Lake to camp by myself for the weekend, and I've already set up a phone schedule with Geoff. He's expecting me to check in with him at 8:00 tonight. I'll only use the phone to check in with Geoff or for an emergency, and if I lose it or drop it in the water, I'll buy a new phone, I promise."

"I don't know," Betty said.

Betty and I had never gotten along, but this was beneath her petty nature. I crossed my arms and forced myself to breathe and remain calm.

Peter, whose office door off the main office stood ajar, must have overheard the conversation because he stood, pushed through the door and walked to Betty's desk. "Betty," he said, "for heaven's sake, give Jane the phone. We don't want her camping in the middle of several hundred bears with no phone to call for help if she needs it."

I saw a grimace fleetingly pass across Betty's face, but then she stood and disappeared into the storage room to retrieve a sat phone.

"What sends you to Karluk Lake?" Peter asked.

I shrugged. "It sounds like a nice, peaceful way to spend a holiday weekend. According to the forecast, the sun will shine until Monday."

Peter laughed. "I don't know how many years it has been since we've had a nice Fourth of July.

Betty handed me the phone, and I scribbled my name on the sign-out form.

"Are you heading out now?" Peter asked.

"I nodded. My charter is at 4:30. I'll have to hustle to make it."

"I'll walk you to the front door," he said.

I inwardly groaned and wondered what Peter wanted to talk to me about. The man always had an agenda.

Peter made small talk until we were out of earshot of Betty in the office. Then, he said, "I think Tamron is close to writing us a big check."

"Great," I said.

"Jane," Peter's voice dropped in volume. "Can I count on you to keep your head down until this deal goes through? Any publicity associated with you will be linked to the center. I know it doesn't seem fair, but it's the way it is."

"Sure, Peter, I have nothing crazy planned except a camping trip."

"By yourself?" Peter asked.

"I have a rifle and bear spray," I said. "I'll be fine."

"Please don't use the rifle." Peter smiled, but I knew he wasn't joking.

PRESENT DAY
Thursday, July 3rd
12:52 P.M.

When they arrived at Kodiak Flight Services, Charli told Patterson that Rusty was on his way back from a charter to the south end of the island. She expected him to land in Kodiak in twenty minutes.

"Don't talk to him too long, he has a busy day of flying."

Patterson could tell the charter service was busy. In one corner of the office, a group of five men stood next to fishing rod cases and a stack of twelve-packs of beer. A couple who looked exhausted sat on one of the couches while their four kids raced back and forth through the room, and an elderly man sat on the other couch, frowning at the parents each time the children ran past him.

"I hate to ruin your day," Patterson said, "but you should probably redo your schedule. We need to take Rusty back to trooper headquarters for questioning."

"Why?" Charlie snapped the word at Patterson.

"We have some questions for him."

Charli shot daggers at Patterson and turned to her computer screen.

"I also have a few questions for you, Charli, if you have a minute," Patterson said.

Charli gestured to the full waiting room. "Does it look like I have a minute?"

Patterson smiled. He realized now he should have asked Charli the questions first before telling her they planned to steal one of her pilots the day before a holiday weekend.

"I know, I'm sorry," he said, "but this will really only take a minute."

Charli let out a long sigh and lifted her eyes to meet Patterson's. "What is it?" she asked.

"Did you know Rusty and Roy swapped flights the morning Jake was murdered?"

"No," she said, turning back to the computer and punching a few keys. "I have Roy departing at 8:50 headed to Uyak, and Rusty leaving at 9:24 for Karluk." She looked back at Patterson.

"No," Patterson said. "According to Roy, his girlfriend's son broke his arm that morning, and when he realized he would be late for work, he called Rusty and asked him to trade flights. Is it possible they could have traded flights, and you wouldn't have known?"

Charli sighed again and then nodded. "Yes," she said, "unfortunately, pilots sometimes change flights and don't bother to tell me."

"But don't they radio the office after takeoff? Wouldn't you have realized which pilot was calling you?"

"If we have a busy office," Charli said, "and people are lined up behind the counter to talk to me, I don't always hear the pilots call, so someone else in the office answers the radio."

"Wouldn't the office staff know which pilot they were talking to?"

"Not necessarily," Charli said. "Roy and Rusty both have deep voices, and it's tough to tell which one is which when they call on the radio. I know their voices, but," she motioned behind her at the three young people working in the office, "we get a lot of turnover in office staff." She shrugged.

Patterson thanked Charli for her time and walked over to Simpton and Traner, who stood next to the coffee pot. Each man held a cup of steaming coffee in his hand.

Patterson picked up the carafe to pour himself a cup, but Simpton said, "I wouldn't do that, sir."

Traner shook his head. "Definitely not. I'm headed to the bathroom to pour mine down the sink. I think this is several days old."

"If it was made this decade," Simpton said, handing his cup to Traner. "Will you dump mine, too?"

Less than twenty minutes later, Patterson watched Charli respond to a radio call. She turned and looked at him. "Rusty is landing now if you want to meet him on the dock."

Patterson understood the meaning of Charli's words. She didn't want the troopers questioning one of her pilots in the main office in front of Kodiak Flight Services passengers. He nodded to Traner and Simpton, and they left the office and walked down the long ramp to the floatplane dock. With the low tide, the ramp tilted at a steep angle, and Patterson gripped the handrail as he descended. He did not want to be known as the trooper who rolled down the floatplane ramp.

The troopers watched two young couples jump from Rusty's Beaver and thank him for a great flight. They must have been flight-seeing or bear viewing because they had little gear other than a purse, a daypack, and a camera bag.

Patterson waited until Rusty's passengers began climbing the steep ramp up to the office before he approached Rusty. Traner and Simpton followed behind him.

Rusty was leaning into his plane, rearranging the seat belts neatly on the seats and replacing headsets on their hooks. When Patterson said his name, he turned quickly and looked surprised to see the three troopers standing on the end of the dock.

"Sergeant Patterson," he nodded. "What can I do for you today?"

"We'd like you to come back to our headquarters with us," Patterson said. "We have a few questions for you."

Rusty frowned. "Can't it wait? I have a full schedule today."

"I'm afraid not, Rusty," Patterson said. "I've already told Charli to give your flights to the other pilots today."

"But I'll lose a lot of money," Rusty said. "Can't you just ask me the questions here?"

"We'd like you to come with us," Patterson said. Patterson wasn't yet ready to arrest Rusty, and he knew Rusty could refuse to accompany them back to trooper headquarters, but Patterson didn't feel he needed to tell Rusty his cooperation was optional.

Patterson couldn't see Rusty's eyes through his dark sunglasses, but the glasses couldn't hide Rusty's red face.

Rusty ran his hand through his thick dark hair and turned to spit in the water. "Let's get it over with, then." He looked at Billy, who stood motionless, watching the exchange between Rusty and the troopers. "Take care of the plane. I don't know who's flying the next trip, but it will need to be ready to go soon."

Billy nodded. "Sure thing, Rusty."

Rusty stared out the window and remained quiet on the drive to trooper headquarters. Patterson led Rusty to the conference room where he had questioned Roy earlier. A carafe of coffee and a plate of sandwiches sat on the table.

Patterson, Traner, and Simpton each poured themselves a cup of coffee and grabbed a sandwich, but Rusty declined Patterson's offer of refreshments. Rusty propped his sunglasses on his head and took a seat at the table.

Rusty's eyes darted around the room, looking from Patterson to Traner to Simpton and back to Patterson again. Rusty's eyes were the color of a spring fawn, and while Patterson guessed Rusty was in his mid-thirties, his eyes made him appear innocent and youthful.

Patterson read Rusty his rights, but Rusty said he didn't want an attorney.

Patterson decided to start with an easy question. "How long have you been with Kodiak Flight Services?" he asked.

"This is my sixth year," Rusty said.

"Who did you fly with before then?" Patterson asked.

"I flew for Emerald Island Air for a year," Rusty said, "and before that, I flew for an outfit in Montana. My dream was always to be a floatplane pilot in Alaska, so when I got a job in Kodiak, I thought my dreams were finally coming true." A single tear slid from the corner of Rusty's right eye, and he swatted at it.

"What happened?" Patterson asked.

"What do you mean?" Rusty cleared his throat.

"You said you thought your dreams were finally coming true when you moved to Kodiak. Did something happen to spoil those dreams?"

"Could I have a glass of water?"

Simpton stood. "I'll get you some water."

"My wife didn't like Kodiak, and I work long hours, so I wasn't home much," Rusty said. "She left with my baby girl three months ago." This time, Rusty couldn't stem the flood of tears. He pulled his handkerchief from his pocket and mopped his face. "Sorry," he said.

Simpton placed a bottle of water on the table in front of Rusty, and Rusty screwed off the top and took a long drink.

"That must be tough," Patterson said. "I'm sure you are under a lot of strain."

Rusty nodded but said nothing.

"We talked to Roy this afternoon," Patterson said, "and he told us that the morning Jake was murdered, the two of you changed flights."

Rusty looked at the ceiling and seemed to be lost in thought. Patterson didn't know if Rusty was trying to remember what had taken place the morning of Jake's murder, or if he was trying to formulate his answers so he didn't incriminate himself.

"Right," Rusty said. "Roy was late because his girlfriend's son broke his arm, and Roy drove them to the hospital. He called and asked me to take his flight. I think the flight was scheduled for 8:30 or so."

"And you flew the plane Roy usually flies?" Patterson asked.

Rusty nodded. "I flew 16 most of the morning, and Roy flew 14. We finally traded back to our usual planes around noon."

"Rusty," Patterson said, "If you and Roy traded flights, then you flew to Uyak and Roy flew to Karluk."

Rusty blew out a breath and slowly nodded. "Sounds right."

"Then, why was your plane spotted over Karluk Lake?" Patterson asked.

"Because Roy was flying it." Rusty's hand flew through his thick hair, leaving it standing on end.

"I'm not talking about N4414, Rusty. The plane you were flying, N4416, was seen not only over Karluk Lake near the time when we believe someone murdered Jake, but you were observed flying low near the spot where Jake's body was discovered."

Rusty drained the rest of the water from his bottle. "I guess I did fly over Karluk Lake that morning, but I was just goofing off for a few minutes. Karluk is just on the other side of the mountain ridge from where I was in Uyak."

Patterson pushed the copy of Jake's journal in front of Rusty. "This is the journal Jake kept. He wrote everything in a sort of shorthand." Patterson said. "Does this entry mean anything to you?" Patterson pointed at *6-24 R -DWF -S? – FAA?*

Rusty stared at the notation for several minutes. Patterson, Traner, and Simpton remained silent, while the ticking of the wall clock marked the passage of time.

Patterson finally decided Rusty wasn't going to respond to his question, so he said, "We heard a rumor about Jake confronting a Kodiak Flight Services pilot for drinking alcohol while flying passengers."

Patterson waited, but Rusty said nothing, so Patterson continued. "Mark," he said, "Why don't you tell Rusty what we think Jake's June 24th journal entry means."

"Sure," Traner said. "We think it means, Rusty was drinking while flying, and Jake was wondering whether to tell Steve or report it to the FAA."

Rusty's body began to tremble, and for a moment, Patterson thought he was having a seizure.

Rusty choked back a sob and looked at Patterson. "I think I want a lawyer."

Patterson nodded. He was disappointed, but he didn't fault Rusty's decision.

"Rusty Hoak," Patterson said. "I'm placing you under arrest for the murder of Jake Shepherd."

"What?" Rusty said and jumped up, knocking his chair on its side.

Simpton and Traner hurried to block the door, so Rusty couldn't flee the room.

"I didn't kill Jake," Rusty said. He looked Patterson in the eye. "I couldn't kill someone."

"Do you want to continue our interview?" Patterson asked.

"No," Rusty said. "I'll wait for my lawyer."

1976
NOVEMBER 11TH
6:00 P.M.

Bently stood at the edge of the lakeshore, while Schwimmer sat on his duffel. It was 6:00 p.m. and getting dark. Bently knew they wouldn't be rescued today. The snow stopped the previous evening, and the skies had cleared. This morning, the men packed their gear, took down their tents, and hauled everything to the edge of the lake. They'd waited on the shore expecting the plane to arrive at any minute, but now, it was time to haul their gear back up the trail to the stomped-down area of their campsite. They couldn't leave anything on the narrow ribbon of shoreline where waves would flood it.

It took them an hour with the aid of flashlights to erect their tents and stow their gear. Bently assumed it must still be snowing in town or snowing somewhere between Karluk Lake and town, making it impossible for a plane to either fly through the mountain passes or skirt the outside of the island. He wondered how many days they would go through this routine of dismantling their camp, packing everything to the lake, waiting all day, and then returning to their campsite to set up their tents again. They only had two granola bars left, and they hadn't eaten yet today. Schwimmer already had given up hope and barely said two words all day. You'd think by now he'd realize the old man wasn't coming back to kill them. Bently looked for the trapper while they sat on the lakeshore and saw no sign of him. He didn't have a good view from this low vantage point, but he could scan the shore, and the shore was the only place the old man could walk in all this snow.

He'd tried to reason with Schwimmer and tell him the old guy was not a threat, but Schwimmer just stared at the ground and said nothing. Bently decided he didn't care if Schwimmer was scared, depressed, homicidal, or suicidal. Bently would keep his gun and knife handy and a wary eye on his hunting partner. When they got back to Anchorage, he'd move away from Alaska as fast as he could and tell Schwimmer he never wanted to see him again.

PRESENT DAY
THURSDAY, JULY 3RD
4:02 P.M.

Sara, Simpton, Boyle, and Traner sat talking and eating Irene's cookies when Patterson entered the conference room. As soon as they saw him, the four troopers stood and began to clap. Patterson couldn't quite manage to suppress a smile from spreading across his face. He held up his hands, though, and told his troopers to sit.

"It's a little too soon to be patting ourselves on the back," he said. "Without a confession, we have nothing but hearsay evidence against Rusty."

"He practically admitted to drinking on the job," Simpton said.

"Yes, but he didn't confess to it. Instead, he asked for a lawyer." Patterson said. "Even if he had admitted to it, the crime of drinking while flying passengers is a long way from murder."

"But you think he's guilty, don't you, sir?"

"I do think he's our guy, but I don't have enough evidence to hold him for the murder of Jake Shepherd. I have him on a forty-eight-hour hold right now, but we need to find more evidence against Rusty."

"Where?" Sara asked. "If Rusty doesn't confess to murdering Jake, we'll never be able to find enough to prove he did it."

"We can get a search warrant for Rusty's house and vehicle to see if he owns a gun that fires .30-30 ammo," Boyle said.

"Good, Peter. You're in charge of obtaining a search warrant," Patterson said. "Let me know if you need me to talk to the judge." Patterson scanned the troopers' faces. "Any other ideas?"

"We need to find more evidence suggesting Rusty has a drinking problem," Traner said. "If we can get Rusty to crack on the drinking issue, he might decide to confess everything."

"I agree," Patterson said. "This is a far from perfect approach, but I think we're more likely to find additional witnesses to Rusty's drinking problems than we are to Jake's murder. Look through his trash for alcohol bottles, check his truck for a flask or open bottles, and talk to his friends and find out if Rusty has been drinking heavily."

"We could also re-interview campers and rafters and ask them if they remember seeing the tail numbers on any planes over the lake near the time when Jake was shot," Simpton said.

Patterson nodded. "I think it's a long shot, but we probably should re-interview campers and rafters and ask again about planes. My opinion is most people don't notice airplane tail numbers unless they're pilots themselves or have friends who are pilots."

"Like Jake's last passenger," Traner said.

"Exactly, and he's the one who told us he saw N4416 flying low near the spot where Jake was murdered. Jason Meckel also told me he saw Roy's plane over Karluk that morning, so we should talk to him again."

"Maybe we should concentrate on radio communications," Sara said. "We've never asked the pilots or the biologists at the research center if they heard two pilots talking on the radio about landing for a meeting."

Patterson nodded. "Good idea, Sara. We did ask everyone if they saw planes over the lake around the time of Jake's murder, but we never asked about radio calls. Why don't you see what you can find."

"Wouldn't Jake have conversed with another pilot on an airplane frequency?" Simpton asked. "I doubt anybody on the ground would be tuned to those frequencies."

"Not necessarily," Patterson said. "The planes all have VHF radios, too."

"Still," Simpton said, "if two pilots wanted to have a private conversation on another frequency, they'd have to make initial contact on a standby frequency."

"Good point," Patterson said. "Sara, call Charli and ask her how two of her pilots would initiate contact for a private conversation, and how they'd hold a private conversation. They all carry sat phones, so maybe they call each other on those."

Sara scribbled in her notebook and then nodded to Patterson. "I'm on it."

"Mark," Patterson said. "I want you to grab a few troopers and organize a canvas of the bars and liquor stores in town to find out if Rusty was a frequent customer, if bartenders ever saw him intoxicated, et cetera. Make it clear we are not there to arrest anyone for serving alcohol to an intoxicated patron. We're just collecting information about Rusty Hoak."

"Yes, sir," Traner said.

"Brad, I want you in charge of finding and talking to Rusty's friends. If Rusty had a serious drinking problem, someone knows about it. His wife recently left him and took his little girl with her, so Rusty's friends must know he's having problems."

"If any of you can think of another approach for gathering evidence against Rusty, give me a call anytime. Also, let me know immediately if you learn anything. We're racing against the clock."

1976
November 15th
3:00 P.M.

Where is that damn plane? Bently's headache was finally gone, but his stomach roared with insistence for food. Yesterday, Schwimmer had refused to pack his gear and head to the lake for another day of waiting, so Bently had gone by himself. Today, though, even Bently stayed in his tent. If the airplane came, the pilot would have to wait for them for a change.

Could the weather still be bad in Kodiak after so many days? Bently knew the answer was "Yes." The town of Kodiak sat in a rainforest and near one of the stormiest mountain passes on the island. A winter storm probably could last for two weeks there, but he hoped it cleared soon. They'd already waited eight days, and his fantasies had switched from women to steaks.

PRESENT DAY
THURSDAY, JULY 3RD
5:15 P.M.

Geoff slid his phone in his pack and grabbed his jacket. He looked at the stack of files he should take home for the long weekend, but he didn't want to work this weekend. He hoped for a weekend of R and R with his buddies.

A sharp knock rattled his door, and he glanced at his watch. He didn't have time for an interruption; he was already running late. The jet should be landing in twenty minutes, and he wanted to be there waiting when his friends deplaned.

"Yes?" he called.

Betty pushed open the door and marched into his office. "I believe I heard Dr. Marcus say she has an 8:00 phone schedule with you this evening."

"That's right," Geoff said.

"I have a message for her," Betty said.

Geoff couldn't imagine what type of message Betty would need to pass to Jane on her camping trip.

Betty handed Geoff a slip of paper. He started to read it but returned his attention to Betty while she explained the note.

"Jane's Uncle John called and said he's trying to locate Jane because there's a family emergency. I guess he thought she'd be at work."

"Should I have someone fly out to Karluk and pick up Jane?" Geoff asked.

"I asked the uncle the same thing," Betty said, "but he said it was a situation more than an emergency, and Jane could just wait until after the weekend to call him." Betty shrugged. "I thought she might want to call him sooner, though, since she has a phone out there."

"Did you explain to the uncle she was camping in the middle of the wilderness?" Geoff asked.

"Yes, I told him she was camping at Karluk Lake, but I didn't mention she has a phone. I thought I'd leave it up to her whether or not to return her uncle's call."

"Good thinking," Geoff said. "As long as we have a good connection tonight, I'll pass this on to her."

1976

Bently rubbed his bruised right knuckle. An hour earlier, he'd punched Schwimmer in the nose as hard as he could, knocking the man flat and causing a river of blood to flow from his nose, coloring the snow crimson. Schwimmer hadn't even screamed; he'd just grabbed his nose, staggered to his knees, and crawled in his tent.

Bently now sat in his tent, his rifle cradled in his lap. He was expecting Schwimmer to arrive at any moment to try to kill him, but he had been sitting here for a long time, and he hadn't heard a sound from the direction of Schwimmer's tent.

Had he hit the guy hard enough to give him a concussion? Maybe Schwimmer had crawled in his tent and died. Why had he hit him in the first place? He couldn't remember. Had Schwimmer said something to him? Maybe he was just tired of looking at Schwimmer's face.

They had been waiting for the floatplane to pick them up for nearly two weeks, and they'd been without food for almost as long. Rain and fog enclosed the lake today, and he could understand why a pilot might choose to not fly in this weather, but before today, they'd had a long string of cold, clear days when it also must have been clear in Kodiak. *Where is the plane? Why had they been left here?*

Schwimmer had given up several days earlier, and he believed they would starve to death. Bently hated to admit it, but he was beginning to agree with Schwimmer. He kept expecting Schwimmer to kill himself, but he didn't think the guy had the nerve to do it. Bently had no intention of taking his own life. He wanted to live, and he would go down fighting. If only they had wild game to shoot. Sitka black-tailed deer were common around town, but there were few this far south on the island, and he hadn't seen a single deer since they'd arrived here.

The old trapper had not been a problem so far, and Bently suspected the guy was all talk and no action. He'd had fun scaring the Chechakos, but he had no intention of harming them. They had seen no sign of the trapper since he'd approached Bently on his glassing hill. The old man was probably miles away by now, trapping a different area.

Bently placed his rifle next to his sleeping bag and crawled into the bag for a nap. Anymore, all he wanted to do was sleep. He was getting as lazy as Schwimmer.

PRESENT DAY
THURSDAY, JULY 3RD
5:50 P.M.

I wiped my hands on my jeans and stepped back to examine the tent. It looked secure, but I knew I should tie it to a few more trees. Correction, I should tie it to a few more bushes. Except for scrubby alders, there weren't many trees here. I'd carefully studied the forecast for the next several days, and while no wind or rain was predicted, this was Kodiak, and I knew the wind could howl for no reason at all.

Once I stowed my gear in the tent and unrolled my sleeping bag on the pad, I decided to take a hike. I still had plenty of daylight to begin my bone search. Before leaving my tent, I covered my body with insect repellent, heading straight for the hard-core poison. I hated spraying the stuff on me, especially my face, but several mosquitos already had dive-bombed, and I knew the situation would deteriorate as the evening progressed.

I grabbed my camp shovel and hiked for twenty minutes until I found the area where we'd discovered the bones. I spent the next hour looking over the area we had already searched. The job proved much more difficult than it had in May after the fire. Vegetation had reclaimed the scorched earth, and I now had to push aside sedges, cow parsnip, and other plant life to look underneath it. I hadn't considered the vegetation would have sprouted and started to grow again by now. I should have left this task until winter or early spring.

My search seemed futile, and I was about to quit for the day when my eyes caught a glimpse of metal in a clump of alders. I dropped to my hands and knees and gently pushed aside undergrowth as I crawled toward the object. The trees blocked out much of the ambient light, and I hadn't brought a flashlight, but after ten minutes of careful searching, I found what I was looking for. Only the end of the object emerged from the ground, but the round surface with the small indentation in the center told me I was peering at a shell casing. I carefully dug the casing from the muddy ground with my shovel and moved out of the brush and into daylight. I knew Patterson would say the casing might be related to my bones, or it could be present here for any number of other reasons. I knew it had been in the ground for a long time because instead of shiny brass, it wore a patina of flat, dark browns and blues. If I gave this casing to Ying, could she or another anthropologist determine if it or one like it unleashed the bullet that caused the hole in the skull?

With a start, I looked at my watch. It was 7:28 p.m. I'd lost track of time. I dropped the shell into my jacket pocket and hurried back toward camp. Geoff would be waiting for my call at 8:00 p.m., and while Geoff seemed laid back, I knew him well enough to know he would worry if he didn't hear from me at 8:00 p.m. on the dot.

I'd been walking for ten minutes when I heard a loud "Huff," followed by breaking branches and pounding feet. I froze and held my breath. The bass-drum cadence of my heart pounded in my ears. Within seconds, a brown bear popped out of the brush, twenty feet in front of me on the trail.

The creature blocking my path could have been a huge Kodiak bear, a medium-sized bear, or even a small bear, but to me, he looked enormous. He lunged forward on his front feet, foam dripping from his bared teeth.

My survival instinct finally kicked in, and I dropped my shovel and fumbled at the bear spray canister on my belt. The seconds it took to remove the can from its holder seemed like long minutes.

Before I could remove the safety and place my finger on the nozzle, the bear turned, and after shooting me one last, disgusted glance over his right shoulder, he entered the thick brush and disappeared.

I began to shake so violently, I could barely get the canister back into the holder on my belt. I placed my hands on my knees, bent over, and took several deep breaths. I would not tell Geoff about the bear when I talked to him. The story would only serve to worry him, and I'd have to listen to him say, "I told you so."

I picked up my shovel and walked as fast as I could down the game trail. When I reached the fork in the trail, I planted the shovel in the soil where I could grab it the following morning when I continued my search. *Will I have the nerve to walk down this trail again?*

I followed the left fork of the trail and arrived at my tent with three minutes to spare. I removed the sat phone from its case and walked to the lakeshore and out of the brush, where I was more likely to pick up a satellite signal. The clock on the phone read 8:02 p.m. I waited several seconds until I had a signal, and then I dialed Geoff. He answered on the fourth ring.

"Doc, is that you?" From the background noise, I assumed Geoff had collected his friends, and they'd found a bar. "Hang on," Geoff said, "I'm walking outside where it's quieter."

A moment later he said, "This is better. Can you hear me?"

"Just checking in as ordered," I said. The usual static crackled over the satellite phone, but the connection sounded strong.

"Doc, I have a message for you."

"What?" I asked, and hoped Peter wasn't ordering me back to town for another dinner date with Corban Pratt.

"Someone called our office and talked to Betty," Geoff said. "He told her he's your Uncle John and he wanted to contact you about some sort of family emergency."

Uncle John?

When I didn't immediately reply to Geoff, he rushed to fill the silence. "Don't worry too much. He said whatever it is can wait until after you get home."

"He didn't explain the emergency to Betty?" I asked.

"No," Geoff said, "but if you have his number, you can call him on the sat phone and find out what the problem is."

"I don't know his number," I said.

"I can find it for you," Geoff said. "What's his last name, and where does he live?"

"Geoff," I said. "I don't have an Uncle John. I don't have any uncles who are still living."

Geoff said nothing for several seconds, and then he replied in a low voice, "Jane, this is weird. Why would some guy call the marine center pretending to be your uncle?"

"I have no idea." I reviewed the events in my life over the past several weeks, but I could remember no strange men. Except for my obsession with the bones and my call to duty to help Peter win a grant for the marine center, everything in my life had been routine. *Maybe one of my students is stalking me to find out how he did on the exam.*

"I don't like this strange guy calling to learn your whereabouts when you're camped alone in the middle of nowhere."

I shivered and wrapped my jacket around me. "Did Betty tell him where I was?"

"I can't remember," Geoff said.

I laughed. "I'm sure there's an innocent explanation for this. I'll call my Dad and make sure he and everyone else are okay, but as long as no one is injured or dead, I'll wait until I get back to town to sort through this."

"Be careful," Geoff said. He lingered for a moment, and I knew he wanted to say more, but he finally told me goodbye, and we disconnected.

1976

November 28th
11:10 A.M.

Bently awoke slowly. He strained his ears to hear if it was still raining, but he heard nothing. It felt colder this morning than it had the last few days. The constant rain over the past week had melted most of the snow. The rain had also leaked into his tent and gotten his sleeping bag wet in spots. He had to curl into a ball at the top of the bag just to stay warm and dry.

Suddenly, he opened his eyes wide and stared into the darkness. *Had he imagined talking to the old trapper the previous evening? Had the old man been in their camp? Was he still here?*

Bently grabbed his flashlight and climbed from his sleeping bag. He didn't bother to put on clothes or his boots but untied the tent flaps and walked out onto the wet ground in his socks. He swung his flashlight from side to side but didn't see any sign of the trapper.

"Terry," he called. When there was no answer, he walked over to the tent adjacent to his and yelled, "Schwimmer!"

He waited. Had the trapper killed Schwimmer? Should he look in Schwimmer's tent to see if he was still alive? He stood frozen with indecision.

"What do you want?" Schwimmer finally said.

"Was the trapper here last night, or did I dream that?"

"He was here." Schwimmer's voice sounded tired and weak.

"Why didn't he give us some of his food?"

"Don't you remember?" Schwimmer asked.

"No." *Why don't I remember?*

277

"He said he was going to let us starve to death to teach us and everyone else a lesson."

"What lesson?"

"Not to trespass on his land."

"I yelled at him." Bently's memory was returning.

"Yeah, and he nearly stabbed you. We have no chance of getting help from him now." Schwimmer's voice sounded more resigned than accusatory.

"He never would have helped us. He just wanted to amuse himself. He wanted us to grovel for food so he could tell us no."

"Whatever, man."

"Terry, I think we need to drink more water. Our cooking pot is full of water, so let's split it."

"I'm not thirsty."

"Hey, man, you'll die if you don't drink water. A human can last a long time without food, but only a few days without water."

"Okay," Schwimmer finally said, and Bently suspected he'd agreed to drink the water only so Bently would leave him alone.

A few minutes later, Schwimmer untied his tent and crawled from it.

"Man, you're not wearing any shoes," he said.

Bently looked down at his feet, surprised to see his wet, muddy socks.

"Aren't you cold? You're just wearing your long johns."

"What's wrong with your face?" Bently stepped closer to Schwimmer, studying his face with the beam of his flashlight.

Schwimmer reached up and shielded his eyes. "Get that out of my eyes," he said.

Bently quickly pointed his light at the ground. "Sorry," he said, "but what happened to your nose? It looks broken."

"Are you serious?" Schwimmer grabbed the cup of water from Bently's hand and sipped.

"What?" Bently asked.

"You did this." Schwimmer pointed at his nose. "You don't remember?"

Bently took a step back. "I did?" *Why had he broken Schwimmer's nose?*

"Man, you're losing it," Schwimmer said.

PRESENT DAY

THURSDAY, JULY 3RD
8:22 P.M.

Patterson was sitting in his master bedroom watching Jeanne sleep when he felt his phone vibrate in his shirt pocket. When he'd arrived home at 5:30, Jeanne finally seemed ready to talk, and Patterson thought this was a good sign. Thirty minutes later, though, she began sobbing uncontrollably, and he helped her to bed. She finally fell asleep around 8:00 p.m., and the last thing he wanted to do now was awaken her.

He tiptoed from the bedroom and walked to the family room at the other end of the house. By the time he got there, his phone was silent. He didn't recognize the number of his last call, but he pushed re-dial anyway. At this point in the investigation into Jake Shepherd's murder, he didn't want to miss any important calls, and for all he knew, one of his troopers had used his wife's or a friend's phone to call him with critical information about Rusty Hoak.

"Geoff Baker," the man said into Patterson's ear.

Patterson had to think for a minute. The name sounded vaguely familiar, but he couldn't place it in relation to the Shepherd case.

"Do I know you?" Patterson asked.

"Sergeant Patterson," Geoff said. "Jane Marcus is a friend of mine. I'm sorry to call you on your personal phone, but I had the number from when you asked me to send you the photos of the bones."

"Now I remember," Patterson said. "You two were together when you found the bones. You took the photos and GPS bearings."

"Yes," Geoff said. "That's why I'm calling you."

"I don't understand."

"Something strange just happened, and it might mean something or nothing, but I'm worried about Jane. Do you know she's camping at Karluk Lake by herself this weekend, hoping to find more bones or other evidence related to the bones we found?"

Patterson exhaled a breath. The woman was a pain in the butt. "By herself?" he asked.

"Yeah, I tried to talk her out of it, but she insisted. I just talked to her on the sat phone, and she's fine, but something happened at the marine center today, and I'm worried about her."

Geoff proceeded to tell Patterson about the strange call from the man claiming to be Jane's Uncle John.

"And Jane had no idea who this man is?" Patterson asked. "He wouldn't necessarily need to be an uncle. He could be a close family friend, someone her parents referred to as her uncle when she was young."

"Maybe," Geoff said, "but Jane couldn't think of anyone who would refer to himself as her Uncle John."

"Can you call her back?" Patterson asked. "After she thought about it for a few minutes, she probably figured out who the guy is."

"No," Geoff said. "I screwed up. I should have told her to call me back in an hour, but our next schedule isn't until tomorrow morning at 9:00. She doesn't have a sideband, only a sat phone, and I'm sure she turned it off as soon as we finished speaking. She'd want to conserve the battery, and she probably has to walk from where she's camped in the woods down to the lake to get a signal. When we were camped at Karluk Lake in May, we couldn't get a sat signal unless we walked down to the lakeshore."

"She does have a sat phone, though," Patterson said. "She can call if she has a problem. I'm sure she's fine but call me right away if you hear from her."

"That's not all," Geoff said quickly, just as Patterson was getting ready to disconnect. "I called Betty, the secretary at the center who talked to the strange man. I asked her if she told the guy Jane was camped at Karluk Lake for the weekend, and she said yes, she told him Jane flew to Karluk Lake to camp over the holiday weekend. She said the guy kept asking where Jane was at that moment. He said he needed to get this emergency message to her. Once Betty told him Jane was out of town and unreachable, he pushed her further, wanting to know exactly where Jane was. Betty thought she should divulge Jane's location and ask him if he wanted to send a message to Jane via one of the airlines. Once she told him Jane was camping at Karluk Lake, he suddenly downplayed the urgency of contacting Jane immediately and told Betty he would wait to talk to Jane until she returned to town. Betty told me she couldn't get the call out of her head and felt she'd made a terrible mistake by telling the man Jane's current location."

"Karluk Lake is a big area," Patterson said. "Betty didn't tell Uncle John exactly where at Karluk Lake Jane would be camping, did she?"

"No," Geoff said. "I asked Betty, and she said she didn't know where Jane planned to camp, and he didn't ask. Could this man have something to do with the bones we found?"

"Geoff, I'm worried about Jane running into a bear at Karluk, but I can't believe those old bones could cause her any trouble. I appreciate you calling me, but I don't think Uncle John is a threat. It's possible Jane has a stalker, and when she gets back to town, she might want to report the incident to the police, or at least take precautions and record her phone calls."

"I guess you're right," Geoff said. "I have an active imagination, and I'm protective of Jane. She tends to get herself in trouble."

Patterson laughed. "Yes, she does. Call me when you talk to her again, and let me know how she's doing."

Patterson slid the phone back into his pocket and poured himself a cup of coffee. He sat in his recliner in the family room and tried to relax. He wasn't worried about Jane—or at least, he wasn't worried yet. He hoped to spend the long weekend with Jeanne, and maybe he could help her work through her grief. He couldn't shake the Shepherd case, though, and he knew he should be out there with his troopers, talking to people and trying to make a case against Rusty Hoak. Without a confession, they didn't have enough evidence to charge Rusty with murder. The prosecutor would laugh him out of the room if he suggested they charge Rusty with what they had.

Patterson retrieved his pack from where he had dropped it by the front door. He pulled out the copy of Jake's journal, returned to his chair, and turned on the floor lamp next to the chair. Had he missed something important in the journal, something about a planned meeting with Rusty? He began rereading the entries from the last month of Jake's life, but he saw nothing new. He dropped the pages on the table by his chair and leaned back in his recliner.

Patterson drifted into a light sleep but then jerked awake, sat forward in the recliner, and stood. He began to pace and could feel the blood pumping through his body. Why hadn't he thought of this before now? *It isn't what Jake wrote in his journal, it's what he didn't write.*

He pulled the Shepherd case file from his pack and found the number for Lance Crane. He punched the digits into his phone, but his call went to voice mail. Patterson hurried to his small home office and booted up the computer. Five minutes later, he had a phone number for Lance Crane's home in Oregon. He placed the call.

"Hello," a pleasant, elderly female voice answered the phone.

Patterson asked to speak to Lance Crane.

"He isn't here," the lady said.

"This is Sergeant Dan Patterson with the Alaska State Troopers. Are you Lance's wife?"

"Yes, I'm Emily Crane. Is everything okay?"

"Yes, ma'am. I need to speak with your husband about a case we're investigating."

"The dead pilot," Emily Crane said. "Terrible thing. Lance told me about it."

"Do you know when he'll be home?" Patterson prodded.

Emily Crane laughed. "No, sir. My Lance is a wanderer. He should be home by now, but he called me from Anchorage and said he was flying back to Karluk Lake for the Fourth of July weekend. He said the forecast was great for the entire weekend, and he didn't want to miss it. We had plans to attend a holiday party here, so I'm not happy with the man, but that's Lance."

Patterson thanked Emily Crane and then called Sara.

"Sir," she said on the second ring.

"Sara, a few days ago, did you say Lance Crane once flew on Kodiak."

"Yes, sir," Sara said. "He was a pilot for Jarvin Flight Service for a year or two before moving to Southeastern Alaska."

"You said he knew Jake from back in the day."

"I don't know for a fact they knew each other, but they must have. The air charter businesses in Kodiak form a tight-knit community. All the pilots know each other."

"Yes, they do. Thanks, Sara." Patterson disconnected and continued to pace.

He placed a call to Sid Beatty, hoping the old trooper was within cell range and not out on his boat fishing.

"Beatty," Sid said.

Patterson said, "Sid, Dan Patterson. I have a quick question. Do you remember a pilot by the name of Lance Crane who flew for Jarvin Flight Service back in the seventies?"

"The name sounds familiar," Lance said, "but I don't remember anything about him."

"You don't know if he was the pilot who dropped off the stranded hunters you told Jane Marcus about?"

"Until I talked to Jane today, I thought those missing hunters were a crazy rumor. I've been beating myself up all day for not taking the rumor more seriously when I first heard it."

"Sid, there wasn't anything you could do," Patterson said.

"Maybe not, but I'm sure you now feel the same way I did. When something bad happened on this Island, I felt it was my responsibility to take care of the problem."

"I know exactly how you feel," Patterson said, "and I fear we have a problem now."

"Something to do with the pilot you mentioned?" Sid asked.

"Lance Crane was Jake's last passenger. He was camped on the other side of the lake from where Jake was murdered, so I didn't consider him a suspect, but I just took another look at Jake's journal. The man was anal. He wrote down the exact time of departure for every flight he made," Patterson said. "I was so busy trying to decipher what Jake had written in his journal, I failed to notice what he didn't write in his journal."

"I don't understand," Sid said.

"There's no entry for when he left Karluk Lake after dropping off Lance Crane."

"He could have forgotten to write in his journal before he took off."

"Possible," Patterson said, "but several people I interviewed told me he religiously recorded every flight."

"Can you bring Crane in for questioning?" Sid asked. "Does he live on the island?"

"He lives in Oregon," Patterson said, "but I fear he's on his way back to Karluk Lake now." Patterson told Sid about his conversations with Geoff and with Emily Crane.

"Sid," Patterson said, "Lance Crane flew for Jarvin Flight Service in the mid-seventies."

Sid didn't say anything for several moments and then asked, "You think the dispatcher Jane talked to this morning called Crane to tell him Jane was asking questions about the stranded hunters?"

"I think it's possible," Patterson said. "I think after talking to the old dispatcher, Crane called the marine center to find Jane. After the secretary told him Jane had gone to Karluk Lake for the weekend, he changed his plans to go home and decided to return to Karluk Lake."

"But why?" Sid asked. "What is it he's afraid Jane knows, or what is he afraid she'll find at Karluk?"

"I don't know," Patterson said, "but I am worried Jane's in danger. I'm flying out to check on her."

"I'm going with you," Sid said.

"Sid, you're retired."

"Not tonight," Sid said. "I sent Jane down this path, and I don't want any harm to come to her."

Patterson knew he'd be disobeying regulations if he let a retired trooper accompany him to Karluk Lake on trooper business, but there was no one other than Sid he'd rather have with him if they encountered a problem. Patterson knew he could trust Sid. The man had been a trooper for nearly forty years, and while he might not be able to run as fast as some of the young troopers Patterson commanded, Sid possessed something far more valuable than the dexterity and speed of youth. Stories abounded about Sid's steadiness under fire. He functioned flawlessly in stress situations, and if Patterson's worst fears proved correct, he'd need Sid's steady hand this evening.

"I'll pick you up in ten minutes," Patterson said.

Patterson wrote a hasty note for Jeanne and left it on the kitchen cabinet. He then called her friend, Lois, and asked if she could spend the night at their house because he had to be away on business. Lois didn't ask him any questions but said she was on her way.

1976

December 1st
9:20 A.M.

Bently felt cold and wet. He opened his eyes. Where was he? He was sitting on the ground in a patch of alders. He looked down at his clothes. At least he was wearing his parka, boots, and gloves, but the seat of his jeans felt soaking wet from sitting in the melting snow. Had he come out here in the middle of the night? He couldn't remember. He recalled going to bed last night, or at least he thought it was last night.

He looked at the watch on his left wrist and cursed. Why had he worn this useless piece of junk on a hunting trip? He knew the answer, of course. He wore it because Julie gave it to him, and he could still remember how thrilled he'd been when he'd opened the box on his birthday three years earlier. Julie had saved up her money to buy him the digital watch he'd been eyeing. Instead of hands, the watch showed the time in red, glowing numbers on the black watch face. The gold watch was beautiful but impractical. If the temperature was too cold or too hot, the watch stopped working, and it never worked in high humidity. Since it had been exposed to rain and snow for several days now, Bently doubted it would ever work again. He unbuckled the clasp and threw the watch into the woods. It was gone, just like Julie.

He needed water. He really needed food, but he kept telling himself he would survive this nightmare as long as he kept himself hydrated. He slowly pulled himself to his feet. His arms and legs trembled from the cold and from hunger.

He was only a few feet from his tent, and he staggered toward it. He picked up the pot sitting between his and Schwimmer's tents. The pot was half full of water they had collected either from rain or melting snow. At first, they had been diligent about drinking only clean water, but now the water looked brown, and particles floated in it.

Bently took a small sip. His cracked lips burned, and the sores in his mouth screamed at the insult of the invading liquid. Schwimmer rarely drank water because he said it hurt too much. Bently had tried to convince him to fight against the pain because he would die if he didn't drink. Bently no longer cared about Schwimmer and had even stopped checking on the other man. At this point, Bently's only concern was saving himself, and he was beginning to doubt even he would survive.

PRESENT DAY
THURSDAY, JULY 3RD
9:03 P.M.

Geoff's call rattled me. I immediately called my father and woke him. It was three hours later in Kansas than it was at Karluk Lake, and I could tell from the sound of his voice the late-night call scared him. I didn't want to worry him, so I didn't mention I was camping alone in the Kodiak wilderness. If he wondered why my satellite phone call sounded strange, he didn't say anything about it. I said I'd missed a call at work from someone who said he was my Uncle John.

I asked Dad if I had an Uncle John or anyone who would refer to himself as my Uncle John. He sounded groggy and cranky but assured me I didn't have an Uncle John and then said he thought at my age, I should know who my relatives are. When I asked him if everyone in the family was okay, he growled a yes, and I told him goodnight.

I decided to delve into the mysterious caller when I returned to town. I'd been shaken twice since I'd arrived at Karluk Lake, once by the bear and once by the strange phone call. I now sat on a rock outside my tent, studying the shell casing I'd found earlier. What did it mean? Was this casing from the bullet that had killed the young man whose bones we'd found, or was it unrelated to our case? Plenty of people tramped the area around Karluk Lake, from bear viewers, rafters, and fishermen in the summer to hunters in the spring and fall. This bullet could have come from a thousand different sources, and I knew I'd hear similar words from Sergeant Patterson when I talked to him. Hopefully, tomorrow I would find something more definitive.

I decided to get ready for bed and crawl into my bag before it got dark. I'd brought two flashlights with me, but no camp light. Since the ambient light wouldn't fade until after midnight, I didn't think I would need anything more substantial than a headlamp or a flashlight.

I pushed myself off the rock, and as I wiped dirt off the back of my jeans, I heard a roaring sound, and I walked from my campsite down the short trail to the lakeshore to see if I could determine the source of the noise.

I reached the shore in time to see a plane skim the surface of the lake, land, and then taxi into a cove, out of my view.

"I have neighbors," I said.

1976
DECEMBER 10TH
2:00 P.M.

Bently heard the buzzing noise but didn't know what the sound was or what it meant. He again sat outside on the ground. The air felt crisp, and no clouds marred the perfect blue sky. The sun hovered so low on the horizon he couldn't see it, and the muted daylight had an eerie blue tint. He smelled earth and decaying leaves. Most of the snow had melted and then turned to ice, but he sat on a patch of wet dirt. He couldn't feel the wet seeping through his jeans. *It must be cold*, but he couldn't feel the chill either. He didn't feel anything. He was happy he no longer felt hungry, and although he didn't desire water, he still forced himself to drink.

He'd seen Schwimmer drink some water over the past few days, but Bently knew neither of them was drinking enough. *What did it matter, though? They would both die from hunger in a matter of days.* He was so weak now he could barely stand, and he saw Schwimmer stretched in front of his tent on a patch of ice, staring sightlessly at the sky. Maybe he was already dead. Bently knew he should call Schwimmer's name and tell him to go into his tent and get in his sleeping bag, but Bently didn't have the energy. Instead, he sat and stared at his hunting partner.

PRESENT DAY
THURSDAY, JULY 3RD
9:12 P.M.

Patterson called trooper headquarters on his way to the boat harbor and asked Sienna, the night dispatcher, to call the charter services in town and find out if any of them flew Lance Crane to Karluk Lake in the last few hours.

"Sir," Sienna said. "The air charter services are probably closed for the day."

"Then call the dispatchers at home," Patterson said. "Call Irene. She'll know how to get ahold of them. Tell her it's an emergency."

"Yes, sir," Sienna said, her voice trembling.

"I'm flying to Karluk Lake, and if it gets too dark to fly back to town, I might have to spend the night there," Patterson said. "I'll be leaving town in the next twenty minutes, and before I take off, I want to know if any of the charter services flew Lance Crane to Karluk Lake in the last few hours and if so, where they dropped him."

"I'll get on it right away, sir."

Patterson screeched around the corner to the boat harbor and found Sid Beatty standing in the parking lot waiting for him, a backpack and a rifle case slung over his right shoulder. As soon as Patterson pulled to a stop, Sid opened the back door of the SUV, deposited the pack and rifle on the seat, and then slid into the front passenger seat and slammed the door behind him.

"Do you have camping gear in your pack?" Patterson asked.

"Yes, sir, and at this late hour, I reckon I'll need it."

Patterson groaned. "I hope not. My back hasn't recovered from my last camping adventure."

Sid laughed. "Come on, now, you're just a kid."

Patterson sped to the parking lot above the floatplane dock, and he and Sid grabbed their gear and trotted down the ramp to the plane. Patterson checked to make sure the plane had plenty of fuel, and then climbed in and began warming up the engine. Sid stored their gear in the rear seat, climbed in the front, and buckled his seat belt. Once Patterson untied the plane and began to taxi, they both slid headphones on their heads.

Patterson's phone vibrated in his shirt pocket.

He pulled his headphones down around his neck and held the phone to his ear. What do you have?" he asked.

"Sir," Sienna said, "Charli and I called all the charter dispatchers on the island. "None of them flew Lance Crane to Karluk this evening. As a matter of fact, none of them flew anyone to Karluk this evening."

"Okay," Patterson said, "thanks."

"What?" Sid asked.

"None of the charter companies on Kodiak flew Crane or anyone else to Karluk this evening. Maybe we have nothing to worry about."

Sid shook his head. "No, the guy probably chartered straight out of Anchorage and got someone to fly him down to Kodiak and drop him at the lake."

Patterson nodded slowly. "Possible," he said. "We're here now; let's fly out and take a look."

Sid remained quiet while Patterson talked to the flight controller in the tower at the airport. Once they were airborne, Patterson circled back and headed for Sharatin Pass.

"Tell me your theory," Sid said when they were through the pass. The clear sky and calm air made flying as easy as it ever gets on Kodiak. Unfortunately, they would run out of daylight in a few hours, and when it turned dark, Patterson wouldn't be able to see to navigate through these mountains. They could predict darkness, though, so while they might have to spend a night in a tent, darkness should not be a threat. At least it shouldn't be a threat to flying, but it might impede their ability to find Lance Crane.

"I need more information from you, first," Patterson said. "I regret I only half listened to Jane today when she told me what she learned from the Jarvin Flight Service dispatcher. I had a lot going on at the station at the time."

"Jane told me the dispatcher, Abby Long, admitted Jarvin Flight Service dropped off two hunters in late October 1976 and forgot to pick them up," Sid said.

"How is that possible?" Patterson asked.

Sid explained about the calendar and then continued to relay the story to Patterson.

"But Jane didn't know who the pilot was who finally went to check on them?"

"Abby told her the pilot who dropped them off was the same pilot who went back to look for them, but she said she couldn't remember who the pilot was."

"I don't believe she couldn't remember," Patterson said.

"Of course, she remembered," Sid said, "and I kick myself because I should have told Jane the first thing Abby would probably do is contact the pilot and tell him Jane had just been at her house asking questions about the incident."

Patterson shook his head and looked over at Sid. "Not your job anymore, Sid. I'm the one who should have told her she might be in danger. I didn't even take the time to listen to her closely. I simply thought I could put the matter on the back burner and deal with it after I closed the Shepherd case."

"I still find it hard to believe those old bones are related to Jake's murder," Sid said.

"I'm only guessing," Patterson said, "but I think it's too big a coincidence that Jake and Crane were both pilots on Kodiak in the seventies and Jake ended up dead after flying Crane to Karluk. This case has had more than its share of coincidences, though, so maybe I'm wrong."

"I'm not questioning your instincts," Sid said. "I think you're right to be worried about Jane. Why else would Crane turn around and fly back to Karluk Lake? Jane's inquiry into the Jarvin Flight Service incident must have spooked him. I'm trying to understand how Jake was involved in all of this."

"I don't know," Patterson said. "All I can guess is that Jake said the wrong thing on the flight from Kodiak to Karluk Lake, and Crane thought he knew too much and decided to get rid of him."

"Now he thinks Jane knows too much," Sid said. "I hope we aren't too late."

1976

The buzzing sound grew louder and louder. Bently looked up and saw a white plane circling above him. He thought it might be a de Havilland Beaver. *Maybe it's our plane.* He tried to yell as the plane circled again, but only a strange croak escaped his lips. He drifted to sleep.

PRESENT DAY
Thursday, July 3rd
9:35 P.M.

I awoke with a start, my headlamp still glowing and my right hand clutching the Greg Iles novel I'd been reading. I pushed the book into my pack, and turned off my headlamp, placing it within easy reach beside my sleeping bag, next to my rifle. I hoped I could fall back asleep before it began to get dark. I knew if I were still awake by the time darkness fell, sleep would never claim me. I'd start at every noise, imagining a huge bear outside my tent.

I curled into a ball in my sleeping bag and thought I heard someone call my name. *I must have fallen asleep again and started dreaming.* A few minutes later, I again heard a male voice yell my name. The voice sounded closer, but I couldn't identify it.

I crawled from my bag and pulled on my Xtra Tuff boots. I unzipped my tent flap, climbed through the opening and stood alert. After a few minutes, I heard breaking brush. *Did Geoff fly out here to check on me?* I remembered the plane landing earlier, but the man who'd called my name didn't sound like Geoff.

A man walked out of the brush fifty yards in front of me. I'd never seen him before.

"Are you Jane?"

"Yes," I said. The man was probably in his late sixties or early seventies, but he looked thin and fit. As he neared me, I saw the smile on his face. He seemed friendly, but I felt vulnerable. I'd left my rifle in my tent and now considered scrambling back into the tent to grab it. Instead of following my instincts, though, I stood motionless and watched the man advance.

When he got within thirty yards of me, he lifted what I'd thought was a sturdy walking stick and pointed the end of it at me.

"Stay right there," he said and leveled the rifle at my stomach.

My heart slammed in my chest. *Who is this guy?*

"Do you know who I am?" he asked, as if reading my mind.

"You're the pilot," I said. My words surprised me, but I saw from the expression on the man's face, I'd hit the mark.

"No one thought about those hunters for forty years until you started asking questions," the guy said. "Not even their families cared about what had happened to them."

"What did happen to them?" I asked.

He ignored my question. "Did your carelessness start the fire that uncovered the bones?"

Abby Long must have called the old pilot after I talked to her this morning. I knew she'd been lying to me when she said she didn't remember the name of the pilot who dropped off the hunters and then flew to Karluk to search for them. Of course, she remembered who he was. I didn't think I'd told Abby about the fire, though. *Where did this guy get his information?*

"How do you know about the fire?" I asked.

"The article in the Kodiak Mirror a few weeks ago," he said. "The article was the reason I flew here in the first place. I wanted to make sure no other bones had been exposed. I buried everything at the time, but the ground was mostly frozen when I dug the graves so I couldn't dig very deep. I guess over the course of forty years of wet Kodiak weather, the ground releases its skeletons." He shrugged and smiled.

"How did they die?" I asked. I knew the one guy died from a shot to the head. *Had his hunting partner shot him, and if so, how did the partner die?*

The old man laughed, "You still haven't put it together, have you?"

1976
DECEMBER 10TH
2:20 P.M.

Bently opened his eyes and saw a man approaching their campsite. Were they about to be rescued? He knew he should be excited by the prospect, but he couldn't summon the energy. Maybe they would live through this after all. He had given up hope several days ago, but maybe they'd make it.

PRESENT DAY
THURSDAY, JULY 3RD
10:03 P.M.

"What irritates me," the man said, "is now I have to kill Abby, too, and I like Abby."

"Why kill Abby?" I asked. I knew I had to get away from this man, run into the woods and hide. The sat phone and my rifle were both in my tent where I couldn't get to them now. He'd shoot me if I tried to crawl into my small tent. I didn't see how I could hide in the woods all night, but if I lured him away from my camp, maybe I could sneak back to my tent, grab my rifle and call for help. It was already getting dark, however. *Even if I call for help, it will soon be too dark to fly, and help won't arrive until tomorrow morning.* I could think of no other plan, though. Fleeing seemed to be my only option.

"I don't have any choice but to kill her," the man said. "You aren't even law enforcement, and she told you everything." He shrugged. "Well, she told you everything she knows, except my name. I am grateful to her for withholding my name, but it wouldn't take the troopers long to run down all the pilots who flew for Jarvin Flight Service in 1976."

"What didn't she know?" I asked.

"What?" The man looked confused.

"You said Abby told me everything she knew. What didn't she know?"

The man laughed. "Honey," he said, "Old man Jarvin and I told her I couldn't find the guys. I said I found their abandoned campsite but saw no sign of them."

"You didn't tell her they were dead, and you buried their bodies." Now I was beginning to understand what had happened, or at least I thought I was until the old man spoke again.

PRESENT DAY

With clear skies and no wind, Patterson opted to fly high over the spine of the island. He willed the plane to move faster, but de Havilland Beavers weren't built for speed. He estimated they would arrive at Karluk by 10:30 p.m.

"Do you know where Jane camped?" Sid asked.

"I know where they found the bones, so I'm sure she camped near there," Patterson said.

"Crane would know where to find her, too," Sid said.

"I'll circle the area before I land. If we see another camp near Jane's, we can assume Crane found her.

1976

The man said nothing as he approached, which Bently thought was odd. Shouldn't he ask them how they were or apologize for arriving so late? Of course, maybe he was talking, and Bently couldn't hear him.

This was definitely the same pilot who had dropped them off. He had the same, stupid long hair tied into a ponytail. His skin looked darker than Bently remembered, though, and then Bently recalled the guy had been about to leave to go on a vacation to Hawaii. *His vacation must be over, and he is home looking tan and rested. Except he didn't look rested. He looked angry, his jaw set and his eyes narrowed. No, he looked determined, not angry.*

The pilot was carrying something in his hand. It looked like a club, but then he lifted it, and Bently saw it was a rifle. Bently watched in fascination while the pilot walked up to where Schwimmer lay on the ground. He kicked Schwimmer and Schwimmer moaned. Apparently, Schwimmer was still alive.

The pilot calmly raised the rifle and fired a shot at Schwimmer's head. Schwimmer's body jerked in response, and then red began to flow from his head. Bently wondered why the pilot had shot Schwimmer. Bently decided he must be hallucinating again because it didn't make sense for the pilot to kill Schwimmer.

Next, Bently watched as the pilot approached him. Bently wanted to ask the man why he was killing them, but he couldn't form the words. He couldn't even manage to be scared or angry. He just watched the man walk closer, aim the rifle at him, and put his finger on the trigger.

PRESENT DAY
Thursday, July 3rd
10:08 p.m.

I backed to the edge of the clearing while the old man talked. He was so caught up in his story, he didn't seem to notice me move.

"Those hunters ruined my life," he said. "I had big plans to buy Jarvin Flight Service from old man Jarvin. He hadn't agreed to the sale yet, but I believed he would have. I had just proposed to my girlfriend, Emily, and we were excited about our future. She said she'd help me run the air charter business, and I'm sure we could have made it work."

He stopped talking, and I took another small step backward toward the brush. "What happened?" I asked.

He seemed surprised by the sound of my voice as if he'd forgotten I were there. "I came home from spending a month in Hawaii with Emily. I went in to work, and Abby asked me if I remembered dropping off hunters at Karluk Lake. She said a woman called looking for her nephew and said the last she'd heard from him, he was planning to fly down to Kodiak for a bear hunt. The aunt didn't know which charter company her nephew and his buddy had used to fly them to Karluk Lake, so she called all of them. Abby told her we weren't the ones who flew them, but then Abby checked the logs and saw we did fly them to Karluk. What Abby couldn't find was any record we had ever picked them up." He took several steps closer to me, but the barrel of the rifle now pointed at the ground instead of at my stomach.

"It wasn't my fault," he said, "but old man Jarvin blamed me. I was on a beach in Hawaii, how could I have known?" He shook his head. "I still can't

301

believe Abby and her office staff managed to lose track of our passengers. It was their incompetence and the fact that Jarvin no longer cared what happened at his air charter business. They were the ones who killed those men. I just pulled the trigger."

"What?" I said. "They were alive when you flew out to Karluk Lake looking for them, and you shot them? Why?"

"Jarvin said to make the problem disappear. He suggested he wouldn't sell me his business until I solved this little problem. If those men had survived, they would have sued Jarvin for all he was worth, and he wouldn't have had a business left to sell."

The man's words paralyzed me. "Were they at their campsite when you flew out to Karluk?"

"They were nearly starved to death. The first guy I shot looked like he would die any minute. I put him out of his misery. The second guy had a little more life but not much. He watched me kill his buddy, but he didn't say anything or even try to move." The man shrugged. "I did them a favor," he said.

My stomach lurched. I tried to imagine the horror the young hunter must have felt at seeing his buddy killed in front of him and knowing he would be next.

"I thought that winter day at Karluk Lake was long behind me, but then you found some bones and your curiosity got the better of you. You just couldn't leave it alone, could you?"

He laughed. "I flew out here to make sure the rest of the skeletons were still buried, and who did I get for a pilot but a guy who flew for another Kodiak charter service back in the seventies. When he remembered I flew for Jarvin Flight Service, he asked me about the old rumor." He shook his head. "I still don't know who started the rumor. Abby must have said something to someone, or maybe old man Jarvin opened his mouth. I think he was senile. Anyway, there was a rumor that we'd dropped off a party at Karluk Lake and hadn't picked them up. It was so long ago, I couldn't believe anyone remembered the rumor." He barked a short laugh. "So, here I am flying out to Karluk Lake to make sure the skeletons from my past remained buried, and I get Jake Shepherd for a pilot. When he asked me about the old rumor, I knew I had to kill him."

My mind raced ahead of the man's story, and I understood seconds before he confessed that he was the one who had killed Jake Shepherd. I turned and ran into a thick mass of alders and willows. The rifle blast nearly deafened me, but somehow, the bullet missed me. I pushed through a willow thicket and found a narrow game trail on the other side. I could move much faster on the game trail, but so could the man, and I was also a much easier target out in the open.

I ran a short distance down the trail and heard the loud report of the rifle again. A bullet struck a tree in front of me, and I darted back into the thick brush and pushed through the undergrowth. This area showed no damage from the fire in May, and I struggled through the jungle-like growth. I lost my sense of direction while fighting through willows and alders, and I didn't know if I was heading toward the lakeshore or away from it. I did not want to emerge on the open shore where the guy could easily spot and shoot me.

I tried not to make noise but found it impossible to hurry through the willows without breaking branches. When I exited into a small clearing, I expected my assailant to be waiting, but I saw no sign of him. I found another game trail leading back toward my camp, and I ran down it, tripping once over a fallen branch. I recovered my balance and began to feel I'd temporarily lost my pursuer when a powerful force slammed into my left shoulder and sent me toppling. I lay on the ground dazed, unsure what had happened. I didn't remember hearing a blast, but there must have been one. I'd been shot.

PRESENT DAY

Thursday, July 3rd
10:25 P.M.

Karluk Lake materialized below the plane, and Patterson worried they were too late. A part of him believed Crane hadn't flown to Karluk. If the secretary at the marine center told Crane that Jane planned to camp at Karluk for the entire weekend, then he'd have several days to get to the lake and find her. Of course, the longer he allowed Jane to search for more bones and artifacts, the more she might find.

Sid hadn't said a word for several minutes, and now he stared out the window at the lake. Daylight was beginning to fade. Unless they could wrap this up quickly, they'd be forced to camp at Karluk Lake until daylight.

Sid pointed to a spot on the west shore of the lake. "She's over there somewhere?" he asked.

Patterson nodded. "I think I'll circle the area a few times to get a feel for what to expect."

Sid nodded. "If she crawls out of her tent and screams obscenities at us for waking her from a deep sleep, we'll know she's okay."

"And if a guy greets us with a rifle, we'll know we have a problem," Patterson said.

Sid unbuckled his seat belt and reached for his rifle in the rear seat. He unzipped the gun case, pulled out his rifle and propped it on his lap.

"Good idea," Patterson said. "If he approaches the plane with a gun leveled at us, shoot first and ask questions later."

Sid nodded. "I have no intention of ending up like Jake Shepherd."...

PRESENT DAY
THURSDAY, JULY 3RD
10:33 P.M.

Flames seared through my shoulder. *Will I die here tonight? Is this it?* I flashed on the face of my boss. Peter told me not to shoot anyone, but he didn't say anything about getting shot myself. If I survived this night, would Peter fire me? I brushed the worry aside. How could I think of something so trivial with imminent death facing me?

I pushed myself to my feet with my good hand. I didn't know why the man simply didn't walk down the trail and finish me, but perhaps he didn't know the bullet hit me. I looked down at my left shoulder. Blood seeped through my jacket and down my arm. I knew I needed to apply direct pressure and elevate the wound, but I didn't have time to doctor myself now.

I hurried as fast as I could down the uneven trail. The open ground made me an easier target, but if I entered another willow thicket, I would never fight through it with one good arm. Another shot rang out, but I didn't hear or feel the impact of a bullet, so it must not have been close. With each step, my shoulder screamed in pain. I held my left arm against my body and cradled it with my right arm as I ran.

I looked behind me, searching for the old man. I didn't see him, and I also didn't see the rock in front of me on the trail. I tripped, flew into the air, and crashed into an alder. I felt dazed and confused and wondered how much blood I'd lost. I pushed myself into a sitting position, and my right hand brushed against the canister attached to my belt. I'd forgotten to remove the can from my belt before crawling into my sleeping bag. I pulled the bear spray from its holder and removed the safety.

Pepper spray was no match for a rifle, but the spray was my only weapon, and I knew I couldn't run from the man much longer. If my shoulder continued to bleed, I'd soon lose consciousness. *Did the bullet hit a major artery?* I put the can of pepper spray on the ground behind me and slid my right hand inside my coat, directly over the wound. I pushed as hard as I could and bit my lip to keep from screaming in pain.

A few minutes later, I heard footsteps on the path. I withdrew my right hand from under my coat and gripped the pepper spray. I kept my right hand on it but slid the cannister under my leg where the man wouldn't be able to see it when he approached.

PRESENT DAY
THURSDAY, JULY 3RD
10:42 P.M.

"There's her camp," Sid said.

Patterson piloted the plane in a tight circle while they surveyed the small, blue tent staked to the ground. "I don't see any sign of her, do you?"

"No," Sid said. "Let's look for a nearby camp and then circle her again."

Patterson made a wider circle, and when they saw no sign of other campers, he increased the radius and circled again.

"I don't see any sign of Crane. Maybe he isn't here yet."

"But where is Jane?" Sid asked. "Either she is a very sound sleeper, or she's not in her tent."

"I'll circle one more time, and then we'll land and walk up to check on her."

PRESENT DAY
THURSDAY, JULY 3RD
10:40 P.M.

"There you are," the man said, his voice low and friendly as if he'd just discovered the hiding spot of a child in a game of hide-and-seek. He held his rifle loosely in his right hand, apparently judging I was not a risk to him and was in no condition to flee again through the underbrush.

"I hit you," he said. Just then, a plane circled low overhead, and the man briefly looked up at it but then returned his attention to me and my wound. He bent down to take a closer look at the damage his bullet had inflicted on my shoulder.

This was it, my one chance to survive. I waited until his face drew within two feet of me, pulled the can of pepper spray from beneath my leg, and pushed the nozzle. I sprayed directly into his eyes.

The man stumbled backward, his left hand on his face, his right hand still clutching his rifle. "What the . . ." he screamed. "What did you do?" He struggled to breathe and fell forward onto the ground.

I hadn't yet formulated part B of my escape plan because I didn't think I'd succeed with part A. I needed to do something. I wasn't sure how long the effects of the bear spray would last, but I recalled Geoff telling me they last several minutes.

I pushed myself to my feet. Unfortunately, the old pilot had fallen on his rifle and seemed to be clutching it. I continued down the trail toward my tent and my own rifle. Burning pain coursed through my body and spots danced in front of my eyes. My feet felt like concrete blocks, and I had trouble lifting them. I hoped I didn't have to go far. Overhead, I heard the plane engine, fainter now.

I walked several more steps to a point where the trail divided, and I realized the trail snaking to the left was the one I'd followed in my search for more bones. I saw my small camp shovel stuck in the ground at the fork in the trail where I'd left it a few hours earlier, planning to retrieve it the following day when I continued my bone search. I knew where I was now, and I still had too much ground to cover before I reached my tent. At my best, I could cover the distance to my tent in a few minutes, but with my gunshot wound, I didn't think I could make it that far.

I pulled the shovel from the ground and retraced my steps to where the pilot lay writhing on the trail. The plane passed low overhead again, and this time it sounded as if it were flying through the trees. I didn't have the strength to wave to it and try to summon help. I poured what little energy I had into dealing with the old pilot and his rifle. When I reached him, he lay hunched on the ground, head in his hands, and his rifle still underneath his body.

I didn't know how much damage I could inflict with waning strength and only one good arm, but I lifted the shovel with all my might and brought it down on his head. His body relaxed, and his moaning stopped. The barrel end of the rifle protruded from under his body. I pulled on it until it was free. I crawled several feet away from the man and sagged against an alder. My next goal was to remain conscious.

PRESENT DAY
Thursday, July 3rd
10:56 P.M.

"I'll make one more pass over Jane's tent," Patterson said. "I'll buzz the tent, so while I concentrate on not plowing into the trees, will you watch for Jane?"

"I'm on it," Sid said.

Patterson circled the plane and came in low, barely above the thick brush.

"I don't see her near the tent," Sid said.

"Where is she?" Patterson asked. "There's no way she could sleep through this much noise."

Patterson lifted the nose of the plane and began to gain altitude.

"Wait," Sid said, "I see movement in the brush. I think it's Jane, but I can't tell what she's doing. She is walking very slowly and not looking up at the plane. Something is wrong with her."

"I'm landing," Patterson said. He circled the plane in the opposite direction and brought it in for a smooth landing. He pulled up to the beach and cut the engines.

"You tie up the plane," Sid said. "I'll start toward the spot where I saw Jane." He gripped the stock of the rifle in his right hand while he jumped off the float into knee-deep water. As soon as he reached the beach, he broke into a run.

"Be careful," Patterson yelled to his fleeing form. Patterson hurriedly tied the planc to an alder on the bank, and then he grabbed his rifle and followed Sid into the brush.

PRESENT DAY

THURSDAY, JULY 3RD
11:08 P.M.

"Jane? Jane, can you hear me?" The hand lightly caressed my cheek, and I opened my eyes to see Sid Beatty kneeling on the ground in front of me, a frown on his face.

"Where did you come from?" My voice was just a whisper. *Why am I sitting on the ground, and why am I so weak?*

"Shhh, don't try to talk," Sid said. "You're okay now."

"Is she okay?" I heard another man speak. Was it Sergeant Patterson?

"She's been shot," Sid said. "We need to get her to town."

"What about him," Patterson asked.

"I didn't check him," Sid said.

A moment later, I heard Patterson say, "He has a pulse. I'll cuff him, but I think we'll have to wait for him to regain consciousness. We can't carry him to the plane."

I heard a loud moan, and Patterson said, "Lance Crane, can you hear me?"

"I don't think we can wait much longer to get Jane to a hospital," Sid said.

"Grab the first aid kit out of the plane and start applying pressure to the wound," Patterson said. "I'll walk Crane to the plane, and then we'll carry Jane."

Sid ran toward the plane to retrieve the first aid kit, and when he returned, Patterson said, "We found the rifle."

"What?" Sid asked.

"The gun beside Jane's leg is the weapon Crane used to kill Jake," Patterson said. "This old Marlin rifle takes .30-30 shells."

Sid said something, but his words faded into nothingness as I drifted to sleep.

PRESENT DAY
FRIDAY, JULY 4ᵀᴴ
2:33 P.M.

Sid Beatty's face was the first thing I saw when I opened my eyes.

"Hey there," he said. "You had a nice, long nap."

I tried to sit up but groaned in pain and fell back onto the bed.

"Whoa," Sid said. "If you want to sit up, push the button." He leaned over the arm of the bed and found the proper button for elevating the head of the bed.

"Where am I?" I asked. My voice sounded wispy and disconnected. I looked up at the bags hanging on a stand next to my bed. One was clear and the other scarlet. I traced the tubes descending from the bags into my arm.

"You're in the hospital," Sid said. "They're feeding you blood and antibiotics. Do you remember being shot?"

My brain worked on the puzzle. I looked down at my bandaged shoulder and my swathed left arm, immobilized against my body. *Someone shot me?*

"The old pilot," I finally said. "He murdered the hunters."

Sid nodded. "He confessed everything to Sergeant Patterson last night."

"Why?" I asked.

"He was young and very stupid," Sid said. "He thought Mr. Jarvin would sell him the air charter business if he took care of this little problem for him. As it turned out, when Crane returned from killing the hunters, Jarvin told him he had one month to find a job somewhere else other than Kodiak Island. Jarvin ended up liquidating his assets and didn't sell his business to anyone."

"Did Jarvin want Crane to kill the hunters?" I asked.

"According to Crane, Jarvin told him to get rid of the problem if one still existed. Crane said he had no doubt in his mind what Jarvin meant." Sid shrugged. "Of course, we'll only ever know Crane's side of the story."

"What about Abby Long?" I asked.

"Patterson arrested her."

"For the old crimes?" I was surprised Patterson would arrest her for her involvement in the old murders.

"No," Sid said. "She is an accessory to attempted murder."

"I don't understand."

"She called Crane, and he tried to murder you."

I pulled the blanket tighter. For a minute I'd almost forgotten my brush with death.

"Do you think the hunters would have recovered if Crane brought them back to town when he found them?"

Sid nodded slowly. "I do, and I blame myself for not investigating the rumors I heard."

"No," I said, "you can't blame yourself for their deaths. If you'd investigated every rumor you heard, you wouldn't have had time for the real crimes. Besides," I added, "by the time you heard the rumor, the hunters were already dead and buried."

"Crane murdered Jake Shepherd, too," Sid said.

"Jake asked him about the old rumor, and Crane thought Jake knew too much," I said.

"Crane is an idiot," Sid said. "If he had simply ignored the article in the paper about you finding the bones, Patterson never would have collected enough evidence to charge him with those murders. Even if Patterson questioned him, he could have stuck to his story saying that when he flew out to Karluk Lake, he didn't see any sign of the two men. Patterson might have suspected Crane knew more than he was saying, but Patterson couldn't rule out the crazy, old trapper for killing and burying those men."

"Wasn't Jake Shepherd found in his plane on the other side of the lake from the bones? How did Crane kill him?" I asked.

"Crane shot Jake as soon as he pulled up to Crane's camping spot and unloaded Crane's gear," Sid said. "Crane said he maneuvered Jake into a conversation about the types of rifles they used to carry in their planes for emergencies. Once they landed, Crane told Jake he still carried his old Marlin and wanted to show it to him. Jake sat in his plane with the door open while Crane pulled the rifle from his duffel, walked up to Jake and shot him in the head. Crane said Jake never saw it coming, but I imagine confused terror filled the last second of Jake Shepherd's life." Sid lowered his head and shook it slowly. "Crane then flew Jake's plane to the other side of the lake because he knew Jake was planning to pick up his next passengers over there."

I pondered the situation for several moments. "I understand Crane is a pilot and could easily fly the plane to the other side of the lake, but how did he get back to his camp?"

"He walked," Sid said. "He said it took him the rest of the day and most of the evening, and he had to avoid other campers, so he stayed in the brush. He said he jumped from the float of Jake's plane into the water, so he wouldn't leave footprints and then cut up into the brush once he'd walked several hundred yards."

"I can't believe no one saw him," I said.

Sid shrugged. "Karluk might seem busy by Kodiak standards, but it is still the wilderness."

A knock sounded on the hospital room door, and a nurse whisked in carrying two vases of flowers. One had a "Get Well" balloon attached to it.

"Let's see," the nurse said, "the one with the balloon is from Geoff. Is he the guy with the red ponytail?"

I laughed and nodded.

"He brought both of these." She glanced at the card on the other arrangement. "This one is from Peter Wayman." She placed both cards on the table by my bed. "We've been holding your calls at the desk. Do you want me to send them through to your room?"

"Sure," I said, wondering with a start what had happened to my phone and camping gear.

As if reading my mind, Sid said, "Your stuff is in my truck. Do you want me to get it?"

"You can bring it to me the next time you visit" I felt my face flush. "Sorry," I said, "I'm not usually so bold. I must be pumped full of pain medicine."

Sid smiled. "I'd love to come back and visit you again. I'll bring you your pack the next time I visit you here, and I'll hang onto your camping gear, so I'll have an excuse to see you again after you're out of the hospital and feeling better."

My stomach fluttered, but Sid saved me from saying anything else stupid when he said, "I should get out of here so you can read the cards that came with the flowers."

"One is from a friend and colleague, and the other is from my boss, probably telling me I'm fired. The last thing he told me before I flew out to Karluk was to stay out of trouble. If I brought negative publicity to the marine center and screwed up the grant he was trying for from Tamron, I'll be searching for a new job."

The telephone beside my bed rang, and Sid handed it to me. "I'll be back later," he said.

I watched him walk out of my room and then answered the phone.

"Jane?" A male voice said.

"Nick? How did you find me here?" I asked.

"Dan Patterson called and told me you'd been shot and nearly died." FBI Agent Nick Morgan said. "I've been trying to call you for the last several hours, but the nurses wouldn't put my call through, and of course they wouldn't give me any information about your condition. How are you?"

"I hurt, but I should heal," I said. "I haven't talked to the doctor yet."

"Look," he said. "I'm getting ready to head up there."

"Thanks," I said, "but I know you're in the middle of a big case, and all I want to do is sleep, so let's save our reunion until we can both enjoy it."

"I miss you, Jane. I'll do a better job of staying in touch. I promise."

I disconnected and lowered the head of my bed. I thought about Nick Morgan and Sid Beatty. *What am I doing?* I glanced over at the envelopes on the table beside my bed. I'd wait until after my nap to find out if I still had a job.

AFTERWORD

Kodiak Island lies 250 miles (402 km) southwest of Anchorage, Alaska. The island measures 3,588 square miles (9293 km²), and much of it is part of the Kodiak National Wildlife Refuge. There are no roads on the refuge, and the only way to access the island beyond the road system is by floatplane or boat. Most of the 13,500 residents of the island live near the town of Kodiak, but even there, less than 100 miles (161 km) of road lead away from the town.

Karluk Lake, the largest lake on Kodiak Island, spans 12.2 miles (19.6 km) in length and 1.9 miles (3.1 km) in width and sits in the southwest region of the island. The Kodiak National Wildlife Refuge and Koniag lands surround the lake. Karluk Lake and its contiguous lake and river systems boast one of the largest salmon spawning grounds in the world. The fertile soil around the lake produces rich vegetation and berries, and the salmon and berries provide the dense population of Kodiak brown bears in the region with a bountiful supply of food and nutrients.

Karluk Bones is loosely based on four true stories. A few years ago, I began writing a newsletter about true crime in Alaska, and two of the tales I covered for my newsletter provided me with part of the plot for Karluk Bones. An incident relayed to me by a friend offered me the idea for another portion of this novel, and finally, I glued the story together with a tale I knew from personal experience. If you would like to know more about the true stories behind Karluk Bones, drop me an e-mail at robinbarefield76@outlook.com, and I will be happy to share them with you.

Kodiak Island is beautiful, wild, mysterious, and sometimes dangerous, and it provides the perfect backdrop for my novels. Kodiak offers a vivid stimulus for my creativity, and the four stories I mentioned above set the plot of Karluk Bones in motion. The people and businesses in this novel are a figment of my imagination. None of the airlines or pilots referred to in this book are real. Kodiak is a difficult place to fly a plane, and the pilots who fly here are talented individuals who take their jobs seriously. The Kodiak Braxton Marine Fisheries Center is not an actual facility, and none of the troopers in this book represent actual law-enforcement personnel. I am responsible for any mistakes in this novel.

Thank you to Evan and Lois Swensen at Publication Consultants for their guidance and assistance in publishing this novel, and thank you, Evan, for going above and beyond to point your authors in the right direction. Thank you, Deirdre Stoelzle, for meticulously editing my manuscript. I would also like to thank Loren Wilson and Mary Ann Poll for reading my manuscript and offering valuable suggestions, and thanks to all the authors in my Author Masterminds group for their weekly inspiration and support. Thank you, Dave Embry, for a great story. Without you, this would have been a different book.

Finally, I would like to thank my husband, Mike Munsey, for his patience with me and my writing addiction. From reading everything I write to offering advice and ideas, he is always in my corner. Mike is also my weapons expert.

Please check out my website at http://robinbarefield.com. While you are there, you can sign up for my newsletter and follow the link to listen to my podcast: Murder and Mystery in the Last Frontier.

I have written three previous novels: Big Game, Murder Over Kodiak, and The Fisherman's Daughter. You can find all my books at Amazon.com, barnesandnoble.com, and other online booksellers.

I invite you to join me on:
Facebook: https://www.facebook.com/wildernessauthorrobinbarefield/
Twitter: https://twitter.com/BarefieldRobin1
LinkedIn: www.linkedin.com/in/robin-barefield
Pinterest: https://www.pinterest.com/robinbarefield7/
Author Masterminds: https://authormasterminds.com/robin-barefield

Printed in the USA
CPSIA information can be obtained
at www.ICGtesting.com
LVHW050244230424
778173LV00003B/12